Griswoldville

Also by Jordan M. Poss:

No Snakes in Iceland
The Last Day of Marcus Tullius Cicero
Dark Full of Enemies

GRISWOLDVILLE

A NOVEL OF THE
AMERICAN CIVIL WAR

JORDAN M. POSS

NEOCLASSIC BOOKS

Set in Walbaum
Map by Jordan Poss
Author photo by Scott Poss

for my grandfathers

J.L. McKay   Edwin C. Poss

Rabun County native   Clarke County native
(1932-1998)   (1927-2017)

THE STATE OF **GEORGIA** & ENVIRONS
DURING THE WAR BETWEEN THE STATES

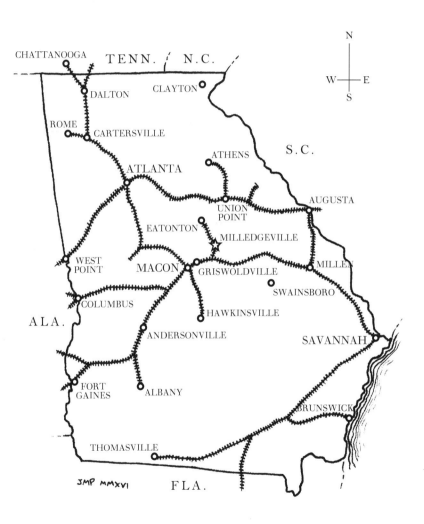

It is good for everyone to ally himself at one time with the defeated and to look at the 'progress' of history through the eyes of those who were left behind.

—Richard Weaver

Adversity toughens manhood—and the characteristic of the good or the great man is not that he has been exempted from the evils of life, but that he has surmounted them.

—Patrick Henry

Where now the horse? Where the rider?   Where the gift-giver?
Where the feast-settings?   Where the joys of the hall?
Alas, bright beaker!   Alas, bold warrior!
Alas, for the glory of the prince!   How that time is gone,
darkened under night-helm,   as if it never were.

—The Wanderer

I

ANTE

IT IS STRANGE NOW to see my grandfather's face, etched by light upon this browning bit of tin. This old man is hollowed out, bonier, his eyes fiercer than the man I recall, and I do not remember not knowing him. He lived but two miles off by road—a mile over the hill and through the woods, if one could get away with jumping a property boundary or two. He was omnipresent in my childhood, whether in person or in spirit. Plowing, reaping, and the winter slaughter had work-strengthened him from youth, and even in old age his arms were as pieces of brass or bars of iron. He seemed an immensely big man—though I know, as an intellectual matter, that I now stand taller than he did by five inches—made of hide and sinew and gunmetal beard stubble, smelling of rust, earth, mules, the warm friction of his clothes, pipe tobacco, and healthy sweat. I recall this all upon an instant merely by recalling his embrace; to hug him was to be enfolded in a great quilt of a man, for despite his strength and hardiness he was a tender and loving man. He had great black brows and a bald head full of stories, jokes, and lore. He knew every sign to look for to find the wild blackberries and muscadines secreted in a roadside hollow, the proper moon phase in which to dig a posthole so that it would stand unwobbling for years, and all the roots, herbs, blossoms, and barks needed to remedy the ailments common to the laboring yeomanry. He loved to read and to read to us, an ever-appreciative audience, and knew Dr. Gunn's *Home Medicine* and *The Book of Common Prayer* and a host of songs, hymns, and verses by heart. He had a lively, raspy chuckle that he employed often. Indeed, he wears the start of a grin in this photograph, his mouth blurred in his striving to suppress it. He never could for long.

How things had changed by the time we sat for those tintypes. My own is lost, I fear, but it was never as dear to me as this image of my grandfather.

This was the first change—when he came to live with us the summer the war began.

My father volunteered for the Georgia infantry after he had finished the spring plowing and ensured that we were set to tend and harvest the crops. There were five of us by then—he and my mother, my two younger brothers James and Jefferson, and I. Two more children, one of them a baby sister, had been stillborn between my brothers, a hurt more common at that time, and not often spoken of then or remembered now. I would not turn eleven years of age until October, and my brothers were then aged seven and five. My father had considered long whether he ought to volunteer, but finally decided to for three reasons: he felt it his duty to do so, since Georgia was threatened with invasion after Fort Sumter; he did not want to shame my mother, who, though more sensible than many Southern women at the time, who had hen-pecked their husbands or fiancés into joining, was nonetheless a woman who expected my father to defend her and her children; and he had learnt from my grandfather, his father-in-law, a certain attitude toward politics, and knew that no matter the talk of states' rights and the denunciation of federal power, if war came the John Waxes of the South would be called up from their farms one by one. It was a matter of time.

The day of my father's muster my grandfather came early, on foot, from his farm to see him off. He would not depart our house from that day forward. He arrived with a sack of clothes slung over one shoulder and a box of books suspended from the other by a scrap of hemp rope. He arrived before sunup, and only now do I wonder in what darkness he had left his own house.

I had risen early in anticipation of his arrival and saw him coming from some way off. I spotted his pipe smoke first, rising in wisps above the swell of the hill, and when his old hat and his face came into view on the road I ran to him from our porch.

"Morning, Georgie," he called long before I had even reached him.

"Morning, granddaddy!" I said.

I caught up to him and circled him in the dust, powder-dry and cool in gloaming before the May heat. I indicated the box. "What did you bring?"

"Oh, we'll see."

"Can you read to us later?"

"It's a certainty," he said. "But first we got to see your daddy off."

"He's going to go fight."

"God willing, no," he said. I did not puzzle over-much at this; I was yet a child.

"Wes and Cal said they seen Uncle Quin's rifle. He's going to fight, too."

"That's right. He and your daddy signed their papers together. They're going to meet on the road yonder. Not too long from now."

"Could Wes and Cal come visit afterward?"

"You got work to do, Georgie?"

"Yes, sir."

"I reckon they do, too," he said. "Then—maybe."

He grinned at me from under the brim of his slouch hat. I grinned back. A visit from my cousins, who were near the same age as I and did not live much farther away than my grandfather, was always welcome.

We had by this point reached the shade tree in our yard and my mother and father had come out to meet us. James and Jeff followed, stumbling and bleary-eyed.

I did not mark my father's appearance carefully but I can recall it in detail nonetheless. He already wore his uniform—the soldiers still had them in those early days—a gray shell coat with a row of brass buttons stamped with the seal of the State of Georgia. He had new belts and accoutrements that had just begun to crease and break in, and were bound at the navel with a heavy brass beltplate stamped GA. He carried a rolled dark blue woolen blanket and a canvas poke of personal belongings and toilet goods. My mother had insisted specifically on his taking with him daily changes of socks. On his head he wore a gray woolen kepi with leather and brass harness and on his feet a slightly worn pair of brogans. He was clean-shaven and bright-eyed. It was the last I would see him so, in any of these particulars.

He approached my grandfather and extended his hand. My grandfather took it warmly and they greeted each other and shook for some time. At last, they nodded and broke off. My father looked at me and inclined himself without quite kneeling.

"Georgie," he said.

I was impressed only now, at this moment, that my father was leaving, would be gone just moments hence.

"Yes, sir."

"You take care of your mama, hear?"

"Yes, sir."

"Granddaddy will be staying with y'all like we talked about. He's going to help, and you mind him like you mind me. But you got to be the man of the place, now, hear?"

I nodded. Another word spoken and I risked shaming myself by crying.

He regarded me. His eyes were green, like my brothers', and probing. It was a fearsome thing, when in trouble as a child, to meet them. Now I held his gaze and wished he would never remove it. He straightened to his full height but still met my eye.

"I don't want to leave, you understand. But sometimes a man has got to do things he don't want."

"Yes, sir," I said, and the crisis passed. He was not speaking to me as a boy.

"Sometimes that's by choosing and sometimes it steals up on you. Wouldn't none of us do any of these things on the farm if we didn't have to, but we have to. That's the nature of the curse. This is just a bigger version of that."

"A bigger version of the curse?"

He did not understand at first, but then my grandfather laughed and he laughed too. "Yeah, I reckon so."

Then he held out his hand to me, and after a moment of wonder, I took it.

"I'll be back soon as I can."

I nodded. My grandfather put his hand on my shoulder as my father stepped over to my younger brothers and knelt to say his goodbyes.

"Y'all take care of mama, hear?" he said, and I marked the difference in the way he said it— unseriously, as one does when imparting some grave and momentous task to a child, because it is already in better hands. A wave of confidence and trepidation intermingled and passed over me. My father had recognized me as a man, put me in a position of headship—under the stewardship of my grandfather, of course—and I felt in a moment the glory and weight, the sudden responsibility of it descend upon me. I looked at my mother and saw, despite her calm and the smile she reserved only for my father, how she twisted her hands together in the folds of her apron. I looked at my grandfather, and he, without looking at me, gave my shoulder a squeeze.

At last my father embraced and kissed my mother and tipped his cap to her and set off down our road. The sun was just up.

WHAT I WRITE HERE I write upon reflection—some years' worth. One whose imagination has steeped long in the melodramas and romances of after generations will here advance the story to some time after the tearful goodbye, to see where the figures in our play are now. But, if anxious, our goodbye was not particularly tearful. We had no idea of what awaited us in those early days of brass and polish. And, furthermore, we had work to do. We watched my father until he was out of sight, around the bend in the road that would take him past the Hale, Turner, and Wheelwright farms and onto the main way to Athens, where my uncle Quintus would join him, and others, no doubt, on the way to join their companies and depart for the war proper. All that would play out well away from us. Once hidden from sight, we turned to our work for the day.

The sense of the responsibility imparted to me by my father quickly smothered under my chores. We lived on a fifty-three-acre farm with a barn, smokehouse, chickenhouse, and a good well. We kept hogs, chickens, a few milk cows, and two mules, and grew corn, oats, and a few acres of cotton for a little extra cash. When my father's time to muster came he had been mending a length of fence between our cornfield and the Wheelwrights' cow pasture. An unseasonably early thunderstorm had spooked the Wheelwright's cows and they had broken down a significant length of it along our cotton patch, which we husbanded carefully for the money it portended. Since my father could not finish the work before mustering in with the regiment it fell to me to complete it. Fencework was no joy for me; I was strong but smallish and had never developed the stoicism toward splinters that my father evinced. It was also lonesome work, out at the farm's edge and out of sight of the house, and yellowjackets seemed to favor the fenceline for their underground nests. They had stung me more than once. I was therefore joyed to learn that my grandfather's first task on our farm would be to help me finish mine. Not only was he good company but, in the event of a sting, a wad of his pipe tobacco would come as an immediate and welcome remedy.

We gathered tools for the work and headed toward the fence. I kept up a withering fire of questions out of sheer excitement that he would be staying with us.

"Is Aunt Laura watching y'all's farm?"

"Yeah," he said. Laura was my maiden aunt, my mother's elder sister, and perfectly capable of running a farm on her own. She had been the mistress of my grandfather's farm since my grandmother died some years before, when I was seven years old. Hired help called her Queen Laura.

"Will you have to go back?"

"Probably for a little bit at harvest, and of course we'll all have to go slaughter the hogs. You can help if you want, and if we get the crops in here in good time."

"Yeah!" I said. Any task was an adventure if done at the behest of my grandfather. "How long you staying with us?"

"As long as need be, like your daddy said."

"Until the war's done?"

"Something like that. He might could come home early, if it lasts long enough."

"How?"

"If the war lasts a couple years his enlistment papers might run out. Then he could come home. If he don't sign back up."

"Why would he do that?"

"Well," he said, and thought. "That ain't happened yet. Could be he'll come home when the war ends, if it's short."

"How long will the war last?"

"That I can't say."

"How come?"

He laughed. "I mean I don't know. Don't nobody know. Wars are like that."

"How come?"

"People are involved."

I scratched my head.

"I mean anything folks do, especially if they're worked up about it, is unpredictable. We can't know how long it'll last, how it'll turn out."

We had reached the fence and he gestured to it with the hatchet we would use for shaping the rails. "Look here. We're fixing to repair this fence. When will we be done?"

I looked and pointed to the farthest section of broken rails, about fifty yards off. "When we get there?"

"Right. Now, you ever been in a fight?"

I had, but it had had an embarrassing outcome and I had not repeated the mistake since, despite my temper. I gave a vague and unconvincing answer that lay partway between yes and no.

He laughed. "Well, you see what I mean."

I did. And I felt a sinking again. My father could

not have been three miles off on the road but it felt as though he had flown to Texas or Indian Territory in an instant. I foresaw his and my Uncle Quin's long walk and thought on how far it must be to Virginia, where it already seemed the war was shaping up.

"Have you ever been in a fight?" I said.

"Not since I was a boy," he said, and took up a fencerail. "And not many at that, for what I suspect are the same reasons you got. Besides—men don't fight each other. At least they shouldn't. Not in a fit of temper, anyways."

"No, I mean—have you ever been in a war?"

"Yes," he said, and set to work.

"When?"

"A long time ago," he said. "In the Floridas. I wasn't much older than you."

"How long did it last?"

"I was involved about a year," he said.

"Did y'all win?"

"Well, the Spaniards fussed about it, but the United States government got to keep Florida, so I guess so. At least, the government won."

"But you don't think so?"

"Help me here, Georgie," he said, and I helped him lift the rail into place. The Wheelwrights' cows had by now arrived to goggle and eavesdrop. They swished their tails and blinked in the early morning slantlight. Already the cicadas and other insects had begun their screaming song, which seems to add to the heat of a Georgia summer, and our faces had budded with sweat and taken the first step toward dripping. My grandfather took up the hatchet and tools and we moved to the next section of rail.

"Well," he said, "you're going to hear a lot soon, if you ain't already, about the Cause."

"Independence," I said. "Like General Washington."

"Right. And while I favor that, you don't want to

12

get anything by fighting if you don't have to. You risk too much, and if you lose, you lose too much."

"So—don't fight?" I had never suspected my grandfather of cowardice.

"No, son, you pick your fights. You recognize the danger, and you recognize that you will do evil even if you fight for a good thing. Why's your daddy fighting?"

"To defend us."

"You know how hard he thought on that? Before signing his papers?"

I had heard him and my mother talking on that very subject several times, late at night when they thought I lay asleep. But I had never realized that my father had been weighing a decision.

"So, then he's fighting—"

"For you. For your mama and your brothers. This farm and all of us. Fighting to protect what you love is the only kind of fighting worth doing."

"All the other men was joining."

My grandfather laughed. "Georgie, that's the worst reason to do anything."

He patted me on the back and I took no offense. Our conversation drifted to plants and berries, what would be ripe and ripening in that season and where we should go about looking for it. We finished repairing the fence by noon, had some dinner, and went to work on other chores—checking on the hogs, tending the three and a half acres of cotton on the southern slope of the farm, finally taking down the laundry for my mother—right up until suppertime. By that time I was mostly concerned about my cousins Wes and Cal, the twins, paying us a visit, but that was not to be for some time. Instead, my grandfather showed us that evening what he had brought along to read to us. These books were to change my life.

A WORD IS IN ORDER about my family. My father, John Wax, came from Emanuel County and much of his family remained in that area. Some of his own cousins lived one county over from us, and had even married members of the Thorpe family, which had married into my mother's side, as well. My father was the youngest of four surviving children born to Patrick and Kate Wax, and so my cousins on that side of the family were mostly older than I and I have never known them in the way I know my maternal cousins. My father's eldest brother, Henry, with four girls of his own, also joined the army and would be maimed at Malvern Hill. The younger of the daughters by his second wife—Grace and Elisabeth—were to stay with us as well one summer, but only for a few weeks, as I mean to relate.

My mother's family, on the other hand: they were Eschenbachs, and took great pride in having been among the Moravians who helped settle Georgia in the days of General Oglethorpe himself, of whom reminiscences and anecdotes had been handed down. These Eschenbachs were early acquainted with the Wesleys as well, and that branch of the family had eventually turned staunchly Methodist—strange as it may now seem for staunchness to enter the description of a typical Methodist. My father, raised Episcopalian, had joined the Methodist church upon marrying my mother. It was a less troubling proposition, he said, than becoming Baptist. At least the *Book of Common Prayer*—in its Methodist version—was truly common to both.

A handful of Eschenbachs remained along the coast but most of them had journeyed inland in the early days of the new century. My grandfather—born Lafayette, known to all as Fate—had been born outside Savannah but had lived the last forty years on the farm just over the hill from ours. His brothers Alexander, Tom, Casimir—you may infer from these names that my great-grandfather was himself the son of a great patriot in the Revolution—and Henry, Jr., all eventually moved up to the rolling red hill country of north central Georgia, and, with my grandfather's seven children and their own offspring, there eventually grew a great diaspora of Eschenbachs, spread in a triangle from Jackson to Elbert and to Talliaferro Counties.

My maiden aunt Laura excluded, my mother, Mary Eschenbach, was the eldest and—as was generally acknowledged, even long after her marriage—the most beautiful of Fate Eschenbach's daughters. Everyone knew the tale of my father's courtship of her, of the nervous young man in a borrowed tailcoat who, having spent hours working up the gumption to speak, approached her at a winter dance and found himself talking for hours over books, dead Romans, and how the weather affects the taste of persimmons—with her father. My mother and father had danced precisely once, the last turn of the evening, and my father had proposed as they parted. They were married in the spring—somewhat late, the both of them aged twenty five—and my mother bore me two years later.

Of my grandfather's other children—Charlotte,

Cornelia, Elizabeth, Margaret, and Quintus—my uncle Quin lived nearest us, and was the father of the twins, John Wesley and John Calhoun Eschenbach. Wes and Cal, to keep things manageable. Their younger siblings, Jeremiah and Caroline, were aged three and two when the war began. My aunt Charlotte and her husband Wilfred Thorpe and son Wilfred, Jr. lived across the road from my grandfather and aunt Laura, freeing him to live with us for the duration. My grandmother had died, as I have mentioned, when I was seven years old, and was buried at Barber's Chapel cemetery just up the road near the store.

We were farmers of the yeomanry, with a few exceptions. My great uncle Tom Eschenbach had worked as an overseer on the MacBean plantation and eventually took up blacksmithing and eventually shop-keeping. Just before the war, he set out for Texas, having decided to become a ranchero. My father's cousin Joan had married into commerce; her husband Robert Johnstone was a shopkeeper and leatherworker in Jefferson. My father's older sister Anne had married Walter Lucas, a stonecutter and mason from Elberton who owned three skilled Negroes, a fine house in town, and a thirty-acre farm a few miles outside town. My mother's younger sister Elizabeth had married one Thomas Crabtree, an early dabbler in photography and patent medicines, and had mostly disappeared. My grandfather received the occasional letter from the pair, almost always from Arkansas or some other uncivilized place. Rumor had it that Crabtree had been addled by the chemicals used in his hobbies, and that he was a Presbyterian, too.

Thus the broad-cast net of Eschenbachs and Waxes, which made it possible for my father to go to war and for us to be looked after. One wonders what will replace such bonds.

EVENING OF THAT FIRST DAY descended. We helped my mother clean up from supper and then I stepped onto the porch. The sun had gone down and the land lay bluing but yet visible. I recalled my father's departure. Most evenings he would sit with me outside, smoke his pipe, and whittle or tell stories from his own youth, moral tales of the lessons learned from his own failings. I already missed these times, and would grow to miss them more over the next weeks until my grandfather filled that loss almost totally. I sat alone for some minutes before my grandfather came out and sat next to me.

"Thought you wanted to hear a story."

I brightened—I had forgotten about the box of books. My grandfather brimmed full of stories—not just his own, but those recounted in books, from which he constantly increased his own store. Any book carried by my grandfather was a mystery and a wonder.

"What did you bring?"

"Look in here and we'll see."

He rose and I followed him inside. My brothers had already plundered the books, looking for plates and engravings. They had only just begun to read and still

17

favored those books with lots of pictures, the more lurid or dramatic the better.

"Shoo," my grandfather said. "Let me see them."

My brothers laughed and surrendered the books. He gathered the two they had been looking at and the ones in the rope-handled box and sorted through the stack. They were:

The Age of Fable and *The Age of Chivalry*, by Thomas Bulfinch. "A Yankee," my grandfather said, "but don't hold it against him."

Æneis, by Virgil, translated into heroic couplets by John Dryden.

Ivanhoe: A Romance, by Sir Walter Scott.

The Last Days of Pompeii, by Edward Bulwer-Lytton.

Macaulay's *Lays of Ancient Rome*.

And, last, his personal copies of Æsop, Dr. Gunn's *Domestic Medicine*, and, most importantly, the *Book of Common Prayer*, from which he would read to us daily. In this way I would learn the Psalms almost by heart.

His own interests may be clear from these selections. My grandfather, who seemed to know everyone, had established a friendship with one of the librarians at the University of Georgia in Athens, and by some arrangement—I was never to learn what, precisely— was permitted to borrow anything he fancied. He returned them and picked up new ones when he visited Athens, once every few months. Some he enjoyed so much he had sent away for and acquired by mail; a long wait in those days, and not for the impatient. What he liked tended toward the ancient and armored. I already loved the stories he had retold me from such books. I could not have comprehended what else I was to learn from them, at first through him and then on my own.

My brothers, once my grandfather had told them what a volcano is, begged for Bulwer-Lytton's story of

Pompeii. I asked for *The Age of Fable*. I liked legends and heroic tales. My grandfather set both aside and began that evening to read us *Ivanhoe*. I had heard of the book before—Walter Scott was immensely popular among the boys my age at that time and place, and we had often tilted at one another while playing at knights in the churchyard—but I was unprepared for the glut of heroism and melodrama the book was to present me.

For the next few months—I cannot recall precisely how long—my grandfather read to us nightly from *Ivanhoe* before reading some psalms and remembering our father in prayer. He proceeded sometimes no more than a few pages at a time, particularly as we passed harvest and staggered home ready to collapse at suppertime. But more often than not we bolted his reading down by the chapter. We speculated what was to become of Wilfred of Ivanhoe and Rowena, cheered Robin Hood, fulminated against the Templar Brian, fumed at the unjust governance of Prince John—who we assumed was a Yankee—and wondered not a few times why—with Wilfred incapacitated for much of the plot—the book was not entitled *Rebecca the Jewess* instead.

We did not limit our excitement or speculations to reading time in the evenings. We discussed the plot like gossipy ladies during the day, from sunup to sundown, as we milked, raked, snapped peas, shucked corn, wallowed in the creek to cool off, and plundered the hollows and thickets around the farm for the flora my grandfather prized. The book informed our souls. Once, a few weeks after harvest, while working the okra in my mother's garden plot behind the house, my brother Jefferson called to James and I. When we looked up from our tools, we saw him standing at rigid attention. He then presented his gardening implement, pointed, and said, "Look—I've an hoe."

We did not cease from laughing for some time.

When we repeated the joke for our mother—more than once, I'm afraid—she smiled and chuckled. When we told my grandfather, he slapped his thigh and roared with his high, raspy laughter.

At church on Sundays and any other opportunity to meet, I would catch my cousins Wes and Cal up on the story. We and the other children refined our games of knights—I, for one, much preferred jousting with sticks to mumblety-peg—to incorporate figures from the plot of *Ivanhoe*. Wes, devil that he was, took the Templar Brian de Bois-Guilbert every time. Like any actor, he savored a good villain. Caroline was inevitably Rowena. When Cal performed Wilfred, the girls fought for the part of Rebecca. Rowena may have been Wilfred's intended, but the girls divined where the real amorous interest of the story lay. I preferred to play Robin Hood.

I can remember that we read the novel well past harvest because we had almost finished the story when my father's first letter arrived, wrinkled and water-blotted, from Virginia. This was October 12, 1861, two days before my eleventh birthday.

My mother had sent Jefferson to Dawes's store—a mile or so away, near Wes and Cal's farm—for soap and bluing and he had returned with the letter. We knew about it immediately, for he came running back into sight much sooner than expected, waving the letter high overhead and shouting as he ran. We thought at first something had gone wrong—an emergency at a nearby farm, bad news Jefferson had overheard, or something of the like. We met him by the shade tree and he threw himself into my mother's arms, further deepening her impression of imminent bad news. Only after looking at the letter and the grin on Jefferson's face did we understand—our first letter from Daddy.

"Jeff," my mother said at length, and found herself smiling, "you about scared me to death."

"Sorry, mama."

"Scared me to death," she said, and held the letter up for my grandfather to see. "A letter from John, Daddy."

"Good news," my grandfather said.

She looked back to Jefferson, still panting happily against her apron. "You pick up them other things I sent you for?"

"Yes, ma'am," he said and produced a small flour-sack with the items inside.

"Good boy." She took the items and stood, smoothed her apron, and slid the letter under the apron strings at her waist. "Don't you go scaring me that way again, Jeff."

Jefferson laughed. "Yes, ma'am."

"All right, then," she said, and looked at the rest of us. She regarded us a moment and a look of puzzlement crossed her face. "Well? We got work to do."

"What's the letter?" I said, bewildered.

"It's from your daddy."

I looked at my brothers, my grandfather. "You going to read it to us?"

"This evening, after supper. We got a lot to do."

My grandfather picked up Jefferson where he knelt in the dusty yard and brushed him off. "Y'all heard your mama. We'll see what your daddy wrote us later."

My mother nodded to him, to us, and went into the house to arrange the wash and her other chores. The letter would still be there, folded nearly in half under her apron string, when we came in for dinner, and then supper. I marveled then that she could be so patient, and for the first time, to my recollection, deliberately held myself up for comparison. I gobbled my food, spent every penny I earned the moment I could on some trinket at Dawes's store or out of a catalog, and hurried through everything. How she could deny herself the immediate, tantalizing pleasure of reading my father's words baffled me, and I felt a lack in myself that wanted mending.

Later, much later, only long after she died and after years of reflection, did I light upon another, complementary reason for keeping the letter back: fear. Who knew what it might have said? Women in our part of Georgia had already gotten plenty of bad news just a few months into the war. So her day may not have been spent entirely in hoping and looking forward to the letter. Not at all.

I, for my part, spent the workday in three places: there on the farm, among the corn, chickens, and the tedium of my chores; in the holted countryside of England six centuries before, albeit more actively than Wilfred of Ivanhoe; and somewhere in Virginia, under arms with my father.

I SPENT SUPPER IN SILENCE, too much anticipating the reading of the letter to talk. I hardly breathed. My brothers coped otherwise, through ceaseless chatter, and may well have forgotten the letter. I recall Jefferson had a funny story about Herod, one of our mules, which he spun into an epic by laughing, losing his place in the story, and backing up only to fall to laughing again. I cannot now even remember what the mule had done. I kept glancing at the letter where my mother had finally placed it, resting on a shelf by the stove.

Once finished, my grandfather said, "Now then, Mary, how about that letter?"

"Yes! The letter!" my brothers fairly shrieked. "Daddy's letter!"

I was, by then, enervated through waiting. I sat watching. The moment had finally arrived. My mother smiled and nodded toward the shelf. "Go on ahead."

My grandfather retrieved the letter and offered it to her. She shook her head—another action I mistook for something other than dread.

"All right," my grandfather said. He unfolded the letter and read it to us in the same voice he used for

Ivanhoe, albeit more haltingly. I think now that he looked ahead as he read, watching for anything bothersome, just in case.

August 6 1861
Virginia

Dearest Mary,
I cannot be more exact in where we are as we are prohibited from including such detail in our letters home lest they perchance be intercepted by the enemy & also as I do not rightly know. We have marched & marched since we left a few months back. All ready I have had a boy who workt as a tailer cinch up the waist of my britches. His stitches have held but needless to say they do not have the fine workmanship of yours.

I have writen before but before I could post the letter to you & the boys I ruint them in fording a creek. Only now have I got to replace my paper & ink. I apologise.

We had us a scrape a week or so ago. It was bigger and lasted longer than expected but we are all rite. Do not fret for us. We are well lead & Lieut McBean you may well hear has been promoted Capt of our company. I have also writen to Ellen about Quin. He is all rite just got nickt & needed a few stitches & a stiff drink & is all ready back with us in the company. I mention it to forestall any rumor that may reach you before the truth does. For remember what Fate that is your daddy always says about rumors.

Greet the boys for me & your daddy & sisters to. I love you all & will write again when I can.

John Wax

When my grandfather had finished reading, he passed the letter to me. The paper was worn and creased, and had been dampened and re-dried at some point, but my father's hand was strong and legible.

I read it through again as my brothers asked my mother and grandfather questions. Its content was lucid enough—my father had little formal education but commanded the word well enough to make himself felt and understood, a skill too little valued by teachers of spelling and grammar. He had lost weight, presumably from all the marching. Fording a creek sounded like great fun to me, or at least a chance to cool down after chores. My brothers and I could often enough be found wading in the creek at the edge of our property. The Lieutenant MacBean was Thomas MacBean, master of the MacBean plantation not four miles as the crow flies from our farm, and one of the elected officers of the infantry company raised in our county. He was a planter of but modest means, and had only been voted to one of the most junior officers' billets; the first lieutenants and the company captain were men of greater wealth from nearer Danielsville and Athens. I wondered idly what Mr. MacBean had done to earn promotion to that spot.

The letter was full of such—to me, at that time— pap, and wanting in two particulars: *What about my uncle Quintus, Wes and Cal's father?* and *What about this "scrape?"* I found the letter sadly devoid of battle scenes. My father's "scrape" could only torment, not entertain. He did not even write who had won. I had spent the day adventuring in my mind with him and Ivanhoe, and wanted badly to bring the two images together. My father the warrior, who could tell me again and again of his fights and bravery. I read through the letter a third time, divined no more, and handed it on to James. In my scrutiny of the letter itself, I missed whatever might have passed over my mother's—or grandfather's—face.

My brothers had not ceased from talking since my grandfather read the letter. As I sat and mulled what I had read—and not read—my grandfather grabbed and rubbed my shoulder.

"You glad to hear from your daddy?"

"Yes, sir."

He was quiet. My mother said something to Jefferson. At last, as if waking, I looked at my grandfather. He eyed me from under his bushy black brows, measuring. I tried a smile. My grandfather nodded and said, "He's whole son, and seems to be in good spirits. We ought to be thankful for it. In the morning I'll walk over the Quin's and talk to Ellen."

"Better go pretty early if you mean to go to church with us," my mother said.

"Course."

My mother nodded. "Take something with you for her. I'll get something ready here in a minute."

"That'd be nice," he said. "Want to come with me, Georgie?"

I did, and was instantly excited about it. I could see my cousins—and the day before my birthday no less.

"When we leave their house," I said, "can we walk to church with Wes and Cal?"

"If they feel like going," my grandfather said.

I had never heard *feeling like going* mentioned as a criterion for attending church but, as children are wont to do, I stored it for later.

We cleaned up and made ready for bed. My grandfather read the penultimate chapter of *Ivanhoe* and prayed a Psalm with us, and I forgot my disappointment in my father's letter. I was truly grateful that he was alive, and also well, but after seeing him off in uniform those months earlier and having steeped myself in chivalry and adventure, I expected our first word from him to be of triumph. In the meantime, I would get to spend time with my favorite cousins, and make a special trip—earlier than usual, for a Sunday—to do so.

That night I settled into my bed with James and Jefferson and my grandfather dimmed the lantern before, himself, going to bed. He stopped by the stove and table to say good night to my mother, who—uncharacteristically—embraced him for some time. Then he climbed into the attic and she pulled her rocker around behind the stove where she would not need a blanket and sat and rocked.

I have neglected to mention the size of our house—small. As I lay in bed she, in the kitchen, sat no more than five paces away. I lay on my side, my back to my brothers, and drifted.

One can usually recall only terrible dreams, but this uneventful dream, coming to me still half-awake, I can recall in every particular: My father, in the armor pictured in the engraved frontispiece of *Ivanhoe*, sitting a caparisoned charger in the pecan grove by Wes and Cal's house. The trees sough and creak in the breeze. He faces away from me but I know him to be inattentive, possibly sleepy. The wind kicks up, the leaves show their pale undersides, as before a thunderstorm, and he puts spurs to his horse and gallops away. I find myself—still impassively observing—in armor too, but lacking a horse.

I had begun to follow when I heard a voice murmuring on the breeze, and awoke.

It was my mother, praying. I could no longer see her clearly because of the stove, but I had seen her sit up and pray in her chair so often it should have been unremarkable. Like the dream, nothing about this should have rooted itself so firmly in my mind that I can still recall it after so many years. I lay still for some time, listening to her faint words, softly footed like half-remembered poetry, and realized with a start that she was praying for my father. I discerned then a new force to her words, not so much entreating as asserting, boldly before the throne, that the Lord of Hosts look after John Wax.

Later, in the militia, before our own scrape, I made the acquaintance of a Roman Catholic boy and his grandfather, and had plenty of occasions to watch them tell their beads, cycling through litanies and prayers of such variety that I wondered that anyone could learn so much by heart. Such fervency was to make a deep impression upon me. And yet I only judged their devotion fervent by comparison with my mother, who prayed in the quiet of the night as zealously as ever those others would pray under fire. I had heard her pray so before, but now I saw the truth behind it. And her prayer went on and on, until I slipped into dreams I forgot when I woke.

MY GRANDFATHER AND I ROSE early that Sunday morning, dressed for church, and struck out for the main road and the Quintus Eschenbach farm.

We lived in a solidly yeoman patch of Madison County, but the plantation life was never far from sight. I have mentioned the MacBeans already; their plantation of 322 acres and 31 Negroes lay just down the road from us; we could see the woods along the backside of their property from the upper branches of the shade tree in our yard. Otherwise it was 30-, 40-, and 50-acre tracts sewn with corn, beans, oats, or a little cotton like ours, or orchards like the pecan grove of my dream. This was rolling country veined with creeks and cow ponds and muscled with hard-worked red land. It was hard then to see romance in it—Walter Scott did not encourage any association of the lance with the plow, though I would later learn that the two were as dependent upon each other as our land and the musket rifle—but it was beautiful.

This morning walk proved beautiful enough that I noticed it. The weather had cooled with the corn harvest, and we stood ready to pick and bale our cotton.

The hollows between the blue hills lay dense with fog rising from the creeks and the dust of the road lay still, settled and softened by a fine dew. I relished such weather and hummed as we walked.

We passed our immediate neighbors, the Wheelwrights, on the left-hand side of the road, and Mr. Hale on the other, who lived alone—it was gospel among children of our area that he was a wizard or wanted murderer, but was in fact only a crank—but who had wrung impressive yields of sweet potatoes and cotton from his plot of red clay through hired help and willpower. We shared a pond at the edges of our properties, where my brothers and I swam and he watered his cows and caught snapping turtles to sell for soup to the MacBeans.

As we passed Mr. Hale stepped out of his house in trousers and boots, with his galluses drawn bowstring taut over his naked shoulders. He saw us and nodded. We waved.

"Fate. Georgie," he said.

We wished him a good morning and passed on as Mr. Hale set to work on his woodpile. At the junction of our road and the main road to Athens, we passed three Negroes from the MacBean place—I knew two on sight as Frank and Clovis—on their way to Mr. Hale's. They tipped their hats and we nodded.

"Good morning, Mister Fate, master," Clovis, a big man, said to us.

"Morning," we said.

My grandfather's farm, in the care of my aunt Laura, lay down the road to the left, toward Danielsville and Athens. We turned right, just as the sun rose behind the steeple of Barber's Chapel ahead of us. We pulled the brims of our hats low and walked down into the shadow of a foggy saddle where the creek passed under the road. I had learned from my grandfather that the banks of the creek in its hollow

30

were good for all kinds wild berries and medicinal plants, especially those that grow well in shade— ginseng, mint, blueberries, and blackberries. We had wandered that hollow with hats and buckets many times, but this morning my mind turned elsewhere.

"Granddaddy?"

"Yes, Georgie?"

"Why's Mister Hale work Sundays?"

"That's none of our business, I reckon."

"Is he in trouble?" I thought, perhaps, that his crops were too large for one man to bring in and threatened to rot on the stalk.

"Not any that I ever seen."

"Is he a bad man?"

"Nah. Just a Presbyterian."

I looked at my grandfather, uncomprehending. He started to laugh and then stifled it.

"Naw, Georgie, I don't reckon he's a bad man. I reckon he just don't care about church."

"He don't feel like going?"

Now my grandfather laughed. "Feeling ain't got nothing to do with it."

"So why? He's keeping them niggers from going to church working on Sunday like that too."

"Well, he pays them."

"So it's all right if you pay somebody?"

"Well, maybe not all right, but they mind a whole lot less."

"Hm," I said. "What do them niggers do with their money?"

"Colored boys, Georgie. Colored. Don't talk like white trash."

"Sorry, granddaddy."

"They save it up, sometimes. They save enough, they can even buy themselves and work on their own. I knew a boy out near Lavonia did that. Some of them spend it pretty quick. I seen them buy up eight or nine

31

dollars of stuff at Dawes's store, and not anything useful, neither."

We were, at this point, coming uphill out of the foggy, shady bottom land. The Dawes family's pecan grove loomed out of the mist on our left and I felt eerie looking into its ranked and filed boles, remembering my dream. Ahead, at the fork in the road, stood Dawes's store, and across from it our church with an apple orchard behind for the maintenance of Reverend Asbridge. The sun shone down on us again and we shielded our eyes.

I noticed then, sitting on the steps of the store, a figure whittling and smoking a pipe. I recognized him even from afar as Horace Magruder, a local white trash boy who had worked briefly for the MacBeans. He rose upon our approach and tipped his hat, which had the broad brim fashionable among planters. IIe looked much like white trash everywhere—lean, tallow-skinned, lantern-jawed. The hat looked like it was midway to returning to its primitive state as straw.

"How do you do there, Mister Eschenbach?" Magruder said.

My grandfather nodded. "Horace."

"And young Master Wax. Getting big there. You fixing to join up with your daddy now?"

I was affronted and not a little afraid. Magruder had a reputation as a layabout and had been given the sack by the MacBeans for undisclosed outrages against the slaves there. There were salacious rumors.

"Maybe," I said, and looking upon his outfit narrowed my eyes at him. "When are you joining up?"

"Well, hell—"

"That's enough, Horace," my grandfather said.

"Well, ain't no call being ugly about it. I'm sick if you want to know the truth."

"That's fine, Horace. Apologize, Georgie."

I looked in shock at my grandfather. We had stopped

32

walking now and he looked firmly at me from under those severe brows. I looked at Horace, who had his tongue planted wonderingly behind the corner of his mouth, waiting.

"I'm sorry, Mister Magruder," I said.

"Aw, now, no offense taken. Hey—whereabouts y'all headed?"

My grandfather had resumed walking the instant I had completed my apology. He took out his pipe and clamped down on the stem with his teeth, his sole sign of distress or anger. "My son's place, just up here."

"Well, now, I'll walk with y'all. Damn if Dawes ain't open today."

"It's Sunday, Horace."

"Well, damn if I didn't forget. Aimed to get me some fishing hooks and a sack of flour for the missus. Just have to wait til the morning."

"Hm."

I noticed that my grandfather had greatly lengthened his stride. I had commenced to panting. Presently we reached the track leading to Wes and Cal's house, which stood just out of sight behind the browning corn stalks along the road.

"Wellsir, it's been a pleasure," Horace said.

"You have good day, Horace," my grandfather said, and gave my foot a subtle nudge with his toe.

"Good day," I said.

Horace tipped that hat again and was off.

We turned off the road and my grandfather grumbled and shook his head. I looked at him, at his frown and his furrowed and lowered brow.

"Granddaddy, why did you make me apologize to that man?"

"It was the right thing to do."

"But he's white trash," I said. "And how come he's here when Daddy—"

My grandfather put his hand on my shoulder and

gave it a gentle but fairly seismic squeeze. I hushed. Ahead, Wes and Cal's house hove into view, and their bulldog roused at the end of his rope and barked a welcome. My grandfather took out his pipe and inspected the stem for damage.

"Steady, Georgie," my grandfather said. "We'll talk about all that later." My aunt Ellen stepped out onto the porch, wiping her hands on her apron. I could see even at that distance the inquisitive look she had, occasioned by our arrival. My grandfather waved. "We got something important to do here and now," he said.

I RECALL THE FIRST PERSON I remember dying—my grandmother. She had been a big, hale, hearty woman, an excellent cook, with a gentle touch and a gift for comforting others, a lady singularly well-matched with my grandfather. My grandmother was present at my birth in 1850, and my father and grandfather both credited her with saving my mother's life. A cancer took her when I was seven years old, but well I recall the struggle. She only gradually lost her vitality, and friends joked by way of encouragement of the regret the disease must surely have felt at tussling with her. By the end, she had ceased to leave the house and spent much time on the porch, shelling peas and shucking corn while my Aunt Laura took over the cooking, and when her strength failed her even of those activities, and her great strong hands could only lie in her lap, she lay confined to bed, but still relished our conversation. I grew hesitant to speak to her, after the way of children, who harbor a terror of illness in others, and wish to this day that I had made myself sit and talk to her at greater length than I did—if not for my own sake, then for hers. In the final weeks, she spent most of the time napping, only waking to sip some stew or water.

One evening in the early spring, as we sat down to rest after supper, Chapman, an aged Negro from the MacBean plantation who had been hired out to my grandfather's farm to help, arrived in my grandfather's wagon. We had been sent for; the time was near, he said. We rode with him at breathtaking speed to my grandfather's farm, and I shall never forget stopping in the yard and hurrying to the porch, where my Aunt Laura met us and, without preamble, said, "She's gone."

My mother took me in to see her mother's body. She lay on her back, with her eyes closed and her mouth open where she had taken her final breath. According to my Aunt Laura, she had lain all day sleeping on her side and, in the evening, turned over as if to make herself more comfortable, and begun immediately to struggle to breath. She had passed about the time Chapman was leaving the house with us.

We sat all night together, and spent most of the next day there as friends came and went and more family arrived. I do not recall much else of that time— I spent much of it weeping, and in being comforted by my mother and grandfather—but I well remember the stunned expressions of some of the men. My Uncle Quin, in particular, sat as if struck senseless by a blow. By the time we left for home, I, too, felt numbed by grief and exhaustion, and fell almost instantly to sleep in the wagon driven again by Chapman.

I mention this here because while my grand-mother's death was not unexpected, it still struck hard when it came.

My grandfather spoke with my aunt Ellen there on the steps of their house, with Wes, Cal, Jeremiah, and Caroline listening. This time, undistracted, I watched the faces of others receiving the news, vague as it was. My cousins sat blank-faced, silent, exactly as Uncle Quin had when my grandmother died. They feared not the unexpected, but the long-anticipated worst. Aunt Ellen buried her hands in her flour-dusted apron, wringing them out of sight as her mouth went through rapid evolutions of its own.

"Nicked?" she said once.

"That's all John said," my grandfather said. "He didn't say much more but to say that he was back with the regiment and all right."

Ellen nodded. My grandfather resumed, explaining fully, and I saw her face wash from anxiousness and dread to a settled mix of relief and fear. My grandfather embraced her, and she closed her eyes and nodded against his shoulder as he said one or two more comforting things. But she did not untwist her hands from her apron.

We stayed to walk them to church. I rejoiced to spend the rest of the morning and the lunchtime hours with Wes and Cal, but was surprised they would not stay home given the chance. "I reckon we better go," Ellen had said, smiling, when my grandfather asked. She insisted on including my grandfather and me for breakfast, despite our protestations that we had already eaten, and then got the family ready for the walk to church. Wes and Cal and I played outside until time to leave.

Wes and Cal were towheaded, like their mother's people, and brown-eyed, like my grandfather, mother, and myself. They were but six months older than I and so we could not remember not knowing each other. At eleven years old we had spent years of accumulated time together playing, hunting, swimming, foraging in the woods, and, of course, working. Especially when the cotton came in, we would help out on each other's farms to avoid spending money on rented Negroes or hired trash like Horace Magruder. We prided ourselves on doing our own work, the one point of honor that placed the yeomanry above the planters. On cool harvest evenings we would wash in the cow pond or the creek below our house, rusting the water with red clay, seeing who could stand the frigidity longest, and chase each other through the woods. The preferred game of this season, as I've mentioned, was knights.

We arrayed ourselves around their bulldog and menaced him with branches, three knights trying to attack a nimble and aggressive dragon. The bulldog barked and bounded happily at us on his rope as we feinted and called to each other. He managed at one point to snap Cal's lance in half, which sent Cal shrieking and laughing to the woodpile to recover his courage. We shouted that Cal was a knave thus to flee. We stood winded and sweating in the cool morning air by the time my grandfather stepped down off the porch with Ellen and the younger children.

"You boys ain't hurting that dog, are you?" he said.

"No, sir!" we said, and laughed. The dog barked at us for stopping the game. Cal returned and hugged it about the neck, laughing.

My grandfather grinned. "Good boys. Come on— let's go to church."

Barber's Chapel Methodist Church stood just back down the road across from Dawes's store. It had started as a log meeting house set up by the first planter in the area, a man named Barber, long since deceased. Over the last fifty years it had grown, burned, and been rebuilt two or three times. The oldest grave in the cemetery was an infant, Julia Barber, aged three months, buried in 1804. A reminder.

There was an unusually large congregation that morning. We were not, it became apparent, the only people in the area to receive letters. The old men who stood smoking and spitting by the hitching posts spoke knowingly about a big late summer battle in Virginia. A railroad junction, name that sounds like *molasses*. Word had gotten back via newspaper but with letters arriving the details—reliable details, eyewitness details—began to fill out the story. Georgia regiments involved, yes, in the thick of it. Someone knew someone in Sanford, outside Athens, who had been killed. But they spoke with little mournfulness—the battle had put the invaders to flight. The rumor, repeated from newspapers, was of pell-mell retreat in the face of Southern fire and bayonet. Perhaps the war was over? Nah, the Yankees are too damn arrogant to let one setback stop them. A passing lady clucked her tongue at this last, and the Reverend Asbridge stepped into the church door to bring in the flock. We filed in, singing by the time we crossed the threshold, but my mind wandered, distracted.

The Reverend Asbridge, a bespectacled man of about thirty years, made up for his relative youth with fervor. Since he had come to Barber's Chapel a few years before the war, he had driven up church attendance through vigorous—though not what one would call "fire and brimstone"—sermonizing and regular activity among the farmers of all classes. He stopped by every farm in the area for a visit once a month and would find chores to help with if he could. He even dismissed the Negroes usually seconded from the MacBean plantation for the care of the apple orchard behind the parsonage, preferring to learn how to do it himself. Activity was a sort of Gospel to him. "Good, honest, vigorous work is the calling of every man," he had said. He said it so often that an old lady had stitched and framed it for him. It hung on the back wall of the sanctuary, above the door.

I appreciated the Reverend Asbridge because, following the Creed, the various other offices, collects, readings, and rites prescribed for a given Sunday by the *Book of Common Prayer*, his homilies were short and delivered on a concrete point a child could understand—usually hard work and holiness, which seemed synonymous. His sermon this Sunday was, at first, not markedly different from those before. He had only made passing reference to the politics of secession and the outbreak of the war, and had evaded or dismissed questions on the topic until none bothered to ask anymore. Such questions seemed to confuse him. One or two ardent fire-eaters had even quit the congregation because of what they deemed his "feminine impassivity before the face of aggression." Or so Tom Streets, my grandfather's neighbor, wrote in a handbill crudely printed up at the newspaper office in Danielsville and distributed at Dawes's store until Mr. Dawes himself ran him off.

I was sitting between Wes and Cal with my mother behind—so she could administer correction if our minds wandered too visibly—when the Reverend Asbridge, having stopped in the middle of a sentence with his head bowed, closed his Bible, removed his spectacles, and stepped down out of the pulpit. So far as I can remember he had never done this before.

He walked to the first pew and asked the lady sitting there whether she had a man in the army. Three, she said. A husband with the First Georgia Cavalry and two brothers in the infantry.

"Officers or enlisted men?" he said.

"Enlisted all."

He went to the next lady with the same question. One—a brother. And the next. Two—an uncle and a near cousin, raised with her like a brother.

On he went, through every pew in the building, which, while not large, held enough people. It took some time. Perhaps someone grew bored during the proceedings but I did not. I watched, rapt, unsure of what the Reverend Asbridge intended and astonished at how many soldiers could be connected with one congregation of yeoman Methodists.

Wes and Cal stirred as he got closer to our pew.

Preachers made them nervous, even Cal, the more pious of the two, who had sometimes entertained notions of becoming a preacher himself, if he could not be Wilfred of Ivanhoe or brave Horatius, the captain of the gate.

"He ain't going to get us to talk, is he?" Wes said.

My Aunt Ellen shushed him.

And then there Reverend Asbridge was, looming over us. My impression to this day is one of looming, though I know he could not have stood more than five feet, four inches and appeared shorter due to a general roundness of figure. He smiled gently.

"Missus Eschenbach, have you a man with the army?"

Aunt Ellen nodded and took my mother's hand. "Yes, Reverend. My husband, a brother, and my brother-in-law. Enlisted men."

Reverend Asbridge looked at my mother and made the same inquiry.

"Yes, Reverend."

"How many?"

"My husband and my brother-in-law."

"Officers or enlisted?"

"Enlisted."

And then he moved on. It was exhilarating, having the preacher pass by during the service itself, when he was usually safely anchored to the pulpit. I felt I understood somewhat Moses's feeling when the Lord showed him his back parts in a blinding rush.

At last, the Reverend Asbridge walked in great state back up to the front of the sanctuary and turned to face us.

"Consider, brethren, the danger each of these men is in, and consider how tenuous our hold on life regardless. Make me to know mine end, and the measure of my days, what it is, that I may know how frail I am. Recall that all flesh is as grass, and that our days are but a shadow or a vapor. Already I have learnt of men attached to this congregation by blood and friendship, grievously wounded or killed. Pray for them, and attend to their families. For within the body of Christ, if one member suffer, all the members suffer with it. Let us consider the cost of this war, for what king, going to make war against another king, sitteth not down first, and consulteth whether he be able with ten thousand to meet him that cometh against him with twenty thousand? Or else, while the other is yet a great way off, he sendeth an ambassage, and desireth conditions of peace. If he does not, consider what will become of the ten thousand. Would it not be mere vanity and vexation of spirit?"

At that, with a smile and a nod, he fell silent. After some while, and many sidelong, questioning glances, we rose one by one and departed the sanctuary. Outside, in the churchyard, the old men resumed their stations by the hitching post and scratched their heads and muttered at the ground. The Negro members of our congregation stood by, somehow even more silent than usual.

My mother took Jefferson by the hand and we walked home. She and my grandfather smiled and spoke kindly to us, and answered some of our questions, but said nothing of import about the sermon.

THE NEXT FEW WEEKS PASSED with some general consternation among Barber Chapel's parishioners—enough so that even a boy aged eleven could not be wholly unaware of the upset. The Reverend Asbridge's departure from the liturgy and even his own habit, exceptional by any standard, proved impossible to interpret through any available hermeneutical scheme. Some took him to be evoking the sacrifices of the men already fighting the Yankees; others were convinced that his speech—these uniformly resisted calling it a sermon—was a covert condemnation of the fight for Southern independence, and dispatched letters to the president of the North Georgia Conference of the Methodist Episcopal Church, South; others felt discomfited but put it all out of their minds. Tom Streets printed another handbill based upon the rumor and hearsay, causing my grandfather to remark that Streets had the makings of a career journalist.

The controversy fizzled as the last of the harvest came in. By the time my hands healed from the annual cotton picking, which wore and tore them bloody every year, the consternation had dwindled to suspicious looks thrown Reverend Asbridge's way as he passed some quarters, and one or two poorly attending members disappearing for good.

We brought in three bales of cotton on our farm and two and a quarter on my uncle Quin's, all of which we sold through the cotton factor that visited the MacBean place every fall. We picked and bagged the terrible bolls until our hands hung so bloody raw and abraded we could not reach into our pockets without agony. A blind gypsy could have read our fortunes sniffing the blood caked in our lifelines. A team of Negroes arrived and loaded the bales onto wagons and carted them off to the railhead in Athens, from whence they would ride to Savannah. I found out later that the price was a great disappointment, as the Confederate government in Richmond had ended exports of cotton in an vain effort to bring some European power into the war, and we were not to plant it again until years afterward. In between there would be much worry over cash, even for farmers. We brought in good crops of oats and corn and fairly stuffed our hogs—who were already nigh spherical with acorn mast—with the latter. Slaughter approached, and we needed the pork. With harvest ended and hog-killing time not quite upon us, and the frosts arriving and our breath coming like broken glass when we ran or worked outside, my grandfather oiled his rifle and shotgun and took me hunting.

I had watched him hunt before, and even taken potshots at squirrels and raccoons, but now he let me carry the guns and taught me in earnest how to bring down small game.

"Your father left you in charge," he said, "and a man ought to be ready to provide, any time. I'm just here to help."

He taught me to clean and skin the game on my own and—when my fifth or sixth squirrel dropped out of the trees too torn up to be good for food—a trick of his that I never forgot.

We had just left the porch one morning and by accident flushed some squirrels from my mother's garden patch, where they had been foraging among the stalks and remains of what we had missed in the picking. They scampered to the fields, up the side of the house, behind the muleshed, and into the shade tree.

My grandfather produced his powder and measured a charge for the rifle. "Let's get started with these rats here."

I grounded the shotgun and brought out my powder and pellets.

"Not this time, Georgie. I want to show you something."

He loaded without looking at the rifle. He regarded the two or three plump squirrels watching us upside down from the shade tree. The tree was a great white oak, older even than the state, five feet wide at the base and better than seventy feet tall. In the high summer we watched the yard like a sundial with the tree as its gnomon.

My grandfather brought the rifle to half-cock and fastened a percussion cap to the nipple. He nodded toward the tree.

"See that fat one there, bout halfway up?" One of the squirrels sat, contented with his distance and sanctuary, dead center in the thickest part of the trunk, about twenty feet up.

"Yes, sir."

"Watch, now. My granddaddy taught me this."

He thumbed the hammer to full cock and raised and sighted. The squirrel moved its head minutely, taking in this new intelligence. I heard my grandfather softly breathe out and he fired. The ball struck the trunk of the oak just above the fat squirrel's head with a sound like a hammer on a loose plank—a miss. And the squirrel flopped backward to the ground anyway.

My grandfather and I stood wreathed in the sulphurous reek of the rifle. The surviving squirrels skittered up and down the tree; a distant dog commenced to barking. I looked at the lifeless squirrel in the yard and up at my grandfather, who grounded the rifle and grinned wide, pressing his tongue against the back of his teeth and chuckling.

At last, he said, "Whew!"

"How——"

My mother burst out of the house, black hair loose, apron in hand.

"God sakes, Daddy!"

"Fixing to rid your okra patch of squirrels, Mary," he said.

I pointed, awed. "He killed it without even shooting it!"

"If you possess such power why don't you forebear to shoot at all?"

My grandfather retrieved the squirrel and handed it to me.

"Georgie's got to learn. He needs a teacher."

My mother shook her head and strode back into the house. From inside, I heard her declaim to one of my younger brothers about being startled half to death. I laughed and looked at the squirrel. My grandfather grounded the rifle and set to measuring out his powder again.

I turned the squirrel over in my hands. It was still warm and completely unmarked. I looked at its yellow maloccluded teeth and felt an uncanny prickle of fear—I had seen boys with fingers bitten clean through by squirrels and did not want this creature awaking in a fright in my still-tender cotton-raw hands.

"You know what concussion is, Georgie?"

I looked at my grandfather. He stowed the ramrod and waited. "No, sir."

He balled a fist and struck the open palm of his

46

other hand. "That's concussion. Shock—the force of smiting something. It's the concussion, of a kind, that knocks a man down when you strike him. The concussion of your fist on his skull. Now, you knock a man hard enough, the concussion on his skull knocks his brains into his skull. You can do a most powerful lot of harm to a man, you strike him hard enough. You understand?"

"Yes, sir. That's why you don't want us fighting? That's why you say men don't fight?"

He chuckled. "Naw, men don't fight each other cause that's the worse way to go about settling things. But we can talk on that later. Now, what I said about concussing a man's brains? This bullet—" and he produced one, a .32 caliber lead ball, "—when it strikes a thing, concusses everything around it. You feel a cannonball strike close by, you feel the earth shake. You feel a bullet pass close by your face, you feel it clap the air by your cheek. You hit a tree trunk like that close enough to a squirrel's skull—not too close, not too far—the concussion knocks its brains and kills it dead just like that. Don't tear up the meat, don't hurt the squirrel."

I marveled over the squirrel. He took it and handed me the rifle. It seemed suddenly like a more powerful instrument than a mere squirrel gun. My grandfather had ennobled it.

"Your turn, Georgie."

It took some practice, but by the end of the fall I had brought in twenty-three squirrels—including seven in that way—and further trained my eye to strike rabbits, raccoons, possums, and groundhogs without damaging the meat. In my greatest coup, on the first morning of December, we surprised three turkeys in the woods by the creek, and I brought down the tom with a shot to the eye. With plenty of game, garden vegetables, and corn, we prepared for

47

hog-slaughtering and looked forward to eating like kings.

My grandfather, James, and I had just sat down on the porch with the knives and a few whetstones, the scalding pot by the pigpen already at a boil in the frosty morning air, when my father returned.

HE HAD RECEIVED A FURLOUGH to come home and help us with the slaughter, and arrived in the yard already apologizing for missing the harvest. We fairly smothered him with hugs and kisses, and brought him inside to stuff him with food and ask him no end of questions. My mother, once recovered, sat beside him and held his hand in both of hers, and did not once cease from smiling. I thought it at the time mere happiness, or—I was at the age when I was becoming aware of such things—romance. I understand it now to have been gratitude—to my father, to his regiment, to God—immense and deep.

As he sat at our table I marked the changes in him: he was skinnier to be sure, and his loosened jacket somewhat faded and ineradicably stained at the elbows. His pants were new, and of a different shade of gray, and stained at the cuffs, way up the inseam, and at the knees, which were patched. He wore the same brogans, also patched, also worn. I watched his face for some hint of the adventures upon which he had quested. His cheeks had hollowed out somewhat and the bones showed more clearly, but his smile and the glittering of his eyes as he chattered happily with us were those of the man who had marched away seven months before.

"Uncle Quin get to come back, too?" Jefferson said.

"No, I was the only man in the company to get to come home," my father said.

"How come?" James said.

"I don't rightly know. A lot of us put in for them. All but me got a 'no' back."

"Aw," Jefferson said. He was the tenderest of us three boys.

"I'm most thankful," my mother said.

My father squeezed her hands. "The boys in the company give me letters and money to bring back to their folks. I'll help y'all slaughter the hogs and then I got to make my rounds."

"Like the Reverend," Jefferson said.

"Ha! Just like."

"Well," my grandfather said, "they picked a most trustworthy man to carry their dispatches."

"Thank you, Fate. Just thankful to be home for a bit."

"How long?" I said.

"I reckon I can get away with a week. I saved up my pay and took the train all the way from Richmond to Athens. Made the trip in two days!"

Such speed beggared my imagination. I had seen trains once or twice but never up close, and never had I gotten to ride on one.

As with his departure, so with his arrival—after the initial greetings and excitement and a little visit, we set to work. The slaughter would take the better part of the day, and we did not want to lose the daylight.

James and Jefferson stoked the scalding pot back up and my father, grandfather, and I set to work with the hogs themselves. I had never enjoyed this part, but as my grandfather had reminded me the day before and the morning of, a man must do things he does not like if he wants to perform his duty—not sometimes, but often.

My grandfather would prod one of our corn-swollen hogs up from the mud and hustle him out of the pen to us by the pot, where a ditch for this purpose could drain downhill, and keep the creature still while my father dealt it a blow between the eyes with an ax. It was my job, as the youngest and quickest of us three, to cut its throat, slashing "right across the gullet," as my grandfather put it. This was a most important task—a poorly aimed thrust of the knife and the animal would merely suffer and shriek—and the one I liked least of all. After the sickening tension and give of the hog's skin, perceived clearly through the tip of the blade, came the plunge and the blood. The notoriety of the proverbial stuck pig's jugular spray is well earned.

After the gouts of blood slackened and the hog lay certainly dead, we hoisted and heaved the carcass to the scalding pot and Jefferson and James scraped the hair from the hide. Then we strung up the hog from a pole we had set up the day before and commenced the real cutting—carving clean around the spine to remove the head, cutting away the fat and beginning to render it into lard, removing the intestines rectum first and separating the major organs, setting some of the latter aside to soak and dropping the former into a tub, and my mother cutting up the meat and taking it into the smokehouse to cure. It was a kind of triage. And so through fifteen of our fattest hogs, until, in the waning light of dusk, with the operation ceased, aching through all our muscles and covered head to foot in a slurry of red clay and blood, we sat down, still daubed in gore, to eat a late supper. After dark, we washed away what we could into the drainage ditch and cleaned and put away our tools. Then, before my mother allowed us near the house, we washed, outside in the cold, under the dark of the moon.

We had waited unusually long in the year for two reasons: first, as my grandfather had pointed out, slaughtering on a new moon like the one at the beginning of that December would ruin parts of the hog; and second—a point my grandfather never made but I could not miss—we were shorthanded at harvest. It was a good harvest, but everything took longer, and put us behind in bringing in the hogs from the woods.

It did not seem a problem then, merely an inconvenience. And we were, above all, thankful for my father's brief return.

AFTER SLAUGHTERING THE HOGS at our farm, we helped with the same at Quin and Ellen's, and then at my grandfather's farm under the watchful eye of my Aunt Laura. With Wes and Cal's help the work went somewhat faster, and I was glad for someone else to handle the spurty job. My father's fourth day home saw us sorting the meats for curing and generally tidying the farm. That evening, my father took the three of us boys hunting in the woods that verged our property. I attempted to demonstrate my grandfather's technique for concussing squirrels, albeit with no success.

After supper my father asked if I would like to join him in delivering the letters and things he had brought home. I was delighted—an entire day with my father, walking the greater part of our corner of the county. I could hardly sleep that night, the first since May in which my mother's prayers and the creaking of her rocker did not lull me to sleep from behind the stove.

We departed, just the two of us, before dawn. The mid-December air bit the cheeks and woke the respiratory system with a rush of pure, thin cold. It felt good to breathe deep. I imagined the insides of my lungs frosting, the way I had seen empty bottles left on our porch do in the chill. My father fell naturally into a quick step march that forced me into a light trot to keep up. Familiarity with this pace would prove handy later.

We walked out past Dawes's Store and the church toward the MacBean place, to a twenty-nine-acre farm I had passed many times but seldom visited, run by a family named Neal. The Neals were tenants of their neighbors, the McAbees, and tottered on the edge separating the ordinary yeoman farmer from white trash. The house was old and in poor repair, and not only because the man of the place was away fighting. My father delivered to Mrs. Neal three letters, dictated to him by Mr. Neal—that is, Private Neal—who was unlettered, and a handful of carefully folded bills. My father asked whether all was well with her and the children; she complained of nothing but thrush in her youngest, a child of about ten months, and my father said he would tell my grandfather about it. Mrs. Neal thanked my father and asked whether he could take a letter with him when he returned. He said yes, and we tipped our hats and left. I looked back as we walked away and saw Mrs. Neal sitting down with the letters, her six children emerging from hiding to listen. I did not know them—the Neals were notionally Baptist, and their children seldom appeared at school—but something about the scene remained with me long after.

We visited four more farms out that stretch of the road before doubling back toward Dawes's Store. My father generously gave his time to each family we saw, and offered to stop back by and perform any chores or heavy labor that was needed around the place. He was refused—though thanked profusely—but the offer meant a great deal to the families we saw. All the while, I marked my father's demeanor—warm and deferential, as was his way, and obliging with information about life in the camp when questioned. He told amusing stories about local notables: enlisted silliness, pratfalls and misunderstandings, near misses on picket duty with amusing outcomes, and the foibles of the officer class— the MacBeans and their like. One thing he did not talk about: the fighting, the war proper.

When we stopped at the McAbee farm on way back, Mrs. McAbee came closest to asking the questions I wanted.

"And how are things out there?" she said near the end of the conversation.

"Tolerable," my father said. This was a less optimistic answer than he gave at the other farms. He had, apparently, adjudged Mrs. McAbee a serious seeker of the truth, not someone seeking mere reassurance or a diverting anecdote. "We make do."

"How are you men holding up?"

"Tolerable, ma'am. We got what we need."

"I hear fearful things, Mister Wax."

"Yes, ma'am."

"My late father, you know, who passed away from consumption here two years ago? He fought in Mexico. He told me things—you know. I never did want no war, not after what he told me."

"No, ma'am. Me neither, and for the same reason."

I looked at my father. I recalled that my grandfather had fought—when? where? I had always known this, and he had never spoken of it, not in detail. And when he taught me how to kill squirrels without shooting them, his examples—the earth-shaking crash of a cannonball, the clap of air against your cheek when a bullet whistles past. He knew these things firsthand. I stood dumbstruck as my father and Mrs. McAbee talked on.

"Well, you men make us right proud. I'd've rather not had war, but if it comes, let Southern men fight it and God will see us through."

"Thank you, ma'am. We do what we can. Sometimes a man's got to do things he don't like."

"That's right, Mister Wax."

She thanked us for the letters and the cash—a thick roll of bills here—and sent us off with three fresh biscuits wrapped in a handkerchief.

"Bout lunch time," my father said as he unwrapped them. "I was getting hungry. How about you?"

"Yeah."

He handed me two of the biscuits. I looked at him. "Go on," he said. "Everybody in the family knows they're your favorite."

"Thank you." I took them and ate absently as we walked.

"I was going to get us a bite at Dawes's Store. Reckon we can get us a little something else. Piece of rock candy, maybe?"

Something in me perked up at that—we had candy so seldom in those days—but I could not rouse myself to excitement.

"Daddy, when was granddaddy in a war?"

"Long time ago."

"I know, but—he didn't want a war?"

"No, Georgie."

"And you didn't?"

"Don't nobody with any sense want a war, Georgie. It's the worst way available to get things settled, bar none."

"I know," I said, and took a bit and thought. The biscuit was still warm inside, and buttery. I could not help but savor it as I thought.

"Something wrong, Georgie?"

"No, sir."

Presently, we reached the store. My father used the quarter dollar he'd brought with us to buy a tin of crackers, a scoop of roasted peanuts, and a stick of rock candy for me. He also procured a few small items for my mother and brothers. While I waited, I looked at a series of advertising bills tacked to the walls, giving special attention to the firearms. Since honing my aim under the guidance of my grandfather, the rifle had become my favorite tool. Leaflets and brochures of all sizes—from Colt's, Springfield, Savage, and their many imitators to the strange patent models of engineering cranks—cluttered the walls, abounding with engravings that showed the weapons in action and anatomical cross sections of their inner workings.

When my father had finished, he and Mr. Dawes walked up to me.

"Looking at them repeaters?" Mr. Dawes said. He was a bluff, hearty man with a very red face, probably due to drink, though he never showed it.

"Yes, sir," I said. I had just then been looking at the illustrated parts of a rifle action worked by lever, which could load a new, brass-cartridged round without having to ground the weapon or fool with a ramrod and powder. The two or three gears, pins, and springs seemed an unfathomably complex machine to me.

"Ah, the Henry," he said. "New Haven Arms. Seen one shoot a while back and it's a sight. No chance getting one of them now, though." As if to emphasize this futility, he untacked the flyer from the wall.

"How come?" I said.

Mr. Dawes laughed and his face reddened even more. He rolled up the flyer for the marvelous rifle. "Yankees, son. Ain't going to do business with us!"

We left the store and sat on a stump in the yard, near a group of old-timers who haunted the store and talked gossip and politics for lack of entertainment. It was still cold, but the sun felt pleasant enough as we ate our crackers and idly shelled peanuts for a time.

"Daddy, what was the battle like?"

"Aw, we didn't do much of nothing in the battle."

"That ain't what Wes and Cal said."

"Oh?"

The day we helped with the slaughter, my cousins had made a cryptic joke about all the killing in Virginia. A jet of blood from one of the hogs provoked another laugh, and a remark the gist of which was, "Just like daddy wrote us!" I told my father, and he chewed a handful of peanuts in silence for a while.

"We did do a little fighting, back in July. I wrote y'all about it, Georgie."

"I remember, but you didn't say nothing about what it was like."

"That's right."

I was bewildered, and fought against the child I still was to keep my voice steady. "Why?"

"Well, it ain't nothing your mama needs to hear about. A man's got to think about others, Georgie, hear?"

I was stung—he was right. "Yes, sir. Yes."

"And, well, I don't need to talk about it."

"Did you shoot anybody? Did you shoot any Yankees?" My father looked at me, and I knew in an instant that I had asked the wrong question. To this day I cannot describe his look—you would have had to know the man—but it lay somewhere between irritation, fear, and abject sorrow. "I'm sorry," I said. "I'm sorry, Daddy."

He put his hand on my shoulder. "I don't honestly know, son. There was a lot of smoke. But yeah—I shot at some Yankees."

Some inward part of me thrilled at this, but I said nothing for a while.

"That's why you tell the good stories," I said at last. "The funny ones."

"Don't want to worry folks none. Least of all your mama."

"The war is hard."

"The hardest," he said.

I remembered, of all things, Wilfred of Ivanhoe and his trials, and more importantly, the new book my grandfather had begun to read to us—Bulfinch's *Age of Chivalry*, with King Arthur and Sir Launcelot and all their sufferings. The seed of a new romance planted itself in my imagination—the adventure of hardship. If we were not to grow weary in welldoing, well, something had to be working against us, wearying us, tempting us away from our striving. I said nothing of this. I wish, now, that I had. I may have learned something then that I would need later.

"Sometimes men got to do things they don't like," I said.

My father smiled and gave me a shake. "That's right." He stood. "Come on, son—we got a ways to go today."

I rose and we set off for the next farm at the quick step.

II

THE PISTOL

WE WOULD NOT SEE MY FATHER again for two years. His furlough passed like a shadow, and we saw him off with the new year. He departed with his haversack again stuffed with letters and his person laden with gifts—socks, scarves, twists of favorite tobacco, the occasional embroidered handkerchief, little mementoes from the hands of children. He took the dictation of no few letters himself and delivered a few remedies from my grandfather—a tea made from leaves saved from our shade tree to the Neal child with thrush, catnip tea with honey for another family's colicky baby, a peachtree root poultice for another child's pumpknot—all of which he did for his fellow soldiers. I was present—he kept me with him through his errands in the countryside.

He left in much the same way as before, but in the cold of a winter morning and with new trousers, shirts, and long underwear sewn by my mother. She even managed to replace some of his issued brass buttons with new ones, complete with the seal of the State of

Georgia, procured by some means unknown to me.

We, however, were much changed by his visit. This departure we took harder. We had felt his lack for some months and now knew how badly we would miss him once gone again. Furthermore, it was now the dead of winter, with little to do to keep us occupied or his absence off our minds.

My brothers and I walked to school on days we were not much needed, which were most of them through the beginning of February. Our education was irregular but enough. We could all read by the age of six and do enough arithmetic to get by. We improved ourselves on our own with my mother and grandfather's tutelage, and constant reading. Everything else we learned by doing on the farm or from the stories our grandfather told or read to us. *Ivanhoe*, *The Age of Fable*, Macaulay's *Lays*, Dryden's *Æneis*, and his other favorites—*The Pilgrim's Progress*, *Paradise Lost*, *Two Years Before the Mast*, *The Pathfinder* and *The Deerslayer*, Defoe's *Crusoe* and *Journal of the Plague Year*, which interested me mightily, Chapman's *Iliad* and *Odyssey*, a book of stories condensed from Shakespeare. I mulled Macbeth, Lear on the blasted heath, Æneas leaving proud Troy with his father upon his back, and especially Horatius. I could not read those lines

> *Then out spake brave Horatius,*
> *The Captain of the Gate:*
> *"To every man upon this earth*
> *Death cometh soon or late.*
> *And how can man die better*
> *Than facing fearful odds*
> *For the ashes of his fathers*
> *And the temples of his gods?*

without thinking back upon my grandfather's talk as we worked on the fence that first day.

All of these books proved entertaining, a sight better than the lessons in our school readers, and a good store of parables besides, but they soon were not enough for me. I read and reread them through the winter months, inquiring of my grandfather to understand difficult passages and retelling the stories in heightened form for my younger brothers and Wes and Cal. I wanted and asked for more.

"Soon, Georgie," he told me. "We've yet to finish reading these through with James and Jefferson. We'll get us a new batch then."

In mid-February we received our first letter since my father had left again.

January 12, 1862

Dearest Mary,

I am returned to Virginia and the regt. Quin & the boys in my section done built a house, chimny & all, while I was away. They thank all for their letters & gifts & promise to respond accordingly. We are safe & show no signs of fighting any time soon. Right now it is all drill drill drill & boiling our hardtack to make it edible. The officers they have balls & social calls to keep them intertained. It is a tolerable winter all things considered.

Mary it is hard being away again having seen the boys grown so much while I was away. I pray I may return soon & especialy that the war ends so it dont have to be on furlow. I wish to stay in Georgia & grow old with you & see our boys grown into men of there own. Georgie is well on his way & no thanks to me being gone. Your daddy is a fine man & I thank him for being there for you & the boys.

John Wax

More letters followed, filled with the details of camp life and more amusing stories. Many involved my uncle Quin, a notorious trickster—Wes and Cal came by it honest—taking the starch out of young bucks fresh to the theater. I had learned more of the "scrape" of the July previous from Wes and Cal, from newspaper accounts, and from eavesdropping upon the old men hanging about Dawes's store, and realized that the new men who were so full of themselves were fresh recruits—replacements. And one did not replace living soldiers.

I kept much of this to myself. It seemed of no consequence, and the war lay dormant far from Georgia.

DORMANT, COURANT, RAMPANT, salient, guardant, regardant. Even now these words put me in mind of lions. I do not now recall when, but sometime during the spring of 1862 my grandfather found and gave to me a handbook of heraldry, full of the component parts of chivalric display. Here was grist for the taxonomical mill of a boy's mind, perhaps the finest sorting instrument in creation—blazons and escutcheons and ordinaries, charges like the chevron and saltire, fleurs, crosses, lions, gryphons, horses, and boars, every attitude and posture and tincture subject to classification under arcane schemata of French jargon.

I practiced the formulæ on the animals around the farm or those I happened to encounter. Wes and Cal's bulldog was a particularly fruitful source of attitudes. "Dog sable couchant regardant," I might say, whereupon he would usually rise and become "Dog salient." "A cock argent courant" once pursued Wes clean out of their yard and into a tree. We avoided the "ox tenné" in the MacBeans' back pasture, and once, while out walking with my grandfather in search of blackberries, we chanced upon "a hind lodged regardant," nursing a newborn fawn, for which wonder even heraldry had no word. I drafted for myself, my brothers, my cousins, and many friends coats of arms with fantastic beasts in every conceivable variation of what I knew from the handbook. We imagined these designs onto sections of board, jousted one another, and went on quests interrupted only by church.

Furthermore, I was to find myself later in the war understanding more of what was happening. When a literary-minded newspaperman—they still existed, in those days—described a general as "rampant," or the warring sides as "combatants," or of an action taking place in desperate defense of a "salient," I grasped almost by instinct what he meant, and could see an image of it in my mind to boot.

One night, as my grandfather neared the end of the story of Sir Launcelot's humiliation in the cart—in Bulfinch's King Arthur book—I asked whether our family had a coat of arms.

"I don't reckon so, Georgie."

"How come?"

"Well, those are for knights."

"But knights are soldiers, ain't they?"

"Yes, of a sort. They're soldiers all the time. Professionals—er, of a sort."

I considered this. "The king pays them?"

My grandfather chuckled. "In a way. He gives them land to look after. That's how they can afford to get all that armor and them horses."

"So they're—farmers?"

"They defend farmers. It was different back then."

Knights, land and horses, but not ordinary farmers. I puzzled it over.

"Are the MacBeans knights?"

My grandfather burst into a full laugh from deep in his belly. "Well, they certainly think so."

"Daddy," my mother said.

I looked back and forth between them. "I don't understand."

"Your granddaddy was making sport of the MacBeans. Tell them, Daddy."

"Yes, yes, I confess," he said, and wiped a tear. "I'm sorry, boys. The MacBeans have a lot of land. They ain't plain farmers, like us. And they do fight. Hell, they read *Ivanhoe* just like us, and think of themselves as latter-day knights."

"Daddy, don't you go cussing in this house."

"Sorry—forgot myself." My grandfather couldn't help another chuckle. "No, Georgie, things are different nowadays. There ain't no knights no more, not really. But we can act like them."

"Jousting!" Jefferson said.

"Naw, I mean what folks like the MacBeans call chivalry. It's about respect—for your elders, like in the Bible, and for ladies like your mama, and for yourselves. Everybody deserves a certain amount of respect."

My brother James, ever the silent of the three, spoke up. "That why men fight duels?"

"Yes, exactly."

"That's a joust!" Jefferson said.

"In its way, certainly."

James was still at work. "Because—because of disrespect."

"That's right. You disrespect a man, it's a wound to his honor."

"And everybody deserves some."

"That's right."

James bit his lip and rolled his eyes, his habit of hard thought. Jefferson said, "You ever fight in a duel, Granddaddy?"

"Naw, Jeff, I haven't. I figure real men ought to settle their differences some other way, though I can't say I've ever seen or heard of a duel in these parts as long as I've been alive."

It was true. We had heard about duels, and boys being boys we reenacted some of the greats—Jim Bowie on the sandbar, Andrew Jackson taking a ball to the chest before laying Charles Dickinson in the dust, Hamilton and Burr, despite its less exciting outcome—but duels even then existed in the fog-shrouded frontier between fact and legend. Besides—the yeomanry seldom if ever dueled. Some of our class even viewed it as a dishonorable hobby of the planters, though, again, with few or no concrete exempla to speak of in decades.

"What if somebody challenged you?" James said.

"That ain't happened, thank God."

"But what if?" Jefferson said.

"Folks like us just don't duel, Jeff."

"But what ifffff—"

"Well—I'd try to see what I done wrong, and make amends. Give him satisfaction. It don't progress from the challenge to the duel directly, you know."

"Oh," Jeff said, and lowered his head, defeated to find reality so dull, as procedural as the morning milking.

"What if he wouldn't accept?" James said.

"I reckon I'd have to fight him."

We were silent. After a moment, my mother stirred nervously from her place by the stove. "I think maybe you boys should talk about something else."

"Is there anybody don't deserve respect?"

"No," my grandfather said.

Something struck me, something from weeks before. "Even white trash?" I said.

"Yes, even white trash. They're folks, after all."

"I remember you told me not to be ugly to Horace Magruder. Made me say sorry."

"You think you didn't ought to?"

He raised his dark and pointed eyebrows, a rarity and a sign I had better reconsider my present line of thought. I was taken aback.

70

"He's trash," I said. "He's a drunkard and a lay-about. Mama said so."

"Oh, no you don't," my mother said.

My grandfather smiled and regarded me patiently. "Georgie, them things may be true. But that don't change how you treat a man. Horace Magruder don't have the blessings we do. He'll have to answer for what he done with his life, given what he does and don't have, but it ain't for us to treat him ugly on this side of the grave."

"Even though he's trash?"

"Yes."

"What about niggers?" Jefferson said.

My mother strode over. "Don't you go being ugly now, Jefferson Wax. Georgie, look where you've took this talk."

My grandfather raised a hand. "Jefferson, why do you honor your mama?"

He had to consider this. "Cause the Bible says so."

"They stoned children didn't honor their elders," James said.

"Why else?" my grandfather said.

"She'll whip me." This was no small consideration. My brothers and I, despite much discussion, had never settled whether my father's strength or my mother's passion made for the worse whipping.

"Why else?"

Jefferson was silent.

"Do you love your mama?"

"Yes, sir."

"Does she love you?"

"Yes, sir."

"If you love somebody, you respect them and obey them. Ain't it so?"

"Yes, sir."

"Now, do you respect your Aunt Laura? Your Aunt Ellen? All of you boys."

We nodded.

"Why?"

"They're our elders, too," I said.

"And kin," James said.

"Now," my grandfather said, "how about Missus Bower?" Mrs. Bower was a widow woman who lived on her son's land behind Dawes's store and had midwifed half the ladies in the county. We saw her often when walking to see Wes and Cal.

"Yes, sir."

"Why?"

"She's a lady," James said.

"But not kin? Not your elder?"

James scratched his head. I said, "Elder, but not kin."

"And a lady," Jefferson said.

"You respect and honor some people just because of who they are," my grandfather said. "And everybody got a 'who they are,' even beyond what they got in land or cotton or money. And so you ought to treat them right, regardless. Colored folks got nothing at all, not even what drunks and white trash do. You go and mistreat a slave, you may have got away with it cause a slave got no honor to speak of, and no wherewithal to go after you. But you've wounded the honor of God, who made them too, though foolish and weak, base and despised of the world, and God don't never lose a duel."

"Yes, sir," Jefferson said.

"Think on Wilfred of Ivanhoe. He stuck up for Isaac and Gurth, despite them being a Jew and a hog farmer. Didn't get much lower than that back then— something we all might should remember next time we slop the hogs. Wilfred wasn't the king, or the most powerful knight in the land, but he used what he had to do the best he could for the folks around him. Leastways till he got laid up later in the book."

I mulled all this over. I had absorbed certain ideas, like all Southerners, with my mother's milk. We knew honor like the inside of our clothes. But with this explication, I sensed its subtleties opening to me, another system like heraldry.

When I spoke again, my grandfather and Jefferson were laughing at a remark the latter had made about Wilfred's relative inactivity in the later developments of the plot.

"So," I said, "all this is like rules for how to treat folks? Like the Ten Commandments?"

"Yes and no," my grandfather said. "It ain't so easy. You can learn a list of rules by heart but you got to live respect. There's officers—folks like the MacBeans, though we can't say nothing about the character of Mister MacBean himself, now—there's officers know all the rules of a dress parade and a Christmas ball but make asses of themselves over who gets to sit at what seat at dinner."

"Daddy."

"Ain't nothing wrong with *ass*. It's in the Bible and it describes a lot of folks."

"So's *piss*," Jefferson whispered.

"I think it's time we all went to bed," my mother said, and demonstrated the power of the respected lady.

THE NEXT YEARS PASSED. Time got away from us in the interlocking cycles and epicycles of the yeoman life: the daily routine of early rising, breakfast, chores and labor, play if we had time, supper, and time reading with my grandfather; the weekly routine of church and meals with family at our farm, Wes and Cal's, or my grandfather's with Aunt Laura, followed by the six days of labor decreed for man these many millennia; and the seasons, with the hunts and slaughters and play of the winter giving way to the plow, hoe, and scythe for most of the year. With the last frost we set to work plowing and planting, and as the cool mornings disappeared we would break a sweat walking out the door in the morning. The sky over the furrowed red hills blanched white and the air grew heavy with heat and moisture, and we hastened through our chores when possible and spent the late afternoons cooling off in the pond or the creek, where we could distract ourselves catching crawfish, salamanders, or turtles. When at last the heat began to drain away and the whited sky turned blue, we brought in the oats and corn. Then came slaughter, first at our farm, and then at Wes and Cal's, and then the winter.

My grandfather took me hunting, and in the following year instructed James in shooting, too. And so on again the next year, with us growing and reaping and my father so far away.

Beginning in the late summer of 1862 I sprang up some five inches, my voice deepened, hesitantly at first before bellying out much later, after the war, and strange things happened to my body. I took more notice of the girls at church and school and about the county, but was too ashamed to talk to them. I noticed, in particular, the unattainable—Eliza MacBean, daughter of Thomas MacBean, planter, lawyer, and, by the end of '62, major of volunteer infantry. She and her elder brother, Pritchard, who was a year and a half my senior, took to long horseback rides through the countryside around their plantation. I saw them sometimes when I had to run to Dawes's store, or walking to Quin or my granddaddy's farm. She rode always impeccably dressed, if not in the great state of the large planters of the Black Belt, and had long wavy auburn hair and freckles. Ladies considered freckles a blemish in those days but, I confess, they did something powerful to me. I looked forward to seeing her and her brother on the road. I do not believe I ever spoke to Eliza before the war ended, but Pritchard will figure into my story again.

We felt other changes as a family. My father continued to write letters, but they arrived erratically, sometimes in batches covering three months at a stretch, with gaps in his narrative where we had already received a letter from between the new arrivals. We began to lose track of him from afar. The newspapers did not help, in accordance with their nature, especially as reports of vastly bloodier campaigns arrived—on the Peninsula, and then Maryland, and again in Virginia at Fredericksburg, and, in the spring and summer following, both Virginia and Pennsylvania—and in just enough detail to know nothing. When my father's letters did come, they reassured us that he and those we knew were whole, but little else. For example:

September 25, 1862

Dearest Mary,

I write to you from Virginia having returned from Mary Land. We are well despite a fight of some proportions up there in Union territory. We was spared the thick of it thank God & our gravest hardship is want of food & shoes, which is a blessing all things considered. Quin is newly recovered from a stomach complaint & sends his thanks for the chimny soot remidy you taut me some years ago. The regt has had three days rest & the talk is of quiet til spring. I have put in for a furlow but there is no talk of anyone getting them this year. I saw Genl Lee himself on the march & a fine old man he is. I will write again as soon as poss. Thank your Daddy for me & kiss the boys.

John Wax

One would never divine from this missive that my father had lived through the near entrapment and destruction of the army in a bend of the Potomac at Sharpsburg. Not that my father intended to deceive us—far from it.

Other changes stole up on us. With a few years of conscription—as my grandfather had predicted—the manhood of the county thinned out, and foot traffic along our road increased as families attempted to work multiple farms at once. The Reverend Asbridge left Barber's Chapel to serve as a chaplain with a regiment in the west. As we no longer planted cotton, we planted more beans or potatoes or simply let the cotton acres lie fallow. Prices of goods climbed as the several states of the CSA issued paper currency, and a dollar didn't go nearly as far as it had just two or three years previous. Merchants like Mr. Dawes began shamefacedly to insist on payment in specie. We felt the pinch, enough so that even I was aware of it in the prayers of my mother and the hard calculation in my grandfather's eyes when he looked across our fields of a midsummer's day, assessing. But we ate well enough, and what we needed but didn't already have we could borrow from family or neighbors. War, thus far, was an onerous inconvenience, but not ruinous. And still my father lived.

Others did not enjoy such luck. Ned Kirk and Isaiah Medford, acquaintances of my father and grandfather, with farms a few miles away, died in the spring campaigning of 1863. Another, John Woodley, returned that summer with a leg missing below the knee. Reports and rumor, exchanged at the store or at church, ran rampant, of whom had been wounded or taken sick, how, and whether they would live. Mrs. Neal received word in August 1863 that her husband had died of dysentery. A cousin came out to oversee the sale of their farm for her and she left for her in-laws' farm with her—now seven—orphaned children in tow. Horace Magruder, called up from the ranks of the poor whites to the infantry a year after my apology, died when a Yankee cannonball struck him full in the face at Salem Church. The same ball maimed three others, only two of whom made it home. Despite my regret and inquiries after the war, I never learned what became of Horace's widow or children.

THREE VISITS STAND OUT to me from about this time. The first came during the stay of my Emanuel County cousins Grace and Elisabeth Wax in May and June of 1863.

My uncle Henry had been gravely wounded in the slaughter at Malvern Hill. He had, with his regiment, advanced into Yankee crossfire and, with his regiment, been mown down. He had dragged himself wheezing from the field with three shots through the musculature of his thighs and a perforated lung, a sucking chest wound. The surgeons pronounced it a miracle that he had lived. Today I find it more a miracle that the Minié balls that struck him had all missed the femur, limiting themselves to massive damage to the soft tissues. Had any one of them struck bone, he would lie to this day in an unmarked grave on the field. That was July 1, 1862.

The following spring, Henry, whose wounds had still not fully closed, took a turn for the worse. He lay dying from late April onward, and my aunt Dinah, in hysterics, according to my cousins, distributed their children among family. Grace and Elisabeth—known as "Bit"—traveled up from Swainsboro to stay with us.

They were bright, pretty girls who strongly resembled my brothers and were similar in age. Jefferson and Bit got along particularly well, and for those few weeks were inseparable. They helped in our mother's chores where they could and generally enlivened the farm with their chatter, which was endless but of an innocence and good humor which did not make it burdensome. My mother, for her part, seemed greatly to enjoy having daughters for a few weeks, and fussed over their hair and the particulars of their dress. The girls beamed when she did so—they had not gotten much attention at home for nigh on a year.

Yet Grace and Bit are not who I mean when I remark that a visit from this time stands out vividly to me—I mean the man who came to fetch them when Henry recovered.

My uncle Henry, remarkably, miraculously, rose from his bed one day and—so family lore has it—said, "I'll be God-damned if I'm going to lay there and die like a God-damned cripple. I'm tired of laying there. Where are my britches?" and traipsed outside in his sweat-sodden and pus-crusted long underwear and set to work in the garden. Henry was an irascible man. Nor was he churchgoing.

Thereafter, Henry recovered but for a permanent halt in his step, "Where are my britches?" became a recurrent joke in our family, and the Emanuel County Waxes sent a hired man to escort the girls home.

I cannot recall the man's name but he stood over six feet tall and looked like he'd cured in the smokehouse too long. He plodded and had a schoolmasterly air about him. I believe I heard he had been a seminarian at one point but had run out of money. He stayed overnight with us and departed with the girls the next day; my grandfather and I drove them into Athens to the train station, which was for me a great and distracting adventure.

But I marked something else odd about this wizened man—his speech. Even Jefferson noted later that "He talked funny." He drawled more than was usual in our county, and spoke breathily, lighting gingerly on his vowels and pronouncing them just differently enough for mere boys to notice. When I asked my grandfather about it, he said the man came from Savannah. He had known the moment the man opened his mouth.

I puzzled over this for some time, and realized that I had noted peculiarities in Grace and Bit's speech as well. I knew enough of the wider world to know that people from far away spoke strangely, but my family, Grace and Bit, and the lean hireling all came from Georgia. Could Georgia be so large that the people spoke with discernible differences in different parts of the state? I asked my grandfather.

"Well, yes—Georgia is a big state. One of the biggest, matter of fact. And people do talk different in different parts. But it don't take much of a distance to put space between the ways people talk."

"What do you mean?"

"You go up in the mountains, up near North Carolina, and seems like the folks up there talk different in about every hollow. You might not even understand some of them, Georgie."

I marveled at this and returned to it many times over as I went about my work. I would have cause to ponder it again.

The second visit I recall in particular detail was with Pritchard MacBean, whom I have already mentioned, scion of the nearest plantation.

As I have related, Pritchard was a year and a half my elder, and though of an entirely different class we did know one another well enough to say hello in passing, though I had not yet found the temerity to say hello to his sister. He was a well-built, ruddy boy whose jaw had already squared off above a bull neck by the time he joined the cavalry.

I had heard somehow that he had joined up and was to head west to help in the campaigning near Chattanooga when we met one day near Dawes's Store. It was late summer of '63. It was not quite time to bring the corn in and so when my chores were done I had as much as remained of the afternoon to myself. That day I had finished particularly early and made for Wes and Cal's. Pritchard and I crossed paths in the low-lying place where my grandfather and I had walked through the morning fog two years before, over a brick culvert through which ran the creek that fed our pond further down.

Pritchard rode high on his favorite stallion, the finest horse left on their plantation after his father had taken many of them and the Confederate States of America had requisitioned others, and he was in uniform. Eliza did not ride with him this time, but his manservant—what the British call a valet or batman— a dark, heavy, bearded Negro of twenty-five or thirty named Anchises, rode a dappled mare beside him.

I nodded and touched the brim of my hat—broad-brimmed, unmilitary, weather-beaten. "Pritchard," I said. "Anchises."

"George Wax," he said.

"Young Master Wax," Anchises said.

"Right fine uniform, Pritchard," I said. I was excited. I had seen plenty of uniforms—though most of them had been pretty shabby for the last year or so— but the thought of someone mine own age in uniform, off to the war! I took it in. He wore a finely tailored shell coat with yellow cuffs and collar and his own fine riding boots in soft tan leather to the knee. He wore a blue-grey kepi with the chinstrap tight under his jaw. A steel cavalry sabre clattered at his thigh and all his brass buttons, buckles, and tack shone burnished in the summer sun. I thought of gleaming armor, of my conversation with my grandfather about knights, of my dream of the pecan grove. I grinned.

Pritchard narrowed his eyes. "Something funny, Master Wax?"

I realized he may have taken my remarks as sarcasm. "No, no—you're just a sight!"

Pritchard looked at me. Anchises looked at Pritchard.

"I mean it. And to think—somebody our age!"

"Well, you do what you got to."

I nodded. "What outfit you joining?"

"Wheeler's cavalry."

"Fighting Joe. My word."

"Well, I aim to fight. I wanted to go to Virginia with my papa and fight for General Lee but they need me here."

"I imagine!"

"Yes, sir, I'm proud to defend the State of Georgia. The Yankee invader will rue the day he crosses swords with us."

I whistled. My enthusiasm was manifest, and, I feared, embarrassing. But I was overcome with excitement. I nodded and grinned like a simpleton. Pritchard saved me; he looked off to the horizon like some hero in a bookplate.

"Well, George, I'll be seeing you."

"Yes, sir," I found myself saying. "Farewell. God speed."

"Thank you, George. Let's go, Anchises."

Anchises tipped his hat as he passed. "Master Wax."

I nodded and watched them go. Private MacBean jangled and winked and flashed uphill and out of sight. I dashed the rest of the way to Wes and Cal's and related every detail.

Wes screwed up his face when I told them. "Shit, he's been riding around three days now hoping people will talk to him about his uniform."

82

I balked at Wes's language. He had begun precociously to experiment in obscenity after listening in on the old men at the store and had gotten a few soapy mouth-washings from my aunt Ellen for it. "You don't say."

"Yeah," Cal said. "He's awful full of himself."

"Puffed up," Wes said.

"Yeah, but how about that uniform?"

"How about it?" they said.

"Forget for a minute Pritchard MacBean was wearing it," I said. "Wasn't it smart? Didn't he look most like a soldier?"

Wes and Cal looked at each other. "Well," Wes said.

I clapped my hands and pointed at them, victorious. "Yes! And think of it—boys our age, going off to fight! In uniform, Wes! In uniform, Cal!"

This had not occurred to them, and deeply impressed them as it had me, to my regret.

THE FINAL OF THE THREE visits came October 15, 1863, and was the greatest surprise and the most melancholy. As with the receipt of my father's first letter from Virginia, I recall the date precisely because, in this case, the visit occurred the day after my thirteenth birthday.

We were about to sit down to breakfast when the man arrived. Mr. Dawes brought him in his wagon and stood by while we spoke. When I first spotted them rounding the bend, coming up the road from the direction of the Wheelwrights' and Mr. Hale's farms, I knew something unusual had happened. Mr. Dawes never absented himself from his store on a weekday. I shouted to my mother and grandfather and we all stood assembled in the yard by the shade tree but a moment later. Something bade us wait.

Mr. Dawes reined up his team in the yard and the man lowered himself from the seat. He stood a rangy five-foot five, with long, thin hair, a long, bony nose and high cheekbones in a long, thinly bearded face. He regarded us in our gathering shyly and held his hat—a shapeless slouch hat with a faded blue infantryman's hatcord—in both hands. He worked it nervously with his knuckles.

"Missus Wax?" he said at last, and I recalled what my grandfather had told me earlier in the year about accents. This man's voice wavered between throaty and nasal, and he had drawn our family name out to a full two syllables. Even his speech was long. I listened the more intently for being distracted.

"I'm Mary Wax," my mother said. "This is my father, Lafayette Eschenbach."

My grandfather stepped forward and shook the man's hand. "You can call me Fate."

"Abraham, ma'am, sir. Abraham Keener." He bore down hard on his Rs, chewing on them, pronouncing each and every one, unlike the folks of our area.

"You have news for us, Mister Keener?" my grandfather said.

"Yes, sir, of a kind. And you can call me Abraham, sir."

"You serve with my husband, John Wax?" my mother said. I noticed she had pulled my younger brothers in close to her skirts, and I forgot, for a moment, the man's accent.

"Not rightly, no," he said. "I was with the Twenty-fourth Georgia? Compny E, Rabun Gap Rifles? That's us out of Rabun County, up north yonder."

"Yes, sir," my grandfather said. "I been there onve or twice. Lovely country."

Keener seemed to relax. He shifted his weight and grinned shyly. His teeth looked poorly, and I noted bright red gums. The edges of his eyelids were red and inflamed as well. The man had made this trip though wholly unwell to travel.

"Yes, sir, that it is, and I caint wait to get back. My connection to John, see here..." he looked at his feet and searched for words. "Well, I'll just come out with it. We was wounded, the both of us." My mother made a choking sound and stiffened. Keener raised his hands. "He's all right. He was all right last I seen him."

My grandfather took him by the shoulders and beckoned him inside.

"No, sir, I reckon I might shouldn't. I'm a little poorly, to tell you the truth."

"Then here—have a seat on the porch step."

"Thank you, sir. I appreciate it."

Keener sat and my grandfather offered him tobacco. He filled and lit his pipe and seemed at real ease at last.

"Tell us your story, Mister Keener," my mother said. "Just tell it to us right on through from the beginning."

"Yes, ma'am." He took a drag on his pipe. "Y'all done heard of Gettysburg by now. Well, I got myself hit in the attack, as we passed on through this wheat field there. Canister shot from this ridge yonder, coming right down on us as we moved up. I took shots through this calf, here, and one through the middle, right here." He clapped a hand against his left side, below the armpit. I saw when he did so how thin he was under his clothes, which I now recognized as the remnant of a uniform. "Took a bite outn my leg and busted a couple of ribs. Wasn't too bad as compared with some of what I seen happen to boys in my compny, but I couldn't hardly walk and so two boys drug me back to the rear and I wound up in a hospital. Surgeons fixed me up and laid me in a barnyard. I was lucky there, too. Got a spot in the afternoon shade. Yes, ma'am, it was hot, and that shade might've saved my life. Well, I slept a bit and woke a bit, specially when I got hungry, but wasn't nothing to eat so I mostly just layed there. Right along about sunset they brung in your husband John, ma'am."

He hesitated, and took refuge in a slow pull on his pipe. My mother said, "Don't spare me nothing, Mister Keener. I brought these three boys into the world right here in this house. I can hear what happened to my husband here just as easy."

Keener did not look at her but nodded. "Well, John—he looked pretty busted up. Seems he caught some canister shot, too, and something else besides. Surgeons told me they took a couple of pistol balls outn his shoulder and chest. Whatever he'd got up to, he'd got up to it good and close. The canister had struck him above the hip and below the ribs, here, and they was worried it'd tore through his stomach and he'd get took off by sepsis or the gangrene. They told me straight out I wasn't to give him no water or nothing, just in case. Well, night come on and the boys around me in that yard was crying something pitiful. They was still cutting on them in the tents, too. You ain't never smelled nothing like that. John, he commenced to groaning. He was thirsty, he said, and needed water. I told him what the surgeons done said, and he made me to know in no uncertain terms that he needed water. Not that he was ever rude, you understand, ma'am—he was only ever a gentleman, even in pain."

My mother smiled through her tears and nodded, mouthed, "Go on."

"Well, I said—well, I reckoned the least I could do was give this man some water. I thought on the rich man and Lazarus and I thought if I didn't dip my finger in some water for this poor man I might just wind up needing a drink myself, if you follow me. So I give him a sip from my canteen, and he near guzzled it down. I prayed mercy on me for maybe killing this man—the bandages on his stomach was something frightful—but nothing ever come of it. Fact, he quieted down and slept. Next day I give him more water, since I was getting around better than him, and we shared some hardtack and whatever else we could come by. He told me he was from Georgia, too, and I'd be lying if I didn't say that was joyous news. You spent a lot of time with Alabamians and Texans? Well, day after that we was heading back for Virginia.

87

"I seen a lot of boys die on that march—retreat's hard on the wounded—and others fall back and get captured, but I told myself I couldn't very well let a fellow Georgian fall behind or die, so we looked after each other all the way to the Potomac. After that we made it into a good hospital. I was patching up just fine—no infections, they told me—and got around on a crutch pretty good. John was getting better, too. Took a while, but they let me out and give me a furlough for disability and reenlisting to boot. Fore I left, John asked me to see y'all on my way home—don't worry, it ain't too far out of the way—and to give y'all this, so's you'd know he was all right."

Keener produced a thick letter and handed it to my mother, who rose, nodded, stuck it into her apron, and smoothed Jefferson's hair. At last, she took a deep breath and looked at the man.

"I'm most grateful, Mister Keener."

"You're welcome, ma'am."

"Most grateful," my grandfather added, and shook Keener's hand again.

"Where do you go from here, Mister Keener?"

"On up north, ma'am. Railroad don't run to Rabun County, so it's walking or wagons where I can get them."

"Is it a hard road?"

Keener grinned shyly. "Ain't much of a road at all, to tell the truth. And they's some mountains and a good-sized gorge between here and there. But I know the country. It's home, after all."

"You wait here," my mother said. She left my brothers, grandfather, and I there on the porch with Keener—and Mr. Dawes watching at a respectful distance—and entered the house. The door sighed shut behind her.

My grandfather offered Keener his tobacco pouch. "Take the rest of it with you."

"I appreciate it," Keener said.

My grandfather nodded to me. "This here is George, John's oldest."

I stepped forward and offered my hand. "Thank you, Mister Keener."

"Abraham, please. Pleased to meet you Georgie. Your daddy's right proud of you, looking after the place."

My heart could have burst—not merely with pride, but with missing my father. "Thank you, Abraham."

My grandfather nodded to my brothers and introduced them as well. "Tell Mister Keener thank you for coming. He come a long way to tell us your daddy's all right."

My brothers thanked him. Jefferson seemed to want to cry. Keener leaned in close. He was a frightful sight but my little brother did not flinch or back away.

"You miss your daddy?"

"Yes, sir."

"He'll be home soon enough. He's doing this for y'all, you understand?"

"Yes, sir."

"He's a good man. You be proud to have such a daddy. They don't stamp men like him out in factories."

He settled back on the step and seemed to sink in on himself a little. He puffed on the pipe. Some of our chickens bestirred themselves in the yard and pecked at the quiet sunlight. Mr. Dawes's horse shifted idly in the traces.

At length, my grandfather said, "Has it been hard fighting?"

Keener tamped another pipe full and appraised my grandfather. At last, he looked away and said, "Yessir."

My mother returned with our entire breakfast wrapped and bundled. In the October morning air it

89

began to steam through the cloths my mother had folded around it.

"You take this on with you," she said. "We got plenty."

Keener raised his hands and shook his head. "Aw, now, Missus Wax—"

"You take it, Mister Keener. It's been hard, but not that hard. We can't say thank you enough."

Keener rose and accepted the food. "Thank you, ma'am."

"Thank you."

We saw him to Mr. Dawes's wagon. Mr. Dawes tipped his hat and rode away with him. I have neither heard of or from Abraham Keener since. I imagine he would be well into his nineties by now, should he have survived the war.

When they had gone, Jefferson looked at my mother.

"Is Daddy hurt?"

"He was hurt, Jefferson. Mister Keener came to tell us he'll be all right. God seen him through it."

"Was he bad hurt?"

"Sounds like it."

Jefferson hugged my mother about the waist and rested his cheek against her hip. She patted his head and looked off down the road where Mr. Dawes and Keener had gone.

James spoke up. "Is that a letter from Daddy?"

"It is," my mother said.

"Can we read it? Now, this time?"

She seemed to brace herself and nodded. "All right. Let's get on inside. I'll fix y'all something simple for breakfast."

"Ain't there nothing left?" I said.

My mother gave me a look that withered me.

"Shame, Georgie Wax. Ain't nobody here needed that food more than Mister Keener. Think on what he done for us. For your daddy."

I blushed and stammered—I had not meant it that way, but any response would have been inadequate. I remembered my father's praise of me, relayed through Mr. Keener, and felt more a child than ever. I had, in some way, let my father down in the instant of his pride. I followed everyone into the house.

My grandfather patted me on the back as we sat down to the table and I hid my face. Shortly, my mother gave us plates of grits and stale cornbread. She gave the letter to my grandfather. We ate in silence, and then he read to us before we set to work.

September 12, 1863
Richmond, Va.

Dearest Mary,
I am sending this letter on with a friend & fellow Georgian Abraham Keener. He done a lot for me as I will relate to you someday. I know you will treat him right.

I have been grevously wounded in the fighting up north. I feared for my life & the lives of you Mary & our boys who I miss so dearly & I had a hard time of it. But I am thankful to report that I am getting better & the surgens tell me I walk no longer through the valley of the Shadow of Death, so I may fear no evil. Be that as it may I am still not whole & do not expect to be for some time.

It is hard so hard to be away. I aim to request a furlow but can not expect to get it. It is money I must not spend before I get it. I hope to see you & the boys again soon none the less, be that on furlow or when this war is over. I would give all for it to be so. Many has already.

I have much more I mean to write or say to you Mary, but I hope this letter will suffise.

91

Abraham tells me he will leave on a furlow of his own in the morning & he has agreed to see this letter delivered into your own fair hand. Greet the boys & your daddy for me.
John Wax

I looked over the letter when my grandfather finished reading it through. My father's hand, I could not help but note, was large and shaky.

My mother's prayers increased in frequency and intensity. Three months later, after hunting and the slaughter and curing of our hogs and long after the end of harvest, my father came home.

I N THE MEANTIME, my grandfather began training with the state militia. I do not recall precisely when, as Governor Brown and the general assembly fiddled with the militia throughout the war, but it must have been sometime in the late fall or early winter of 1863 when my grandfather first mustered in. If Pritchard MacBean's jining the cavalry had excited me, my grandfather—someone of my own family, in our household!—training with the militia did so to an even greater degree. I begged him to let me go with him and, to my great delight, he consented.

The handful of times we went that winter and spring, it was a small, almost informal affair. We hitched our mules and traveled by wagon to the designated place and camped out that evening—another adventure—before my grandfather spent the entire next day drilling. I generally found a convenient fencepost or tree and hitched myself up into my improvised grandstand to watch, and then followed hours upon hours of the thirty or forty militiamen marching, wheeling, dressing, moving through their evolutions, bringing their arms to various positions, and practicing the movements from column to line of battle. The adventure of the thing usually wore off by midday, but I did not lose interest in the systems of the training. Like heraldry, drill boasted an endless variation of a few basic components, and I studied them eagerly. I hungered to partake.

Only on the third or fourth drill did I notice that the men were uniformly old. My grandfather—aged sixty-three at the time—was not even the eldest among them. The youngest was a Mr. Gibbs, a man I recognized as a carpenter from Wilkes County, who had built and delivered some furniture to the MacBeans; he was certainly forty years old at least.

The meaning of these old men's drill was not difficult to divine—most of the men of military age were away, encamped with the armies in Virginia, Tennessee, northwest Georgia—alarmingly close, had I but thought about it—Mississippi and the incredibly distant "Trans-Mississippi." Militia, after all, comprised those available to defend a place. I marked it but did not worry overmuch about it. Furthermore, with my grandfather's example before me, I figured that the majority of them must have had military experience. These men were veterans, reared in a difficult school, and the lifetime of toughness they would bring to bear would enable them to forego heavy training. So I reasoned.

I asked my grandfather about it once, as we returned from a day of drill.

He puffed on his pipe and regarded me. At length, he said, "Georgie, how many men you reckon have been in the army?"

I blinked. "Those men?"

"Men generally. How many?"

"Well—most of them?"

"I'm afraid that's the case now. But before this war? Not many."

"You were in the army?"

94

"I was in a militia, yes, down in the Floridas. Long time ago."

"What about them others?"

"One or two. Mister Gibbs was in Mexico eighteen-odd years ago. Few others spent a few years guarding forts, places like Texas, Minnesota Territory. Not a lot of fighting experience."

"Y'all look right smart drilling."

"Drilling has its uses."

"Like what?"

"Discipline. Like reciting your lessons in school. You do that often enough the basic evolutions, the basic maneuvers, become memory. Don't even have to think about them, you just do them. That frees up your mind for more important work, so you're not getting shot at and trying to remember if 'shoulder arms' means the right or the left shoulder."

I looked at him. He sat in the wagon seat beside me, a big man hunched in his blue greatcoat, hat pulled low against a cold breeze. He took his dark and deep-set, beetle-browed eyes from the road ahead and smiled at me. I remembered how he had explained concussion to me—the passage of a bullet past one's face, the shake of the earth beneath the blow of a cannonball.

"Granddaddy, you ever been shot at?"

Something in his smile changed. He seemed to look at me from far away, as if taken to a place he had long forgotten but now remembered. "Yes, Georgie."

"In Florida? In the militia?"

"Yes."

"Did you show great courage?"

My grandfather chuckled. "Well, I didn't run."

"Did you charge the enemy?"

"Wasn't much of an enemy to charge at. Just staying put was hard enough."

"Who were y'all fighting?"

"Seminoles," he said. I recognized the name as an Indian tribe, one of which I had only dim awareness. "They'd been raiding across the border—the Floridas belonged to Spain in them days—and General Jackson went after them."

"Did y'all beat them?"

"I reckon you could put it that way. They had to do what we wanted in the end. We whipped them pretty good and Spain give Florida to us in the end. But beat? War ain't exactly a game of cards."

"When boys fight, somebody's got to win and somebody's got to lose."

"That's the truth, but think of thousands of boys fighting on two and sometimes three or four sides, all at once. It ain't always so neat and clean. Ain't nothing involving people is."

I remembered our conversation by the fence the day my father left for the war. It seemed a long age past.

"You think this war might not have a winner? Or loser?"

"Folks up in Richmond sure hope so."

"What do you mean?"

"Well, they hope to make enough of a fuss that the Yankees will get sick of it all and give up, let us go, leave us alone. They're impatient folks, Yankees. They got problems of their own and it ain't all gone their way, and folks is upset about it. If the generals and politicians can go on making the Yankees more and more upset, the war might just end and, in a way, we'll have won just by getting what we want."

I watched him throughout this explanation, observing his face as he looked past Herod's back at the road ahead. When he had finished, I said, "Do you think that's how it's going to happen?"

He shook his head. "I don't rightly know. Can't know. Can't nobody know. Accident and mishap pursue the man who commits himself to war, and with thousands and thousands of men caught up in it the mischance and damn fool bad luck pile on up with every passing moment. War ain't a machine. It ain't predictable or governed by laws, scientific-like, though some folks persist in believing so. Like I said, so long as people are involved, it ain't given to us to know the outcome."

I considered this for a long time. He puffed on his pipe, a warm tobacco scent in the chilly air.

"What was the war like? Fighting the Seminoles."

"Well, I didn't see much of it. Got in a scrape or two but never did see much of the Indians. Old Hickory was intent on using his federal troops to do his work. Us militia mostly got caught up by accident."

"Did you get shot at?"

"Yes, once or twice."

I asked the following with some trepidation, recalling as I did how I had transgressed some hidden boundary when last speaking with my father.

"Did you ever shoot any of them?"

He paused, actually thought on it, which came as a relief. "So far as I know, no. But I did shoot at them."

"How come you don't know?"

"All the smoke. And I don't know about this present war, but fighting the Indians—it was like fighting the haints and boogers folks think live in the woods. I only recollect seeing them in the flesh three or four times. Most times the first sight you got of them was the billowing of their musket. Then we'd billow right back and pretty soon the fight would be over."

"You couldn't see nothing?"

"Not a blessed thing."

"So it wasn't scary?"

"Scarier than I can express," my grandfather said. "Think how long it took Jefferson to get to where he'd go outside to the necessaries at night. Scared silly of

97

the dark, and wasn't nothing in the yard going to get him."

I laughed. James and I had made great and cruel sport of Jefferson's fear, the way boys do. I felt a stab of remorse, and realized something had changed in me in the intervening years.

"Well," my grandfather continued, "fancy yourself in the dark, or in a fog, only it's alive with bullets—you can hear them when you're the target, you understand—and there are men in the fog who most fervently want you dead."

I nodded.

"What happened to them?"

"To the Seminoles?"

"Yeah, the Indians."

He sighed. "Beat them. Jackson forced them into a treaty. John Calhoun—Cal's namesake, you recollect—he was hopping mad about the whole thing. Said Jackson had no authority to do what he done and I reckon he was right. But that was Jackson's way. When he become president a few years later he took those federal troops of his again and forced the Seminoles and the Cherokees and a whole pack of other Indians out of their territory and away west."

I had heard a little of this. Cherokee territory in northwest Georgia was yet a fresh memory in those days.

"I got to feel a little bad for them," I said.

"I think that's the right way to feel, Georgie."

"You say the federal troops. You mean—"

"The United States Army. This time around, the bluebellies. The Yankees."

"And they're trying to whip us the way they did the Seminoles?"

"In a way, yes."

"Where are the Seminoles now?"

"Out west, with the Cherokees and Creeks and a

98

whole bunch of others. And the Creeks were our allies when I marched south with General Jackson."

"That don't seem fair."

"Don't to them neither. They didn't appreciate being pushed around then any more than we do now. Whose side you reckon a lot of them Indians are on in this war?"

I had much to think about, but not nearly enough age, wisdom, and experience to do it with. While my grandfather's explanations and stories sufficed for me at the time, only much later, with the accumulation of the things aforementioned, would the significance of his words begin to make sense to me and to form a coherent set of ideas and beliefs. But by then it was too late for men of his kind.

IF I HAVE ELABORATED upon some of my youthful political conversations with my grandfather, I fear it has given a false impression of him. I have thus far recounted every word of politics I had heard him express in the two and a half years of war through which we had lived. To this day I do not know how he voted, so to speak, that trait which in the present seems to have unseated faith, creed, and even color as that which defines a given man. I know what my grandfather would have thought of such misplaced worth. He seemed to hold much political talk in scorn. When visiting Dawes's Store, for instance, he avoided the chatter of the old men outside or the enthusiast gaze of his neighbor, Mr. Streets, the local Unionist and peddler of crank literature like the pornographic anti-Roman book *Maria Monk*, a man whose presence was tolerated almost as a curiosity. Had he had actual influence in the neighborhood he may have found himself tarred and feathered. We had heard of such incidents, but never seen any. For another instance, with the departure of the Rev. Asbridge a new preacher arrived at Barber's Chapel, an older man named Jones or Jonas. This new reverend preached on politics more and visited our farm less. He gave rousing patriotic sermons, sometimes reading newspaper accounts of the goings-on in Virginia or Mississippi from the pulpit. I found it all very exciting. My grandfather, despite not wanting to make a show or draw attention to himself, sometimes excused himself after communion and settled in with a pipe outside during such homilies. But never did he explain why. It was as though the mere idea of high emotion in the employ of politics offended him, and it strikes me now as telling that his lengthiest conversations on such topics he held with a thirteen-year old boy.

WE HAD A WEEK'S WARNING of my father's arrival on his second furlough. In the middle of January 1864, we received the following letter:

> *December 25, 1863*
> *Richmond, Va.*
>
> *Dearest Mary,*
> *I am now well enough to leave the hospital &*
> *am happy to say I have rec'd a months furlow.*
> *The best gift I have ever rec'd for Xmas! I send*
> *this short letter ahead to let you all know I am*
> *coming home & I pray to see you & the boys*
> *soon.*
>
> > *John Wax*

It was a miracle, in those days, that the letter did arrive before he did, though in this case there is also a more mundane explanation: my father could not afford train fare this time. And, except for stretches where generous ladies paid his way for a leg or two of the journey, he walked much of the distance from Virginia to Georgia.

My Aunt Ellen and Wes, Cal, Jeremiah, and Caroline—now aged not quite six and five, and hardly remembering my father—joined us at our farm to await his return. My Aunt Laura came out once we sent word he had arrived, which he did six days after we received the letter. I can express neither the anticipation nor the rejoicing.

He arrived in the middle of the afternoon of a cold January day, borne by cart from the Athens rail depot. He had been relieved of walking the final stretch from Crawford to Athens by the grieving mother of two young men killed in the war. An Athens lawyer—who had also lost a son—gave him the cart ride to our farm, a generous help.

Jefferson had climbed into the upper reaches of the shade tree and so saw him coming while he was yet a great way off. At his cry of joy we gathered instantly and moved in a rush to meet the cart. We fairly hoisted him down from the seat and fell on his neck and kissed him, embracing him and each other and shouting thanks and gratitude to the stranger who had delivered him to us. For my part, I had grown fleeter of foot in the two years he had been gone and was, with Cal, the first to meet him on the road, but not by much—my mother nearly bowled us over. Once on the ground with us I hugged him and pressed my face hard against him, and his voice and bearing and smell told me *Yes, this is my father.* Only when the throng broke up and we all walked to the house did I trust my eyes, and discern how much this, my father, was changed.

He was much diminished. Everything about him had receded and thinned—his face, his hair, his frame entire. His uniform—such as it was—draped in angles from points of bone at his shoulders, hips, knees, and elbows. His cheeks had sunken and his eyes seemed unnaturally large for the dark patches encircling them in their sockets. When he grinned—as he did continually all that day and for a week or more thereafter—he showed two missing teeth in what once had been a whole and winsome smile. The only thing about him that was increased was his beard—where once he had gone clean-shaven, he now wore a thin and curly beard that hung down over his collar. My mother, weeping with joy and laughing at the same time, fingered it delicately.

"How striking," she said. "Never once have I seen you bearded, John Wax."

"It is the fashion, ma'am," he said, and grinned once more.

"How modish."

"As ever, as you know."

My grandfather slapped him on the back and boomed his thanks and congratulations on returning home, and enlisted me to help carry his things in.

My father's things, all his worldly goods in his service in the army: a canvas haversack, much worn and patched; a canteen; cartridge and cap boxes with a shoulder strap and belt for securing them about the waist; a bayonet, much dinged and notched, albeit not in combat; a pair of woolen blankets; an oilcloth; his rifle, an Enfield with its stock polished smooth by the action of his hands, like an axhandle; and a large oilcloth poke weighted heavily at its bottom. Even has he proceeded in triumph to the house, my father caught sight of us unloading his goods and called out, "Don't go opening that sack, hear? I'll tell you why presently."

I looked at my grandfather.

"Go ahead and tote it on in," he said. "But you heard your daddy."

I nodded and hefted it over my shoulder with the leather belt and accoutrements of war.

My mother begged the lawyer to stay with us for supper but he apologized, said he had to be getting back. It was a long ride from Athens but he had been glad to do it. We thanked him again and again and brought my father inside.

We brought out bacon, beans, crackling bread, grits liberally buttered and honeyed, and buttermilk. My mother despatched Jefferson to my grandfather's farm—with permission, for the first time, to jump fences and cross Mr. Street's back acres to reach it faster than by road—to alert Aunt Laura, and when she arrived that evening she brought cake. We feasted like kings. Crowded elbow-to-elbow around the table in our small dark house all through that winter night, with only the light of candles and oil lamps and the warmth of our wood stove, I imagined that the feasts of Arthur and his knights on those exotically named holidays—Michaelmas, Whitsuntide, All Souls, Twelfth Night, and Epiphany—must have been something like this. I understood the joy and relished it. We all did, and in that way fed and increased each other's joy all through the night.

MY FATHER SET TO WORK on his own chores around the farm as soon as he was able—and my mother would let him. She fiercely attended his health. She concealed it well, but I understood later that his thinned appearance had alarmed her as it had me. He looked markedly healthier after just two days of hearty eating and long, heavy sleep. We all noted his sleep—so deep that once, when Jefferson, in helping my mother, dropped a cast iron pan against the stove and onto the floor, he did not stir at all; so light, that he once shot out of bed at the creak of a board underfoot. But rest he did, and for that we were grateful.

He had never been particularly talkative nor taciturn, but he talked continuously and animatedly those first several days. He had questions about everything, wanted to know the latest about everything, and remarked upon everything that caught his attention with great surprise. He spoke spiritedly and in good humor except in noting how much James, Jefferson, and I had grown, which sobered him. I noticed him a few times, during other conversation, regarding us boys in sad wonder, but he seldom made mention of it.

He enjoyed walking with us. Sometimes, when our chores were done, we would set out on walking tours of the farm, making laps around the property until sunset. Once, I asked if he weren't tired of walking after nigh upon three years in the infantry.

"Oh, you get used to it," he said. "A man can get used to anything."

"Did y'all do a lot of marching?"

He laughed. "Georgie, this is my thirteenth pair of shoes in the last two years, and I'm lucky just to have them."

He raised one foot and the brogan's sole flapped as if in applause.

He walked with me and my grandfather to Dawes's Store once to see the neighborhood and talk with anyone he happened to meet. Mr. Hale and Mr. Streets were there, shucking peanuts on the steps, while old Mr. Woodward leaned against the building nearby and whittled. They greeted my father excitedly and asked him a great deal of questions, not all—in the case of Mr. Streets—of charitable intent. I recall he made remarks about "a rich man's war and a poor man's fight" to which my father responded that he didn't think himself poor, thank you kindly.

"To hell with your pamphlets, Tom," Mr. Hale said. "Let John alone for just a damned minute. The man's home for the first time in years."

"I'll not take profanity from the likes of you," Mr. Streets said.

"Complain to your missus and your reverend, then. And mayhap Old Abe, if you're in a praying mood."

"Blasphemer."

"Presbyterian."

"Oh, enough with that already," Mr. Woodward said, and spat in the dust. Of the old men who gossiped at the store, he was widely reputed the most sensible.

My father and grandfather laughed and Mr. Streets and Mr. Hale nodded apologies to one another.

We walked quite a bit in our part of the county, and pitched in on chores at Uncle Quin's farm. Quin had not once gotten or taken a furlough, and I believe my father felt badly about it. We helped all we could and had Ellen and the cousins over for meals two or three times per week for the duration of my father's stay. For he had to return—one of the reasons he had received this furlough was his reenlistment.

I do not recall my mother and father discussing the reenlistment, but what I know of them and what I remember of their behavior in the days leading up to his departure suggests that neither of them enjoyed the prospect of his return to the war, but neither would they back down from what they considered a duty, however onerous. My father had given his word, and to this day I respect him for keeping it. He did not desert—how seldom the veterans' magazines make mention of this epidemic—even for understandable reasons, the way many men appeared, uniform and all, at harvest or slaughter time, before disappearing back to the war. My father kept his word. So had Uncle Quin, so far.

My mother, for her part, could never have depended on a man who did not keep his word. Her standards were too rigorous. But that does not mean she did not mourn his leaving again, and bitterly—ever more bitterly as time went on.

One Sunday near the end of his stay, my grandfather took us boys and walked us to church. Our mother and father needed rest this Sabbath, he told us. And so we dressed as quietly as we were able—probably as quietly as a train of newly shod mules on a corduroy road—and slipped out into the blue country morning.

"Granddaddy," I recall Jefferson asking at length, "why's daddy got to go back?"

"They need him in the army, Jeff."

"Can't he stay?"

"No, they'll send folks after him." We had heard about the home guard, albeit as rumor, and well knew what happened to deserters. The stories that had reached us out of Bragg's army, even accounting for the perversions of newspapers, were hair-raising.

"Why'd he reenlist?" James said.

"They'd have come for him anyway," my grandfather said. "It was a formality."

"A what?" Jefferson said.

"A formality," I said. "Means they were going through the motions. He didn't have no choice either way."

Jefferson looked at my grandfather.

"Georgie's right, I'm afraid."

Jefferson pouted. I would have too, but was too full of growing up to mourn like either a man or a boy.

"How come they got to take everything?" James said.

"It's the way of the world," my grandfather said. "Has been ever since Eden."

Presently, we reached the church, where after the hymns and creed and rites which in their rhythms seemed so holy, we heard a sermon on the folly of placing Joe Johnston in command in Tennessee, and how God, despite it, would use the foolish things of the world to confound the wise. I agreed, in my way, but with the approach of my father's departure, and feeling even his mundane absence in church that morning, I would have preferred prayer.

THE OILCLOTH SACK my father had forbidden us to open when he arrived contained gifts. He gave them to us one morning in the first week of February, the day before he left.

For my grandfather: a battered copy of a French novel popular among soldiers for its great length and faraway setting, *Les Miserables*. Every man in the company—every man who could read—had taken a turn through it. "Some boys call us 'Lee's Miserables,'" he told us, and laughed. "The newspapermen do, anyway."

For my mother: a bundle of letters. "Read these whenever you like. These in particular I wanted to make sure got home."

For my brother Jefferson: a child-sized forage cap and a drill manual. "I recollect hearing that you march around the garden with a hoe at shoulder arms, so I reckoned you and your brothers could put this to use."

For my brother James: a section of toy soldiers, whittled of hickory by my father. He pointed out one, showing a private at trail arms, he intended as a self-portrait. "The fine detail work I had help with."

He gave me my gift last. When it came time, he paused and regarded me quietly.

"Georgie, I want you to know—like I said through Abraham when he come by—that I'm proud of you. You've taken up a burden of responsibility here just by accident of birth as my firstborn. Some boys might've said it was unfair, they didn't ask for this war and they didn't want the farm to look after, but you never questioned it."

My cheeks burned. I looked at my mother and grandfather. "I had help," I said. And the truth was, it had never occurred to me to question the duty my father had lain upon me. If it had, I might have.

"Still," my father said. "I hate it, but I've missed every one of your birthdays these last three years— same for your brothers. But you've become a man and are shaping up to be one I can go on being proud of. A lot of responsibility still goes with that, of course. But I want to thank you for taking care of our farm and taking care of your mama."

"You're welcome," I said. He spoke so softly and seriously, with such weight, that a sense of dread had built inside me for no reason that I could name.

"This farm means a lot to me—to us. All three of you was born here, and your baby brother and sister is buried here. I bought the land from your mama's daddy and you and your brothers will get it from me when I'm gone. It'll happen one of these days, sure as the sun comes up."

"Daddy—" I said before my dread could choke me.

He looked into the oilcloth poke and pulled out a long heavy object bundled in canvas cloth. He unwrapped and presented to me a six-shot revolver, a pistol. My mother and brothers gasped. My father smiled. All my dread and anxiety at his talk of land and legacy and mortality disappeared.

"Take it."

I took it by the grip and he let me have its full weight. It bore my hand floorward at first and I had to heft it to keep it upright. It was a Colt's Navy-pattern revolver with a long round barrel, polished grips, and a brass frame, a solid ingot of machine-fashioned steel and brass. I turned it over and over in my hands, wondering at it—a firearm of my own.

"My land," my mother said. "John, where did you get that?"

"A gift, from an officer in the hospital," he said. "Wanted me to have it."

My grandfather whistled. "A Colt's?"

"Even better—Griswold and Gunnison, made right here in Georgia. I'm right proud of that."

"Augusta?"

"Griswoldville, outside Macon. Yankee industry man, used to make cotton gins."

I did not care about any Yankee industrialist or his pistol factory—this wonder, with its gleaming brass and carefully polished parts, might have been hammered out on the anvil of Vulcan himself. I read glorious scenes of war and Southern victory into the burnished metal. I looked at my father.

"Thank you."

My father beamed. "You're welcome, Georgie."

"Can we shoot it?" Jefferson said.

"Sure enough," my father said. He produced the oilcloth bag's final contents—a small powder flask, a pouch of pistol balls, a pouch of percussion caps, and a bullet mold. "How about it, Georgie? It's your pistol."

Naturally, I agreed. There is little more romantic than firing a pistol to a boy accustomed to squirrel guns; the only thing moreso may be firing a pistol of one's own. I leapt up with the great weight in hand and fairly bounded to the yard.

Outside, my mother kept pace with me. "George Wax, you know to be careful with that instrument."

112

"Yes, ma'am."

"Don't you never, ever point that thing at another person."

"No, ma'am."

"Don't you never, ever point that thing at anything you don't want to see killed."

"No, ma'ma."

"All right, then. Don't you make me regret your daddy's generosity."

My father smiled and clapped her on the shoulder. He said something in a soft voice. I could not hear it well, and was not intent on anything much besides the revolver, but I believe it was, "He's growing up, Mary."

My grandfather set a weather-warped board across two large rocks under the shade tree, naked now this deep into winter, and set six old cans in a single rank across the board. He and my father showed me how to load the pistol, an involved process, as this revolver did not take brass cartridges. Powder and ball into each chamber of the revolver's cylinder, with a tamp into each from the hinged ramrod under the barrel, and finally a minuscule percussion cap on each nipple of the cylinder. It took a respectable amount of time to prepare this half-dozen shots, trying with one hand to rotate the cylinder while at half-cock and with the other to position the cap onto the nipple. I fumbled a great deal.

"You'll get better the more you do it," my grandfather said.

"Like drill, ain't it?" I said.

My father and grandfather laughed, but I marked a note of half-heartedness in it.

"Well, something like that," my grandfather said.

"Got to learn it like any skill," my father said.

At last, the pistol was loaded and ready. My father and grandfather stepped back. My mother shooed my brothers farther back from me. The world narrowed to me and those cans under the shade tree in the clear and frosty February morning. I drew in a great lungful of the cold air and relished the weight of the pistol.

"You know what to do from here, I reckon," my father said.

I raised the pistol and, with some effort to keep the weight balanced level in my hand, thumbed back the hammer, past half-cock. The cylinder gave a hesitant turn in my near vision and I felt transmitted into the tip of my thumb the delicate tumble of gears, springs, and levers—the pistol's inner workings. The hammer clicked to a stop, full-cock. My father and grandfather had trained me well enough to control my breathing while I aimed, but my excitement overcame me. I tried to draw a bead on a can near the middle and watched the tiny sight at the end of the barrel waggle and yaw. I shut my left eye tight and gritted my teeth. My arm ached at the weight. I squeezed the trigger.

The pistol barked and jumped and yanked itself almost free of my hand, and I heard the shot whack into the bark of the tree. A cloud of blue smoke twisted away from me and I saw all six cans standing yet where they had. My brother James whooped and Jefferson laughed. I exhaled lustily. A miss. But I was not disappointed.

"Try again," my father said. "It takes some getting used to."

We practiced much of that day, my father, grandfather and I long after the rest had gone inside or found other things to interest them. Out of perhaps thirty shots I fired from my Georgia-manufactured Griswold & Gunnison .36 caliber revolver, I hit the cans seven times. Again—I was not disappointed. Aunt Laura came over in the evening with a cake for my father's send-off, and Wes and Cal walked over on their own.

In the morning, we saw my father off much as we had in the early summer of 1861, only we wept more. He left better fed than when he arrived, and had recovered much of his color, and he had shaven the sickly beard he had brought home. I said good bye to him with the pistol stuck in my belt. He hugged me warmly in a new coat my mother had sewn for him, told me to take care of James, Jefferson, and my mother, and marched off again. We then commenced with our chores for the day.

IN THE SPRING OF THE NEW YEAR, 1864, the Yankees pressed hard on the states of the Confederacy, Virginia and Georgia foremost. I do not remember being much concerned, personally—we had plowing and planting to do, and much more besides. We pitched into the plowing and planting as we were accustomed to do, difficult as it was. But by the end of the spring and the approach of summer, with the land heating up and the sky whitening with haze, the State of Georgia called up my grandfather for the militia and, what is more, called me up too.

III

MILES GLORIOSUS

WHEN THE STATE created the Georgia Reserve Force in accordance with the general assembly's Third Conscription Act, Madison County was redistricted, lumped into a new military department with Elbert and other counties to our east. In April the government began to reorganize the militia in earnest, to refit it with men after the attrition of three years of inactivity and careful husbandry.

The state called up enough men from our corner of the county to form half a company; and we filled out a half-strength company otherwise raised across the line in Elbert County. I say "men"—their number included my grandfather, soon to be aged sixty-four; myself, who would not be fourteen until October, by which time we surely would be home; and my cousins Wes and Cal. Our neighbor Mr. Hale received the call as well, despite being a bachelor aged fifty-five with no one to look after his farm with him gone. I believe he made arrangements out of his vast savings— probably with the MacBeans, although they were known to be stretched thin as well—for hired help to look after everything as long as necessary. It would be harder for us.

For three years the farms of our nearest family—my grandfather and Aunt Laura, the Thorpes, Uncle Quin and Aunt Ellen, and my family—had leaned one upon the other for help: to bring the corn and cotton in, to plow and sew, to slaughter and put up the winter's meat. Every one of us had worked hard to sustain the others, and no member now seemed dispensable. There was other family, to be sure, but the distances were such that it would have been hard as well as inconvenient, and the plan would have failed. In the days leading to our mustering in, we fretted considerably over what was to become of the crops.

"How long do you reckon they'll need y'all?" I recall my mother asking my grandfather.

"I don't know," he said.

"Where will they send y'all?"

"I don't rightly know. North of Atlanta, probably. That's where it's gotten bad."

"Not out of the state, surely?"

"I can't say. There's been some states' militia in Virginia this whole time. Governor Brown has mostly kept the Georgia boys home. I pray he will yet."

She looked at me where I sat at the table, watching and listening. Something passed over her face, the import of which she artfully concealed. She looked back at my grandfather and spoke softly.

"They won't put y'all in the line, surely? In—battle?"

My grandfather took a long time answering. "Can't say. Pray it don't come to that."

She nodded.

I recall waking one night to go to the necessaries and hearing her, in a much deeper watch of the night than usual, rocking and praying. I stole a glance behind the stove at her and realized she was not praying at all—at least not at that moment. She had open in her lap one of the bundled letters my father had left with her. The rest of the stack lay open in her lap beneath it. She read softly to herself, her voice a rhythmic lilt like mumbled song, and folded the letter. She prayed. Then she moved the letter to the bottom of the pile and read the next.

We were able, in the end, to get some help, but only enough to get by. My brothers were old enough to do some of the heavier chores, but it was fortunate that we already had the plowing done. A few cousins on my father's side pledged to come up from Swainsboro at harvest if need be, but would need help with train fare if their trip was to be expeditious. There were also still in the area older white trash men whose health was too poor for military service whom we paid for some work. Laura, Ellen, and my mother pooled some of their meagre savings and my grandfather matched it, but most of their cash since the beginning of the war was in greenbacks and got them much less help than hoped for.

A final complicating detail: My mother had, within a month of my father's departure, discovered she was in a delicate condition, as we said in those days. She was with child. She wrote immediately to tell my father the good news, but worry could never stay far off. The memory of the two stillborn children, the second of whom had almost taken my mother with her, lived unspoken but ever present in our home. Bearing me and my brothers had not proven easy either. And now my grandfather and I, the two men of the place, and the two with the most responsibility for her, were to depart indefinitely, possibly into battle.

It can be no coincidence that, on the morning we left, I noticed her first gray hair. She had always had a thick head of jet black hair that had retained its luster well past the time most women of her age had turned

121

half gray. Only now had gray appeared, a leaden gunmetal hue at the temples and in her widow's peak. She had braided it under and out of sight beneath the rest, but I noticed it.

It was Thursday, June 16, 1864. We departed as my father had, just before sunup, when the world lay yet in the nighttime cool despite the brightening dawn.

My mother and brothers saw us off. She sent me with a new pair of brown trousers, newly patched brogans, a blanket and homemade canvas haversack with some biscuits, salt pork, a sack of hominy, and salt, a book and some stationery for letters, a dark blue knitted scarf and fingerless gloves, and my overcoat, made of light brown wool but with some newly sewn patches at the elbows. I had tried to avoid carrying the overcoat, but my mother had insisted.

"Think ahead, Georgie. You don't know how long you'll be," she said. I am grateful she did.

I also packed my Griswold & Gunnison revolver in a homemade calfskin holster which rode at my hip on a baldric of my own design, based upon illustrations in Scott and Bulfinch. The powder, balls, caps, and bullet mold I carried in their own box in my haversack. That was the end of my equipment; all else would be issued to us.

I remembered as I embraced my brothers how my father had deputized me, handed on his authority those three years before, and I thought for a moment I should do something of the sort. I stepped back from James and looked at him. He stared at me wide-eyed, and at that moment tears started to his eyes. He had not even cried over my father's going; his grandfather and brother were finally too much. Jefferson, always sensitive to others, commenced to crying too. At last, I simply leaned close, as though sharing a secret, and said, "Y'all take care of mama, like Daddy said."

They nodded.

We hugged and kissed my mother. She grasped and held me close a moment longer than usual, then sighed and broke the embrace to step back. She clasped her hands as if about to set to work.

"Georgie, you do your duty, like a soldier. Like your father."

"Yes, ma'am."

"Don't never forget to whom you owe your duties."

"Ma'am?"

She held perfectly still but seemed to rise in height, as though becoming a colossus before my eyes. Her eyes grew fierce. "God. Us. The State of Georgia."

I stared and, finally, nodded.

"You remember, Georgie."

I nodded again. She smiled and seemed to relax, and kissed my grandfather.

"We'll be back soon as we can, Mary."

"I know, Daddy. Y'all stay safe."

"We'll do our best."

We walked off the way my father had left, three times now in three years. We met Wes and Cal, similarly burdened with goods by their mother, on the main road and walked on toward Athens and our mustering in. I tried not to look back as we marched away, and succeeded, but wish to this day that I had.

WE MUSTERED IN and entrained in Athens and rode packed into boxcars to Union Point, on the main Georgia Railroad line between Augusta and the great endangered city, Atlanta. That ride was my first aboard a train. I had seen them a few times, and heard their chugging and whistling at a distance a few others, but never had I been aboard one. I found it exhilarating. I had never moved faster than I could sprint or a horse could carry me, and to be borne along behind the loud and powerful machine at the head of the rattling chain of boxcars both terrified and thrilled. I sat by the open door the entire way, watching for three hours as the countryside swept past like so much dust brushed out the back door. The ride impressed me anew with the size of Georgia. I saw forest and river, the towns along the line, many scores of small yeoman farms—the fields, now that I think back on it, subtly emptied of men and worked by children, women, and hired Negroes—a few smaller plantations like the MacBeans', and one or two of the great plantations that took some minutes to steam past with dozens of colored folk scattered across the ripening fields. The whole ride made a curiously silent tableau; any noise arising from the work or play of the landscape tossed helplessly and drowned in the thumping tide of sound issuing from the locomotive—the chuff and chug, the metallic scraping, the hiss and clatter of the rails, and all the other mechanical rhythms of our journey.

We disembarked and made camp just outside Union Point. The ladies of the town, well known for their liberality toward returning or wounded soldiers, met us at the station and walked with us some way down the street, thrusting gifts, homemade articles of clothing, prayer books and religious pamphlets, and food into our hands as we marched. A number of them, when they looked at us, placed their hands over their mouths or their faces. Their eyes welled. I took it at the time as a show of appreciation for the courageous soldiers; I believe now that they stood shocked to see this gang of old men and boys, most of whom had never shaved before, marching as soldiers through their town. Some of them openly wept to see us.

I tented with my grandfather and cousins and we shared out our rations around a fire, just like camping. We rose early, clumsily struck camp, boarded train again and rode on east to Thomson to join the rest of the new militia. Here we detrained and formed up—again, with the exception of some old-timers, clumsily—and marched out to a broad fallow field for drill.

We had barely begun to make camp when the non-commissioned officers arrived and bawled for us to form up on the parade ground. By this they meant the field, late a pasture and much used by cattle as a jakes. We would drill among the cowpies. The sun shone hot and the smell proved potent enough for even farmboys to object, which we did as we lined up, slowly, lazily.

A few officers stood along the fence by the road. One or two sat on the top rail. Most of them smoked their pipes; I saw one whittling. All regarded us in silence. At length, I saw one shake his head and spit tobacco juice between his feet. He did not look back up. Nearby, the Negroes holding their horses stood still but for their swatting at flies and watched us.

I turned to ask my grandfather—who stood next to me in the line—about the officers' behavior when a sergeant appeared before us. He wore an actual uniform jacket of gray, with the blue stripes and diamond of a first sergeant on the sleeves, and a great black slouch hat with a blue hat cord. His face was heavily and darkly bearded, almost up to his eyes, which were narrowed in the glare and deeply lined, as if he had been fashioned from a dried up creekbed. He sidled along slowly but stopped when he saw my grandfather.

"Well, Fate Eschenbach."

My grandfather nodded and extended his hand. "Nick. How you doing?"

The sergeant shook his hand and looked back and forth along the line, which was still forming up and making considerable noise in the process. "Better than some." Nick angled away and spat in the grass. "How long it been?"

"Long enough."

"Been a long war." Despite his words my heart stirred; the romance of the army was rekindled. This sergeant was my grandfather's friend! "How y'all been?"

"Tolerable. Sarah died a while ago."

"I heard. I was sorry to hear that, Fate. I truly was."

My grandfather nodded. "She's better off now. Back together with her mama and sisters."

"Won't we all be."

My grandfather and the sergeant stood in silence a moment and regarded the sun where it glanced across the field full of militia men. Finally, my grandfather turned and put his hand on my shoulder. "Nick, I

126

apologize. These here are my grandsons. My eldest, George Wax. Mary's boy. You remember Mary."

I straightened and thrust out my chest. The sergeant held out his hand and I took it as firmly as I could. "Nichols Sloane," he said. "I remember her well. How are you, son?"

"Fine, sir," I said.

"You make granddaddy proud, hear?"

"Yes, sir," I said.

"He already does," my grandfather said.

Nichols Sloane nodded. "A fine boy."

My grandfather nodded and I sensed that I could relax, recede from the scene and regroup. He introduced Wes and Cal, with much the same pleasantries. With the introductions over, he said, "How'd you get into this line of work?"

"Oh, you know. Joined up at the beginning. Spent a while out west til I got wounded. Ain't fit for nothing but militia work, now, but I'll do it."

"Nothing wrong with that."

"Well, a body does what he can, then part of you just up and quits on you." He slapped his left thigh just above the knee. "Canister shot, Champion's Hill. Lucky I still got the leg."

"Nothing wrong with that," my grandfather said again.

"Well, I best be getting on. You boys listen to your granddaddy, hear? We got a lot of work to do to get ready. Then we'll whip us some Yankees."

Wes, Cal, and I cheered at that. First Sergeant Sloane nodded to my grandfather, said, "Fate," and moved on. I saw then that what I had taken for a lazy amble was in fact a limp. Canister, he had said. I recalled Abraham Keener, in his visit the fall previous, mentioning canister in the stories of both his and my father's wounding. I had heard of canister shot—it was somewhat like grape, but instead of a cluster of balls

127

like giant buckshot, canister was a tin or sack of even smaller musket balls, which when fired would spray in a cone from the muzzle of the cannon. I had heard of artillerists improvising their own such shot with nails and other debris. I watched First Sergeant Sloane limp and wondered that I had heard so much more about canister than rifle shot from men who had been in combat. I was still watching him when the group of officers, heretofore resting by the fence, broke up and strode out into the field toward us.

"All right, boys," my grandfather said. "Wes. Cal. Georgie."

"Yes, sir," we said. I brought myself to the best "attention" that I could muster, based on my repeated perusal of James's drill manual. Silence fell along the ragged line. A team of sergeants met the officers and fell in behind them. At last, an older officer in a smartly tailored uniform—a twisting line of gold embroidery on each sleeve, a fine dark blue standup collar with a single gold star on it—a major—stepped up in front of us and assumed the posture of a gentleman preparing to hold forth: one foot forward, as if about to lunge, chest and head thrown back, one hand held behind the body and the other in a relaxing position at the breast. I had seen this posture in the newspaper engravings many times before and knew what it meant. This man was a politician.

He introduced himself as Major Frady and made a speech. I learned over time that he had a plantation of nine hundred acres and thirty-two slaves in Taliaferro county, near Vice President Stephens's farm outside Crawfordville. I do not now recall much of his speech. It reminded me of our preacher—Rev. Asbridge's successor—and his patriotic sermons. He talked about the Yankee invaders and driving them out, and of the glorious cause of our great new nation and the inevitable victory that must result from the strivings of

128

Southern men, inured to hardship by a life of work and virtuous self-discipline. He punctuated his speech, which he delivered in powerful stentorian tones, with bold and sweeping gestures, much practiced in a legislative chamber somewhere. His performance elicited some cheers, but seemed—certainly in the case of myself— only to generate real interest and enthusiasm when he mentioned defending hearth and home, the wives, mothers, sisters, and sweethearts we had left behind. I thought of my own mother, who was just beginning to show, whose face had been so drawn, whose hair had finally begun to gray with our call to the militia. The Major seemed to sense that these homlier themes drew greater response, and rounded out his speech with repeated emphasis upon them. A band played "Dixie" and "The Bonnie Blue Flag"—an example of which flag I never once saw during the war, incidentally— and another officer stepped forward.

This man was younger and bore what I recalled from my book of Shakespeare stories as "a lean and hungry look." He stood tall and thin as a post, with fine features, the most prominent of which was a Roman nose above a thin but long and drooping mustache. He wore a less impressive uniform—his jacket was a brownish color, his trousers light blue, and he was shod in ordinary infantryman's boots—but had as erect and soldierly a bearing as the Major. He introduced himself as Lieutenant Huger Guerard, commander of one of the militia companies mustering there, and ordered those of us still unarmed to fall out by squads to receive weapons.

Again, clumsiness and disorder. It took some time and consultation of the rosters to sort the gaggle into squads. Once accomplished, our squad was as follows:

Sergeant Burrell. I never learned his first name, but I believe he came from near Elberton, hard by the border of South Carolina. He was about fifty years old.

Private Hoyt Burrell, his young cousin, heavily favored to make corporal, aged 17.

Private Lafayette Eschenbach, aged 64, my grandfather.

Private George Wax, aged (almost) 14, myself.

Private J.W. Eschenbach, aged 14.

Private J.C. Eschenbach, aged 14.

Private Shannon Halloran, aged about 60.

Private Peter Halloran, his grandson, aged 15.

Private Alfred Massey, aged about 60.

Private Dempsey Bell, aged about 55.

A squad, I learned, consisted notionally of ten privates under command of a sergeant and corporal. One man on our roll, whose name I have forgotten and can therefore avoid mentioning, appeared some days late for muster and disappeared for good after a few weeks, and we had no corporal, at least in the beginning. Such imprecision governs military life, I was to learn.

Under the direction of our sergeants and officers we filed past tables set up by wagons with State of Georgia markings. The quartermasters performed a sort of triage, roughly going over each man and issuing him only those necessaries he had not brought from home—so long as they had them in store. Many men had arrived with rifles of their own, or shotguns or bird guns. A few had brought rust-dappled flintlocks that long dead quartermasters may once have unpacked and handed over to the service of His Majesty. These men received powder, lead, and cartridge paper, and went away cursing. As neither I nor my grandfather had brought longarms, the state quartermaster issued me my rifle, an 1853 Enfield in .58 caliber; with it I received a cartridge box, cap box, bayonet, canteen, and belt with an oval brass beltplate marked GA. I was most proud of these accoutrements. The heart still swells a bit to remember receiving them and first strapping them on, and especially hefting and turning over in my hands that beautiful rifle. It had, stamped upon the plate beneath the hammer, a crown and the word TOWER; the Enfield had come into my hands by a circuitous route that included the stores of the State of Georgia, a port somewhere, the Yankee naval blockade, and a smuggler's hold, but had begun in England, the land of Ivanhoe, Robin Hood, and Arthur. I could not have been prouder had I been issued Excalibur.

Further, we received bits and pieces of uniform to improve our civilian motley. We had arrived in every conceivable mode of dress—farmers in straw hats, a dandy or two who owned brightly colored cravats but no working clothes, white trash in plug hats who went barefoot already and, in their rags, presaged everyone's later appearances. I even saw absurdities like men carrying umbrellas, canes, or pairs of unworn silk gloves. Some of us received new brogans; I was not such a one, as my feet were too small for the few men's sizes they had. Others got caps, hats, coats, and jackets. The few items of uniform I ever wore I received here: a blue-grey kepi and a gray jacket with brass buttons marked GA.

Once dressed and equipped, my cousins and I showed ourselves off like so many beaux preparing for a ball.

"Right smart, right smart," Cal said of my uniform jacket and kepi.

"Damn right," Wes said. He glanced at my grandfather, who stood a short way off talking to the older men in the squad, to be sure he hadn't overheard, then looked back at us. "Damn smart."

"Y'all don't look too shabby, yourselves," I said. Wes and Cal had both received brown shell jackets and kepis in different colors, Wes a yellowish brown romanticized now as "butternut," Cal a gray kepi with an infantryman's blue band.

Hoyt Burrell, an older boy and cousin of our sergeant, sidled past. He wore all homespun in various shades of tan and brown. His only stitch of uniform was a blue hatcord and a couple of stamped brass letters—G and A—on his hat. He raised his chin at me.

"Well, what we got here?" he said. "Where'd you get that pistol, sonny?"

"His daddy give it to him," Wes said. "Got it off a dead Yankee."

I shook my head. "Ain't no Yankee pistol. An officer give it to him. It was made right here in Georgia."

"Mind if I see?"

I put my hand to my holster. It had not yet occurred to me that others might want more than a gander at the pistol. I remembered too, from my books, that no good came of a knight giving up his sword. "Nah, I keep it on my person at all times."

Hoyt smirked and spat in the grass at his feet. "Suit yourself, sonny. Ain't no use less you're within sniffing distance anyways."

He walked off casually and began to pick at his fingernails with his knife.

"Hey," Cal said, "member the fable of the fox and the grapes?"

We laughed. My grandfather had read through his copy of Æsop for us a half-dozen times during the war. Jefferson was particularly partial to it.

"He ain't no count anyway," Wes said. He licked his thumb and ostentatiously polished a brass button on his jacket. "See them rags? Ain't nothing compared to the likes of us." He feigned hooking his thumbs through suspenders.

My grandfather happened past as we laughed. "Careful with those rifles, boys," my grandfather said as he passed by. "Careful. And don't be getting uppity about a couple of brass buttons."

"Yes, sir," we said.

He stopped and looked around, then leaned close and said, "And watch your mouth, John Wesley."

"Yes, sir," Wes said, and we laughed.

Once all had passed through the lines to receive weapons, accoutrements, and uniforms, we were ordered back to the field for drill. We walked to the cow pasture again, heads held high. We felt like soldiers, and Hoyt was by no means the only man to show interest in or jealousy of the Griswold & Gunnison my father had given me. The adventure had well and truly begun. Drill was to begin something new, the discomfiture of our adventure.

I SHALL NEVER FORGET that first afternoon of drill. We marched and countermarched and worked through the evolutions and maneuvers I had seen my grandfather perform so often, with which I was so familiar from the neat diagrams of my brother's drill manual, but which thwarted and frustrated our attempts at mastery for hours in the heat and the pasture's dunghill smell. The sun grew oppressive as it beat upon our new wool jackets and unfamiliar caps and hats. Our frames, unused to such burdens as cartridge boxes or slung rifles, ached and chafed at the straps and belts, which dug into our shoulders and hips. I say "our," and mean primarily the boys among us, who formed a great part of the "men" mustering for militia duty there. The afternoon stretched on and on; it was, with the exception of the afternoon I first took up pen to relate, the longest of my life.

Added to the mere physical discomforts I have described was a quantum of terror—the sergeants. These men acted as drillmasters. I had never heard such abuse in my young life. Even when my grandfather slipped up and uttered a *hell* or a *damn* or even a *son of a bitch*, he had done so accidentally, and

134

invariably apologized—especially if my mother overheard. The sergeants exercised mastery of a library of incomprehensible abuse, with which they countered every mistake or misstep on our part, and in the loudest and harshest possible voices. Some of the recruits objected. One man stepped out of the ranks and argued strenuously with a sergeant. Never in his life, he said, had he suffered anyone to speak to him in such a manner. The sergeant redoubled his abuse and another joined him. The man's squadmates beckoned to him to let it go, to rejoin the line. Eventually, he did, cowed. All such incidents ceased after the first few hours.

The sergeants' purpose, my grandfather told me later, was to test us mentally as well as martially. A man of unsound or disturbed mind could not be expected to move from column to line of attack; not, in any event, without thorough and repeated practice. Failing that, a man should at least be so used to abuse and chaos as to greet combat with a shrug. Such a state will never actually occur, but the closer a man can get, the better. And so—the haranguing and hectoring.

One recruit in another squad was a boy perhaps a little older than myself, who arrived for drill wearing a pair of oversized knee-boots that reached to mid-thigh on him. "Come on up out of them boots, boy!" the sergeants shouted. To a man with spectacles: "What you got behind them windows, shopkeeper? Ain't no use pretending you're closed—I can see you in there." To a tall man, the tallest I have seen to this day: "Come on down from there and join us!"

Within our own squad, the sergeants somehow discovered that Shannon and Peter Halloran—another grandfather and grandson—were not only Irishmen, the grandfather native-born, but Catholics. They had at one time or another two and even three sergeants hanging on them, shouting at both the old man and the boy.

135

"You pray to Mary all you want, ain't nobody going to save you from me."

"You spect the pope will show up? Spect that old buzzard will swoop in and stop the war? Or maybe just nibble us some?"

"How many babies you strangled, Paddy? How many nuns you go through fore you get this red-headed thing here?"

I sensed a kindred spirit for Mr. Streets. The old man and the boy, for their part, neither flinched nor broke. After a time, the sergeants left them alone. They recognized good soldiers.

Other abuse was not meant to prove, but served as punishment earned for failure. Once—I am not sure at what point in the afternoon, so long did it seem—I fell out of step when marching through a left wheel, causing me to tread upon the heels of Wes, who marched in front of me, thus throwing us both out of step and causing a general upset. Before the files could collapse into utter disarray, a Sergeant Hopkins called a halt and stalked up to us.

"Damn your eyes, boy, what the hell do you think you're doing?"

The boy in question was me—I stood dumbstruck. Sergeant Hopkins towered over me. His face reddened.

"I said, God damn it, what do you think you're doing? Left wheel turn! Left wheel! How many God-damn times we have to go through it? Look at your feet! I said look at your God-damned feet! You don't march worth a pinch of shit, boy. Raise your right foot. Right! There! Now the left. God damn it to hell, the left!" I had lowered and then raised my right foot again, dumbly, as though I knew no more of right or left than the common mule. "You're awful heavily armed for a Sunday Soldier. Left! Left!" At last, I complied. Ahead of me, Wes had half turned wide-eyed and giggled in terror. Sergeant Hopkins noticed and pounced.

"What in God's name are you chuckling at, you towheaded piss-ant?"

Wes gawped like a landed trout. Cal, beside him, shrank deep into his uniform.

"You know how to make a left wheel, boy? I said, you know how, shitferbrains? Christ." He yanked away Wes's rifle. He thrust out a hand to me. "Give me that rifle, boy. Now, get down and crawl. Don't you little shitbirds look at each other, look at me. You can't wheel about like a soldier, you crawl along like a baby. Get down and crawl!"

Wes feebly gestured to a cow-pie directly beneath him. His mouth worked but no coherent sound came out. Hopkins shook him by the collar.

"What you afraid of? Shit? Get down in that shit and crawl, God damn it!"

I glanced at my grandfather, who stared ahead. We prostrated ourselves. I recall the feel, the smell of that hot grass on my face and palms as though I had just come in from that field today before sitting down to write. Wes lay down directly in the dung, heroically routing a troop of blowflies.

Sergeant Hopkins stepped back and pointed. "All you fellows look at these here sonsabitches. You can't march, you might as well take to the dirt like a worm. Yankees'll plant us all in the dirt with the worms, you can't march. Now—attention! Forward, march!" And he led them off on a lap of the field.

We rejoined the column a few minutes later, covered in dirt, grass, and, for the unfortunate Wes, cow manure. When Sergeant Hopkins bade us rise, my grandfather stole a moment to pat us both on the shoulder. He nodded to us and mouthed, "Steady." I read in his look that it was ever always thus—this was army life. We had best embrace it. And so I did. While we had crawled along, Wes cursed Sergeant Hopkins and every cow on those thousand hills; I purposed

137

within myself never to grant Sergeant Hopkins or any other drillmaster the opportunity to punish me so again. I still feel some pride knowing that, through the rest of our rudimentary training, I did not.

I must also admit pride in my grandfather's summary of our first day at drill. When at last the sergeants released us, and we fell out for supper—cornbread and salt pork, with whatever we wished to add from our personal stores—my grandfather gripped us each by the shoulder and told us that he was proud, that we had done well.

"Thank you, granddaddy," I said when he told me.

"You done good. You'll make fine soldiers yet." I imagined myself in armor, or on horseback, lance couched, in pursuit of some black-hearted enemy, but before I got far along that path he added: "Though I pray you won't have to prove yourself. You or any of these boys."

I searched his face in the light of the cookfires. "What do you mean? Like you said men shouldn't fight? Should settle their differences some other way?"

"It ain't just that, boys. We're doing things the right way around so far. A man fights if he has to. But that don't mean fighting—that don't mean war ain't one of the worst things there is."

"You think we ought to give up?" Wes said.

"No, course not. But it's gone on an awful long time and it's only gotten worse the longer it's gone on. I can't imagine what it'll be like if it keeps on going. If it's long enough, it'll consume us all, old and young, the way it's eat up so many men your daddies' age."

We considered this. Wes scoffed. "I can't wait to get in a scrap."

My grandfather laughed and tousled Wes's hair. "You couldn't never wait for that, could you, you towheaded rascal?"

Wes must have remembered Sergeant Hopkins's

abuse, because he blanched and shrank a bit from my grandfather's playful roughness. My grandfather looked at me again, and after a time said, "Nah, scrap don't begin to describe it. But I hope you won't never learn the difference."

I would not begrudge my grandfather his opinion, but I must admit—I inwardly hoped the opposite. He had seen war and combat; I would, too.

SLEEP PROVED DIFFICULT AT FIRST. Tired and bonesore as I was, I woke repeatedly from dreams of the sergeants. When I rose for breakfast, I felt as though I had drilled all that night. Despite the June weather I had also woken with a runny nose, something common enough to me through the winter but alien to the summer months. We ate and fell in for more drill, broke for a midday meal and fell in for more drill, and at last broke for the day. All that day, as I had promised myself, I had avoided punishment by the sergeants. I had mastered—or felt I had mastered—the myriad steps of the maneuvers we practiced. Despite my exhaustion, I had begun to respond more quickly to the shouted orders for arms. As a squad and company, our performance had already smoothed out some, and pure correction had slackened, if but a little. I slept more soundly. The third day I stood my first guard duty, and lost my unreasoning fear of the sergeants. That night, I slept like the dead. On the fourth day word reached camp of the gruesome death of Bishop Polk, shot through the middle by Yankee artillery. The boys asked for more detail and marveled at the idea of a man blown nearly in two by cannon shot. The older

140

men shook their heads at the news, but said little else. My grandfather said nothing. By the end of our first week, I and many others, despite the growing summer heat as July neared, had nagging colds and coughs. Every morning filled the camp with a rustling sound, the sound of a few hundred men coughing, clearing their throats, hacking up phlegm, and blowing their noses. We sniffed continually. A few days later, and much improved as marching machines though still somewhat clumsy and accordion-like, alternately stuttering and racing along the route of march, we struck camp and entrained for Atlanta. Despite my excitement to board that mechanical marvel again, I slept through several stops. We would all need it.

I DO NOT INTEND to recapitulate the campaigns that took Atlanta or brought about the destruction of Georgia. For one, our regiment was held in reserve through much of anything that may interest the casual reader, especially the man who likes to refight great battles in the clear light and stillness of his sitting room. Furthermore, men more directly involved in the planning and ordering of events—and with more of their reputations at stake—have rehearsed them in weighty memoirs themselves, and the succeeding generation of historical enthusiasts have recreated their movements in the minutest detail over and over again. Nor do I mean to repeat every sentimental camp story one finds in magazines for veterans or church readership, or in the conciliatory essays of well-intentioned ladies. Such things have their places—most of them, anyway—but that is not what happened to me. I mean to write events as they came my way, and as we in the Georgia militia infantry—and we, my family, particularly—heard of or lived through them. Such has been my approach and such shall continue to be.

So—we had heard rumor of Bishop Polk's death, and of the movements toward Atlanta by the enemy, and a little something of our own dispositions. All were the subject of intense and often abusive debate by the men. No group is so sure of the right course of action than a bunch of privates criticizing a general. A congress is not more savage in its denunciations. Johnston had plenty of detractors, especially those men much given to reading newspapers, but one man had fought under him before Lee took over—what seemed ages before, when my father was not long gone from home—and cautioned against rash condemnation of him. Others were certain every rumor they heard of the fighting around Marietta was true, and that it demonstrated decisively their opinion that such and such was correct, or incorrect, or what have you. These were small but loud arguments; the greater part of us, especially those of us yet boys, concerned ourselves more with things like food and gossip about the officers and easing the agonies of our blisters and diarrhœa. I shall have more to say about that later.

We rode about 130 miles from Thomson to Decatur, detraining once between Rutledge and Social Circle to drill and make camp. It was during this first move that we properly joined our regiment of the Georgia militia and that I made the acquaintance of Peter Halloran, the Catholic boy in our squad.

He stood not quite five feet tall, the shortest of any man in the squad, not to mention the company. In bayonet drill, and when loading his rifle, he stood eye-level with the muzzle of his Enfield. I noticed early on that he stood on tiptoe to direct the powder from his cartridge into the bore, and when we cocked our rifles, he had to bring his whole hand up and lever the hammer back with the heel of his palm. His hands were too small, his fingers too short to permit the use of a thumb only. Despite these seeming defects or clumsinesses, the sergeants early abandoned their abuse of him—he had been for a time "you redheaded papist

143

piglet"—because he was an excellent shot, never erred in drill, and never showed fear.

We struck up a friendship one evening as I sat reading the sole book I had brought along, *A Tale of Two Cities*. He sat down near me by the fire and looked at my book.

"What's that you're reading?"

"*Tale of Two Cities*," I said. I was distant, not from meanness or hatred of Irishmen or papists—too abstract a loathing for me to comprehend at that age—but my own shyness and a suspicion that came from the hatred heaped on him and his grandfather by the sergeants and a few others.

"What's the two cities?"

"Paris and London. I think. They're the only cities in it so far."

"Is it a good story?"

"Oh, yes. My grandfather give it to me. He only picks out good ones."

"What happens in the two cities?"

I summarized what I had read so far, which was about half the book. I mentioned at some point Lucie Manette, who, like Wilfred of Ivanhoe, seemed to faint all the time. Peter laughed.

"My mother's that way," he said. "Every little thing comes along—whoops! Down she goes."

"Maybe she's got an affliction?" I said, and felt real concern.

"Nah, she's what they call historical."

"Hysterical?"

"Yeah, that. She's shrill and squeaky, keels right over like a possum. We seen her do it so much it don't much concern anyone any more. Except maybe my granddad there."

I paused to consider my next question: I did not want to cause offense, and Wes and Cal were less inclined to talk about stories than my grandfather or this boy. In the event, I asked the Southern way: a statement shaped like a question. "He's from Ireland?"

"Yeah, born there. His mama and daddy sailed over when he wasn't no more than a baby and he's lived here in Georgia forty-five years."

"It bother y'all? What the sergeants say?"

He waved a hand. "Ain't nothing we ain't heard. It's just louder now. Maybe less cussing." We laughed. "Nah, speaking of stories, my grandfather's told me stories from his grandfather, who stayed over there and I never knew. About the English and what they all done in Ireland, taking land, clapping folks in jail, bringing in soldiers. My grandfather tells me them stories to remind me getting called a Romish dog over here, or maybe having neighbors whisper the name of Maria Monk, ain't so bad."

So he had heard of Mr. Streets's *Maria Monk*. My father and mother and grandfather had always fastidiously kept any of Mr. Streets's Presbyterian literature out of our hands, which had only made it more an object of curiosity. I asked about it.

"Damned horseshit," he said warmly. "Every word of it lies. Writ by some preacher wanted to tell stories about titties and fornication and get away with it. We's just a handy whipping boy. Same's in France in your book there."

I looked at the book in my hands. The author had made little or no mention that I had noticed of religion.

"I mean in real life," Peter said. "That's stuff actually happened. The gillatine and all that. Beheaded a whole mess of priests and folks like us."

"I'm sorry to hear that. Awful sorry."

He settled and waved a hand again. It was pale and smooth like a small child's in the firelight. "Aw, it don't affect me personal like. But it happened and it don't take much of an excuse for the big men to stomp

145

on little men. Leastways that's what my granddad says. Maybe it's a little easier for us to spot, being outsiders in our own state sometimes."

I thought on that. "Why would folks talk about y'all like that?"

"Same reason anybody tells stories about other people, I reckon."

"What is that?"

"Settle with themselves that they's right and the other folks ain't. My granddad says both sides of this here war been lying about each other since before he sailed over. Says all this was inevitable."

I would think on that some more. But as is the way with conversation between children, the talk drifted quickly to another subject. We talked about our rifles and drill, and how badly our feet ached. He complained of a stomach ailment that he blamed on the Negro cooks, who were careless and sloppy with the Yankees so close. At length, Wes and Cal joined us and warmed quickly to Peter, so that by the time we retired to our tents—or, were made to retire by our grandfathers—we had been through a great deal of talk and several games of checkers using Cal's board.

It was but a day or so afterward that Lieutenant Guerard promoted my grandfather. He called my grandfather out after morning parade.

We had already made our way toward breakfast but stopped when we heard. Lieutenant Guerard walked up quietly and when he spoke, spoke softly. His accent and speech were more different yet from the Savannah man, my Swainsboro cousins, and the man from the mountains. Lieutenant Guerard came, I was to learn, of prosperous South Carolina French Huguenot stock on both sides of his family, but had left the low country behind as a young man and, prodigal-like, with his share of his father's fortune, invested heavily in some industrial and rail concerns in Atlanta and Augusta. He

146

had flourished for a time but in the end circumstances put his wealth to flight and he fell back into the yeomanry, a prosperous middling farmer from somewhere on the Savannah River near Augusta. He had retained only the reputation and, especially, the connections for a commission.

"Private Eschenbach," he said when we approached. Wes, Cal, and I remembered ourselves and came to attention. My grandfather had stood at attention the moment the lieutenant had called his name.

"Rest," Lieutenant Guerard said. "Private, your squad has been less one deserter since Thomson, and wants one corporal yet." Each squad required a sergeant to lead it and half of the privates, and a corporal as second in command and leader of the other five privates. We had mustered in shorthanded and without a corporal. "I've spoken with First Sergeant Sloane about making up this lack and he put forward your name as a suitable non-commissioned officer. You have past military experience, I gather?"

"Yes, sir," my grandfather said. "Though by past, you mean when Old Hickory was just a general and not even president yet."

Somewhere under his moustache, Lieutenant Guerard smiled. "Good enough. You are hereby promoted corporal in second squad. We'll see about some stripes."

"Yes, sir. Thank you, sir."

"Dismissed, corporal. Boys—er, privates."

We saluted and once Lieutenant Guerard had gone, gaped at each other and at our grandfather. He seemed ten feet tall, and smiled down upon us from Olympian height.

"This mean we got to salute you?" Wes said.

My grandfather laughed and slapped his stomach. "Nah, but I'm more responsible for you boys than ever."

"Think one of us might make corporal?" Cal said. Cal was not one for thinking big, as they say. I was standing there imagining myself a lieutenant.

"Nope," my grandfather said. "*Corporal* come from the French word for *body*, and y'all's bodies ain't big enough."

We looked at each other, taking his explanation for gospel until he laughed again, and we joined in. Once he and Sergeant Burrell had talked it over, we found ourselves in my grandfather's half of the squad, along with Private Bell. The other half, directly under Sergeant Burrell, included his cousin, whom we had expected to be made corporal, Peter Halloran and his grandfather, and Private Massey. This arrangement made it certain that my grandfather, cousins, and I would march and deploy into line together, which excited us at the time.

I remember this excitement vividly because it was so short-lived. I had expected the dash and pomp of Walter Scott, as most of us did then—boys riding off to war, brotherly bands covering one another in glory, protecting the flower of womanhood. Indeed, for a certain school this has continued to be the usual way of talking about the late war. When I had once expressed this excitement about going off to militia training to my grandfather, he had fought against a grin. He knew; I was to learn.

We learned through that summer that war is mostly a matter of wagon trains, quartermasters and commissaries and teamsters, tabulations and maps, railway timetables, unanticipated changes of weather and rain, the condition of roads, and waiting. Even that great purveyor of modern war—whom I shall not name, though he figures into my story—deceived when he declared that "war is all hell." If this be so, hell is disproportionately Limbo. The screams and terrors that populated the mediæval mind have little place; instead, war is mostly sighs and boredom and retiring footsore to a threadbare tent to resume the ordeal the following day. Despite the attention lavished upon fighting and combat by unblooded enthusiasts, there is little of those things in it. Combat is the prettiest girl at the ball—a rare beauty, the recipient of many attentions—and the cruelest.

DURING THIS TIME I saw the first man I ever saw killed in the army. He was a private about my own age in another company. We had marched fifteen miles and had just been ordered to fall out and bivouac in a pecan grove by the roadside when he walked behind a pack mule. I do not know whether it was something the boy did, or an accidental flash of sunlight on a buckle or bayonet or tin cup, or just a mule being a mule, but the mule planted its forelegs and struck back with both hindlegs and caught this boy full in the side of the head with one ironshod hoof. I saw it happen—he went down like a cut clothesline, just sank in place, his head spilling into the ditch. The mule made not a sound, even when a weeping Negro teamster commenced to whipping it.

We gathered in a crowd around the boy while his squadmates—two brothers, his father, and an uncle among them—stood over him, beseeching him return. I saw clearly the shoe-shaped stamp in the cranium, the warping of the temporal and parietal bones underneath the broken and bleeding scalp. The eyes rolled unfocused in their sockets as the men cradled and shook him. They ceased only when the surgeon came and examined him. First Sergeant Sloane came and dispersed the rest of us.

We felt low for some time after that. I recall settling down in the shade of a big pecan tree, unbuckling my belt, and unshouldering my pack, canteen, haversack, and cartridge box, with no enjoyment of the rest whatsoever. Cal wiped away tears. We broke out rations and ate in silence for some time.

At last, Wes said, "What kind of—of dummy walks behind a mule like that?"

"Come on, now, Wes," Cal said.

"Ain't no more sense than a chicken."

"Speak no ill of the dead," I said.

"Aw, hell, we're all sitting here mooning over him. He wasn't looking out. Everybody knows you don't walk behind a horse or a mule like that."

"That's enough, Wes," my grandfather said. Wes hushed. My grandfather put away his mess kit and brought out his pipe. "He was tired. Could've been any one of us."

I thought about that for a long time.

Not long after, a man in our own company accidentally shot himself with his musket. When we first heard of it, we took it to be a self-inflicted wound—we had all heard the stories of men shooting off their thumbs so they could go home without giving in to the craven urge to desert. But soon the whole camp was full of the sound of his dying, and we went to have a look. He lay gut-shot in the shade of the regimental surgeon's tent. They had pulled aside his shirt so that the belly lay exposed among a wreath of bloody rags that had been his uniform. A thumb-sized hole with ragged arms like stars opened his insides to the world and fairly poured out blood, which the surgeon and his orderlies were much busied in washing away and trying to stanch. He moaned and moaned and occasionally cursed. I reckon now that he was shot through the stomach and a part of the liver, and that the vital organ took some persuading to fail. To this day I do not know how he did it. He lasted four hours, well into the night as we tried to sleep. When he finally died, the silence disturbed us.

There were other losses. Two of the older men died of pneumonia and another lay down after a long march in the heat of August and never got up. I saw some of the preparations for their burials, and silently compared them to the funerals I had attended back home—I thought often of my grandmother. Here was a different rite: whatever prayers and scriptures were read when the body lay finally interred, here the late soldier's fellows—full of regret, yes, but eagerly—divided his wealth, if not his garments, and wound him in a blanket. Someone might say a prayer of his own invention, tailored to the dead man, and then drill, or inspection, or pitching or striking tents, or the march would resume.

DURING THE MONTHS we spent in reserve we marched hundreds of miles, never coming nearer the combat than earshot, and at distances at which the cannonade proved indistinguishable from the afternoon thunderstorms Georgians know from birth. We ran out of good food and meat and ate into our stock of hardtack. Sometimes we had to boil it to render it edible, and more than one man broke teeth trying to eat it, especially when our lack of vitamins weakened our gums' hold on our teeth. Any fruit or bread the militia acquired through requisition we immediately gorged ourselves upon. We used the bayonet for digging more than anything else, and used the shovel and pick more often than the rifle. Our collars and caps wilted, browned, and warped. We sweated our brogans full to sloshing and our socks rotted on our feet; holes bloomed at our knees, elbows, and armpits as we marched, as we worked, as we drilled. The lice multiplied. Our war was dust and fatigue and stops to dig trenches or prepare breastworks for the army to fall back to when, inevitably—and to the great fury of the newspapermen and the enlisted strategists in our camp—it did.

I learned also that we were not all of us soldiers in common. Despite President Davis's urging forward of conscription for the national armies in the East and West—as if in fulfilment of my grandfather's pre-sentiments—Governor Brown husbanded Georgia's resources, especially its manpower. While the volunteer regiments went off to Virginia or elsewhere, the militia remained at home, subject to militia authority and militia command and resistant to all efforts by the commanders of the national army to commandeer them. This dispute was part of the reason we remained in reserve, and a great part of the reason the national soldiers grew to resent us.

Once, while digging earthworks and placing chevaux de frise on the west bank of the Chatta-hoochee near Buckhead, a squadron of Wheeler's cavalry rode by, heading north to Marietta. A young lieutenant at their head nodded to Captain Guerard as he passed, but the men following showed no such deference to their peers.

"Well, if it ain't Joe Brown's pets," a corporal called out. This was the first time I heard the nickname.

"Here's your mule," a man shouted back from down the line.

"Y'all be careful," another cavalryman said. "I hear there's folk around these parts that'll shoot a body if'n you cross them."

"Yeah," another said. "Lucky they's easy to identify. Y'all seen any men in blue coats?"

"Bugger off," Peter's grandfather said.

"Now now," the corporal said, and laughed. "Y'all see any strangers wearing blue, you just send for the cavalry, hear? Don't want to ask too much of the upstanding yokelry."

Thereafter we heard the name "Joe Brown's Pets" nearly every time a unit of the Confederate army passed, which—the more we worked on Atlanta's fortifications, and the nearer the enemy pressed upon them—was often. It often came goodnaturedly, but even when delivered with a grin and a comradely wave it had a sting in it, and like all such jokes it grew tiresome. It proved especially hard to take coming from the lean and battle-weary men who threw the epithet our way, some of whom had bloodstains on their coats. The more bitter among them passed stories, generously leavened with oaths, that the governor aimed to settle separately with the enemy and thus betray the rest of the Confederate states. We gritted our teeth and endured it, and sometimes shouted back. I thought of Sir Launcelot, the noble knight humiliated by his ride in the cart, and longed for a chance to prove ourselves in battle.

Our daily duties grew especially onerous under this barrage of resentment. I looked forward with dread to picket duty, not because of danger but because of boredom. My mind wandered; I wished I could read instead or be back on the farm swimming. I cleaned my pistol or simply worked the mechanisms, wondering at the soft and precise clicking as I spun the cylinder or cocked and lowered the hammer. But I had to limit my use of the pistol—I was afraid to break it. Conversation, which was forbidden on picket duty anyway, proved little help in assuaging the boredom.

"Ivanhoe never stood watch in no picket line," I said to Wes one night.

He shushed me.

"King Richard the Lionheart never stood no picket duty," I said.

He shushed me again.

"Nor Robin Hood neither."

He did not immediately shush me. I waited. "What about his merry men?"

I had not anticipated this tack. "What?"

"Who guarded Robin Hood's camp in Sherwood Forest?"

I said nothing.

"Surely the merry men stood picket duty?"

"Don't go being foolish," I said, feebly.

"The sheriff was all the time looking for them—surely somebody kept an eye out for him, too."

"I—"

"And most of the time wasn't nothing for them to see. But they had to be ready. Just like picket duty."

"Oh, hush."

"Look who's telling who to hush now."

"Maybe the Sheriff of Nottingham was a Yankee," I said.

"Say what?"

Before my feint could work, the third man at our post, Peter's grandfather, shushed the both of us.

When I had to stand watch without my cousins, or alone, I passed the time by mulling my favorite stories, making up a few of my own, or, especially, concocting heraldic blazons for our regimental and company colors. The state flag proved easy enough—*gules, an arch and three columns or* &c.—but I spent long hours puzzling over our battle flag. After some days, I had settled on *gules, a saltire azure charged with thirteen mullets argent.* I remained unsure how to account for the fimbriations, the white borders of the blue cross, and occupied myself for hours yet in shifting this subordinary back and forth through my primitive blazon. I did the same with the many other flags I saw as the army I wished I belonged to passed us by.

Illness struck the camp. After the first few weeks, every man and boy in the camp rose with a cough every morning. The elder men spat huge quantities of phlegm; the boys hawked and hawked and produced little, but nevertheless strove for the appearance of a manly pulmonary complaint. This cough only worsened when the weather turned cold, with even my grandfather stricken and struggling, as I shall relate.

Other problems were acute—diarrhœa in particular, looked upon now as an inconvenience and sometime subject of fun but which killed a few of the older men in the late summer. Every halt saw men hastening to fencerails and fallen trees to squat shivering on the side of the road until we marched on again. Serious cases fell out while still marching and then hastened to catch up; there are few sights more pathetic than an old man with the trots trying to run while burdened with gear to reclaim his place in a moving column. A few men tried to remedy such complaints by eating nothing but fresh fruit—purloined from orchards we passed—but more often this only aggravated the condition.

In our squad alone, Cal, Peter, his grandfather, Private Bell, and Hoyt Burrell were all stricken with diarrhœa at the same time. We were marching and making poor time because of it. Fortunately, we halted once by a farm beside the road.

There were peach trees growing along the road and some of the men set to picking their fruit. The lady of the house appeared and stepped down from the porch, causing a few of the men to fall back to the road and shamefacedly hide their plunder. She waved them back over.

"No, no, no—you men's welcome to them. Ain't no help to pick them no more. The peaches might as well go to the army, too." She was a plump but pretty woman no older than thirty. A pair of small girls who much resembled her appeared in the door of the house. I looked at the woman again and noticed she wore her mourning. "Come on, now," she said, and waved again.

I looked across the road to where half my squad and a good portion of the company sought a place out of sight of the lady to do the quick step, and looked back at the lady and the house. I stepped up to her and removed my hat. She looked me up and down, expressionless.

157

"Yes, young man?"

"I'm sorry to see you're in mourning, ma'am."

She took a moment in answering. "Thank you, son."

"Your husband, ma'am?"

She nodded. "Joined at the start of it. Kilt two years ago. And my father and brother, too, God rest their souls."

"I'm most sorry, ma'am."

"I appreciate it. The Lord gave, the Lord hath taken away. Him and the Yankees."

"Blessed be the name of the Lord," I said, and ignored the Yankees. "My father been gone since the beginning, too. I'm thankful to say he's well—least, the last time we heard from him. Now I'm gone from home."

She simply nodded.

"I don't mean to be improper, ma'am, but our company is afflicted. I don't want to impose, but if you'd allow me to, I'd appreciate some soot from your chimney."

She seemed surprised by that, but after a moment, said, "You learn that from your mama?"

"Yes, ma'am. And her daddy, too. He's here with me and two of my cousins."

She surveyed the men in her trees, resting in the road, or trying to conceal themselves to conduct their agonized evacuations. She looked at me again. "All right. Come on in."

The house was not much bigger than our own. The two girls shied from the door and watched from behind the table as I entered and went to the chimney.

"Private, uh—"

"Wax, ma'am."

"Private Wax, this here's Ruth and Rebecca. Say hey, girls."

They greeted me. I said, "Why, there's a Rebecca in one of my favorite stories. *Ivanhoe*. Y'all read it?"

Ruth and Rebecca shook their heads. Their mother stepped past me to the hearth and said, "Can't nobody read in this house now their daddy's gone."

I looked at the girls, who still stood watching me. I thought I saw some trace of shame cross their faces. While the lady swung the pot out of the embers, I dropped most of my equipment, especially the cartridge box. I took my knife and tin cup from my haversack, pulled my handkerchief over my nose, and leaned into the chimney from the hearth. The fire had burned very low but the chimney was stifling hot; I scraped as quickly as I could against the blackened back of the fireplace and caught the soot and ash in the cup. This accomplished, I lurched back out of the fireplace and caught my breath.

"Thank you," I said. I indicated the cup of chimney soot. "I appreciate it."

The lady nodded. I put my gear back on and stepped outside. Lieutenant Guerard had just ordered the men to fall in; the march would continue.

"What you got there, Private?" he said as I fell in.

I showed him the cup, careful to hold it level, and gestured toward where the last of the stricken men hobbled back to the column from the weeds. He did not seem to understand but grunted and mounted his horse again.

I tipped my kepi to the lady and her girls as I left. The younger of the girls waved.

At our next stop on the march, my grandfather had every man afflicted with diarrhœa produce his cup and a spoon, and I mixed in a measure of the soot. They stirred in the ash and let it settle, and then drank all but the dregs. I also warned them off of unripe fruit. Later, as we bivouacked for the night, my grandfather found a patch of blackberries, from which we gathered both overflowing hatfuls of berries and a good amount of the roots, which he boiled to

159

make a tea and then passed around to the men. The affliction did not disappear entirely, but most of the men had recovered by the next day. Hoyt, who had used to pester me about my pistol, proved especially grateful, and began to treat me less like a boy and more like a fellow soldier. A few who knew me as *Georgie* began to call me *Surgie*, and came to me for other ailments. Between myself and my grandfather's prodigious memory, we could often provide remedies—the soot, blackberry root, and peach tree root for the flux, mayapple for its equally painful opposite, onion poultices or raw peppermint leaves for the colds and coughs that woke us daily, walnut leaf poultices for open sores and infected blisters, peach tree leaf poultices for poison ivy or the stone bruises that afflicted men as their shoes gave out, and others without number. The many older men came for help with their arthritis, for which I had to consult my grandfather—I was yet unacquainted with arthritic pain in those days. He foraged for ginseng and found some on the north-facing bank of a cool hollow through which a creek flowed; he dug up the fleshy white roots, made a whole pot of tea out of it, and had the men rub the leavings on their joints. One old man from another company had been carrying a buckeye in his pocket as a magical cure; my grandfather told him to throw it away and gave him a canteen full of the tea instead. Other remedies proved hard to come by—anything we knew that involved honey, especially for coughs, proved difficult, since honey was hard to come by except by the good graces of farmers past whose farms we happened to march. We did what we could with what we had or could come by. I pray that we did some good.

I thought often of the lady and her daughters after that, and wished I had left them with something as thanks and to help, if only slightly, to relieve their situation. But I do not know what I could have given. I have passed back through that part of Georgia since, but found no trace of them, their farm, or even the peach trees along the road. The war, in one way or another, took all.

I RECALL THAT VISIT in particular detail because it occurred the morning we heard of the fall of Atlanta. Despite change of command and a more aggressive strategy—or perhaps because of these things—the army defending the city lost half its strength, retreated, and gave up the city without the advantage of retaining its strength. General Hood, the great favorite of the newspapermen, the guardhouse generals, and the president himself, lost Atlanta, and—we knew immediately, though we denied we would let it happen—Georgia. This was the beginning of September 1864.

The spirit in the camp was low. Much of the militia received thirty-day furloughs, and those that did not sank lower still. Several men of our company deserted and were never seen again. We cursed them, wished the Home Guard to find them and stretch their necks for us, and wished we could have got away ourselves. A number of times on picket duty, especially at night, we sighted fugitive Negroes, picking their way through the woods toward Atlanta, and we did not bother to stop them. The cries of "Joe Brown's Pets" became more obviously jeers. A few, like Peter's grandfather, openly grumbled about planters and politicians. Rumor of the enemy's intent filled the camp, and was itself full of lies. He would strike next at Griffin, at Macon, at Madison and Milledgeville, at Augusta, or he would feint west into Alabama, into the Black Belt, where most of the planters and Negroes were anyway. Retreating soldiers from the main force of Hood's army said little and explained less, and were no help. The wounded streamed away from Atlanta and intermingled with us on the march. Our movements—the purpose of which had never been clear to us poor marchers—grew obviously confused for a time. Whoever was in command could not decide what to do with us. We marched every direction of the compass. And yet, with Atlanta captured, the enemy did nothing.

I had found soldiering difficult enough thus far, but this situation bothered me enough that I sat down in camp one day and wrote the following letter to my mother:

September 15 1864

Dear Mother,

You have no doubt heard of the fall of Atlanta. It is two weeks now since the city surrendered. There are many rumors in camp about what will happen next. I shall refrain to discuss them for fear this intelligents may fall into enemy hands. I am afraid I do not know anything, I recognize now why daddy wrote so little because there was nothing much to write, but I pray you remain safe. We are all yet safe here & have not seen any fighting, though when the yankees leave Atlanta you can be sure we will try & put a stop to them if they put us into the line. Pray for us. I miss you Jeff & James.

Love,
your son Geo. Wax

I read this letter to my grandfather before I folded and mailed it. He listened and nodded as I read to him and, when I had finished, sat for some time puffing thoughtfully on his pipe.

"They's waiting on the election," Private Bell said. I looked at him. We sat around a fire beside our tents, but I had not expected anyone to be listening to the letter I wrote my mother.

"Election?" I said.

"Yankees got an election coming up," Sergeant Burrell said.

"Don't want to bugger old Abe's chances," Peter's grandfather said. *Bugger*, I had learned, had a deeply obscene meaning to the old Irishman.

"What do you mean?" I said.

"He's safe there, in Atlanta, now," Private Bell said.

"Cept for his supply train," a man from another squad said.

"He leaves, and gets slaughtered by Hood, Lincoln loses," Sergeant Burrell said.

"And it'd serve the son of a bitch right," Hoyt said.

"Damn right," the other man said.

"What we're saying," Peter's grandfather said, "is the Yankees be biding their time. As the sergeant here says, if they make a mistake now, it could cost them in Washington. Meantime, the longer they wait, the more likely we be to make a mistake of our own."

"That's enough of that, you bastard," Hoyt said.

"Shut your trap, Hoyt," Sergeant Burrell said.

I looked at my grandfather, who had yet to speak. He raised his eyebrows and gestured with his pipe. "Shannon's right," he said, meaning Peter's grand-father.

"Ha!" Peter said, and shook his fist at Hoyt, who scowled at him.

My grandfather puffed again at his pipe, consid-ering. "Politicians make wars nowadays, and wars help

164

make politicians." Someone scoffed, and my grandfather looked at him but did not bother to lower his pipe. "Who you think shed Joe Johnston in favor of Hood? Wasn't a general or a soldier made that decision, though I reckon plenty of y'all would've done the same. And the Yankees are up against it just the same as us—politicians running things, making the war do what they want, trying to buy votes. And now they're bargaining with Atlanta, seeing how much the city weighs in the scale against all the blood up to now. Seeing if they can get Lincoln and their war another four years instead of having to quit and count their losses."

He was silent again. At length, Sergeant Burrell said, "Well?"

"What you reckon's going to happen?" Private Bell said.

He laughed and shook his head. "Aw, hell, I don't know. The Most High ruleth in the kingdom of men, and giveth it to whomsoever he will. But I'd bet on one thing—if capturing Atlanta does get Lincoln elected again, the Yankees won't stay bottled up there for long. No, sir. And when they leave, whithersoever they go, there'll be hell to pay. They won't have no reason to hold back, and they'll be out for blood."

"Yeah," Private Bell said, and scoffed, "there ain't been too much bloodshed up to now."

My grandfather shook his head. "I don't mean that. I mean—think on this: in the old days, wars was like duels on a grand scale. You read about the wars in medieval times, and everybody in them was kin. The armies was small. And they fought all the time, not because they was so bloodthirsty, necessarily, but because they negotiated so much. They held back and made agreements and come out against each other every summer only when they could spare a few men to fight. A good king or a good lord didn't need votes,

165

he just needed enough success to keep his people safe, keep his knights loyal, and pass the land on to his children."

I thought, again, of *Ivanhoe*, and it occurred to me for the first time how little war was in that book. I thought of others I had read, whether history or legend, and how personal the combats seemed, how intimate, as opposed to the brutal sprawl of more recent histories—Washington, Napoleon and Wellington, Jackson against the British and Indians, Taylor and Scott in Mexico. My grandfather leaned forward and furrowed his brow. As if anticipating my line of thought, he went on:

"Now, consider wars nowadays. It ain't a king or lord making the choice to go to war, and there's no pope to tell them no. It's the people decides that, through politicians, and it's all the people that have the horror visited on them. Look at the war in the back country in the Revolution, or what the French got up to in their revolution." I thought of what Peter had told me about *A Tale of Two Cities*. "And then Napoleon and Wellington and the Russians—all the kingdoms and empires of Europe armed and blowing theirselves to pieces, everybody caught in the midst and nowhere to escape to. And now the whole of everybody can be called up by everybody else, and so these here huge armies move against each other with their supply trains stretching all the way back to factories that keep on cranking out locomotives and rails to move them and their provender. Armies of strangers fighting in a country too big to ever hang together. The soldiers is just one piece of a huge machine with the politicians and the people at the levers, and it don't end until one side is destroyed entire. The people and the politicians won't let it, and if one lets up or wearies, the other keeps it going."

"You don't think—" Sergeant Burrell said.

"I don't know what I think. But we done it already. You remember the Indians, and especially the Mexicans. Now it's us is on the receiving end."

"But they was—" Hoyt said, and fell silent.

"Yeah," Private Bell said. "Don't feel too good being on the receiving end, now does it?"

The mood had darkened considerably. Sergeant Burrell said, "What do you reckon happens afterward?"

"Things'll be different. Politicking will go on, but it'll go on with a war like this under its belt and forevermore looked at as a choice, there for the picking if need be. If we lose—and I ain't saying we will, now—if we lose, won't nobody, whether state or county or anything smaller than the whole nation ever have its own way in its own business again, right or wrong."

We considered this—or, at least, I did. The sun had fully set while he spoke and the camp lay dark but for the flickering of the cookfires in the night.

"That was a mighty enlightening excursus, Private Eschenbach," Lieutenant Guerard said from the dark. He stepped into the firelight and we rose to salute. He waved us back to our seats. "But I wonder what it had to do with the young private's letter here?"

"Aw, we was just pondering over the enemy's next moves, Lieutenant," Sergeant Burrell said.

"The enemy is stalled in Atlanta," Lieutenant Guerard said.

"Yes, sir," I said, "but after that."

"I have it on good authority that we mean to strike in the enemy's rear, and soon."

"The supply train!" the man from the other squad said. "Like I said—he's weak there."

Lieutenant Guerard nodded. "Cavalry have probed and shown the enemy has reached too far, too fast. We will strike behind him and behead the serpent."

"God willing," my grandfather and Peter's grandfather said, nearly simultaneously.

"Of course. God willing."

"Can we expect to get in on the fighting?" Wes, heretofore silent, said.

"I hope so," Lieutenant Guerard said.

Wes, Cal, and I roused and grinned at each other. I recall clearly how impish the twins looked, laughing squint-eyed in the firelight. My grandfather tamped new tobacco into his pipe and lit it, and looked not into the fire or at Lieutenant Guerard but up, at the stars as they appeared.

Later, as we retired into our tent, I went to him alone and asked him about my letter to my mother. He laughed and put his arm around my shoulders—I was struck for the first time that I was tall enough now for him to do so.

"It's a good letter. Sorry I got side-tracked back there."

"I reckon I understand now how little anybody knows about what's going on," I said.

"Yep," he said, and laughed again.

"Was it like this when you fought the Indians?"

"Worse. We didn't know nothing. No newspapers, no mail to speak of, nothing but rumor—there wasn't even no roads through most of south Georgia and the Floridas."

"So it's got better?"

"Don't nothing get better. It's just got different. Newspapers ain't much of a help, at least in my opinion. Know nothing about what's going on, or know a heap of lies and speculation?"

"What about the telegraph?"

"Tell your lies faster."

"You don't think things will get better still?"

"Georgie, you wrote your mama a good letter. You told her the truth and you did it so she wouldn't worry—not too much, anyhow. That's all a man can do. Anything else, any embellishment, is vanity. More so trusting in something like the telegraph wire. If you think wire will improve men, well, you're mistaken."

"Do you really think we'll lose?" I had felt a dread build through our conversation, and it broke over me when I asked him this. My voice shook and I found myself tearing up. I fought mightily against it, but the tears flowed.

My grandfather half-bent and looked me in the eye. The stern face with those menacing brows softened. He took me by the shoulders with both hands.

"Georgie, we don't know what tomorrow will bring. And what I was saying back there about the war— when a man gets mixed up in something this big, and this powerful, and he's at the beck and call of oh, such destructive principalities and powers, he can only do what's right, where it's right in front of him. You and me, Wes and Cal, and your daddy and Uncle Quin— we're fighting for our homes. Parties and politicking be damned. You understand?"

"Yes, sir."

"Whether we win or lose, we do the right thing. It's what a man does, whether he likes it or not."

"Yes, sir."

He clapped me on the shoulders again and embraced me. He had that same old pipe tobacco, earth, and sweat smell about him, mingled now with damp-crackled leather, wool, and brass, and cookfire smoke— the smells of the army. I embraced him back, and found I wished I were home.

IV

MACON

W E HEARD NOT LONG AFTER of the visit of President Davis to the front, and of his laying plans with General Hood to exact revenge upon the enemy and drive them from Georgia. We gathered—from rumor, hearsay, and newspaper reports of the president's own speeches on his trip back to Richmond—that Hood meant to strike against the enemy's supply train and cause him to double back toward Tennessee.

"If we know——" my grandfather said.

"The Yankees sure as hell know, too," Hoyt said.

We marched. The railroads were in a state of disarray all around Atlanta, and so we often followed the tracks—as a more direct route—until we either arrived at our destination or met a train sent to pick us up. Most often we marched.

We left the first rail line we had ridden at Madison and marched south by road to Eatonton and thence along another rail line to Milledgeville. We bivouacked by the Oconee River that night and I spent the evening in touring the town with Wes, Cal, and my grandfather, who had been there several times before. I was excited and amazed to pass through the capital of the state, to behold the medieval battlements of the capitol building. I marveled to think that the men who governed our state met in a castle, and imagined knights, in their particolored blazons, crouched behind the crenellated walls, flinging stones or dousing Yankee sappers in boiling oil.

Milledgeville was, with Athens, the largest city I had ever visited, of about four-thousand souls at that time, but further swollen with people fleeing Atlanta and points north. Our militia did not live in the only tent city around the capital. Fine ladies and old gentlemen, disheveled and distressed, the women wringing their hands and the men unshaven, wandered the town. We saw many old men, some supporting themselves on two canes or walking only with the help of Negro manservants, awaiting an audience with Governor Brown outside the mansion, or coming and going to the capitol in varied states of anger, but all with resignation. Large numbers of the yeomanry— mostly women and small children, the menfolk of all ages being eaten out by the war—milled about with no connections to call upon. Slaves and white trash completed the throng, though not as many slaves as might have been the case even six months before. All lived on handouts and the few things they had hauled with them in wagons, carts, buggies, or wheelbarrows. I saw women of our station feeding infants, their faces, even while looking into the faces of their babes, masks of sorrow, and thought of my mother. She would have the baby any day, had she not done so already.

We observed at least two funerals for soldiers, and I thought of my father.

We overheard stories exchanged by the fugitives, but our grandfather prevented us listening in too intently—or completely. "It's rude to eavesdrop, boys. Come on," and off we would go to see some other part of the town.

Rumor drifted among the crowd and the camp. Hood had gathered his strength and struck northward toward the enemy. Beyond that we knew nothing with certainty. I only credited this particular rumor because we had learned we were bound for Macon or Jonesboro, which made sense if Hood were to depart with the bulk of the army in order to draw the enemy away. We would serve as the rearguard again.

WE ENTRAINED IN MILLEDGEVILLE and rode the sixteen miles to Gordon. A guidebook to the Confederacy's railroads, acquired by Sergeant Burrell, described a ride of about two and one quarter hours between the two towns, with one stop; the ride took half a day, and in Gordon we disembarked to await another train, which would take us to Macon along the main line of the Central of Georgia R.R. We camped for two days before we moved on. Once we did, I caught my first sight of Griswoldville.

The weather had cooled from the high summer but remained warm, and so we rode in our boxcar with the door open. My grandfather and I sat beside it in the light—for him to read, for myself, as I had long since finished *A Tale of Two Cities* and was in no mood to read it again, to watch Georgia roll past.

"Look here," my grandfather said. He leaned over and showed me Sergeant Burrell's timetable. "The only stop between Gordon and Macon is listed here as Griswold. That's the factory town where your pistol come from."

I perked up. "Say what?"

He showed me. I pulled out my pistol and turned it

over again and felt its weight, almost a warmth, in my hands. We approached the town and slowed. Rail sidings appeared, another locomotive—in obviously poor repair—waiting, huffing steam with mechanically impatient rhythm. The cars stood packed with soldiers, all wounded, many of them laid on stretchers in the doors of the cars. They watched us with faraway stares as we rolled past. A few waved, and at least one shouted "Give them hell!" Then we were past, and I saw the town.

Griswoldville bustled despite its small size. Carts and wagons waited to cross the road as we passed, ladies nursed bandaged men on the station platform, a troop of motley cavalry moved along the road at a walk, and workers streamed into the factory, which billowed steam and smoke like the locomotive. And it was loud, even for someone now used to the clang, whistle, and roar of the trains.

I paid special attention to the gun works, and ran my thumb over the brass and steel of my pistol. This machine had come from this place, here in Georgia, milled and assembled by men in this factory. I marveled at it and reseated the pistol in my holster.

My grandfather patted me on the shoulder. "Something, ain't it?"

"Yes, sir!" I said.

"This where they made your pistol?" Cal said.

"Yeah, right yonder in the factory," I said.

Cal and Wes leaned out of the boxcar door to get a glimpse as we slid further and further onward.

"Wish we could stop," Wes said. "I'd go get me a pistol."

"You done spent all your money in Milledgeville," Cal said. "Wasted it all on sweets."

"Did not."

"Sure did. Wasn't even good ones, neither."

"Hush your mouth."

"That's enough," my grandfather said.

"Don't none of us have enough cash to buy a pistol, anyhow," Hoyt chipped in.

"Ain't that the truth," Private Bell said.

"Besides," I said, and nudged Wes and laughed, "Cal's right."

All laughed but Wes, who sulked another mile and a half down the track. I turned back to my grandfather.

"You say that was a Yankee town?"

"A Yankee industry man started it, building cotton gins. Used the machinery to start building pistols for the war."

"They expensive?"

"I reckon he made plenty on them."

I felt the pistol again and considered the factory town. Pistols were luxuries—I had learnt as much by observing my fellow soldiers, only a handful of whom carried sidearms. How many pistols could the factory turn out for sale to the Confederate States government or private soldiers? I was used to thinking of guns as particular articles, things of themselves, that had no origin meaningful to me and were in most ways unique. Perhaps that had been the case in the past— our neighbor Mr. Hale kept an ancient shotgun hand-made for his grandfather just after the Revolution. The rifle muskets and pistols we carried in the militia had all been turned out, copies of copies, en masse, by machines, not gunsmiths. So here we sat, I thought— with our machine-spun clothing and machine-turned weapons, borne Macon-ward on machine-crafted rails by a machine more noisy and powerful than any living creature. I wondered at the tools at man's disposal.

Once clear of Griswoldville's sidings, our train picked up speed and we chugged on to Macon proper in less than half an hour. We climbed down from the train outside town, fell in on the main road, and marched across the Ocmulgee and through the city.

178

Macon now took its place as the largest city I had ever seen—twice the size of Athens or the capital, spread across a hill above the river with church spires and belfries crowding the sky and the smoke of iron-works and the main rail station rising in white and black plumes amidst the thinner wisps of civilian hearthfires. No crowd turned out for us. A few children—not much younger than myself or my cousins, and not much smaller than Peter—regarded us with interest for a moment before going back to games or chores. A few ladies brought us loaves of bread or small sundries, but nothing compared to the outpouring in Union Point a few months before. We were dis-appointed—every new town brought the hope of handouts, for our own stores were desperately short—and became as sullen as the townspeople. The Negroes went about their errands and pointedly ignored us.

We bivouacked a half-mile north of town on the Macon and Western line running north toward Griffin, Jonesboro, and, one hundred miles off, Atlanta, the Yankee fortress. Where we would go next, none knew, not even Lieutenant Guerard or First Sergeant Sloane.

This was the middle of October—I had turned fourteen on the fourteenth of the month—and the dank summer weather had given way to dank autumn weather. The pages of our books grew wavy in the humidity and our clothing clung to us as we marched or worked. We sweated continuously. It filled and soaked through our brogans and some of us chose to march or work barefoot instead. The fall of Atlanta lay now a month and a half in the past, and so the fleeing populations of Fulton and the surrounding counties had either settled into nearly permanent tent dwellings outside towns like Macon or dispersed to family or fortune elsewhere. The old gentlemen I saw in Milledgeville were nowhere to be seen; instead we saw great troupes of ragged women and children, who were

179

so humiliated and needy that they came even to us for charity. A few men gave up bread that had already been donated once—to us—while others produced a precious bit of remaining salt pork or beef. Wes hesitated at the approach of one band of children but, in the end, brought his remaining sweets out of his haversack and gave them all away.

All that had remained to us for some time now was hardtack and white beans, and peanuts. "Mule fodder," Hoyt called it. Our supplies of meat had waned almost to nothing; what little we ate was given to us by women whose farms we passed on the road, or purchased from the sutlers who followed the army like locusts and sold nearly spoiled meat for a month's pay. Salt and sugar had grown even scarcer than they had been in the last year on the farm. I must own that some of us stole food; during our time around Macon, Hoyt and Wes left camp as often as possible and roamed the countryside, foraging. They would return with the occasional hatful of eggs or bread, poor-looking potatoes, crabapples, and other such foodstuffs. My grandfather and I were much busied with remedying the complaints these things brought on.

The first time they went on such an "expedition," as they called it, I asked how they had come by their booty.

"Paid in gold bars," Wes said. They settled in by our cookfire and put a skillet on over the coals. Wes commenced to blowing on the embers.

"Come on," I said.

"Took it, shitbird," Hoyt said. "What'd you think?"

I stared at them. Wes looked at me and nudged Hoyt. "Go easy—he likes to do things by the book."

"You didn't pay them nothing?"

"Who?" Hoyt said.

I gestured feebly. "Whoever you took this all from."

Wes looked steadfastly at his feet and shook his head. "Georgie, what would we pay them with?"

"They going to put you in a barrel shirt if—"

"You want to eat any of this or not?" Hoyt said, and dropped a fist-sized slab of bacon into the skillet. I looked at the bacon, which served as the vanguard for a column of fresh eggs to follow. As the skillet heated, the food softly crackled and I took in the smell. I sighed. When they had finished cooking up their spoils, I—along with the rest of the squad, who had gathered silently in the meantime, my grandfather included— held out my plate and said nothing.

I thought their theft a crime at the time. I was to see worse, much worse.

HOOD'S ARMY HAD, by this time, moved against the enemy's supply train, between Chattanooga and Atlanta. Our cavalry under Wheeler and Forrest—both of whom we unquestioningly admired as bold scourges of the Yankee rear—had already stricken the enemy in this long and vulnerable neck to some effect, and, based upon what rumor we received, some of us entertained hopes of what such an expedition might accomplish—the enemy's distraction, his luring away from Atlanta, his retreat north, his destruction.

While this proceeded, causing the young among us to gaze northward with longing for glory, we were set to work digging entrenchments, throwing up breastworks, and repairing the rail lines. Large gangs of Negroes conscripted from among the slave population joined us. Some of our men refused to work beside them, but others felt ourselves already so degraded by the endless marching and the spadework and entrenchments elsewhere that our dignity could suffer little further harm. A few men, some of them conscripted white trash, stood on what passed as principle among them and refused to work. When such circumstances arose, work slowed, frustrating the already put-upon officers yet more, and they would threaten, harangue, and curse.

After one tongue-lashing from Lieutenant Guerard, occasioned by the refusal of three long, tallow men—whom I seem to recall being brothers—to dig any more, we set back to work with our tools and a low murmur of grumbling, like a field full of bumblebees, could be heard all along the earthworks.

"Just a chance," I heard Peter's grandfather say between shovel strokes. "Just a chance and I'll tell that Frenchy bastard to bugger off back to Carolina."

"I'd like to see how well he wields a shovel," one of the white trash brothers said.

"A man got no call saying such things to a man," another said.

"Aw, hell, he's just aggravated he can't beat us like his niggers," said yet another.

Laughter along the line.

"Ain't that the truth," Hoyt said. "For all of them."

"And they call us trash."

Others among us fretted less about their standing than their safety. One man from another squad in our company made himself sick and intolerable from his questions about our arms.

"Lieutenant, sir," he would say, several times a day.

"What, Greeves?"

"Our rifles, sir. You ain't concerned the niggers will get them?"

"Your rifles are stacked and under guard, Private." Indeed, a small number of us, usually the youngest or smallest, like Peter, were detailed to watch our rifles where we had stacked them before beginning work. Guarding the rifles and equipment was reputed the most tedious task ever given to a soldier. Servile theft of a weapon did not seem an especial danger, but Greeves could not be mollified.

"Sir, I know the nigger. My uncle had four worked with him in his sawmill. They're sneaky as hell and—"

"Any man here," Lieutenant Guerard called out, "unacquainted with colored folk? The dusky-hued persons one sees at work in the fields? Working harder than some private soldiers, I might add."

We stopped and stared at him, at Greeves. Greeves looked at his feet. Guerard waited.

"What I mean, Lieutenant—"

"I never seen a nigger sneakier than he was lazy," Guerard would say. "Your rifles are under guard. Get yourself to work."

A similar scene would recur not long after a ten-minute break for dinner, and at least once more before we retrieved our weapons and marched back to camp for the evening. After a time even his fellows treated Greeves as a nuisance, though all would admit that he had some kind of point—we had all heard of servile insurrections, and many of us had marked, as I have mentioned before, the occasional lone Negro or small group of dark figures slipping through the woods past our picket lines of a night. We noted as well the way our Negro laborers dwindled in number the farther north we worked the line.

When not digging entrenchments, we worked on the railroads. The work seemed after a time to have no end—it was pointless. The tracks had suffered severe damage at the hands of Yankee cavalry in July, and new rails were not forthcoming. We stole rails from disused lines and sidings and hauled those to the sections that wanted mending. Railroad ties proved easier—we wielded the ax as often as the hammer, and more often than the rifle at this time. We were one of a handful of companies detached from General Smith's Georgia militia and detailed to such work. We marched up and down the line, making camp elsewhere on occasion, usually falling back to Macon when the work was done to be directed elsewhere for further tasks. We marched along the line as far north as Fayette, over sixty miles away, and spent some days digging entrenchments there. This was our longest departure.

We returned to Macon, wasted by lack of food and excess of work, on November 11, 1864. The next day, after we had begun to enlarge and strengthen the earthworks in the hills around the town, I received a letter from my mother:

September 30, 1864

My dear son
I write to inform you that I have rec'd a letter from your father, that he is returned with his reg't to Georgia! He & your Uncle Quintus fight now with Gen'l Hood, who so bravely defended Atlanta these months past. I know little else regarding their situation & the dispositions of our soldiers, but perhaps you two will chance to meet each other one day in the defence of our state. My condition is good, do not worry. I progress well & Mrs Bower stands ready any day to midwife. Your brothers are well & truly helpful to me in my condition. I pray for you & your father both & for John Wesley & John Calhoun. I pray as well for daddy, do tell him I wrote saying so. God guide you & keep you in spite of tribulation, distress, persecution, famine, nakedness, peril & sword.

  Love,
  your mother,
    Mary Wax

I read this letter to my grandfather as we sat with the squad near our tent that evening. "Daddy's here, in Georgia!"

He nodded and clamped down on his pipe.

"What is it?" I said.

He sighed a great cloud of fine-smelling smoke. "If your daddy is in the army of General Hood, he is in great danger."

"Ain't all war dangerous?"

"Certainly. But not all generals know best how to handle their men when in danger. Your daddy thought highly of General Lee. I can't say as I do of General Hood, though some of our fellows here surely do."

I considered my father marching northward with the army, into the enemy's rear, a move sure to provoke battle. I realized as well that this was the first time I had heard my grandfather speak of the danger of battle, pure and simple.

"Will he be all right?"

"I hope so, Georgie."

"And Uncle Quin?"

"I hope so, I surely do."

I ached with dread. I sought words but came up only with, "What can we do?"

My grandfather shook his head and sighed. "Pray."

Peter looked up from a game of checkers nearby.

"Y'all are welcome to come pray with us in the morning."

Peter's grandfather, at the other side of the board, shook his head. "They don't want to be doing that, Pete."

"Aw, well we're just going to the church right here in town."

"For the Mass, Pete. They can't join in if they come."

"Well, I thought they could come pray leastways."

My grandfather removed his pipe and nodded. "We appreciate it, and we will join y'all, if you don't mind."

Peter looked at his grandfather, who raised his eyebrows and said only, "All right."

186

My grandfather rose and tapped out his pipe. "Gentlemen, I mean to retire. Mister Halloran, Georgie and I will see you in the morning. Good evening."

He entered the tent amid a chorus of gruff "evenings" and lay down among his blankets. Peter and I looked at each other in wonder. I had never been to a Catholic church—those reputed dens of Babylonian idolatry and popish servility—and had no inkling what had possessed my grandfather to join the Hallorans there. Peter's grandfather said all we could do was pray. My grandfather must have aimed to do some serious praying.

We rose before dawn, shucked off our blankets and met the deepening November cold. My grandfather coughed a full five minutes before his throat was cleared and, with watering eyes, he bundled up for the walk to church. Wes and Cal did not stir when we tried to rouse them, so my grandfather and I stepped out into the gloom and met Peter and his grandfather, who regarded us with friendly suspicion.

"Morning," we all said.

Peter's grandfather led the way toward the city. We walked up into the town along the streets, which lay quiet but for a few stray dogs—as poorly fed as we were—and a few enthusiasts on their way to church early bearing dishes or cumbersome Bibles. Peter's grandfather led us to the Catholic church, a former Presbyterian sanctuary converted for use with tabernacle, icon, and crucifix.

"If Mister Streets could see this," I whispered to my grandfather, who laughed heartily.

Peter's grandfather turned to us as we ascended the stairs, and I realized he may have taken my whisper and my grandfather's laugh uncharitably.

"Now, I don't mean no offense, but it's a closed communion. Y'all understand?"

"I do," my grandfather said. "We mean to sit in

the back and pray, that's all."

"Protestants can't receive the host."

"Aw, we ain't Protestants, we're Methodists."

Peter's grandfather stared and, when he saw my grandfather grin, smiled despite himself. "All right. Come on in."

We entered the church, which stood empty but for the priest and a deacon near the altar. I watched and wondered at Peter and his grandfather's practiced motions—the removal of their hats, the dip into the basin of holy water, the sign of the cross, the humble shuffle down the aisle and the genuflection before the altar. Watching them and these simple gestures, I felt for the first time that the Almighty was indeed present, and waiting. They knelt in the front row and my grandfather and I seated ourselves in the back.

My grandfather had brought his prayer book and a small book of prayers and hymns given away to soldiers by some charitable ladies that summer. He handed the latter to me and found the daily reading in the former. Choked, nigh suffocated with this newfound sense of God's presence, I read a prayer and a few hymn texts while my grandfather read the prescribed psalm. When he had finished, he handed his book to me, knelt, and began praying himself. I looked at the text: Psalm 118, which begins, "O give thanks unto the LORD; for he is good: his steadfast mercy endures forever," and which I could recite by heart. I paused over these words in particular:

> *I called upon the LORD in distress: the LORD*
> *answered me, and set me in a large place.*
> *The LORD is on my side; I will not fear: what*
> *can man do unto me?*
> *The LORD taketh my part with them that help*
> *me: therefore shall I see my desire upon*
> *them that hate me.*

*It is better to trust in the LORD than to put
confidence in man.*

*It is better to trust in the LORD than to put
confidence in princes.*

*All nations compassed me about: but in the name
of the LORD will I destroy them.*

*They compassed me about; yea, they compassed
me about: but in the name of the LORD I
will destroy them.*

*They compassed me about like bees: they are
quenched as the fire of thorns: for in the
name of the LORD I will destroy them.*

*Thou hast thrust sore at me that I might fall: but
the Lord helped me.*

*The LORD is my strength and song, and is
become my salvation.*

*The voice of rejoicing and salvation is in the
tabernacles of the righteous: the right hand of
the LORD doeth valiantly.*

*The right hand of the LORD is exalted: the right
hand of the Lord doeth valiantly.*

*I shall not die, but live, and declare the works of
the LORD.*

I recalled asking him many years before—even before
the war—what *compassed* meant. "Surrounded," he
said, with a weight that told me he knew what it
meant to be surrounded.

"And tabernacles?" I had said.

"Tents, like the Tabernacle of the Lord in the
wilderness, or at Shiloh, where Hannah brung Samuel
when he was a boy."

I read this psalm with new interest. A life of tents
and campaign, of distress, even thrusting—as in
bayonet drill. I had never before considered God a
valiant general, but I imagined Him now as Lord of
Hosts, saddled on a charger of pure light, an officer's

sabre in hand and the drums tolling the call to form up, into line of battle. In the name of the Lord will I destroy them, I thought. I knelt beside my grandfather and prayed for our success as soldiers, for my father and uncle, for the hosts at the command of General Hood and the wisdom of the political men laying plans at the far end of the telegraph wire.

When I had finished, I retook my seat buoyed with confidence. My grandfather remained kneeling for some time. I watched him, and he reminded me— with the intensity and forcefulness of his counte- nance—of my mother in her prayers through the watches of the night, though he remained silent throughout. My confidence slackened somewhat to watch him, and I considered whether I had given adequate time or fervor to my prayer, whether I had come too boldly before the throne. Just as I made to kneel again and more humbly beseech the valiant right hand of the Lord, he opened his eyes, straightened, and sat beside me. He rubbed his knees for some time but said nothing, only looked ahead toward the altar with his great black brows furrowed. The priest had just lifted the consecrated host before the congregation and begun to sing.

I had time to watch Peter and his grandfather— and a few other Catholics of the neighborhood—in the last steps of their devotion, praying, signing the cross, speaking in murmurs to the priest, and receiving the wafer and wine. By this time newcomers had lit several candles and a surplice boy moved about the sanctuary preparing censers, which already filled the old chapel with a sweet-smelling savor.

I looked to my grandfather, who still sat motionless.

"Granddaddy," I whispered.

"Not now, Georgie."

I indicated the candles, the censers, the ministra- tions of the priest. "What are they—"

"Not now, Georgie. Pray."

I hushed, but was too confused to pray further.

Peter and his grandfather concluded shortly thereafter and we stood and followed them from the church
as they left. Before we spoke again, I saw Peter's
grandfather nod and pat and clasp him by the shoulder,
as my own grandfather did me when particularly fond
or proud of me. I looked back at the church building,
with its foreign images and idols—according to those
like Mr. Streets—and looked at the cross at the top of
the steeple. I would think more of Peter, his grandfather, and their religion in the coming days and years.

Once in the street outside, my grandfather put his
hat on and nodded to Peter's grandfather. "Thank you
for having us along."

"You're welcome, Fate. Georgie."

"We head on back we might catch some of that
sumptuous breakfast they've laid on for us."

Peter's grandfather actually laughed at that. "Better
hurry, then."

The streets had woken and busied—a few men in
rags or bits of uniform stirred where they had slept in
corners and byways; men and women in Sunday dress,
considerably nicer than back home, this being a city,
made their ways; and a handful of less Godfearing
persons walked mules or drove wagons. Far off, I heard
the whistle of a train. As we walked I considered how
to ask my grandfather about his prayers, about the
psalm for that day, about the liturgy through which
Peter and his grandfather had worshiped.

I recall all this in some detail because of what
occurred next. We had neared the edge of town and
the cookfires of the camp were in sight when a sutler's
wagon jangled into view from a side street. My grandfather looked up at this and stopped, frozen, in the
street. I looked at him, at the wagon, at him again.
Peter and his grandfather stopped, too.

191

"Well, by——" my grandfather began. I looked again. He stared at the man driving the wagon, an older man with long faded, red side-whiskers but a cleanshaven chin and lip. He had hauled back on the reins and looked as though he were about to give my grandfather a fearful tongue-lashing, but I saw him startle and a change washed over his countenance. He completed my grandfather's thought.

"By God," he said. "Mister Eschenbach!"

"Thomas Crabtree," my grandfather said. "Now where have you been with my daughter?"

"I—I see you done got yourself roped into this war."

"I see you didn't."

I looked up at this man on his wagon. We gaped at each other. At last, my grandfather turned to us and said: "My apologies, gentlemen. This here is Thomas Crabtree, one of my sons-in-law."

PETER AND HIS GRANDFATHER returned to camp while my grandfather and I, after guiding him to a place where his wagon and wares would be most noticeable to the militiamen, caught up with Thomas Crabtree, my aunt Elizabeth's husband. He had a strange accent, not Southern at all, jabbered rather than drawled, and had a strange way of pulling at his side whiskers as he talked. I only realized much later that he was nervous.

He had wandered for some time through the western territories and a variety of trades, and with the outbreak of war had been part owner of a dry goods store in Fort Smith, Arkansas. He had speculated in cotton along the Mississippi before the enemy had issued a general order expelling the Jews from their theatre of war, which damaged Crabtree by proxy. Thus divested of a considerable part of his trade, and with the Yankees closing down the Mississippi mile by mile, he invested in a stock of goods valuable to soldiers, unpacked his photographic equipment and chemicals, and sent my aunt back to Arkansas and safety. He had not heard from her in a year.

"Ain't heard from either of y'all for nigh on three,"

my grandfather said. He had listened to Crabtree's account—delivered mostly in a tone of complaint, but wryly so, as though he only were to blame, and knew it—with mere toleration.

"It's the war, Fate."

"John's got letters through pretty regular, and him up in Virginia with Lee."

"Up til now," I said.

"What's that?" Crabtree said.

"John—Mary's husband, if you remember. Been in Virginia since pretty much the beginning but now's here in Georgia with Hood. But I believe my point stands."

"She'll be fine, Fate. I apologize we haven't writ you more often."

My grandfather stifled a cough but did not break off his stare. At last, he said, "Apology accepted."

"Fort Smith is safe enough from all this, and I give her instructions to remove to Texas in the event—"

"Where at in Texas? Texas is awful big, as I believe I've heard from a Texan or two."

Crabtree slapped his knee in a pantomime of joviality. "Beaumont, specifically. I got people there. Inland from Galveston. Piney country, not too different from here. Just hotter. More skeeters."

"All right."

"Safer than here, by God. What you think the Yankees are going to do once they're finished with—"

My grandfather raised an eyebrow, and Crabtree stopped. I believe now that Crabtree had been about to say *finished with Hood*. He had nearly spoken doom on my father.

"We're safe enough, Thomas."

"Hood's a fool, Fate. Davis, too, for putting him in charge. Going to be the death of us all."

"You give politicians and generals too much credit. Better not to put your confidence in princes."

"Say what?"

My grandfather shook his head. He brought out his cash, Confederate and Georgia greenbacks. "Enough of this talk. I reckon you recall I never had much use for it, back when y'all were around here. What you got in the way of pork?"

Crabtree did not seem to regret the change of topic, and eyed my grandfather's cash for a moment before he seemed, with great effort, to purpose something within himself.

"I won't take a cent of your money, Fate."

"Nonsense. What you got?"

Crabtree produced some salt pork, fresh sowbelly, and a sack of white beans. He steadfastly refused—as one does when discovering principles out of embarrassment—to accept our money for the meat, but did take it, all of it, in exchange for salt, sugar, and some cornmeal, of which he had somehow procured plenty. He put our haul in a burlap poke and, just as he made to hand it over to us, stopped short.

"Say, now," he said, "how about one last thing, by way of apology?"

"You done apologized plenty, Thomas."

"No, no, no, not like this I ain't." He turned from my grandfather to me, whom he must have reckoned more impressionable. "You ever had your picture made, son?"

"Georgie," my grandfather said.

"Georgie, you ever—"

"No, sir, never!" I said. I was truly excited.

"Well, all right, now! Fate, let me make a photograph of the two of you. Have something lasting to take out of all this mess. How about it?"

I looked at my grandfather. I had never before had my photograph taken. It was still an adventure and a luxury in those days. My grandfather glanced at me and softened.

"All right, Thomas."

"It's a deal, then!"

"One of each of us," my grandfather said.

Crabtree shied a bit, but recovered and pushed forward in the traces. "Done! You'll appreciate this the rest of your days. Something to show your grandchildren. Haha!"

Even my grandfather laughed at that, and so Crabtree unloaded his photographic equipment and we sat for our portraits, one at a time, there before a canvas backdrop on a chilly November morning. I posed with my beloved revolver drawn and lain with casual ostentation across my lap and my rifle—bayonet fixed—propped nonchalantly against my left shoulder. I made certain all of my remaining brass buttons and my State of Georgia beltplates were visible, and wore my kepi smartly—so I thought—low over one eye. My grandfather sat with his rifle grounded and gripped in his right hand and his pipe held in the other, as though he had been interrupted in a contemplative moment on the picket line. I insisted he doff his greatcoat so that the camera could capture his corporal's stripes. We did not smile, either of us, for the time to expose the plate lasted so long—Crabtree timed about eighty seconds on his pocketwatch. And so we made the photographs with which I began this reminiscence.

By the time we had finished, a dozen other soldiers had seen Crabtree at work and gathered to do business. I overheard a threesome pooling their cash for a group portrait; others negotiated with each other to borrow pistols and bowie knives for the maximum appearance of ferocity. My grandfather tried again to pay Crabtree but the latter waved him off.

"A gift for kin," he said. "I'll throw in a couple of handsome frames."

"When will they be ready?" I said.

"It'll be several hours, especially with all these boys

196

waiting. Possibly in the morning. I could mail them to you—if you'd rather not have to come back."

"That'd be fine," my grandfather said. When I protested—my curiosity to see myself on the finished plate, resplendently uniformed, framed in brass, was overwhelming—he smiled and grabbed my shoulder. "Aw, now—we know what we look like, but I reckon your mama would be glad to see us."

I could not argue with that. As we left my long-lost uncle behind at his sutlery wagon and struck back toward the camp, I thought of her at home with James and Jefferson. The new baby would surely have arrived by now. I fretted. I knew the dangers of childbirth—they were at that time more familiar to me than combat, despite my months of soldiering—and I found myself praying again, and for the rest of the day.

MY GRANDFATHER'S DECISION to have our portraits mailed home was a wise one. We learned from Lieutenant Guerard that afternoon that we were to entrain for Jonesboro soon, to join the rest of General Smith's militia outside Atlanta, where we would confront the rear of the enemy's forces as they would inevitably pivot to pursue Hood, who thrust now from northern Alabama into Tennessee, a floodtide reaching into the sandy foundation of the enemy's salient. The young among us grew particularly excited—my cousins, Peter, and I cheered when the word came. Some of the old men grinned and chatted among themselves of finally getting a chance to face the enemy, even if it were to be a rearguard action. To see the enemy's hindparts as they passed our cleft of the rock, so to speak, would be satisfying even if it were not to fall to us to deal the fatal blow.

We spent two more days on the entrenchments around Macon, which would be left to the locals and a handful of other militia to keep up, though the feeling was that they would never see use again.

By now our company had reassembled entire, those men who had received furlough hurried back into arms by the cavalry. Our replacements, who had been arriving in trickles for some days, included more old men and boys from the counties surrounding, and their desperate condition—some ill, many barely even armed—did not hearten us. They complained bitterly of having been swept up by the cavalry to fill out the state's ranks. I talked to one boy who said a threesome of horsemen had come for him halfway through his morning visit to the privy. "Won't never move my bowels in peace again," he said.

At the end of the second day, as we returned to camp for the last time, and anticipated striking the tents the next morning to ride the Macon & Western northward, couriers arrived at the gallop and the officers' quarters buzzed. In the hours after dusk, infantry appeared on the roads and threw up tents near us along the Ocmulgee. Few of us slept for speculation about what was happening. By the early morning hours of the next day, November 16, the roads thronged with men and horses, falling back from Atlanta. Swift-winged rumor flew.

At last, at morning roll call, Lieutenant Guerard appeared and informed us that we were not to strike camp, but had orders to await the arrival of the rest of our militia brigade from Lovejoy Station. The day before, the enemy had left the safety of Atlanta—not to pursue the bold and audacious Hood, but to strike into the empty belly of Georgia. He marched with a considerable number of infantry and cavalry raiding in the van, but there was no firm word on his strength, which to us meant that it was overwhelming. It fell to us after all, Lieutenant Guerard said, to defend our homes against the invader. Our days in the reserve, mending track and digging ditches, had ended; the enemy struck in force for Macon, and nothing stood in his way but us.

THE ENEMY HAD LEFT ATLANTA behind with no baggage, cut free of its supply train and the encumbrance of extra artillery and wagons. It moved on foot guided by reconnaissance on horseback and the word of fugitive Negroes, but also by the theodolite and the calculator, by stacks of railroad maps and courthouses full of land surveys, by the census figures of planters and mathematically precise columns of available provender, fodder, and beef on the hoof, and by the prodigious memory of its commander, who had spent time in Georgia long before and professed to love Southerners and the people of this state, whose substance he now proposed to eat out entirely, until they howled.

The militia who marched into Macon at a shaggy route step two days later told us of the burning of Atlanta, its depots, factories, and human habitations alike, and of the pillar of fire and smoke that followed them in their retreat south. With the militia went a new tide of fugitive civilians of all ages, sexes, and ranks, many of them dusted in soot. The elderly, as though in flight from Pompeii, wore ash in the lines of their faces, making them seem hewn of granite. They spoke of the visitation of farms and plantations by hordes of abusive Yankee mudsills; of the theft of furniture, jewelry, silver, and even useless novelties; of the succeeding theft of livestock, the wanton butchery of anything not taken, so that whole farmyards lay littered with carcasses and puddled with blood, turning a family's yard into a tableau of battle; and, finally, of the destruction by fire of the barns, stables, out-buildings, and the house. This destruction proceeded methodically—there was a rhythm to the stories, as of a machine passing through its necessary and carefully purposed motions. The lucky ones fled before seeing all of this befall their property; they were few. Not just Atlanta, then, but anything that lay between its ruination and us.

A few men of our company turned then to my grandfather as if to a prophet, but he said nothing. The smoke of Atlanta's burning could be seen from fifty miles off, the newcomers said, and it had heralded the arrival of our comrades by a full day, as the wind bore smoke and ash out of the north in a yellowish cloud. The sky appeared jaundiced. The weather had been cloudy and cool already, but now we went about our duties with handkerchiefs over our noses.

Every day a new group of soldiers arrived in Macon and filed into our trenches. We took positions ourselves along the Macon & Western, north of the city. The land around the city whitened, fluttered, and crawled with tents, colors and guidons, and drilling soldiers. Within four days, both sides of the Ocumulgee bristled with troops. Most of our number were militia, and similar in ages, equipment, and general want of supply, but other units joined in. I met several boys from the Augusta gunpowder works who had been conscripted into a defensive force from the body of laborers there. They marched, to their endless curiosity, under the command of an Englishman. There came into the area at least

201

one unit of the actual Confederate States Army, though I never saw them. Detachments of Wheeler's cavalry appeared, and rumor followed them with particular fervor.

We waited in our trenches, certain that the enemy would appear at any time. As is their wont, the soldiers debated. Some, enthusiastic for a scrape, mused on our position along the main line north of the city. The strategists, whether eager for a scrape or not, pointed out that we lay on the west side of the Ocumulgee, a fact that spurred forceful debate once rumor came that the enemy had crossed that river, slaughtering worn out mules and horses on its banks by the hundreds and leaving a ruined town behind.

"We ain't going to see no battle over here," such a man would say. "When the Yankees strike at Macon, they're going to do it from the east, hooking around them trenches on the hills yonder."

"Horseshit," the enthusiast would say. "Atlanta's north. We're south. We're in the way."

"Atlanta was north," some wit would put in.

"Shut your damn trap, jackass. No, see here—you got to reckon with the geography here."

"I've had just about enough of you and your geography."

"He's got a point," Sergeant Sloane would say.

"What's schooling got to do with fighting?"

"Now, the two of you are both coming at it back-wards," yet another theorist might put in. "This here is a feint, what they call a demonstration. The Yanks' real intention is to move on... Mobile."

"Haw haw, Mobile."

"I'd lay money on it."

"You know what they say about a fool and his money."

"Hey, now—where's the geography lesson for him?"

And so forth.

After four days of rumor and retreat the weather, which in those parts had always inclined toward wetness, turned to rain, a cold, soaking downpour that left our breath hanging in the air. Those hardy men who had not yet broken out their winter coats did so, though some who had not counted on staying under arms into the fall and winter suffered miserably. I, for my part, thanked God and my mother for my coat. Nevertheless, picket and guard duty, reveille, and time spent occupying or digging trenches grew steadily more miserable. We remained sodden; our fingertips pruned up and stayed that way. The universal cough worsened and men dropped out of roll call to report pneumonia and fevers. The earthworks seemed to melt beneath our brogans—one stretch turned to sucking mud shin-deep. More than one man passing through that place stopped in the rain to curse—and violently—as he fought the muck for his boot.

"Well," I recall one man saying about three days into the rain, "maybe it'll keep the Yankees from burning too much."

"Don't count on it," another replied.

And the rain had yet to turn to snow.

My grandfather's nagging cough, an annoyance at first, deepened and took root in his chest, and manifested itself more and more often throughout the day, but he neither fell out sick nor weakened at his duties, and so it did not occur to me or my cousins to be concerned. Instead, through all of this, I remembered and worried over my mother. There was plenty to distract from such worries. I do not know how others dealt with such thoughts, but for my part, I only grew the more keenly aware of the vast distances that lay between myself and home, between myself and my mother and brothers, between myself and my father, wherever he was. My only comfort at the time was the thought that, with the enemy turning south, away from him, he would be out of danger for the moment. How wrong, how ignorant I was, and how much still a child.

One night my grandfather and I stood picket duty together on the extreme right of our company's picket line, on the bank of the Ocmulgee River. We strung an oilcloth sheet between two tree trunks and huddled together underneath it and endured our watch.

"Wish I could read," I said at some time deep in the night.

"Me too," my grandfather said.

"How'd you like that book Daddy give you? *Less Miserables*?"

"Passes the time. About the good man made one mistake and is pursued forever because of it."

I thought about that. It looked like an awfully long book, and I was unsure I could stand such a story at such length, and said so.

"It's good. Makes a body think about guilt. Don't happen often enough nowadays."

"How come?"

"Aw, I don't know. War don't help. War gets you thinking about what the other party done. But we're called to work out our own salvation with fear and trembling, to think on our own sins. I—well, I don't know what to think of it all."

"Granddaddy," I said again at length.

"Georgie?"

"What did all that mean in the church? The Catholic church, with Peter and his granddaddy."

"That's their rituals—like our Communion."

"Took an awful long time."

"They take it awful serious."

"We don't?"

My grandfather laughed. He reached as if by reflex for his pipe but stopped himself—smoking was forbidden during nighttime pickets. "Well, Georgie, they bind up a whole lot of other rituals with their Com-

204

munion. Confession being one of them. They confess their sins to the priest."

I thought on that and blanched. I imagined relating my sins to our reverend—not only the actions, but also the dark counsels of my heart. Seeing Eliza MacBean out riding with her brother, for example, smiling with the fun of it and her auburn hair a-tumble in the summer sun—such desires may happen naturally to a boy of that age but that does not mean a boy has to pause over them. I may not have gotten up to all the devilry of my cousin Wes, but I had earned a whipping or two as a child and had plenty more coming from the Lord were the truth known.

"They confess—all their sins?"

"That's the idea," my grandfather said and, in the dark, I thought I saw a knowing grin. "The very idea's like to keep you honest, eh?"

I whistled. "How come folks hate them?"

"The Catholics?"

"Yeah. Is it on account of how long and strange their, their rituals are?"

"Part of it, I reckon, but it goes way back. Folks say they worship Mary as a false god but I ain't seen it, not in actually speaking to them. I don't know. I suspect most of the original reasons don't matter no more by now."

Original reasons for dislike—the thought took me to the other event of that day. "What about Uncle Thomas?"

"Crabtree?" he said with surprise. When I nodded, he said, "What about him?"

"How come you don't like him?"

"I didn't say I didn't like him."

I laughed. "I seen it. Could have seen it a mile off."

He laughed too. "Thomas Crabtree was a sporting young man made a great impression on my daughter, your Aunt Elizabeth, who I suspect you've never met."

"No, sir."

"Well, some years ago Thomas asked me for her hand. I liked him well enough but he didn't seem earnest about much of anything, like he wouldn't settle down. And I didn't want to hand off any daughter of mine to a man wasn't going to provide for her. I owed her better than that. Well, he pestered me, she pestered me, so I ended up saying yes. They got married and hightailed it. He had promised her adventure and by God they was going to have it."

"What happened then?"

"I've told you about all I know. I don't reckon they're unhappy, but I can't reckon they are. No children that I've heard of. And now he's here and she's in Arkansas, on the very frontier of Indian Territory, and if anything goes wrong she's going to light out from there for Texas."

"What could go wrong out there? Ain't it safe?"

"No. There's Yankees out there, too, and worse besides. Yankee and Southerner ain't always so clear. What's happening here with killing plain folks and burning their farms has been going on out there a long time."

I thought this over. "So you don't like him because he's put Aunt Elizabeth in danger?"

"I don't like Thomas Crabtree because he's an irresponsible man. Maybe he and my daughter, your Aunt Elizabeth, will come out all right in this thing, but if not he ain't done nothing to guard against it. Ever since they left it's been a letter a year, here and there, and not a visit, not once. Your grandmother went to her grave hoping to see her at least once more. No, a man has to put down roots. That don't mean he has to be bound or chained, Lord knows, but he needs a place to stay put from time to time. Even deer stop to give birth. I can't say I'm surprised they haven't had any children. It's a shame—not for me, but for them."

I thought of my grandmother again, gone seven years at that time—half my life. I thought of her longing to see a daughter again, and thought of my mother, surely longing to see us. I felt something of the weight of that bond, and understood better why my grandfather, among the most charitable of men, viewed Thomas Crabtree so coldly.

"Least he give us some food. And made our pictures."

"Well, there again, he always did think he could buy forgiveness. Like a bribe."

This, too, struck me like a revelation.

"Always watch out for folks think they can buy their way into good standing with you. They'll try to buy everything before it's over."

"That why you don't like sutlers?"

He laughed. "Sutlers want ten times what a thing is worth, and soldiers got to pay it. We don't have too many choices, Georgie."

"I seen he wanted two dollars for a tin cup and plate."

He laughed. "Businessmen, Georgie. Businessmen."

WITH OUR RELIEF from the picket line some hours later we marched back to camp, and I saw that Crabtree's tents and wagon were gone. Not coincidentally, I heard the latest rumor of the enemy's nearness—a day away, and closing on Macon. Were it not for the rain, I was assured, we would see a horizon of solid smoke.

General officers had begun to arrive and for the first time I saw them regularly. General Cobb passed by our camp and our trenches a few times, followed by staff and a handful of prominent local men hunched under greatcoats and tophats against the cold and rain. Lieutenant Guerard made mention of spying General Hardee, and General Smith himself inspected our lines once.

"You ever see so many big bugs?" Hoyt said as we fell out from the inspection.

"Kindly makes a body itch," Sergeant Burrell, walking beside him, said.

"Bugs nothing," another man, Private Brands, said. "I never seen so much braid in my life."

The men howled. Brands was well known as the father of seven daughters.

"We're fearfully well led," Private Bell said. "Two generals for every man."

"One to order the charge," Cal said, "the other to order the retreat."

"That must render at least one of them superfluous," Peter's grandfather said.

"Aw, hell, Shannon," Private Brands said, "there you go ruining a good laugh with a big word."

The men laughed again. Captain Guerard—newly promoted—stood within earshot but said nothing.

The day of the inspection was also the day the Yankees arrived. We had just sat down to our midday meal when we heard what we took to be thunder away to the southeast, across the river and beyond the city. The older men stopped eating and looked up, divining answers through the rain and fog.

"Cannon?" Private Massey said.

Another chain of rumbling reached us.

"Yep," my grandfather said.

At that moment, the drummers pounded out the order to fall in. We dropped our mess and food, grabbed our rifles, and fell in with our mouths still full. Captain Guerard appeared the instant we had dressed our ranks. He gave no speech, but commanded us into marching order. We formed up in the road and faced about and marched at the quickstep into Macon and through the town. The citizenry stirred anxiously or, in some cases, hurried in a panic through the streets with no apparent purpose. A few times we had to break ranks to pass around stalled wagons and buggies. Their drivers sat goggle-eyed and rigid in their seats, impervious to the curses and threats of the sergeants and officers. When at last we crossed the bridge over the Ocmulgee, the artillery fire had sharpened to a steady crack-crack-boom with a lower, thinner rattle of musketry beneath. When we reached the eastern side of the river, Captain Guerard and Major Frady, the battalion commander, appeared before us on horseback, ordering a left wheel, away from the waxing thunder of the guns. We pivoted and headed for some of the very trenches we had ourselves dug and strengthened over the previous weeks.

I found I had broken into a cold sweat. My hands jittered on the stock of my rifle where I carried it at shoulder arms. I breathed spastically. I do not recall my heart beating or pounding, as so many memoirists do— it was as if it had seized and my chest frozen entire. My whole body, though in constant motion as our quickstep was ordered to the double-quick, threatened to stiffen and I imagined myself dropping into the road rigid as a duckboard.

"Steady, Georgie," my grandfather said. I glanced at him; he stared determinedly forward, and coughed through clenched teeth. "Steady," he said, and I steadied.

We filed into the works and fell into place at the direction of the officers and sergeants. First Sergeant Sloane limped along the lines and muttered "Load. Fix bayonets" as he passed. The fateful order—I was a long moment in realizing the import of what he had said. I took a deep breath, filled my lungs with the cold, wet air and imagined the walls of my chest cavity beading with icy dew. I exhaled and looked through the fog of my own breath to withdraw a cartridge from my box. Nearby, I heard my grandfather steadying Cal, Hoyt, and even some of the older men in our company, men his own age.

Our rifles loaded, Captain Guerard ordered the first rank forward.

"That's us, boys," my grandfather said. "Steady."

We stepped up and propped our rifles along the lip of the trench. We had newly reinforced it with pine logs hewn from nearby and it was fragrant with sap and the dry woodland smell of its bark. I looked forward, ahead, northward toward the enemy.

We occupied a place halfway up a gentle slope a quarter mile from the riverbanks. Ahead lay a stand of abatis, brush and saplings cut down or uprooted and lain with the naked and tangled branches facing outward. Through and just above the abatis I could see the downward reaches of the slope, cleared of obstructions for some distance to a rail fence and a stand of trees beyond. I could make out, faintly through the rain and fog, red farmland beyond that. Our position was good. Should the enemy approach, we could see him coming from a long way off. And I had heard enough veterans' stories to know the folly of attacking uphill against such well-sited works. I felt not only steadied, but confident. I looked at my grandfather and grinned. He nodded and patted my shoulder. We waited.

The guns of Fort Hawkins—another position we had worked on with spade and pick—rumbled on the other side of the hill, about two miles distant. The sound came muffled by the wet, heavy air. Faint bursts of volley fire reached us and we twitched like mules. Occasionally we heard, and less often saw, a messenger on horseback riding hard to or from the town. Officers came and went, conferring amongst themselves, but no word of their orders, fears, designs, or intentions reached us. We stood in the muddy trench and absorbed the rain.

Within an hour my coat hung soaked upon my arms and shoulders. My arms ached where they rested on the stock of the rifle and the lip of the trench. I leaned and shifted and fidgeted to ease them without releasing my gun but only introduced new aches to my thighs and knees. Another hour of waiting in the drizzle and I realized I had not paid attention to our front for the greater part of that time. I shook my head—and slung water from my nose, chin, hair, and the peak of my kepi—and tried to discipline myself. Time wore on.

Once, someone down the line fired his musket. I fairly jumped at the sudden and nearby noise, and lost my grip on my rifle for one terrifying second. A few other rifles popped and cracked and an untidy volley rattled across our front and I swept the hazy ground ahead for signs of the enemy. There was none, and a string of curses reached me from the direction of that first shot. A nervous private had fired at nothing. Once recovered, I could not summon any anger or even irritation. It could have been me.

"Steady," my grandfather said. I looked back at him. He had said it not only to me, this time, but to everyone nearby. "Steady, boys."

First Sergeant Sloane passed by with Sergeant Burrell and another squad leader trailing. All three muttered and cursed as they splashed past. The excitement thus ended; we settled in along the line.

The guns boomed and thudded from Fort Hawkins and Dunlap Hill, out of sight of us on our slope. Once, Wes slipped away and climbed up behind our works to see if he could see the battle. He returned not much later, and I saw from his slumped shoulders and the hanging of his head that he had been disappointed.

"Well?" Hoyt and Cal said.

"Couldn't see nothing."

"Nothing at all?" I said.

"The rain thinned out a bit once and I could see the outline of Fort Hawkins, just the shape of it, and a few flashes of light, but that was it."

We were silent. I had hoped to ask him which side seemed to be winning. But the rain and fog had obscured all, at least from Wes's spot.

"Think we'll get to fight?" Cal said.

"Nah," Wes said. "Everything's happening way over yonder. They'd have to circle five miles to get at us."

He trudged to his place in the line and slumped down. He fell asleep.

212

I drowsed, and my grandfather, still fighting against the cold and wet to stifle his cough, noticed and took my place for a time. I slept a few minutes leaning backward against the wall of the trench, and woke when my head tipped back and the rain collected in the recently deepened hollows of my face. Over the next hours, long after the guns fell silent, we took turns watching, craned our necks and angled our ears any time a sergeant or officer passed our way, hoping for word, and ate what little we could—mostly hardtack, which, even soaked with rain, threatened to split incisors and crumble molars. It was difficult even to smoke, and a number of men decided a sodden head was tolerable if they could keep their pipes dry with a carefully manipulated hat. And it was, of course, too wet to read. Thus passed our Battle of Walnut Creek.

We remained in the trench well past dusk, and the temperature—heretofore cold but tolerable—reached freezing. The walls of the trench rimed with frost and the puddles in the mud crusted about the edges. Our breath billowed in great clouds before us and stole the feeling from our cheeks and noses. We shivered under our soaked and burdensome clothing.

At last, near midnight, Captain Guerard came along. He appeared let down; he hung from his own shoulders like a scarecrow.

"All right, boys," he said. "We are relieved. Company C is posting a picket line. Fall in to return to camp."

I rose sluggish from my place and filed out with the rest of the squad. We fell in and marched slowly—despite our eagerness to be back in the shelter of the tents—back across the Ocmulgee, through town, and into our camp. There we fell out, fell into our blankets, and fell instantly to sleep.

I roused at some time during the night on account of my clothing, which clung still soaked to my body on the inside, and looked once about the tent. Wes and Cal lay completely obscured by their blankets and could only be identified by their snoring. At the entrance of the tent sat my grandfather, with the tent flap pulled partially aside. He sat smoking his pipe and looking out in the drizzly dark. Somewhere I heard a horse snort, a voice curse, a few rapid footsteps—the sounds of a sleeping encampment. My grandfather sat still, watching. All that moved was the smoke that curled from his pipe and nostrils. I know not how long I watched him sitting there, but after a time I fell heavily back to sleep. I wonder now whether I dreamt it; I have my reasons for wondering so, but I certainly did not think so at the time.

I WOKE AS SUDDENLY AGAIN a few hours later. I sat up thinking to ask my grandfather what he was pondering, but it was Cal, shaking me by the shoulder.

"Get up, Georgie. We got guard duty."

I rubbed my eyes. The lids seemed made of lead. Cal shifted in the mass of blankets and trod on Wes.

"Aw, godammit, Cal—"

"Wes, you sorry—one of these days that mouth is going to get you in a mess of trouble and you just see if I lift a finger to help."

"Cal—"

"You lay on back down. Georgie, tell him."

I slapped myself across one cheek. "Sorry, Wes. Go back to sleep."

At last, I worked myself to a squatting position and pulled my kepi onto my head. I swished some water from my canteen to cleanse my palate and, as I did so, looked about for my grandfather. He was not in the tent.

We stood guard duty at the far end of camp through dawn and half the morning. Our coats, jackets, shirts—everything down to our drawers—which had only begun to turn from soaked to heavy and muggy hot at the armpits and crotch, were soaked again by the sleety drizzle. We could do nothing but stand guard, staring out across the fields and scrub or across camp toward the road and the rail line, hoping to see something of interest. This proved a futile effort, but had at least one salutary effect—we woke and remained so for our whole watch.

Shortly after dawn—which we marked by the faint lightening of the sky and the somewhat better visibility of the camp around us through the rain, whose particular drops the naked eye could now detect—my grandfather came to us. He walked hunched over a pair of tin cups which steamed in the frigid gloaming. As he neared, he looked up and grinned.

"Morning, boys."

"Morning, Granddaddy," we said.

He motioned to us to sling our rifles. We looked around for Captain Guerard or one of the sergeants— we had seen a boy put through the wringer by First Sergeant Sloane once for napping on duty—and accepted the cups anyway. The heat conducted through the cup stung my fingers wonderfully. I brought the cup into the shelter of my body and inhaled. It was coffee. I had never drunk it before.

"Thanks," I said.

"Ain't never drunk coffee before," Cal said.

"Well, now's the time," my grandfather said.

Cal essayed a sip and gasped. "God almighty!"

I laughed. "What was that you were saying to Wes about his mouth?"

Cal laughed. "It's hot."

"Ain't no other way to drink it," my grandfather said. He coughed once and looked at the sky. "Specially on a morning like this. Here."

He reached into his old blue greatcoat and produced a glass flask. I knew he sometimes carried one but had

216

never before seen him drink from it. Our family were not teetotalers, but neither were we much given to drink. Cal and I looked at each other as he uncorked it and tipped a measure of some dark liquid into each of our cups.

"Y'all are doing the work of men," he said with some seriousness, "y'all deserve to comfort yourselves like men."

"Thank you, sir," we said.

He returned the flask to his coat—not having taken a swig of his own—and nodded to Cal. "Sip," he said. "You burn your throat on it and you'll be in a sorry state for days."

I gave the cup another sniff. It smelled faintly woodsy, as if seasoned with something out of the ground. It also smelled—and I found this remarkable— hot. Heat had never before struck me as a property one could smell, and yet here I stood.

We tried our coffee. I slurped mine gingerly and still nearly gasped at its heat. I gulped it down and noticed my grandfather laughing heartily, a laugh that broke down into a coughing fit.

"Terrible stuff, ain't it?" he said, when he had recovered himself, still laughing.

"How come anybody drinks this?" I said.

"Well, that ain't really coffee."

Cal's eyes widened. He took on the apprehensive look he adopted once he had caught on to a prank but could not yet predict its outcome.

"What—what is it?"

My grandfather waved a hand. "Chicory. Acorns. Peanut shells, I think. Little bit of pepper thrown in. Nah, I ain't seen real coffee in two years. It's a mercy I never drank much of the stuff. But this will keep you warmed up from the inside here."

We sipped again, more confidently this time. If the older men could handle this stuff—

We broke down coughing. My grandfather laughed again.

"And that would be the whisky."

We laughed and went back to work on the cups. It took half an hour or more, but we drank it all, and we were, as Cal noted with a grin, "strangely warmed." In the meantime, my grandfather stood visiting with us, perhaps the last purely enjoyable time the three of us shared.

Upon our relief we walked back into camp in hopes of drying off in our tent, but that was not to be. The call went out to fall in and our consolation was that we already had all of our equipment on our persons. Cal and I were, in fact, the first in formation. I stood waiting as the company formed up and fought to slow my breathing, my pounding heart. I had heard no noise of guns or shouting so far—could it be the Yankees had caught us this much by surprise? At last, Captain Guerard appeared and waited for the last malingerers to slouch into line pursued by our sergeants. He stood stoop-shouldered as the rain ran off his oilskin overcoat in clear crystal runnels. He seemed carved of stone by the waters, like a weathered statue or a pocked and stratted canyon wall.

With all present, he took one step forward and spoke:

"With the previous day's engagement having taken place on the Sabbath, provision has been made by the good folk of Macon for the observance of divine service for our soldiers. All those not on guard or picket duty are thus freed of other duties for the space of three hours, to begin at noon, wherein to conduct themselves to the town square, where a hospital tent has been set up for the purpose. All members of this regiment—this company—shall return no later than three o'clock this afternoon." He hunched to withdraw and check his watch, a fine silver piece he wore with a fob and chain on a civilian waistcoat under his uniform jacket. He returned the watch and straightened again. "The allotted time begins in one and one half-hour. Dismissed."

We fell out and talked about it. I asked my grandfather if we could go—not out of any particular piety, but as another opportunity to leave camp and, especially, get under shelter, even if only for an hour or two. He agreed.

We spent the remaining time trying to dry out, mostly by removing and wringing out our clothing piece by piece. Our bodies were white as ice and we shivered in the cold of the tent, but we could at least be free of the cloying, damp, sweaty clothes for a few minutes. We had changes of longhandles that offered some comfort, and I still had two pair of dry socks— which I had fortuitously wound in a sheet of wax paper I had kept for no reason that I can now recall—which I shared out of my haversack with Cal. Wes protested that he had not changed his socks in a week and a half—and held up a pruny and peeling foot to prove it—but he had not weathered guard duty and so Cal and I voted him down. Knowing what I do now about trench foot, I may not have laughed at Wes, but offered him those dry socks. They felt good for a few minutes, at least. Then we got wet again.

When the appointed time came we wound our scarves and pulled our mittens on and stepped out of the tent with my grandfather, who carried his prayer book in a strip of oilcloth. I went to Peter's tent to invite him and his grandfather along, but they already lay in a deep swoon of sleep. I decided it'd be more Christian to leave them to rest. And so Cal, Wes, my grandfather and I, with a few dozen other soldiers, walked out of camp and up the road into Macon for the penultimate time.

The hospital tent stood on well-churned, muddy ground near the rail station at the south end of town.

As we approached I could hear music, voices, and the high stentorian tones of a preacher which outdid even Major Frady. My heart sank when I saw the tent, though—a crowd of soldiers, fugitives, and onlookers pressed on the tent from the outside. I groaned. Were the tent really so crowded, we had volunteered ourselves for two or three hours of standing in the rain. Or, as Wes put it with his growing brazenness:

"Well, son of a bitch—the tent's all full."

My grandfather patted my shoulder. "It's all right. Let's just see."

We approached and saw through the open flaps and flies an interior ablaze with yellow lantern light. There was a crowd, but not as much of one as I had assumed in my despair. A man with spectacles and great bushy whiskers like Thomas Crabtree's stood in the center of the tent, an open book in one hand and gesturing theatrically with the other. I thought of plates of Cicero, of Caesar in oratorical mode in books my grandfather had lent me over the last three years. I imagined the man in a toga and nearly laughed, but then I saw the girls, the Vestals to this man's Senator. Three beautiful blonde girls of about our age stood near the preacher, with stacks of pamphlets in their small gloved hands and smiles on their faces. It had been so long since I had seen a woman smile—the road and the towns had been replete with faces of stoic resignation, of uncomplaining tragedy, of pure dolor, but few smiling or even pleasant. I wanted to be in the tent with them. Before I knew what had happened, I stood inside, out of the rain, before one of them. She smiled upon me, handed me a booklet, and directed me to a seat pressed close against the rear canvas wall. I smiled idiotically and thanked her and stumbled on across a dozen laps to sit and steam in the hot dry tent.

The others joined me. My grandfather grinned and

nudged my shoulder. Wes sat and congratulated me on my manly boldness and whistled back at the girl, prompting a shush from an old man seated ahead of us. Cal just smiled.

It was some time before I paid heed to the substance of the preacher's sermon. I sat distracted, thinking of the blonde girls, of Eliza MacBean in her horseback rides on sunny days back home, of Rowena and Rebecca, Guenever and Isoude, Helen of Troy, and the heroines of all the other tales I had ingested in the last years. And I recall thinking of my mother, and wondering about the baby again, and remembering her and my father sitting by the stove in the last weeks he had been home. There again was the feminine smile now in such short supply.

I recall thinking of her in particular because it was from these thoughts that the preacher jolted me with the sudden declamation, *"Hellfire awaits!"*

Now, in the decades intervening this sort of preacher has become the predominant type in the imaginations of most people, but they were a rarity even at that time. How else did they attract attention but by their unusualness? God help the denomination that makes such theatrics its standard.

This exclamation made me jump in my seat and direct all my attention back to the preacher. He repeated it and I jumped again. I sat as though struck by a thunderbolt.

He must already have been nearing the end of his sermon, because my memory is of a short, savage assault on the senses and the conscience by his massed ranks of rhetoric and theology. He pointed northward, evoked the coming hordes of Yankees, described the torn flesh and shattered bone he had seen in many a hospital over the last three years, and dwelt in unsparing detail on the fields of nameless graves, the bodies mouldering and worm-eaten in the dark damp beneath spade-turned

221

earth. Death, he said, has never been nearer, eternity never more readily grasped. The former was coming for us, to carry us off into the latter, from whence only one had ever returned. It could be tomorrow by the sword, this evening by a chill or a fever, or this very afternoon, run down in the road by a mad horse. And then what? The only hope, he said invitingly, lay in the arms of the Savior. Only there could our journey well end in anything but eternal flame.

With that, the tent fell silent for a pregnant moment, and then he swept both arms up and called out, "Let us sing!"

We stood. The girls commenced to marshaling the congregants, rearranging them as quickly as any group of company sergeants, albeit much more sweetly. But I could not now be distracted by their comeliness. I stood rooted, transfixed, which, after all, means "nailed through."

The girls and the older people, apparently familiar with what was going on, helped in moving the people and separating them into four groups. Only then did I notice that the chairs had been crammed under the tent in a box shape, all facing inward toward the preacher. The book he held, I marked for the first time, was not a Bible at all, but a *Sacred Harp* songbook. I knew this pattern of singing from visits to another church with a friend as a child, but it was foreign to our Methodist chapel. The people arrayed by voice against each other, the preacher and his eldest daughter led us into the first song, which I can recall as clearly as anything from those months of soldiering:

I am a poor wayfaring stranger,
A-traveling through this world of woe,
Yet there's no sickness, toil, nor danger
In that bright land to which I go.

I'm going there to see my father,
I'm going there no more to roam,
I'm only going over Jordan,
I'm only going over home.

The plaintive, uninstrumented chant swept over me and I wept. And, strangely, I remember no more of the meeting—only leaving the hospital tent, sweating and apprehensive, to find that the last days' rain had turned to a fine but thickening snow.

THE SKY OVER MACON hung low and silver with snow-laden cloud. The temperature had dropped yet further and continued to do so all through that day and into the night. Well before dusk, those of us not on guard or picket duty sat stoking the fire and nearly biting the coals, we huddled so close. We put on every stitch of clothing that we had and bundled ourselves in blankets and steamed by the fire, finally drying out after the days of rain and mud.

There was some talk round the fire, but I did not partake. Governor Brown himself was rumored to have come to Macon. A private from another company swore he had seen him near General Smith's head-quarters, a big brick building in town. The old rumor of his striking a separate peace with the enemy had cropped up again as a result, now with faint hints of hope and dismay mingled with the calumny like gall. I sat in silence. I was low.

Something about the religious service had upset me, as I have related. I worried over it, and my thoughts returned to my mother, my father, the new brother or sister—I knew not which yet—a hundred miles or more distant from us. I felt the weight of danger in the air about us. It hung so thick it seemed wrong that snow could fall through it.

As we ate our evening meal—hardtack, some bread and salt, the last of Thomas Crabtree's sowbelly, and bacon procured through doubtful means by Hoyt and Wes—rumor went round of movement, of our leaving Macon. Private Brands came by and relayed that we were to entrain for Augusta, or—in another version promulgated by our old neighbor, Mr. Hale, not two minutes later—Mobile. Even a day before, such intelligence would have provoked spirited talk. This night, the men responded resignedly.

A few minutes after first hearing the rumor, First Sergeant Sloane halted up to our fire and sat.

"Sergeant," some of us said.

"Boys." He hitched his bad leg out straight and rubbed it. "News from the Captain."

"We're for Mobile," Private Bell said.

"The hell you say," Hoyt said. He was firmly of the Augusta party and had been these ten minutes.

"Come on, boys," my grandfather said without looking up from his plate, "let Nick talk."

"Much obliged, Fate." First Sergeant Sloane sighed. "General Hardee is of the mind that the Yankees have passed us by. Ain't interested in Macon." He said that Wheeler's cavalry reported the Yankees completely over the Ocmulgee north of us, with no sign of turning back. The generals were convinced; the enemy aimed at Augusta. We were to rise early in the morning and march for Gordon where we would meet a train to carry us eastward. "Y'all can look forward to more digging."

"Aw, hell," Wes said.

"Well, the enemy's got no supply line," Sergeant Burrell said. "Time he gets anywhere near Augusta, they'll be weak. Might break theirselves on our earthworks."

This remained the only hopeful remark of the evening. We had all heard the stories—the enemy lived off the land. And while none of us presumed to know the material wealth of Georgia in statistical terms—the enemy's science—we could not assume it was too little to sustain his army. I could feel the spirit about the fire and across the manifold camps about Macon plummet, as though it were a physical thing. Our particular spirits were so many snowflakes—they fell into the mud to be absorbed, or into the fire to sublimate.

The men of Captain Guerard's company drifted away from the fires. With a march eminent, they wanted sleep more than ever. First Sergeant Sloane rose after a time, nodded good night to us, and went off to join some other group at mess. I remained with the handful of old and sleepless men who sat up late every evening, and I stared into the embers and worried. After a time, I looked to my grandfather. Once finished with his meal, he lit his pipe and smoked. I moved over next to him and he took me firmly by the shoulder in greeting and sat with me in silence and the slow whorls of his tobacco smoke.

Sometime around ten o'clock, as I recall, our desperately hot fire had burned itself almost to the embers. One could hear sleepers stirring in their eyes as the fire withdrew its pickets and the skirmishers of the cold crept in. Private Brands, who had settled in for conversation with Private Massey by our fire and sat wrapped in two blankets and his own arms, swore. "Need more wood for this here fire."

"Well then, get to it," Sergeant Burrell said, and gestured to the fire with his pipe.

"Land sakes. Just making an observation."

"Just grab some off the pile."

"Pile's gone."

"Well?"

"Land sakes."

My grandfather rose. "We'll take care of it. Ain't that right, Georgie?"

I stood and nodded. I suddenly realized how numb and stiff at the joints I had gotten.

"All right then," Sergeant Burrell said.

"Much obliged, Fate," Brands said, and dug into his tobacco pouch for a new plug.

"Be good to move around a little." My grandfather stretched, refilled his pipe, and after clearing his throat at length, we set out for Macon in the snow.

The night lay heavy all around us. I could sense the thousands of sleeping men like a weight in the darkness and silence. I thought then that it had been our presence that had deterred the enemy from assaulting Macon—his depredations had only reached so far because only here had he encountered opposition. How wrong I was.

"Where we going to find firewood?" I said after a time.

"Aw, here and there, I reckon."

"We going to have to cut some?"

"Nah, we'll just forage a little."

We walked, he like Saint Nicholas, a bent and coated figure trailing pipesmoke in the snow. I followed. I remembered earlier times, as a boy or even a child, following him on small chores about the farm. I remembered walking with him from the house to the smokehouse one winter evening in shin-deep snow. I had struggled mightily to keep up then, and I marked now how easily I walked beside him, nearly the same height but he undiminished. I strode along with pride, a fellow soldier of my grandfather.

We entered Macon and found our way to a store with an ample woodpile out back. There came neither lamplight from the upstairs windows nor smoke from its chimney.

227

"Just an armload, Georgie. We'll send Brands out next time." He laughed and loaded up my outstretched arms. The wood was old and well-dried by its time in the pile—it would burn well. He then hefted his own load of wood and we headed back to camp.

We met others in the dark along the way—individual soldiers bearing loads of firewood, pairs carrying fencerails or posts, threes and fours with stacks of planks and boards pried loose from porches and steps. We dropped our wood near our fire and told the others to watch it jealously, to no reply. They were too busy piling the new wood on the fire.

"Won't last, you burning it up like that," my grandfather said.

"Shut up, Fate," Private Bell said.

"It's colder than a witch's tit," Private Brands said.

"Just keep it coming," Private Massey said.

My grandfather looked at me and sighed a great cloud of smoke. "One more load?"

"All right," I said.

We set off for the store woodpile again. We passed some of the others at work vandalizing picket fences and front porches. At one or two houses, Negro housemaids bearing lanterns stepped out onto the porches and harangued the men, but they only lowered their heads against the light and bent their backs to the work. The night was so bitterly cold they could not be shooed away.

We found the store and felt our way around back to find the woodpile—gone. Only a bare patch in the snow and a heap of old bark and splinters remained. My grandfather whistled.

"Boys made quick work of that."

"What now?" I said.

"Well, we can hunt around some more, but I reckon this part of the town's been gone over pretty good."

"All right."

"Let's scout a little deeper, down toward the train station."

I thought of the tent meeting and felt my face blanch, almost go numb. "The train station?"

"Yeah, let's go."

We walked. I pondered the preacher—his lovely daughters had not much occupied my thoughts since the service—his sermon, death, hell, and the song we had sung immediately following. I thought again of my mother and father, all the things that had robbed our evening around the fire of joy. After a few minutes' walk in silence my grandfather coughed and said, "What's bothering you, Georgie?"

"Sir?"

"I can hear you worrying. You get it from your mama—like a millstone grinding away inside of you."

"Well, that's just it. Mama."

"I see."

"And Daddy."

"And what else?"

I gestured feebly. "That preacher today. Talking about death and the war. I—I'm bothered is all."

"What about all that's got you so bothered?"

"See, I don't rightly know. I'm worried—about Daddy, in the army, and Mama, back home, with the baby, and it always being so hard on her, having babies, and us not there. Me not there. We're here in the war, and—" I faltered and gave out. My grandfather walked in silence beside me, gave me time. "I reckon I never thought about all them things together, at once, with death thrown in. And it's all that preacher's fault."

"Aw, don't worry none about that preacher."

My grandfather stopped and sat on the step of a storefront. He gestured for me to sit down with him. We sat in the snow on a darkened stoop in Macon, in a spot of soft quiet. We said nothing for some time. My grandfather's hands were restless—I thought he might take out his pipe and tamp in some tobacco and enwreathe us in his pleasant and homey smoke again, as was his wont, but he did not. At last, he pressed his hands against each other and exhaled.

"Georgie, something you got to reckon with—we're all going to die." I looked at him, and willed the tears away from my eyes; I would not shame myself like I had at the tent meeting. "Somehow," he said. "One of these days. Each and every one of us. You understand that."

I nodded. "Yes, but—"

He did not interrupt, but I did not finish.

"You remember your grandma?"

I did. This was the first I had heard him mention her in some time. I nodded.

"Folks will tell you that death is just a part of life, and to a point they're right. It's the end of life. You know what they called Atlanta at first? About thirty years ago? Terminus—the end. The last milemarker for a couple of railroads. And the end of the railroad is a part of the line like death is a part of life—just where it stops. Now, life is a lot more than any locomotive or machine, no matter what some folks say. But death is the end of the line, the empty air past the last page of a book. But the thing is, death ain't natural. It's a fearful thing, and worth fearing, but it ain't the way things ought to be. God made us to last forever, and we done messed that up. Even Jesus had to die. You remember your Creed?"

"Yes, sir."

"What happened next?"

"'He descended into Hell. The third day he rose again from the dead. He ascended—'"

"And at the end—'I believe in the forgiveness of sins, the resurrection of the body, and the life everlasting, amen.' So death ain't the end, not for us, not for anybody. There will be life evermore. What death is in this scheme of things is a graduation, like on a rule or a yardstick. You pass this spot and you're in the next foot. You understand?"

I nodded. "Like seeing the elephant."

"Right. For soldiers it's joining up, and drilling, and learning how to march and handle your musket, and then comes the day it's all been for—seeing the elephant, as they say. Battle. And all soldiers fall on one side or the other of it. But for a man—you're born, and you pass from milk to meat. You grow to childhood and you speak as a child, you understand as a child, and then—then you have to put away childish things. And I'm proud to see you doing that, Georgie. I surely am. You've become a fine man."

I started, puzzled. "Man? What—When—?"

"There's different things folks say makes you a man. You're old enough to father children, that's plain to see—don't blush, now—but that ain't all it takes. You may not be a boy no more but that don't make you a man. No, there's graduations. When you was born your mama and daddy had you baptized. That was one. When you could eat meat, when you could walk, when you could help with the chores—all graduations, milemarkers on your way to manhood. Learning how to take care of yourself, how to hunt and slaughter and grow food, those are important. Learning how to master yourself and your moods and tempers. Learning how to take care of others, even more. Because there will be others. One of these days you'll get married—another graduation—and have boys and girls of your own. And all the time you're getting older and wiser, your mama and daddy, me—we're ahead of you, on our way to death. And that's the last graduation, the terminus. And then beyond that—well…"

And at last I was overcome. I threw my arms around him and buried my head in his coat and sobbed.

"I'm sorry, I'm sorry," I said, ashamed.

He embraced me. "Sorry for what now? Ain't no need."

"I don't want Mama to die."

"We pray she's all right, Georgie."

"Or Daddy."

"We pray he's all right, Georgie."

"I want to be home with them, Granddaddy."

"Me too, Georgie." He looked off into the darkness for a while. "You know the story of your mama and daddy? Him asking for a dance, and proposing that same day? You know how I knew I could trust him, give your mama up to that young man—a boy not a whole heap older than you?"

"No, sir," I said. Though he had retold the story many times, never once had I heard his side of it.

"Because of how he took that whole evening to sit and visit with me. I seen right away what he meant to do when he come to that dance, it was writ on his face plain as day, but he felt he owed it to me to talk to me, to show your mama's daddy some respect, and he give up every chance he had that evening to dance with her—for her."

"Every chance but one," I said.

"That's right. Right there at the end I had pity on him, and let him go." He chuckled, and I could see from his eyes that he loved this memory as much as either my mother or father. His chuckle turned to a cough again, and he hawked, cleared his throat, and spat before he continued. "But you got to be prepared to give up what you want, what you love, for the sake of what you love. You understand?"

"You mean Daddy was the opposite of Thomas Crabtree."

He nodded, surprised, as if realizing this for the first time himself. "That's about right."

"So love is... duty?"

"And duty love, near as I can reckon."

I thought on that. By some mischance I remembered the song, from that afternoon. I said, as best I could, "No sickness, toil, nor danger. I want that. I want to be home."

"That's in the world to come, Georgie. That's our hope. Sickness, toil, and danger is the world we live in, with all that unnaturalness sewn into it."

I thought of the fevers, aches, and diarrhœa of the army, the endless marching and digging, the hoots and whistles and derision of the regular army, the battle we had very nearly fought not two days before, and the rumors of war and destruction reaching us from everywhere.

"Sickness, toil, and danger. I don't want to be in the army no more."

My grandfather patted my back and took out and filled his pipe. "Now you truly know them. You're a man, Georgie Wax."

V

GRISWOLDVILLE

THE DRUMROLL OF REVEILLE WOKE ME from a dream. I stood in the yard back home of a summer day. I recall it as hot but not unpleasant, but I was distracted from the heat by the presence of my grandmother, whose death I have described. She stood with my grandfather, my mother and father, my siblings, including the new brother or sister—whose presence there I felt and understood without seeing him, in the manner of dreams—my Uncle Quin, and also Thomas Crabtree, who seemed uncomfortable with being among us. He stood somewhat apart, whittling under the shade tree. We had just eaten a great meal and prepared to set off walking somewhere together. Suddenly Peter and Hoyt were there, fully equipped for a march, and Hoyt said something mean about Thomas Crabtree. I bristled at this—with all his faults, Crabtree was kin, and I could not allow such a remark to stand—but I could not muster the guts to confront Hoyt about it, and so stood rooted to the spot. No one else said anything, and I fretted that I had shown myself a coward in front of them. I recalled my pistol—in my dream, suspended in a fine polished leather holster instead of the one I had made—but second-guessed the thought of drawing it. All this action took place over the space of a few crowded seconds, but when I woke, I felt I had wrestled with it the whole night long.

Cal shook me. I woke and heard the drums. It was yet dark.

"Come on, Georgie."

"Fall in!" Captain Guerard shouted outside.

I sloughed off my blankets and the cold slipped up into my clothes. I shivered and was fully awake. Cal laughed.

"Chilly, ain't it?"

"Sure enough," I said. "It quit snowing?"

"Nope." Cal drew the tent flap back and I looked out. Snowflakes lolled down through the dim morning.

I pulled my kepi back on and retied my scarf. I thought of my mother, who had knit the scarf for me back in the spring as God knit my new brother or sister together in her womb, and shook the thought away.

"Anything stick?" I said.

"Little bit," Cal said. "Lot of mud. Ground's frozen, though. It's a mess."

I coughed and nodded. We left the tent and fell in with the other men, who coughed and hacked and wheezed. Many heads wrapped in blankets, scarves, or rags bobbed and hocked vast boluses of phlegm into the frost as we dressed the ranks. I felt my own stuffy head loosen with one cough and the mucus commenced to flowing from one nostril. I sniffed furiously as the others continued to cough and clear their throats. My grandfather fell in next to me, bent nigh double with his coughing, and when he righted himself looked at me with red, watering eyes and smiled. I stared. Before I could ask him about it, First Sergeant Sloane appeared, we old men and boys straightened ourselves to attention, and some wit shouted, "Company Q reporting, sir!"

I pondered the dream, which had already faded to the rump I have recounted above. The full moon—which always brought and still brings me spates of strange dreams—was more than a week past, already half-waned to the dark of the moon. I thought of my talk with my grandfather the night before, of my grandmother, dead seven or eight years by that time.

We fell out and ate breakfast and cooked two days' rations for the march. Other troops, also ordered out of Macon for Augusta, marched past. I recognized in the gloaming the ununiformed soldiers of the powderworks with their Englishman commander, an outfit of men in dingy factory work clothes and soft caps—not a stitch of military equipage among them. They made us look like regulars on parade.

That morning's breakfast, shared out among the entire squad sitting famished and half-frozen by the fire:

A pound of sowbelly

A half-pound of bacon

A pound of grits

A pan of stale cornbread, with which we wiped up every spot of grease from the meat

Three spoonfuls of butter, blessedly fresh

Hardtack, all we could eat (not much)

Thus fed for the day's march—a march of at least fifteen miles, according to the rumored location of the train that would bear us onward to Augusta—we struck the tents and packed our equipment. I folded and sorted my equipment into my pack, one of the few to have one; the rest—Wes and Cal, for instance, and Peter and his grandfather—rolled their equipment up in their quilts and blankets and secured them across their bodies. Those of us with rifles of some standard caliber drew a fresh supply of ammunition from the regimental stores and, this accomplished, Captain Guerard gave the order for the company to fall in with the rest of the battalion. We formed up in column of fours on the slick and icy road and waited. I cast a last glance across our former camp. We had remained here, off and on, for some weeks, and left behind a muddy and much-trodden field, with clearly discernible lanes between the tent rows and a filled in latrine at one end. Only now did it occur to me that this land belonged to someone. The army truly did take something from everyone.

Captain Guerard passed on his horse and met the regimental commander ahead of us on the road. They saluted and exchanged words. Both seemed bored, even disappointed.

"What's wrong with them, Granddaddy?"

"I expect they're not eager for the little walk we got ahead of us," my grandfather said. "Can't say I am, neither."

"But the train—ain't we boarding near Gordon?"

He did not answer at first, but not for lack of answer. The struggle was to choose the words. At last, he said, "I don't expect we'll find a bit of useable railroad between here and Augusta."

I gaped. "What?"

"Yankee cavalry ain't going to make it that easy for us."

"What's that you say?" Private Bell said. "Yankee cavalry?"

"Shut up, Bell," Sergeant Burrell said. "That's enough of that kind of talk, Fate. We're all tired."

"And frozen," Hoyt said.

Sergeant Burrell hooked a look at him over his shoulder and shook his head. "Blazes, Hoyt. Would you shut your God-damned trap? Just this one time?"

Hoyt would say nothing more for some hours ahead.

"Grandaddy," I whispered. He looked at me, eyebrows raised, and smiled. I studied his face. "Are you all right?"

"I'll be just fine, Georgie," he said.

I watched him, tried to divine any other meaning from his expression. While I could read nothing else on his countenance, he seemed to understand my concern wholly. He reached over and squeezed my shoulder.

"I'll be just fine."

At last, after a time of standing in the muddy road collecting snow on our shoulders, the order came and echoed up and down the column in the manifold voices of officers and sergeants: "*Company—forward—march!*"

And so we struck out on the road into Macon. We marched smartly through the town—in step, with the colors unfurled and flapping, and the drummers beating away despite the snow—and across the bridge over the Ocumulgee. There, on the other side, we halted as the rest of the brigade formed up ahead of us. Our commanding officer, Brigadier General Philips, who was to lead us to Augusta on behalf of General Smith, rode past at one point, and I could still muster enough interest in seeing a general to watch him go. He was a dark man who sat heavily but tall in the saddle and wore a simple uniform, without as much braid as some others. He roamed back and then ahead again, until at last I lost interest, sighed, and settled as comfortably as possible into my brogans. We waited a little while more, with the snow falling and officers and messengers riding up and down the road spraying us with mud and grit. A battery of artillery, its caissons, limbers, and guns guided by hand over the churned ground and into the road, fell in ahead of us and set off. With the last gun moving, we marched on again.

The weather had lightened enough, with no fog, that I could see the ground of the battle from two days previous. It lay off to the right, at a distance, but I could see the frosted ruts of cannonball strikes in the earth, freshly abandoned earthworks and trenches, broken and discarded equipment, fallen tree limbs, ball-pocked fenceposts, and even—at a great distance, and so uncertainly—a stiff and bloated horse, upturned in a ditch. I had just spied this when we passed through Macon's defenses, rounded a bend in the road, and lost sight of all. The officers ordered us to march at the route step and so we settled in for the long walk.

"Didn't look like much of a scrap," someone behind me said after a time.

"Tell that to the men got killed," Sergeant Burrell said without turning.

I looked at my grandfather where he marched beside me.

"Men got killed? The other day?"

"A couple, yeah."

I frowned. A couple—this did not, in fact, sound like much of a scrap.

"Just a couple?"

"A couple's still too many, Georgie."

"Killed more Yankees, at least," the same voice shouted up.

"Nah," I heard Private Bell say, "I heard we didn't kill a one."

"Wounded some, though."

"Yeah, but you said 'killed.'"

This exchanged withered and died a minute or two later, as we entered a long straight stretch of road and lengthened our stride to keep up.

I thought on the train we were to meet, and what my grandfather had said, expecting the Yankees to leave us no railroad to use on our march. I thought about all the marches that summer, up and down, to and fro across the middle of Georgia. I tried to picture

242

the distance separating Macon from Augusta, and felt my spirits fall. Walking half the width of the state or more in the cold, the rain, tenting in the fog and snow—my spirit sank yet further.

We had not left the defenses of Macon far behind when we came in sight of the railroad again. We smelled it first—a reek of smoldering tar. Ahead of us I could hear coughing again and soon we marched into what seemed at first a low fog, an assumption belied by our first sight of the railroad.

Everywhere along the embankment and bed of the line lay great heaps of ash and ember with the ends of railroad ties lying about the piles like the butt ends of cigars. Many still glowed despite the cold and snow. The stinging smoke hung low all around, as if too lazy even to drift away.

"What'd they do with the rails?" Private Massey said.

Sergeant Burrell pointed. I peered through the smoke toward the ashes. At last, I saw—in the coals of each bonfire lay twisted and blackened rails. Some of them had been bent nearly double. I saw others twisted like a lady's ribbon around tree trunks and left to cool there. When last I was in that part of Georgia, some of them yet remained.

"What in the sam hill—" someone said.

"The hell?" someone else said, more directly.

"They heated them over the fires, heated them till they were malleable," my grandfather said.

"Even a little warping would ruin them," Sergeant Burrell said. "Appears they enjoyed themselves."

All along the line there stood bloody stitchmarks where the ties had been torn up from the gravel to stoke the fires. Had it been up to us, we could not have repaired that line in ten years. Now I knew what my grandfather had meant. We had been safe in Macon—now we marched into the destruction. I wondered how much farther ahead it would stretch.

A mile or so later we passed a farm. The house still stood but not a soul stirred on that place. All the outbuildings had been fired and only the blackened ribcage of the barn yet stood, smoldering like the railroad ties. As we passed closer I saw hogs and a mule dead in the yard, and a pair of bulldogs not unlike Wes and Cal's shot to pieces by the front steps of the house. Only the cold seemed to have kept the flies off—had this befallen the farm in summer, it would have swarmed.

Private Greeves, who had been so concerned about our stacked arms in the presence of the Negro laborers those weeks earlier, broke from the column and dashed into the yard. Someone shouted after him, "Get the hell back here!" but he paid no heed. He searched among the dead animals, ducking this way and that, and at last hauled up the carcass of a shoat and raced back for his place in the column. His sergeant met him halfway and tried to kick him in the rear, swearing the while. Greeves's face glowed as he rejoined us.

"Whew!" he said. "Look at that!"

"Hell, Greeves, you going to tote that all the God damn way to Augusta?"

"Just till we make camp, Billy. Then—slaughtering time."

"Waste of time. You going to throw that thing out in five miles or I'm Abe Lincoln."

"No, sir. This is quite a find."

"You're a fool," another man said. "Ain't you got enough on your back you go grabbing up rotting hogs?"

"No, sir. I ain't that dumb."

"Guess again, blowhard" another man said. "That there shoat's gut-shot. The meat will be spoilt."

A long silence followed this comment, and then laughter, rippling up and down the column. I believe I heard Greeves grumbling, cursing the Yankees, and a few minutes later something heavy crashed down into the brush along the side of the road, and the chuckling resumed. It would have made a lively and charming soldiers' story, had Greeves lived.

A few turns in the road imparted to the column the old, familiar accordion action, and with that stopping and starting and the snow and cold and the reek of the Yankees' destruction, little could remain amusing for long. The officers seemed to sense this. About an hour into the march, Major Frady met Captain Guerard on horseback along the side of the road and conferred with him. When they parted, Captain Guerard suggested to First Sergeant Sloane that the company sing. He then rode forward along the column. Ahead, we heard other companies faintly singing.

"Sing?" Private Bell said. "What on earth for?"

"Preposterous ass," Sergeant Burrell said. "Music was ordained to refresh the mind of man after his studies or his usual pain."

I glanced at my grandfather. I had heard—or read—that line before. He only smiled.

"Say what now?" Bell said.

"I didn't take you for a learned man, Burrell," First Sergeant Sloane said, and, without waiting, hurried into the first stanza of "God Save the South." By the second line, about the South's "altars and firesides," my mind wandered. I thought of Horatius, in Macaulay's *Lays*, and this in turn led me to the hearths and altars of Virgil's *Æneis*, of war undertaken to defend that most sacred of sites, and I wished I had brought that book with me from home. I had not be able to make myself reread *A Tale of Two Cities*, and had certainly not anticipated so much time afield.

After a handful of patriotic songs the tone grew somber. Two or three hymns introduced a theme of mortality and our want of salvation. Someone sang "The Rebel Soldier," and I felt my heart heavy-laden again. Then someone struck up "When This Cruel War is Over," which drew the officers back to us by the second verse.

"Damn it, First Sergeant," Major Frady said, "keep it light. Light."

He waved his hands like a conductor on the upbeat, and First Sergeant Sloane merely nodded. He halted the singing with one upraised hand, called out, "Goober Peas!" and we lit into that deep and weighty ditty with élan. The song seemed appropriate in at least one regard—we were the Georgia Militia.

This began a string of humorous and sometimes vulgar songs that lasted nearly an hour and, I must say, had the desired effect. For some miles I simply enjoyed myself, and was able to ignore the snow and the cold and wet creeping slowly into my clothing. I was a boy—no, a man out for a walk with his fellow soldiers. For a moment, the adventure I had mourned the night before returned. This spirit lasted until we halted outside Griswoldville.

After about three hours on the march, as well as I can recall, word came down the column to halt. A few men who had fallen asleep on the march—a thing I would not have credited had I not seen it so often— bumped into the men ahead of them, occasioning some cursing and amusement. We waited. Private Ames, a white trash boy from another squad, who was possessed of a fine singing voice, called out: "Sing some more, First Sergeant?" Sergeant Sloane shook his head. And so we waited. A few men broke out pipes and tobacco or rummaged in their haversacks for a piece of hard-tack. A rumor reached us that one of the artillery horses drawing the guns at the head of the column had decided to turn mulish and stop, and no amount of whipping could convince it to move again. Some repeated it as gospel; others discounted this tale. Most of us simply stood in place and stamped our feet to ward off the cold. During this wait, the snow stopped falling, and it departed like a fine, misty veil sweeping away from us over the grey landscape. It was thanks to this that I first saw the smoke.

A murmur and a stirring crept up the column. Ahead, over the tree tops, black smoke rose against the snowy sky—great clouds of smoke, far more than had draped the woods outside Macon, or even here, where we had halted. After some time, the rumors included a new accounting:

"Yankee cavalry. Lot of them."

"Burned."

"It's Griswold Station."

"Shit fire."

I stood on tiptoe and craned my neck to see more, but there was nothing else to be seen from that vantage—only the tantalizing black smoke. I felt for the revolver my father had given me. Could it be that the place that produced this pistol was gone? Destroyed? I looked at my grandfather.

"Steady, Georgie," he said.

"What happened, Granddaddy?" Cal said.

"Can't say yet, but I reckon we'll see soon enough."

At that moment we were ordered forward again, and for some minutes we marched stutterstep toward the smoke. No singing now—we moved in silence, like the people in Peter and his grandfather's church going down the aisle toward that terrible presence.

A thin, sick feeling built in the pit of my stomach. I grew hot and clammy in my clothes, like lying fevered under a blanket. My forehead beaded cold sweat and the ice air painfully quickened my senses. I feared what we would see when at last we reached the rising smoke. And slowly the column bore us forward.

Soon the smoke thickened upon the ground and the men commenced to coughing as if they had just risen. The smoke blackened the closer we approached. The silence fell away—ahead, I heard murmured prayers and boastful curses as rank by rank we gained sight of Griswoldville. We caught sight of the factory chimney, reared above the smoking ruin, and the remains of a watertower. Finally, both straining and fearing to see, I got my second look at the town.

I saw, ahead of us on the righthand side of the road, the blackened hulk of a train of boxcars, still linked on the siding, the ties of which had caught fire and burned away beneath the weight of the flaming train above. The whole thing sagged crazily in its ash and guttering smoke. We neared and filed past it, and it gave off the desperate last heat of a dying cookfire, with the hot metal smell of molten lead. I saw in the wreckage the twisted and scattered contents of the cars—some kind of machinery, put to the torch. The main line had been torn up and ruined, the same as outside Macon. All lay in wreck and ruin, still smoking. And ahead lay the town.

As we passed the burned train, my grandfather, struggling in the smoke to tamp down his cough, drew his handkerchief, daubed it with water from his canteen, and tied it about his head. I followed him and breathed somewhat more easily, though my nose began again to run with the inhalation of the cold, wet air. Many other men fixed scarves or handkerchiefs over their noses and mouths.

We reached the crossroads in the middle of the town and Captain Guerard called a halt and rode forward with some other officers. First Sergeant Sloane ordered us to rest, and some men settled right down into the road, their heads lowered.

I looked around and felt as if I would be consumed from the inside out by the sourness in my stomach. All that remained of the factory village of Griswoldville was a big, stately house in the center of town, near the ruins of the pistol manufactory. All else—stores, warehouses, the rail depot—had been burnt to brands and ashes, right down to the sheds and chickencoops in the yards of the houses and shops. Even the shade trees had caught fire and stood a dusty black, with all but the stoutest limbs burned away. Here the smoke rose in pillars and blotted the sky—we stood coughing and wheezing in a manmade midday gloaming, darker even than the grey and snowy day had been already, and instead of snow, ash settled on our shoulders.

"What's that smell?" Hoyt said.

We coughed and sniffed. Amid the smell of fire and ash was a thin sweetness. I shuddered. At last, someone said, "Soap."

"They was a soapworks here," another man said. "Hell if the Yankees didn't burn that, too."

"Look at that," Private Massey said, and pointed at the house. Like the farmhouse we had passed earlier, the structure remained but all the windows had been broken, the front door battered off its hinges, and the house's remaining furniture lay in a wide spray of splinters and broken pieces as though the house had vomited it into the yard. Even a piano lay upended beside the porch. Here as well lay dead dogs, pigs, and a single chicken—a rooster, with its head twisted backwards.

A few of us ventured away to relieve ourselves, though with little urgency. Wes, Cal, and I crossed the ruined railroad tracks, walked through the wrecked yard of the house and around back. I had slung my rifle and hitched up my coat when I stopped. I looked at Wes and Cal—they had not moved, but stared out across the backyard toward the northerly road. I followed their gaze and froze.

The ditch between the back yard and the road lay full to overflowing with dead and stiffened mules and horses. The cold had kept them from bloating, and there was no smell beyond the ash and blood, but rigor mortis had stuck them in place. We approached slowly, solemnly, and looked upon them. A few other men from the column did likewise.

"Better fetch Greeves," someone joked without humor.

"Don't bother," Cal said, and choked on a sob. We looked at him, and he pointed. Every one of the mules had wasted nearly to death before being lined up and shot by the roadside. Their ribs protruded from their gaunt flanks. Their hooves were cracked and bloody and their fur missing in great patches, with bands of open blisters and sores crisscrossing their shoulders and muzzles.

"What done that to them?" Cal said.

"The Yankees," Wes said. "What do you think?"

Cal had always been fond of animals, from the family bulldog to the draft animals of their farm. He had accompanied Uncle Quin at the plow from an early age because of his way with the mules. Now he neared these carcasses and knelt, ran a hand over one of them. I saw then the pattern of sores and wounds on the animals—harness. The animals had been worked to death. For the first time since leaving home, Cal put his head in his hands and sobbed.

"Jesus. Sweet Jesus," he said, the first and last time I ever heard him say such a thing, though I do not believe it was a curse.

My grandfather appeared, pipe in hand, and stopped. He put his hands on Wes and my shoulders and sighed a great cloud of smoke, a little island of that fine, warm-smelling tobacco smoke in the middle of all that death. After a moment, he stepped forward to Cal, slung his rifle, and knelt beside him. He reached around Cal and held him with one great arm for a moment, and leaned in close and whispered in his ear. Cal nodded, wiped his eyes, and stood. He picked up his rifle and together they walked back to us.

"A righteous man regardeth the life of his beast," he said to us.

He spread his hands and turned us back toward the column just in time to fall in again. We did so, with First Sergeant Sloane cursing a few men back into formation with unusual sharpness, and we started forward again at a slow walk. I felt sicker yet.

I never did find out what my grandfather whispered to Cal.

As we left the center of town behind, the column thrummed with grumblings and curses.

"You see them mules?"

"Hell yes I did."

"Not a house or cowshed left in the place."

"Sonsabitches burnt the church, too. The damned church."

"Nothing left but the factory man's house."

"Not a stick of furniture left in it."

"Everything stolen."

"Hell, not everything. Busted up anything they didn't take."

"Not a soul to be seen."

"And they's boys in this brigade from around here."

"Damned Yankees," someone said, and spat.

"God damn them. God damn them to hell," someone else said, and meant it.

We left the worst of the smoke behind and halted again a few hundred yards beyond town. Curses, cries of "What now?" Ahead, some ways off, I saw a knot of officers on horseback, soon joined by others. I caught sight again of General Philips, who rode up with a few others to join the conference. I saw a great deal of pointing and gesturing, some of it agitated. The conference grew so large that the greater part of the officers dismounted, handed their reins to subordinates or to Negro grooms, and gathered around a tree where two rails had been twisted and left to harden. As the offcers conferred, I marked at last that several of them wore yellow trim.

251

I turned excitedly to Wes and Cal and said, "Cavalry."

Their eyes widened. "What?"

"Cavalry," I said.

They looked about in what I recognized as a growing panic. "Yankee—"

"No—ours. Up ahead. Look."

I pointed ahead, and Wes and Cal strained and stood on tiptoe trying to catch a glimpse. When I turned, I spotted a few more cavalrymen riding toward us at a slow walk, hunkered under coats and blankets in the saddle. As they neared, one looked up from under a yellow-banded kepi, almost straight into my face. With a start I recognized Pritchard MacBean.

I stared. He spotted me and a look of recognition and surprise passed over him. "Georgie Wax, as I live and breath."

"Pritchard," I said.

"And Mister Eschenbach, I believe."

"Hello, Mister MacBean," my grandfather said.

"Mister," Pritchard said, and raised his eyebrows. "I fancy the sound of that. Private MacBean ain't kept too well."

Another man behind us in the column called out: "I got some corporal's stripes I'd like to get shed of, too." There was a rustle of amusement, but no laughter. The sight of the town weighed too heavily for that.

"Boys, I apologize," Pritchard said. He indicated the two other cavalrymen with him, privates almost as young as we were. He introduced them as Brooks and Parker and we greeted each other. I saw then that, behind Pritchard, rode his manservant, Anchises. He recognized us too, and nodded.

"Been a while since I seen you out for a ride, Pritchard," I said, and thought of his sister.

He grinned and straightened up, stretched his back. A faded army blanket marked US fell away from his shoulders and I saw underneath a tattered and much-patched coat. The yellow collar of his cavalry jacket, much dirtied with mud and sweat, peaked out at his throat. He had let his hair grow out into unwashed bushwhacker ringlets and these hung over his collar and shoulders. Despite the wear—or perhaps because of it—there was something of the knight in his bearing, as though he had stepped out of one of our romances into this terrible scene.

"Pritchard?" Mr. Hale called from somewhere behind us. "Pritchard MacBean? Thomas's boy?"

Pritchard looked up toward him and tipped his cap.

"How is your daddy?" Mr. Hale said.

"Wounded," he said flatly.

A faint expression of wretchedness, a tragic curl of the lip, crossed his features and he pulled the blanket back up tighter about his shoulders. Thomas MacBean, now among that awful, ambiguous multitude—the wounded. I felt stricken, for him and for his sister.

"How bad?" my grandfather said.

"What's going on?" someone else called. The column came to life, sensing news to be had. "Who you with?"

"Wheeler," Pritchard said. The topic of his father, wounded in some far off place, fell away.

"The cavalry's here?"

"We're a rear-guard, scouting the enemy. The General took most of us off this morning."

"Why are we halted?"

Pritchard addressed his answer to me.

"Yankee cavalry raided here yesterday. Mudsills burnt the town all to hell. Officers slept in the big house back there and moved on this morning." He paused and idly scratched his chin; I marked how thin even he had become. "We scrapped with them some this morning and they moved on. What y'all got ahead of you is Yankee infantry, guarding the rear and the

253

extreme right of the enemy's wing. Where are you gentlemen headed?"

"Augusta," Private Bell said.

"Supposed to entrain somewhere along this way," Wes said. "Near Gordon."

"Well, Wesley Eschenbach—I didn't see you there. And John Calhoun, no less. Wish I could say it was a pleasure, if you catch my meaning."

"I do," Cal said.

Pritchard sighed. "Y'all ain't going to reach Gordon, much less Augusta. Not this way. Not unless you want to tangle with them."

Silence. I felt then something in the air, a tightening. I had not realized, whatever else we felt, how angry we all were. The whole column strained and groaned with it, spiritually trembled like a coiled muscle that must either strike or cramp. I knew then that we would, that we did want to tangle with the Yankees. Joe Brown's Pets had been waiting the whole summer and fall for this chance. The sick fear in my stomach, for a moment, was subsumed in wrath. I felt my face heat up and I gripped the stock of my musket.

Pritchard saw—or felt—all of this. Some of the starch left his countenance. He had brought this thing to life by naming it. He looked up and down the column as if regarding a monster of uncertain appetites.

"Y'all don't think—"

Just then Captain Guerard rode up.

"We're under orders not to engage the enemy, Private," he said. "First Sergeant Sloane, prepare to form line of battle."

A murmur, a rumbling—approval. The column stirred. First Sergeant Sloane saluted and acknowledged the captain. I looked at my grandfather; he might have been graven of stone, he stood so still, quiet, and inscrutable. I looked back at Pritchard, who still gaped at us. He seemed to collect himself, and shook his head.

"Gentlemen," he said to us, "Good luck."

"Here's your mule," I heard Private Greeves call out. No one laughed, but Pritchard nodded at the old joke.

"Mister Eschenbach," he said, "Georgie. Wesley. Cal."

"Private MacBean," I said.

He seemed to fumble for words. At last, he righted himself in the saddle, lifted the reins and tossed his matted hair, said, "Give them hell," and rode off with his fellows to join the other cavalry.

Ahead, the officers' conference had broken up and riders and runners raced up and down the line, shouting, barking, putting us into motion. Far ahead I spied the infantry making way for the artillery, which jangled forward with yells and curses as an officer directed them. I looked to my grandfather again. Now his head was bowed, and he seemed to mouth a prayer. I reckoned that could not hurt, and repeated the Lord's Prayer to myself two or three times, until a new order came: *forward march.*

The column moved quickly into route step again. We kept silent as we marched toward the enemy. I realized after what seemed a long time that I was holding my breath, and gasped and struggled to control it. My grandfather reached across and gripped my shoulder. Though we must have received orders and shouted commands, and we must have given responses or acknowledgements in return, my grandfather spoke the only words I can recall from before the attack: "Steady, Georgie."

Not much farther past the ruin of the town the column turned rightward. I watched the units preceding ours wheel in column and move away from the road at the quick step, forming into line of battle as they went. I caught sight of First Sergeant Sloane, who stopped to sweep the column with his glance, as if to say, *This is why you drilled.* We approached the point where we too would leave the road and I saw among a cloud of aides and adjutants General Philips, astride his horse, watching, in proud command.

I have since heard rumor and complaint, carried on with the usual vigor in the veterans' magazines, that General Philips was drinking that day, and had been for some time prior to its events; others I have seen come to his defense, and denounce such rumors as slander on an honorable but ill-starred man. Among this handful who know or care what happened that day, the implication of the latter seems to be that what was about to fall upon us was foreordained and unavoidable; of the former, that a sober man would not have ordered the attack at all. I cannot say whether he was intoxicated—I saw him so little that day, which to my mind is a more damning charge than drink—but we were surely not drunk, not after what we had seen, and I doubt that his being sober as a Baptist would have done anything to change what was about to happen. The hamartia, the error, lay in neither leadership nor predestination. The old story.

I do not remember the order for quick step but we broke into it nonetheless, and halted a short way south of the Griswoldville road. Major Frady and Captain Guerard dismounted and we militia—boys like myself and Wes and Cal and old men unblooded since before the Mexican War—moved expertly through our evolutions and deployed into line of battle facing the woods past the town. Beyond them waited the enemy.

We had no sooner halted than the sound of musket fire reached us, a dozen scattered shots out among the trees. Skirmishers driving in the Yankee pickets, no doubt. I thought of my many dull watches on the picket line. My chest tensed, my throat tightened. I found myself holding my breath again, and again my grandfather—silently, this time—gripped and steadied my shoulder. We dressed our ranks and received the order to load. Never had loading a rifle seemed so laborious, to take so long. I can recall each movement as if I had set aside the afternoon to study on it—ripping open the cartridge with my teeth, tasting the foul tang of spilt powder, pouring the rest into the muzzle, thumbing the ball into the bore, wadding the cartridge. Midway through, as I drew forth the ramrod to drive the bullet home, I glanced at my grandfather. He stood loading as calmly as on the morning back home when he had shown me how to kill a squirrel without shooting it—the same seasoned movements of his hands, the same steady gaze forward. His breath came easy, with no coughing now.

We finished loading and fixed bayonets. We raised our rifles to shoulder arms. I glanced down at the pistol in my rawhide holster and wished I had time to load it. Perhaps—

A boom from ahead and to the left, over the trees. I and about half the others jumped. Another boom and another, and one responding report from directly ahead of us. An artillery duel, I realized, and soared and trembled on the thought.

Captain Guerard passed along the line with his saber in his hand and ordered us to light order. We shed our blankets and packs and any excess equipment but our rifles, belts, and cartridge boxes. A line of piled gear accumulated behind us. Unburdened, my coat loosened and I felt a quickening rush of cold air come in from the neck of my jacket. I pulled my scarf tighter. The color bearers stepped forward and unfurled the company guidon and the state colors and the regimental battle flag with its saltire azure and mullets argent, the flags loosening into the calm and snow-heavy air. Calls of command descended to us. Captain Guerard shouted and waved us forward, into the attack.

I do not recall entering the woods but I remember

passing through them—a long downward slope of scrubby pine and a few hardwoods, the kind of untended growth common to the middle and south of Georgia. Our line wavered and crumbled as we tangled with the trunks and branches. I had need to duck my head, and my bayonet, riding high above my shoulder, knocked and slashed against the limbs above me. All around I heard the click and thunk of rifles, bayonets, canteens, beltbuckles, cartridge boxes, and bodies as the line moved through the woods. The cannon fire continued sporadically, with the tree-muffled reports coming from above as whumps that grew louder and heavier the further we marched. I could feel the sound. I recalled my grandfather's squirrel-shooting demonstration and his story of cannon—in Florida, in the militia—and that dread word: *concussion.* My heart began to thud slowly but heavily in my chest.

I heard a crash of musketry ahead and a bullet whickered past us through the trees. I heard whoops and a few more pops of rifle fire. A minute or two more and we passed through a thinning pall of smoke—the final encounter with the Yankee pickets—and peering ahead through the eye-stinging reek I spied snowy ground and daylight between the tree trunks. Kneeling at the edge of the wood were our skirmishers. Private Greeves stood among them; he grinned enormously, laughing and whooping to himself as he reloaded. Somewhere to the right I glimpsed the colors dipping under branches. I stepped around another trunk, bowed and brushed away some grasping limbs, and stood up into the open. Ahead and just down the end of the long slope ran a marshy creek braked with grey-white willows. From there the land rose steadily away into a low ridge of plowland, dotted all over with stubble and here and there with tree stumps, and there, across those fields, looking down on us from their works, I saw the Yankees.

We were still a great way off but their activity showed well enough—blue figures moved this way and that through the artillerists' smoke and falling debris.

Major Frady halted us and we reformed and dressed the line. I watched the enemy and thought of an anthill kicked open. Their pickets were just racing to safety at the top of the ridge. Up there I saw teams of men toting railroad ties to throw onto their breast-works. Others dashed this way and that in a crouch, clutching their caps like a lady keeping her bonnet on in a breeze. Our artillery boomed away to our left and cast up showers of dirt and snow. There were no earthworks, no chevaux de frise, no serious defenses of any kind, and the speed and apparent panic of the Yankees' movements steeled me, flushed me with elation.

A cannonball struck their line and threw up a tangle of fencerails and limbs and cut down their colors, the Union flag. We cheered and raised our caps. The flag rose again a few moments later, but a spume of blood across the red and white stripes was visible even at our distance. More cannonballs struck and skipped across the enemy's position, and we cheered again, higher, more spiritedly. I waved my cap and cried out. I saw Wes turn to look at me and realized that I was laughing like a lunatic.

"At the quick step—forward march!"

"Here we go, boys!" First Sergeant Sloane called.

We struck out in step and a cry rose up warbling, shrieking from us. I screamed and screamed and could not hear myself for the artillery and the pounding of my heart. It chills me today to remember it.

We achieved the marshy branch and halted. Captain Guerard gave the order to ready. We were yet several hundred yards off but we brought our rifles from shoulder arms and pulled the hammers back to full cock. In the space to do so, through our screaming and yelling, I heard a distant pattering and saw smoke bloom from the Yankee line away to our left. Ahead, I still saw rushing and preparing. I recall spying one distant figure struggling to fit his ramrod to the bore of his rifle as Captain Guerard shouted the order to aim. I leveled my rifle—uphill, that is—and laid the sight over the Yankee breastworks but cannot say I really aimed. My breath caught again and I struggled to release it, slowly, the way my father and grandfather had taught me, when the final order came.

"Fire!"

I did not even hear the report or feel the kick of the rifle. Our smoke burst into sight, obscuring all, and like machines we reloaded and readied again. I cannot relate how long this all took—perhaps a quarter of a minute. We seemed to stand loading in the haze for an hour. Elsewhere, I heard and felt the cannon fire, and the crackle of Yankee rifle fire, steadily rising.

Once reloaded, we moved again, at the quick, screaming again. We crossed the creek, crunched through its frozen grasses and soft, muddy places, splashed through its shallow sandy waters, and stepped up onto the other side and began to move uphill. We cleared the smoke of our own fusillade and I just had time to spy the Yankees across the field standing in line behind their breastworks at ready arms. I shuddered with the vast amount I comprehended in that moment—I sensed rather than saw our whole line, several thousand strong, stretched over a mile across the field under the grey sky, and the snap of our state colors and battle flags as we reached the doublequick, and the whole field, with its snowy tussocks and stumps, the clapboard farmhouse behind the Yankee line, the smoke sprouting like moss from every corner of my sight, soon to overwhelm all, and the ground sweeping past beneath me and the solid line of men in their caps and slouch hats and with the tarnished brass of their beltplates and buttons showing dully against their blue-black jackets. I gasped. The Yankees fired.

It became a newspaper commonplace early in the war that the flight of bullets sounds like the buzz of a hornet or yellowjacket; every battle seemed to have its own "hornet's nest." I had found so many of my other expectations disappointed that I was surprised to find this one true in every particular. The first real volley of Yankee fire crashed and their bullets passed overhead with a sound like a bee in your very ear. I had to stop myself from crouching and swatting. I looked up and the Yankees had disappeared, hidden in their smoke.

They fired again, far sooner than I would have credited, and I heard a new sound amid the cloud of yellowjackets—a metallic plink and thunk as bullets struck bayonets, rifles, the flagstaffs of our colors, like the opening salvo of a hailstorm on a tin roof. A third volley, and snow and earth burst from the ground ahead of us and the hailstones and hornets rattled through our lines and I heard a terrible soft thump for the first time. A man somewhere down the line cursed and other voices dropped out of our yell into a timbre of concern. Another volley, and the sounds achieved a harmony as the fire passed over and through our lines and men began to fall.

"Oh, God," I heard Cal say.

We advanced uphill, deeper into musket range. The volleys kept coming. The state flag fell once and snapped back up; I heard a strangled cry away to my right and another to my left. We held the line as in all our drill and withstood it. At last, after seeming to walk the length of a day under that fire, we halted.

"Ready!"

I felt grateful for something to do. I thumbed the hammer of my rifle back to full cock.

"Aim!"

I raised my rifle and pointed it into the stinking cloud drifting down around us. I thought I saw a flash

261

of fire from within—another volley burst around our ears—and aimed more or less at that.

"Fire!"

I heard and felt this shot. Our musketry roared and my rifle kicked back against my shoulder. Now all was smoke; we could not even see the enemy, just as my father had said years before. The order came to reload and I grounded my rifle and glanced about as I felt in my cartridge box.

My grandfather stood next to me, grimly loading. His great black brows were knitted almost together as he worked. I saw Wes and Cal, wide-eyed, fumbling with their rifles. I saw Sergeant Burrell telling Hoyt to calm down, and Hoyt cursing his fingers as he dropped a cartridge. I saw Peter and his grandfather. Peter, though standing calmly reloading, was flecked all over with blood.

It took a moment for the meaning to reach me. This was the right time of year, the right kind of weather, for hog-slaughtering. I had seen men and boys flecked—soaked—in blood every year of my life at this time, but I realized with a start that this was human blood. I cast my eyes across Peter and all the men around us and saw no wounds. I looked back to see if I could spy a man fallen, or straggling because of his injuries. First Sergeant Sloane, who stood with his sword drawn several paces behind the line, stepped into my view and pointed ahead like a schoolmistress. I just had time to puzzle over all of this before the order came to ready. I turned back and found my rifle reloaded—automatically, my hands doing the tasks while I gawped around in the smoke. My grandfather glanced at me, searched my face, and nodded. Another Yankee volley reached us as we aimed and fired and the firefight began in earnest.

I no longer held my breath. My mind had become tremendously concentrated. I noted the most minute things: I somehow heard, through the din of four thousand rifles, my grandfather clear his throat and sniff in the cold as we loaded. I saw a tussock of grass uprooted and flipped end over end by an errant ball. I saw a crow above the smoke, making for the woods. I recall these, but not how long we stood shooting at the Yankees. The smoke hung so dense that, once or twice, I felt momentarily alone on the field, and would turn to look for the rest of the line only to bump into my grandfather or Cal or Peter. But for a long time I stood loading and firing in volleys with the rest of the company, and finally firing at will. The roar of rifle fire overpowered all—it was as nothing I had ever heard, not even the huffing locomotives of the railroads. The Yankee fire came continuous and thick and tore the ground in pocks and furrows, rescattered the snow, and whizzed and rattled through our line provoking cries and curses of terrible volume. I thought I felt bullets plucking at my clothes. Certainly, sometimes they passed so close to my head that I did not hear even the hornet buzz, but rather a crack as of the snapping of a tree in a storm.

Then I was moving with the line as we slunk downhill in a half-crouch, still facing the enemy, still firing. I had not even heard Captain Guerard give the order to fall back. I looked back at the line where we had been standing. The snow and earth had been churned to mud. Bits of paper cartridge and spilt powder lay scattered everywhere. I saw a pack and haversack or two, a bent bayonet, and a blanket roll, half unwound, with several holes shot through it. And I saw blood, specks of it like the trails left by wounded deer, and in a few places great fans sprayed over the snow, or long smears leading downhill. Then our smoke closed over the position.

"Granddaddy?" I said. It was the first articulate sound I had made since—I do not know.

"I'm here, Georgie."

"Did we—" I stopped. Did we win? I am unsure what I intended to ask.

"You're all right, Georgie. Catch your breath. You too, Wes."

I glanced back at Wes and froze. His face was as white and blank as the sky. His eyes goggled out of his head. He wore enormous streaks of black powder at both corners of his mouth, like the mustaches of Prussian warlords. He was drenched with sweat.

For that matter, so was I. As we neared the bottom of the hill, occasional Yankee bullets whined far overhead, but with the first fight over, my mind and body began to calm. I was hot, my longhandles and shirt heavy with sweat. My mouth tasted of the awful powder and my feet burned. I glanced at them—soaked from crossing the creek. I had not even noticed. I looked back to Wes.

"Wes?" I said. He was like a puppet, or a stranger made to look like Wes.

Cal, also wide-eyed but not in shock, shook him. "John Wesley," he said.

Wes blinked. He moved and walked just fine, with his rifle in hand and at half-cock, ready for the next order to fire, but it was as though the battle had driven the vital part of him out.

"Catch your breath, Wes," my grandfather said again. "Eat something."

We reached the creek and Captain Guerard reformed us on the other side, near the edge of the woods from whence we had emerged what seemed hours before. As we crossed—I trying to skip along stones and tussocks to let my brogans dry—we saw the wounded.

The first man lay facedown on the creek bank, soaked to the thighs. He had crawled across and fallen. His left arm lay twisted unnaturally beside him, torn open and bleeding. I thought him dead at first but he

264

moaned softly and raised his head and looked at us. His face was caked with mud, snowmelt, powder, and blood, and I saw that he had been shot through one eye, too. He wept blood from the socket. A slave dragged another man, a lieutenant, who bled freely from bullet wounds high in both thighs. The lieutenant scratched feebly at the ground with his sabre as they went, gripping the hilt white-knuckled, still leading his men, still fighting.

I looked for the surgeon, the man who had tried to save the gut-shot man during the summer, but saw more wounded—dozens more. They sat in huddles on the banks of the creek, leaning against each other, holding their heads in their hands or staring into the water, coughing up phlegm and blood. One man missing most of his right calf knelt on his good leg to bandage the shoulder wound of another with their handkerchiefs. Another I saw wrapping his left hand— which had three ragged stumps from the tertiary digit to the little finger—as calmly as if he were at home binding his hands against the cold.

At the edge of the woods I finally saw the surgeon and the crowd of men making their way to him. He knelt by a man whose abdominal cavity had been torn open from crotch to sternum and all his blue-grey an shining insides spilt out into the light. I blanched. I had seen hog guts plenty of times, steaming in the cold just like this, but never a man's falling from between the brass buttons of his coat. Another lay nearby with his leg nearly shot off at the knee, held on only by tendon and threads of skin. A last walked right past me at a calm, even stately trod, with his hand clutched to his bloody face. At first I thought his fingers broken by a bullet, so unnaturally did they splay where he nursed them; but then I saw that his hands were whole, and his lower mandible, the entire jaw, had been shot away, and he went clutching the wound and wheezing throat hole. What I had taken to be a swollen, broken digit was his tongue, lolling unrestrained and homeless through his fingers.

I cannot describe the wailing that went up from the wounded as they gathered.

I felt faint as we reformed the line. I looked again at my grandfather, at Wes and Cal, at Peter and his grandfather. We were a sober lot, now.

Our artillery fired again, with no response from the Yankees. That much at least was a relief. First Sergeant Sloane came up the line, looking, counting. He stopped at our squad.

"Missing?" he said.

"Massey," Sergeant Burrell said. I looked around. Private Massey was gone. He had been standing in rank beside Peter when we had formed for the attack.

"He got hit right at the beginning," Private Bell said. "I seen him fall out."

"Not two minutes in," Peter said.

Burrell and Sloane looked at Peter. Blood still speckled his face and jacket. First Sergeant Sloane nodded and moved on.

"Wounded?" Sergeant Burrell said to Peter.

"I kindly doubt it," Peter said.

Sergeant Burrell nodded. "Load. Eat a bite. They ain't coming to us down here, so we're going to them up there."

Another attack. I had not yet thought so far ahead. I took out a poke full of peanuts and looked up the hill as I shelled and gobbled them. The smoke had cleared somewhat. Slowly the Yankee breastworks emerged, and the Yankees themselves, working. Again, I grew angry. Their mere presence on the low ridge enraged me, and that we had attacked, fired volley after volley into them, and not dislodged them made me angrier yet. I gripped the stock of my rifle until my fingernails turned white and my knuckles felt like they would burst.

My grandfather had taken out his pipe, filled, tamped, and lit it, and stood resting on his rifle, smoking. The smell of his tobacco calmed me somewhat.

"We going to attack again, Granddaddy?" I said.

"Certainly."

"Going to drive them off this time?"

"I hope so, Georgie."

I looked up the hill again and beheld the Yankee line, the bodies where we had stood to fight. "How did we do up there?"

He looked at me, cleared his throat, and tried a smile. "Well, you didn't run."

Sometimes staying put is hard enough, I recalled. We had shown courage. I had to convince myself, because that was not how it felt. He puffed on his pipe some more and patted me on the back. I turned and grinned at Wes and Cal, who grinned back—Wes a mite wanly, but happily nonetheless.

"Steady, boys," my grandfather said and stifled a cough.

I heard shouts up and down the line, orders to dress the ranks, to fill holes, to reaffix bayonets. From up the hill, I heard hoots and whistles. The Yankees, taunting us. My face burned; I gripped my rifle hard. I thought of my pistol, but it was, again, too late to load it.

Captain Guerard appeared, himself sweaty and bloodspattered. He came shouting orders and in moments we stood ready. The order to march came, and we moved toward the creek, toward the Yankees.

I was angry, as I have related, but this anger was of a different kind from that after we marched through the ruins of Griswoldville. I felt this more personally— as though affronted—and therefore more intensely. It burned away the nerves I felt before the first attack. I did not have to fight to control my breath, my chest did not tighten, I did not feel sick, but our squad had

267

to march past the surgeon again on our way to the creek, and I could not help but look. The gutted man lay dead. The man with the ruined leg lay under a blanket, his leg now foreshortened. The man who had fallen by the creek lay on his side by other wounded men, waiting his turn. I saw no sign of the man who had lost his jaw.

I do not recall the march up the hill, nor the fighting with any great detail. We marched screaming into musket range, received fire, withstood it, and fired at the Yankees. The smoke billowed and enveloped us. We made a series of movements—to call them charges seems grandiose—against the Yankees' works, but what this meant for us was marching deeper into the reek, closer to the fire, until we could see the flashes through the haze, and hear them shouting at us and cursing each other, and firing at them. We were so close I could feel the volleys as they fired, the whump of the musketry like a sudden puff of hot wind or the blast of air one feels upon peeking into the oven. We fell back halfway down the hill, reformed, reloaded, and moved back up and did it again.

Sometime during the attack, another great blaze of hailstones struck through our line and Private Bell crashed forward onto the ground. He fell without even a flinch to catch himself—killed outright. This was the first man I had seen killed in this way, up close, despite the battle raging around us, so dense was the smoke and so enervating the noise. Sergeant Burrell knelt beside him a moment, pulled him up by the shoulder enough to see his face, then stood and resumed his place in line.

Only at the end of this attack did weariness turn to shock again. We were falling back from our nearly face-to-face shooting with the Yankees when a lone shot from the enemy line struck Sergeant Burrell down. It slapped into his coat just above the sternum and below the collarbone and he sagged backwards into Hoyt, his young cousin, who stood in the rank just behind him. My grandfather turned to help him and I saw and heard Sergeant Burrell cough. Blood speckled his beard.

Hoyt—where one may have expected, because of melodramas, a rising note of panic or mourning—said flatly, "Well, shit."

My grandfather and Hoyt hooked Sergeant Burrell under the arms and dragged him to the rear. I stood momentarily alone. Wes and Cal stepped forward into the front rank with me and I felt Peter and his grandfather close in behind us. We kept on firing.

My grandfather and Hoyt did not rejoin us—we fell back to them. Back on the other side of the creek, they came up grim-visaged and silent. None of us asked what had become of Sergeant Burrell, not once we had seen Hoyt's face.

Back out of the suffocating smoke I could see somewhat more of the field. To the left and right of us the attack went on, with one regiment advancing and another falling back. Officers both afoot and on horseback issued commands and waved their swords toward the enemy, but there was no plan. I was not to see General Philips or any other officer again. I grew angry again, now that the battle should even happen at all. I looked up the bloodied hill and ached to strike again.

We reformed and closed the gaps in our ranks. Our line shrank considerably, and Major Frady directed us closer, shifting leftward, crabwise, to the next battalion, and we faced a new and slightly steeper slope already littered with gear, crawling men, and motionless bodies. We joined with the neighboring regiment in an effort at coordination and attacked again.

The sky had lightened by this time—the heavy grey overcast that followed the snow had given way to a clear white with dark blue edges behind us, away to the west. The faint shadows lengthened. I cannot say what time we began the attack, but we had kept at it for most of the afternoon and dusk fast approached. With the change in cloud and weather came a soft breeze, and in the final assaults we saw more and more clearly what the hanging smoke had earlier concealed.

In this attack we drew close enough to the Yankee line to catch glimpses of them through the stirring smoke. I recall reloading after a volley—down to my last handful of cartridges now—and glancing up as I raised the ramrod to the muzzle of my rifle and seeing the smoke part just enough to behold a Yankee not fifty feet away. He stood stout, broadshouldered, and had the ruddy cheekbones and bulbous nose of a heavy drinker. His face shone like glass with sweat. I saw that he too was in the act of reloading—he raised his rifle to thumb back the hammer, and I saw in that glimpse that he carried a repeater, one of the mechanical wonders I had inspected on the wall of Dawes's store those summers ago with my grand-father. He did not catch my eye—we did not see each other—but for the space of a second I got my first clear, closeup sight of the enemy. Then the smoke drew together again.

I looked at my friends to see if they, too, had seen this, but my grandfather had knelt to gather cartridges from a fallen man's box and Wes and Cal were busied with reloading. Cal I could see struggling to fit a percussion cap; he was bleeding raw from the fingers as if he had just picked an acre of cotton. Peter and his grandfather worked grimly with their ramrods. Only Hoyt looked back at me. His eyes were bloodshot and welling and tears had run white streaks through his powder-blacked face. He looked the angriest I have ever seen a person. He said nothing, simply acknowl-edged me and kept loading.

The Yankee fire after this grew so heavy that the

line began to come to pieces. Men left their orderly drill manual formations and went to ground like hunted animals. I saw three crowded together behind the same tree stump, all working to reload and fire but accomplishing little in the crush. Two or three crawled on their bellies or pushed themselves backwards away from the fight. First Sergeant Sloane, his head and upper arm now bandaged, roved behind the line and jerked up or kicked such men forward again. I myself had adopted without thinking a half-crouch, and I was not alone—any man still on his feet could not be rightly said to stand. And of course there were the wounded and killed. The enemy fire could no longer be said to come in volleys—it was a continuous storm of shot. The air seemed alive, to crawl with it. We withstood this ferocity for perhaps five minutes before falling back once more.

Then came the final winnowing of our squad. I cannot rightly recall how far we had fallen back—I remember it as on the instant Captain Guerard gave us the order—when Hoyt fell. A ball caught and tore through the flesh above his left knee and he collapsed on it like a broken chair. My grandfather turned to help him and another ball struck Hoyt in the hip. Hoyt dropped his rifle and scrabbled for it.

"Leave it, son," my grandfather said, fairly screaming above the musketry.

But Hoyt would not. My grandfather looked at my cousins, at me, and nodded toward Hoyt. We slung our rifles and moved to help and a bullet whacked into Cal. He tumbled sidewise downhill and tried to right himself, propped on one arm like the dying Gaul, clutching at his face with the other. Blood did not so much stream as simply appear as a bright coating on his face, hand, and wrist.

Wes cried out in a choked voice. We let go of Hoyt and made for Cal and my grandfather called us off.

271

"Georgie, Wes—y'all stay with Hoyt," he said. We took Hoyt—yet silent, yet struggling to get his rifle—under the arms and my grandfather let go and picked up Cal in his arms and bore him down the hill. We struggled to keep up. Peter and his grandfather fell in behind us, between us and the Yankees, and so we progressed back down and across the creek.

Once far enough away from his rifle, Hoyt stopped fighting us and hung loose-limbed from our grasp; his lank legs dragged behind and trailed blood. We stopped before the creek, stripped his cartridge box, belt, and blanket roll, and carried him across as best we could. My brogans filled again with the frigid water as we slopped through. We dropped Hoyt on the other side and fell panting beside him. My grandfather appeared over us, Cal in his arms, hugging his neck like a child.

"I'm taking Cal on to the surgeon." His voice came out gravelly. He heaved and panted, choked back deep chest coughs, and held Cal tighter. His face dripped sweat. He looked me fiercely in the eye. "Georgie, can you get Hoyt there?"

I could not talk, so I nodded.

Wes gasped and spit and got to his feet.

"Cal?" he said. "Cal, you ain't dead, are you?"

"He's not," my grandfather said to Wes. He looked me in the eye again and nodded. "I'll catch up to y'all shortly."

He walked off. Wes bent double and vomited, thin and phlegmy. I turned away and looked to Hoyt. In addition to the gob torn from his knee and the dark patch about the angle of his pelvis, he had been struck again as we fell back in the upper chest, near the conjunction of the clavicle and shoulder joint. His face had begun to go slack. I spoke to him and he rolled his eyes. I slapped him and he gave me a faint but indignant look and said in a low voice, "Don't you bet I wish I had that pistol of yours now?"

I could not help but laugh, though I felt not the least bit merry. I nudged Wes where he stopped huffing and blowing and said, "Come on. We got to catch up to Granddaddy and Cal."

We heaved Hoyt up and set out for the surgeon. The fire had died down by now and our battery of guns had begun to fire again, though with what seemed diminished enthusiasm. All over the field I saw broken squads and companies reforming, scraping together strength out of diffusion. There would be another attack—there was no one to order it, and no one to keep it from being ordered. The world had narrowed to this field. We must drive the Yankees off.

"Come on," I said again. "They're fixing to go."

We found the surgeon at the edge of the woods surrounded by a great drift of wounded and dead. The horrors of the first attack had multiplied a hundredfold. A man knelt on the ground pinching his throat shut, gasping. With each breath, red translucent bubbles sprouted between his fingers. Another had taken a small round, as from a pistol, through the mouth, and stood politely with a bloodied hand pressed to the back of his jaw and a whole hemisphere of his face swelling red. One had been shot in the groin and lay wailing. Others sat with nearly severed arms clasped to their sides, or with protruding bone sheltered in a cupped hand. The gut-shot lay moaning for water with none to respond to them. A hog-slaughtering stink rose from the whole bunch, with the surgeon and a few wounded men working on the others, elbow-deep in gore.

We had not lagged far behind my grandfather. Wes and I arrived just as he laid Cal down at edge of the group, and when we helped Hoyt down and called for the surgeon we got our first look at Cal.

He had been shot in the face, a glancing blow that shattered the cheekbone beneath his left eye. His face was blackened and swollen and stoved in on one side

273

like a windfallen peach rotting under the tree. He cried out and showed broken teeth. I realized after a moment that these noises were our names—he was calling to Wes and me. Something broke inside me and I recall thinking then that I could not possibly hurt more than to see my cousin wounded like this. I was wrong.

"Come on, boys," my grandfather said. He knelt, gasping, and cradled the back of Cal's head and spoke softly to him despite the battlefield noise. "You'll be all right here, Cal my boy. You'll be just fine."

Cal moaned and nodded and my grandfather rose, pushing himself up from his knees.

I saw then that his whole chest and the greater part of one arm were daubed in Cal's blood. His face, like ours, like everyone else's, was nearly black with powder and soot. I realized then how thin he had become in the last months. His coat hung loose from his shoulders like an old shirt drying on a line. The cuffs of his coat and jacket flapped about his wrists. He took off his slouch hat and wiped the sheen of sweat from his bald head and used it to smear some of the soot and powder from his face. He looked down at Cal for a moment, cleared his throat with great effort, and looked at Wes and me. My grandfather nodded as if to himself and took us by the shoulders.

"All right, Wes, Georgie. We're all we've got. Let's go on."

I had been wrong before—the world had narrowed further still, to these: my cousin and my grandfather. Wes and I unslung our rifles and followed him back to the line.

We had lost track of Peter and his grandfather but found Captain Guerard and fell in with him and First Sergeant Sloane and some sergeants from another company. I saw Greeves and Brands from other squads, and men I recognized from other battalions entirely. We formed ranks with men from the Augusta powderworks and a handful of men from the State Line. There were local militia of boys our age and old men with bird guns and flintlocks. Even some of the artillerists in their redbanded caps and shirtsleeves had left their guns and taken up rifles from fallen men to join the assault.

We formed up ever leftward of our original position, and found ourselves facing the steepest part of the slope—a gully that rose sheer from the broadest, swampiest part of the creek, just south of the ruined railroad.

We dressed ranks, loaded, and waited. The sun was almost down, hanging just above the horizon at our backs. The hillside, the bloody, foot-plowed field of corpses lay gilded by the evening stretchlight. I thought that this would be it, the final advantage that would tip the battle in our favor against the outnumbered Yankees—they would be blinded by the sun, blind before our anger and desperation.

At last, our diminished brigade moved forward. This time the attack unfolded under a weary silence— no yelling from ourselves, no taunting from the Yankees. I recall hearing a few coughs as we crossed the creek, and that was all.

I nearly lost a brogan to the mud around the creek and struggled to keep in line with Wes and my grandfather. I stumbled, and he steadied me once more with his great firm hand. I looked at him. He nodded to me and said, absently, looking back up the hill toward the enemy, "Steady, Georgie."

Once across the creek we started up the bank and the attack slowed. The line disintegrated. A handful of younger boys and the sergeants made the top of the bank and waited. Some of the old men struggled most pitifully. One fell on his face until his nose streamed blood, and still he kept trying to muster the strength to climb the bank. My grandfather moved to help him

275

and Wes and I helped each other to the top, where we dropped to our knees and looked up to see the enemy staring at us.

Slowly the rest of the men reached the top of the bank and a crude line formed. Slowly the Yankees raised their rifles. With no order, no drilled set of commands, we leveled our rifles and shotguns and fowling pieces and the two sides blazed away. And we were repulsed—the Yankee fire drove us back, into the gully again.

My memories are confused. The anger of the first hour of the battle and the mingled fear and elation had all gone, replaced by weariness and a frantic activity that approached panic. We reformed in the lee of the ravine and pressed uphill again to be swept away again. Men fell from gunfire or exhausted clumsiness and rolled or slid back down the bank or lay finally still. We tripped over each other. A man with a blood-streaked face lowered himself and sat and said to me, as if to an old friend, "I'm plumb give out." We passed him by. An older man, to avoid another falling down the bank, staggered into my path, said, "Oh—beg pardon," as though we had passed on the streets of Athens, and a ball thumped into his chest and he fell against me. As he slumped onto the ground he turned and I saw his face; he looked surprised, as though stunned and ashamed at his lapse of manners.

At last, Captain Guerard passed among us and pushed us into line with his own hands. When he and some other officers and sergeants and some private soldiers who had simply stepped into leadership out of necessity had formed us up, they waved us forward and we clambered up the slope. This, for me, turned out to be the final time.

Captain Guerard came out on the lip of the gully and turned to us. He had lost his hat and his britches were shredded at the knees. His saber had a dent in it and his scabbard had been shot away. Wildeyed, courageous with desperation, he waved his saber and exhorted us in a voice like the apocalypse.

"This time, boys—this time! They must break! Now yell, boys! Yell!"

As he screamed this final word, three Yankee bullets struck him and passed through him where he stood, half-turned toward us—one through the muscle of the thigh, another through the side at the lower false ribs, and another through the armpit that traversed his shoulderblades and killed him outright. He collapsed onto himself not ten feet from Wes and me.

We yelled, feebly but with all of our remaining spirit, and reached the body-littered top of the ravine and moved forward in good order into the smoke of the enemy's fire. I recall Wes shouting to me but do not know what he said—I doubt that I understood, rationally, even at that moment. We halted and made ready to fire. I looked up and, for only the second time from so close a vantage, saw the Yankees. They rose together from behind their fenceposts and limbs and railroad ties with their rifles at the ready, brought their hammers to full cock, aimed, and fired. There came another terrible rattle of hail, swarming of hornets, and cries and groans as a fresh swath of men fell.

The next that I can recall, I was in full flight. I ran through the woods. My brogans were full of icewater and I had lost my beautiful English rifle. I could see no one but did not feel alone, so alive were the woods with the sounds of fleeing men. The sinewy branches of saplings switched my face and roots and fallen limbs grabbed at my feet. I do not know how long this had gone on or how far I had gotten when I heard a shout I thought to be Wes and turned to look and ran full into a tree.

I fell. I tried to get up but despaired and lay still. The sun was down and the woods rapidly darkened.

All around me I heard movement—shouts, curses, moans and wails, the rustle and crack of men passing through the forest, the whinny of a horse and the faint tinkle of harness, and, away behind me, musket fire, faint, and diminishing moment by moment—but I saw no one.

I do not know how long I lay in the woods, or how the remnants of our brigade passed through and left me behind, but when at last I rose the sun was down and the woods quiet. I took account of myself. I had lost my rifle, torn from my hands by a tree or bush somewhere. My feet had gone numb, my knees felt scraped and bruised, my back and shoulders ached, my face stung with cold and the whippings of tree branches, and I tasted gunpowder, my own sweat, and blood. I realized at length how greatly I thirsted, and drank off what remained in my canteen and fumbled in my haversack for something to eat.

I was arrested by the silence—the woods seemed suddenly quieter. I heard only the creak of the trunks in the breeze. I looked around. Surely, I thought, I would see someone. We had all passed this way in the early afternoon, those few hours ago. But I saw nothing and no one. I felt sick with fear. Where was my grandfather? Or Wes? Or anyone else? How long had I lain here? I forgot food and struck out through the woods again.

Presently I did see some fellow soldiers, but these did nothing to assuage my fear—the wounded, the dying, and corpses. One man sat against a tree with his breast blown open. I could see the broken ends of ribs through the hole in his coat. He stirred as I passed but made no sound and did not even open his eyes. Another man lay stretched upon the ground drawing limbs and sticks to himself to make some kind of cover. Others lay on their sides or leaned against the boles of trees, sipping water, struggling to breathe, or staring back through the woods toward the Yankees. One man crouched against the roots of a dead oak. Upon my approach, he turned and waved his arms and gasped, "Don't shoot! Don't shoot!" He had been shot through both eyes, and continued to beg for his life until I was far away.

I left the woods and saw ahead of me, about a half-mile off, the smoldering shape of Griswoldville. I heard men and horses milling about. I found the remains of our line of abandoned gear and searched for my own, which I found had been plundered by those who took themselves for the survivors; almost all that remained to me was my blankets—even my copy of *A Tale of Two Cities* was gone. I gathered the rest and headed for Griswoldville.

I did not take the road, but cut through the empty fields toward the town. I had crossed one field and climbed a fence into another when I found Wes.

He sat hunched behind the fence with his head down and fairly jumped when I climbed over and nearly fell on him.

"Jesus—Georgie!" he cried.

"Wes!"

We both began talking, but at such speed that neither could understand the other. A moment later we both commenced to weeping, though for what I cannot say—fear and its memory, relief to see each other, and exhaustion, most certainly. We embraced and cried on each other for some time. At last, Wes spoke.

"Are you all right?"

"Yes," I said, though I was still unsure. "You?"

"I think so. I feel sick."

"Where is everybody? What happened?" I was—and remain—unsure about the final moments of the battle.

"Back over that way," he said, and indicated the town. "Some fell back in pretty good order, I think. I seen a lot of men surrendering, though."

"What?" I thought of the blinded man in the woods. Surrender had never crossed my mind.

"We ain't going to attack again, are we? At night?"

I shook my head. "What about Cal? Have you seen Cal?"

"No—I reckon they moved him off. I don't know. I don't know nothing."

"What about Granddaddy?"

Even in the dark, I could see Wes's lip tremble, like a child's. We had been discovered; all along, we had only been playing at soldiers. I waited, but Wes said nothing.

"Where's Granddaddy?" I said.

Wes cleared his throat and looked away. "I—I think he's back there. I think they got him."

"What? Prisoner?"

"I seen him fall—fall down back there."

I looked back toward the woods, the battlefield. A dread rose up from the pit of my stomach.

"What happened?"

"Right before we started back this way, I seen him just go down on one knee and fall. He was helping a wounded man. I think—"

I shook my head. "We got to find him."

"I seen—"

"He'd go back to find us." I thought of the men scattered through the woods. "He's sick, bad sick. What if he's hurt? What if he needs help?"

Wes gestured helplessly. I turned to go.

"Come on," I said.

"They're rallying in the town," Wes said. "We got to go. They—they beat us."

"Oh, no they didn't. Come on."

"We got to rally. You can't desert now."

Wes was crying again, and I began to hate him for it. All his bravado, his bravery in stealing food and cussing, had gone. I did not consider how we had stood beside each other all through that long afternoon, or the months of marching and working, the embrace we had just shared upon seeing one another again, or simply that he was my cousin, and deserved more respect that I was about to bestow. I raged.

"Go on then, you coward," I shouted, to my shame. "Leave me and Granddaddy here. I'll go find him. See if I don't."

With that, I turned from him, felt for the fence in the dark, climbed back over, and made for the woods that fringed the silent battlefield.

VI

UBI SUNT

I RECALLED MY PISTOL. Before I passed back into the woods, where Yankee pickets certainly would have posted by then, I stopped and, guiding myself by touch and by memory through the practice counseled by my grandfather, I loaded the Griswold & Gunnison. What feelings passed through me then I cannot tell. I thought of my father as I held this gift, and I thought of the town that had produced it, lately burnt to ash by the invaders. And I thought of my grandfather, wounded or prisoner of the Yankees, ahead where we had spent the day in battle. I finished loading the pistol. I had fired my rifle all day with no apparent effect, as if firing into an immovable fog. Perhaps now I could fight and kill the enemy on my own, in a daring rescue. I thought of Robin Hood stalking his forest, a yeoman fighting nobly against Prince John and Sir Brian, and rose and put my pistol into its holster and walked into the woods.

I crept along through the dark for some time. The waning quarter moon offered little help, and so I sometimes proceeded by feeling ahead with my hands and feet. I felt nonetheless like a buffalo crashing through the forest, so loud did every broken twig—I had, like all boys of that time, read Fennimore Cooper as well—and every stumble fall upon my ear. Surely I would alert some Yankee sentry to my presence. But I never did; I emerged from the woods near the place where I had first seen the enemy line that afternoon, just above the marshy creek.

I stood a few moments on the edge of the wood and looked out into the dark. My eyes, accustomed somewhat to the darkness of the woods, now made out the devastated and dimly moonlit field.

What snow remained there had been scraped and kicked into heaps and or smeared dark with the dragging away of wounded men. The slopes of the field lay littered with dark objects—broken rifles, empty cartridge boxes, blankets and haversacks emptied of food and spoils, and bodies. Across the field the Yankee line glowed faintly from the light of their cookfires, ribbing the vaults of the trees in red. A low murmur of voices came to me—the Yankees at their ease in victory. Angered again, and emboldened, I stepped out and began my search.

I thought of Cal, and where we had left him with our surgeon, and walked the edge of the woods to find the place. I heard no moaning or wailing to guide me, as they had during the battle, but it did not take long to find the place—a spot where the snow had been churned by shoes and writhing men into an expanse of lumpy black mud, now frozen. Even in the cold the place had the high copper stink of blood and of viscera and offal beyond description. But there were no men there, neither wounded nor dead, and not even the limbs sawn off and cast aside by the surgeon. I kept on.

I walked the edge of the woods for some time and found two other places where the wounded had gathered, both likewise abandoned. Alone in the cold, wandering the scene of such recent violence, I own I began to doubt my purpose. I remember standing in the blackened wreck of snow where another battalion's surgeon had worked and hugging myself and stomping my feet to warm them. I rubbed my face and blew into my hands. The fingerless gloves my mother had knitted and sent off with me during the summer had proven useful in work, drill, and battle, but during my wandering my fingers had gone numb. I pulled the pistol my father had given me from its holster, tested my grip, and thumbed the hammer back to half-cock, full cock, and lowered it. I put the pistol away and looked up the ridge. There, in the field not far from the enemy lines, I saw again the low dark shapes stretched and scattered across the face of the slope. I squinted at them, tried to stare them into compre-hension, and finally saw, raised above the dark masses, an arm with the fingers splayed wide, as if in greeting. The dead.

I swallowed. I had to find my grandfather, and Cal if possible, but I hated the very thought of searching among the dead for them. What if I should find them? And the line where most of the corpses lay—which ran across the slope to near the gully where we had ended the day—was barely fifty yards from the Yankee breastworks. I had penetrated the enemy's picket line; did I possess the daring to stalk right up to their works, to the position from which they had blasted our brigade to pieces that afternoon? Dare I risk capture, or death?

I settled my hand on my pistol. Yes, I dared. I must find my grandfather, or get some word of him and Cal and what the Yankees had done with them. I pulled my scarf up over my nose and mouth and blew into my hands once more, and then set off.

Ahead, the creek trickled quietly and invisibly, sheltered from the wan light of the moon by the lie of the land. I wended my way down the creek to find a place to cross without again soaking my feet or splashing and thus calling attention to myself. Our repeated crossings had flattened the already slow and marshy branch; thousands of brogans had stomped it into a wide and trickling morass. This mud had only partly frozen and therefore crunched underfoot. I crept even slower than before. At last, I found a narrow place, and jumped across. I slipped as I landed and fell headlong, and the fall knocked the wind out of me.

I lay sometime there in the dark and cold, trying to catch my breath and waiting to see if anyone had heard. None came. At last, I got to my feet and began the climb uphill.

I came across many black patches and streaks in the snow, and usually nearby a tangle of abandoned equipment—belts, boxes, pouches, haversacks, tent sections, bayonet scabbards—sometimes a tattered old hat, a home-spun blanket, a packet of letters, a pair of spectacles, a broken pipe, a Bible or prayerbook, bundles of sodden Georgia greenbacks, a photograph in a folding brass frame, or the entire contents of a pack in a pile, emptied and evidently rifled through.

I crouched as I approached the dead through their leavings. By the time I reached them, I went nearly on all fours. I had been closer to the Yankee line during the day, but now, in the cold, clear night, I could see it. I saw men sitting by the fires and men walking slowly back and forth. I saw at least one officer, walking with apparent purpose toward some task. Farther down the line, away to the right and left, I saw sentries, but they seemed slack at their posts; one glowed and darkened in gentle rhythm as he smoked a pipe. I screwed up my courage and made a final crawl to the firing line, to the first of the dead.

There were probably fifty of them nearby. I saw that these, while not precisely gathered for burial, had been neatened, a final dressing of the ranks for parade. I crawled from man to man along the line, toward the great collection I could dimly make out in the dark above the gully. The first man I came to lay under a Yankee blanket. His bare feet, blue with death, were the only visible part of him. I looked around and saw others under blankets, some barefoot, but most still in their brogans, which were so worn and holed that the Yankees did not want them. I took a deep breath and lifted the blanket from the man's face, but I did not recognize him. I did not recognize the next man either, or the next, but then I came to Captain Guerard. His swordbelt and boots were gone and his plain brown uniform coat had been shorn of buttons and rank insignia and lay rumpled open, with the blood-blacked shirt beneath exposed to the night. His moustache stood stiff with frosted sweat.

Nearby lay Private Greeves. Beyond I recognized the old man who had fallen into me, stunned, when the Yankees shot him. A score of strangers, and then I found, side by side, touching elbows as if in a pew, Peter and his grandfather.

I stopped over them. Peter's grandfather lay in his trousers and undershirt, without even the dignity of his galluses left to him. He had been shot high in the forehead, at the hairline, and I saw in the dark the white curve of bone where a quarter of the cranium had calved away. Peter lay fully clothed but for his belts, blanket roll, and haversack. His coat was tattered and bloodied in a dozen places. His eyes were closed and his mouth open in an attitude of beseeching agony. I turned away. My eyes burned—they welled and overflowed and I choked on a sob.

Someone behind me spoke.

"Well, hello there, Johnny."

I started and stumbled backward. There stood a Yankee soldier, the sentry with the pipe. He had his rifle at secure arms, prepared but not threatening. He chuckled and puffed a cloud of smoke.

"Didn't mean to startle you."

I sat too astonished to speak. I searched for words but my throat still had only sobs. I gabbled incoherently for a moment and stopped.

The Yankee grinned and peered at me. I looked him over as well. He wore a lank and much-patched overcoat and a forage cap weathered out of any shape. I saw in the glow of the pipebowl a young and lightly bearded face. He seemed amused when he looked at me and slung his rifle—a repeater, I noticed, though the full meaning of this did not come to me until much later.

"Come to surrender, have you?"

"No," I said.

"That's fine, that's fine. Spying, eh? Gathering intelligence what will help you rebs in planning another attack on the morrow?"

"No," I said, more confused than defensive.

"Well, come now—no need to sulk," he said. I noticed his voice, his accent: not terribly unlike my own, but a more nasal speech I had never heard, and he spoke with a quick, lilting cadence that gave his speech the foreignness of French or Russian. He puffed again at the pipe and looked at me gravely. "What brings you here? Back here, that is."

I gestured at the dead. I was fairly surrounded by now. "I'm—I'm looking for someone."

He nodded. "You find him?"

"No."

"There's a whole bunch more over that way."

He pointed with his pipe away to the right, where we had begun the attack. Perhaps that was why I had not seen Private Bell or Private Massey yet. How many gatherings of bodies like this were there on the field? And how could I search now, with this Yankee? I realized only then that the dread thing had happened—I had been caught.

My face drained of blood; I broke out in a cold sweat. The Yankee seemed to realize what I feared, and waved idly.

"Go on, Johnny. Have a look."

I regarded him with great suspicion for a moment, but when he made no movement to arrest or shoot me, I looked back to Peter and his grandfather's bodies. I felt I should do something for them, but was unsure what. I could not believe there was so great a gulf fixed between Catholic and myself that I could not pray for them. I ended up mumbling from the Burial of the Dead, the passage from St. John: "I am the resurrection and the life: he that believeth in me, though he were dead, yet shall he live: and whosoever liveth and believeth in me shall never die." I touched their hands, as I had seen the women of my family so often do at funerals. Farewell.

I continued my search. The Yankee followed at a short distance on the opposite side of the line of corpses, enjoying his pipe. After some time, unable to ignore him any longer, and in an absurd attempt to be polite, I offered conversation.

"You asked if I was coming to surrender."

"Yep."

"Y'all take many prisoners?"

"Oh, six or seven hundred. They was lining up to surrender there at the end. Couldn't take no more."

"The wounded?"

"Yep. Them what could move. Had to carry off probably fivescore." He pulled on his pipe, mulling something. He gestured with it; the glowing ember swept down through the dark at the end of his arm. "Course, some of them wounded wound up here."

I looked back to the dead and kept moving.

"You ain't going to pray over every one of them?"

"No."

"You knew them two back there, huh?"

"Yes."

"Come now—no need to sull up. We beat you fair and square."

I looked up from the dead man before me—a boy just a year or two older than myself, with half his blackened face shot away—and stared at him. He smiled as if with goodwill and puffed again on his pipe. This man was trying to goad me. I shook my head.

"Leave me alone, please."

"Afraid I can't do that."

I tried again to ignore him, but he lingered a few yards away as I searched. As I neared the end of this rank of the dead, I began to despair. If there were more dead, and hundreds of prisoners—now sent to the rear, I imagined, though they could not have been far away—I might never find my grandfather. And what is more, I had come back alone to search for him and Cal. Wes had mentioned, in warning, desertion. I had not even considered this charge when I determined to come back, but I remembered with a chill the dread penalties for desertion we had all heard of from Bragg's army, from other theatres of the war—the guilty facing the firing squad, seated on their own coffins. What had I done? Perhaps it was best if this Yankee took me prisoner. It was as I strove with this confusion, and with the compounding influence of my tormentor's presence, that I found my grandfather.

He lay somewhat apart from the rest; no blanket covered him. He had been shot through the upper chest—between the ribs and clavicle, very near the heart—at least twice. Rigor had already stiffened him; his head arched back as though trying to see the sky, and though his eyes were mercifully closed, his mouth stood open. His arms crooked upward at the waist and his hands hung stiffly in the air, clenched. He had lost his old slouch hat but his coat had been left him—it was so torn and bloodstained the greater part of it showed black in the thin moonlight—but it had been opened and rifled through. I saw that his watch was missing.

A sob came unbidden when I saw him, and I sought to choke it back. I fell to my knees beside him and tried to reckon with this. I shook my head and my eyes and cheeks burned with tears, my mouth dried out from gulping the cold night air in sobs. Some part of me had dreaded this, yet I could not believe that it was so. My grandfather was dead. Now I was truly lost. I tried to embrace him, but it was not my grandfather; that which had animated him was gone, absent from the body. I might have fainted, had not someone intervened.

"Found who you're looking for, I gather."

I had forgotten the Yankee in that long, terrible moment. I sobbed. I tried to collect myself, and shook my head.

"Leave me alone."

"I'm sorry, Johnny."

"Leave me be."

"Who is it?"

I sobbed again angrily. "My grandfather."

"Hm." He responded with interest but not sympathy. We might have been talking about politics, or the price of corn two counties over. For my part, I could not think of what to do now that I had found my grandfather. I could not possibly carry him away, but I could not leave him. I thought of my grandmother's death and the long watch through the night, that final duty owed by the living. I collected myself again, and reached into my haversack for paper and pencil. The Yankee tensed for a moment, reached down the stock of his slung repeater.

"What you aim to do there?"

I sniffed. I had, at length, produced a sheet of

wrinkled and damp stationery. "I'm writing his name and where we're from."

I had heard of such in rumor and the newspapers. A few bodies had made it home for proper burial in the family plot thanks to such tags, and so I scribbled *Lafayette Eschenbach, Danielsville Rd, Madison Co.* I looked for some way to affix the slip of paper to my grandfather's blood-darkened waistcoat, robbed of its watch chain. The Yankee spoke again.

"You expect us to ship him off somewheres for you?"

"No," I said. I did not much care what he and his ilk did, but would not give him the satisfaction of saying so. I folded the paper with the name facing outward and slipped it into the distended pocket that had once held my grandfather's tobacco pouch.

At that moment, the Yankee exhaled a cloud of sweet-smelling pipesmoke, and I hardened. My child-like sorrowing melted in the heat of a rage so profound I struggle still to recall, much less to describe it. Likely it was not this man who had spoiled my grandfather's corpse of his personal effects—his simple personal treasures like his watch, a gift from my grandmother, or his tobacco—but if not this man, then someone like him. He spoke again.

"We're going to be a mite busy yet to be shipping dead secesh home for burial. Might remember that."

I turned to face him. My movement must have been sudden, because he started, but did not otherwise react.

"Leave me be," I said again.

He sighed. "No."

"This ain't some 'dead secesh.' That's my granddaddy."

He seemed to weigh me, to calculate before going on. He puffed deliberately at his pipe, his eyes sparking red, and said, "You two fought with the secesh army against the Union, and now he's dead. I'd say he's dead secesh enough to warrant the description."

I rose and he stepped forward and shoved me back down. He tapped out the glowing ashes of his pipe and we regarded each other in darkness for a moment.

"I'm sorry," he said, and gestured to my grandfather. "I truly am. But you can't go rebelling against this glorious nation."

I looked back across the dark line of dead old men and boys—laid low on a hillside near a burnt out railroad town by the fire of repeaters—and back to the Yankee.

"Nation?" I had seen quite a bit of Georgia that year and had gotten some notion of it, and to see it suddenly presented by a stranger in opposition to this bigger and vaguer thing, this ghost—my mind sank into unfamiliar waters.

"The Union, Johnny," he said, as if to an imbecilic child.

"You think we deserved—"

"Come now, Johnny—like I said. You can't go following the slave power into rebellion."

"We don't even own slaves."

He jammed the darkened pipe into his pocket and stepped forward. "You think we give a God damn about the niggers? I joined up to preserve the Union. All of us did, from Uncle Billy on down. Shit on the nigger question. 'Down with the traitor, and up with the star.'"

At this I rose again and drew my pistol. The brass frame glinted in the wan moonlight and I saw the Yankee's eyes widen blue-white in the dark. He grabbed my gunhand and wrenched the pistol away, then thrust me back with both hands. I rose again and he pistol-whipped me. I stumbled backward over my grandfather's body and fell hard against the frozen ground. I gasped. My scalp and forehead burned and blood dribbled into my eyebrows. When I looked up, blinking it from my eyes, I expected to see the Yankee turning my own pistol upon me, and readied myself for it. The narrowing of the world that had begun that morning reached this point—that I did not care if I departed this world if I could at least avenge my grandfather. Such is the way of war.

Instead, when I looked up, I saw the Yankee, turning the pistol over in his hands as I had done when my father gave it to me.

"Well, son of a bitch," he said.

"Give me that back," I said.

He laughed, a single, derisive *Ha!* I stood again and he stepped forward, almost treading upon my grandfather's body, and pushed me down one last time. He did not even deign to menace me with the pistol this time. I was no threat.

"My daddy give me that pistol," I said from the ground. I felt tears start to my eyes—for the fall, and for my pistol, and for Griswoldville and Georgia and for my grandfather. I wiped them and the blood from my face. "Give it back."

"No," he said.

I cursed then for the first time. "God damn you," I said, half-sobbing, quavering with rage and sorrow and the certainty that I had lost everything. "God damn you to hell."

He looked at me and stuck my pistol into his belt. He knelt on the other side of my grandfather's body, leaned against his repeater like a staff, and glared at me. Away behind his fellows' breastworks, I heard a stirring, a questioning voice. I went cold all over again.

"You damned secesh think didn't none of you deserve this. Well, this here army is a machine, an engine, and you're the ones what started the boiler and you're the ones what stoked it up and set it going. Now it's riding down the rails and you're all running hell-bent for leather from in front of it screaming, 'I didn't own no slaves!' and 'We never beat our niggers!' And you're going to go on feeling sorry for yourselves and we're going to give you a whole hell of a lot to feel sorry for. You cannot betray this nation and get away with it. You think you ought to be spared because you personally happen to be righteous? Well, Johnny, it's a whole hell of a lot simpler than that. You threw in your lot with the wrong bunch. The Union forever. Death to traitors."

He stood and drew my pistol, thumbed the hammer all the way back to full cock, and aimed at me.

"I thank you for this fine pistol. Now get the hell on back to your ma."

I lay stunned, staring into the barrel of my own gun, its bore a deeper black than even the night around us. He stepped forward, over my grandfather's body.

"Get!"

More voices yet, distinct shouts and questions, calling from behind him, and dark figures moved along the breastworks, peering into the dark. I tried to get up. My forehead throbbed, my back ached from my falls, and my arms and legs seemed disjointed by fear. After what seemed a long hour of struggle he jerked me up by the back of my coat and thrust me away into the darkness. I felt my pistol thump against my back as he did so, and that is the last I ever saw of it, or my grandfather. I did not even get the chance to pray over him.

I PASSED THE LONGEST NIGHT of my life in the ruins of Griswoldville. I found my way back in the dark and, solitary, bereft, the militia having long since formed up and fallen back toward Macon, I found the remains of a corncrib near the ruined pistolworks and lay down there, huddled under my two blankets and my coat, and did not sleep. I dozed but, once unconscious, I dreamt as I once had of the sergeants who drilled us those long months past—I saw again the battlefield in daylight, and saw my grandfather's body again and again, and the Yankee, looming over me in the firelight, and woke with a start. I lay thus until the sky greyed and pinked with morning, and then, stiff and aching from the day before, and from the long, uncomfortable night, I rose and walked home.

I had no aim at first, no intention. So dejected was I that I did not even fold and pack my blankets. I simply stood up out of them and left them behind. I walked into the ruins of Griswoldville and beheld them a moment. There was the Griswold house, the Yankee factory man's home, which I had not been able to bring myself to sleep in, so much did it resemble the haunted houses of Dickens or the gothic novels I had read, and so much did it remind me of the Yankees who had vandalized it. They were yet near—they could return. I looked at the ruined railroad track and the burned train, and the now cold and sodden ashes of the factory proper. All lay cold and still as dawn broke. Away to the west lay Macon, now itself burned to ash for all I knew, and to the east our destination of the day before, Gordon, behind the Yankee lines. I did not know what had become of my regiment, or whether it could in any way be said yet to exist. I had seen my squad sergeant and company commander shot down, and a huge number of my fellows, and knew nothing of what had become of the rest. First Sergeant Sloane? Major Frady? The Englishman, or General Philips? Who was in charge, and where had they led the remnant? I sat down in the ruins and groaned. I was marooned in an alien country—my own home state, made strange to me. But at least I knew where home was, and, at last, I settled on the northward road. I left Griswoldville behind as the sun first lifted above the horizon.

I set out through the burned land, my empty holster flapping at my hip. I was a week or more on the road—I am still unsure how long it took me to walk home. The first day I spent alternately weeping and hiding from phantom cavalry, but saw only a few Negroes moving furtively through the woods, with a pig or two in their train and bundles on their backs, in the direction of the enemy's march. I passed twoscore farms not unlike my own, and a half dozen larger ones, and all lay abandoned and burnt, with slaughtered animals in the yards and the outbuildings and crops burnt to ashes. I spent that night in a one-room cabin that had been left untouched, and slept only out of exhaustion.

I saw more people the next days, both Negroes belatedly slipping away in the army's wake and

299

farmers, white trash and yeomen, emerging from hiding to see what remained. I saw all in passing—I was the only one on the roads.

I am to this day unsure of my precise route, but I wandered through at least seventy miles of devastation between Griswoldville and Covington. Much of the way I walked through ruined and plundered countryside. The refuse of the march littered the roads: cast off packs and haversacks, books, worn out shoes, broken equipment of every description, and the leavings of animals stolen and slaughtered on the hoof. Crows, buzzards and coyotes were busy. Even where the farms still stood, and had not been burned, no livestock or forage remained. Every place of machine work I passed—every gin, every sawmill, every smithy—lay burned and broken. I saw plowshares sitting blackened in the ashes of their frames and moldboards. No one was abroad in the fields, no one at work. The early winter slaughter approached, but in this swath across the broad back of the state, nothing whatsoever remained to slaughter. I passed several large plantations with the houses still standing, but bereft of all life, as dead as a tomb. I avoided the villages and towns but could see at a distance that most of those along my path had been put to the torch. I journeyed slowly, fearful of the dangers of the road. I did not expect to encounter a literal Procrustes or Polyphemus, but worried much about being waylaid by some modern analogue, and so slept out of doors. I had played at Robin Hood often enough as a boy; now, I went in fear of desperate men in the woods, of bandits. None appeared, but there were other dangers. I feared at first to be caught by Yankee cavalry and imprisoned—a fate I had only escaped through insulting indifference—or later to be caught by the home guard and shot for desertion. But I saw neither, and within a few days walked the roads with less caution, and with a growing number of wandering, stunned people.

I ate up the scant rations in my haversack and went hungry. I used what my grandfather had taught me and scoured the woods for signs of late-growing forage, but found nothing. Even nature had given us up. A few times other people, as needy as I, pitied me and gave me a bit of bread, or brought out and shared with me some sowbelly or bacon they had successfully secreted away from the bummers. I declined all offers of a place to sleep and sorely regretted abandoning my blankets.

I thought that the enemy must have struck at the capital, so I stayed west of Milledgeville. I passed Blountsville after a few days and, a day after that, what must have been Hillsboro, though I saw it at a distance from the woods as night fell. I passed the next night in an empty barn outside Monticello, and a few days later passed through Covington. It had been plundered and much of it burned about a week before, and the signs of it clearly remained. Women and children sheltered in leantos among ruined houses and stores. A few finer homes remained, with tents and makeshift shelters in the yards. There were throngs of people but very little noise. I recall it now as if it a dream, or a story told vividly by someone else, so strange was it.

I remembered Covington from the marches and railroad movements of the summer, and followed the tracks—torn up, twisted, burned, and wrecked—to Madison, which had been spared vandalism. The story put about today is of the town's beauty softening the heart of the enemy commander, whom I shall not name; the truth is that a Unionist politician used his connections to have the town spared. There seemed little sense of relief that the town had not been burnt—the survival of the buildings was moot. Everything around it lay destroyed; how long would the town enjoy its good fortune?

From Madison I walked through the wreckage of

the bummers and foragers to Union Point, now so hungry that I no longer felt it; where the ladies of the town had turned out to welcome the militia that summer, I was received by no one. The town was quiet; there were people about, but fewer of them, with no celebration, no help, no charity. From Union Point I turned northward, toward home.

I had left the paths of the enemy's army behind at Madison but the signs of his passing remained everywhere. The scavengers who plundered the farmers to feed his army had ranged far and wide. I walked a full day from Union Point before I left that ruined land behind. Even so, there were signs—like the inflammation of an infected cut. I had yet to escape these. When I left the road south of Lexington and sought a place to sleep for the night, I crept onto a farm and into a curing shed a good way from the house. It stood empty.

I ROSE BEFORE DAWN and snuck into the woods and back toward the road. I knew enough of where I was to pray I could make it home that day. The infantry had inured me to great amounts of walking and so I struck out at an eager route step.

I am unsure what day this was—though certainly, by now, the beginning of December 1864—but I recall what it was like: cold, clear, with a fine frost even in the dust of the road; in better times, good marching weather. And as I was furthermore back in the rolling hill country that marked my part of Georgia as home, I walked with ever greater recognition and correspondingly greater urgency. I abandoned my secrecy and walked directly through Lexington and made for Danielsville, then the rightward fork in the road that would bring me to the junction at Dawes's store, and then home.

I did not know what awaited me; I had heard nothing from my mother or any of my family for two months. My mother's delivery, that most dangerous of moments, was past, and I knew nothing of the result. On my walk back from Griswoldville I had begun to worry afresh. I had passed so many lifeless farms—would I find such when I returned?

My steady marching step hastened through the day; by early afternoon, when I passed the empty house and weed-grown fields of the former Neal farm, where my father and I had visited to deliver letters three years before, I had reached the doublequick. Not far on I caught sight of Dawes's store—closed, shuttered, so perhaps a Sunday? I hoped so—and broke into a run.

I dashed the last few miles home. This was not joy, but desperation—the root of which word, one must remember, is *despair*. I did not know what terrible news awaited me, and must find out. I left the road by the parsonage's apple orchard and dashed through the sanctuary of ranked trunks, overleapt the fence and down the hill through the woods to the creek that flowed beneath our farm. I saw the cow pond away to the left, and splashed through the creek and up the hill, through Mr. Hale's fields and onto the road. I saw the top of the shade tree ahead, and dashed madly, as in a nightmare, into our yard.

Here was everything I remembered from six months before, apparently not changed as so much of the state was—the shade tree, the house, the well, the garden patch, the outbuildings and sheds, and the fields stretching away in all directions. I halted and stared, looking for signs of life. The dreamlike state persevered—it seemed I waited a long time, though it must have been a matter of seconds. Then the door to the house opened and, not my mother, but my Aunt Laura appeared on the porch.

"Georgie?" she said.

She did well to ask. What a sight I must have presented—stooped in the yard, heaving for breath, having grown a few inches in the intervening months, and diminished by twenty or thirty pounds, hollowed out in the face and covered in the dust of the road. I am sure the creases of my skin were still blacked with gunpowder and soot, streaked clean by tears and restained by the blood and bruises of my pistol-whipping and the dirt of the road, and probably made me look forty years older than my fourteen.

Unable to speak, I nodded.

She clasped her face with both hands and cried out, and disappeared into the house. My brothers emerged instantly, as if from nowhere, and clapped onto me and did not let go for some time. They cried and laughed and sputtered questions all at once. Then, at last, my Aunt Laura came out with my mother, who carried my baby sister in her arms. They fell upon me, crying out, and embraced me. I let go and sobbed as I had not since the night on the battlefield.

They had many questions for me, but I recall only one: "What of Granddaddy?"

I could only sob anew, and shake my head, and this proved answer enough. Sorrow accompanied my return. What joy, and what weeping—I cannot describe it.

The rest of that day I recall only dimly. I met my sister, Joan, and learned that her birth went well; Mrs. Bower had midwifed, as planned, and Aunt Laura had assisted and stayed with my mother for the last two months to help, leaving my grandfather's farm in the care of a closely-watched hired man. Joan was a fine, beautiful girl—with a full head of soft, dark hair and large, dark blue eyes, a stare quick with interest and intelligence—and showed every sign of good health. My mother wept to see me, and to learn of her father's death, but immediately cooked me a meal and kept me at the table for hours. My brothers wept over my grandfather but, after a time, and once inside, nattered continuously and informed me of all that had come to pass since I had left. In the evening I washed—I fairly flayed myself with my scrubbing, so thick had the dirt, dust, sweat, blood, and powder residue accumulated—and dressed in clean clothes for the first time in months: a pair of my father's trousers, a pair of socks my mother had knitted for him, one of his good shirts, and one of his old coats. Thus newly attired, I fell into bed and slept.

DESPITE MY EXHAUSTION I woke sometime deep in the night. I think I had dreamt of the battlefield, or perhaps that I was not yet home, and could not abide it. I lay some time awake, and then sat up. My brothers did not stir, but slept the sound and untroubled sleep of boys. I heard the creak of the rocker behind the stove, and rose from bed.

My mother sat in her old place, with Joan at her breast. Her eyes shone in the dim light. She said nothing at first, but beckoned to me with one outstretched hand. I drew a chair over and sat beside her. She tousled my hair and smoothed my cheek, and I marked a minute flinch of surprise at the hint of beard about my chin. She sniffed and gathered herself, and looked to Joan, who suckled undisturbed.

"My firstborn, my Georgie," my mother said. "What has soldiering done to you?"

Love, pride, sorrow, and regret mingled in one voice and touched something within me. Tears started to my eyes, but I kept them at bay for the sake of the pride in her voice. We sat some further time in silence, and at length my mother sat Joan up, rested her at shoulder arms, and began to pat her on the back.

"Tell me what happened, Georgie. What happened to Daddy?" And, when I hestitated: "You tell me straight out. Don't spare me nothing."

I remembered her instruction to Private Keener, who had brought us news from Gettysburg, and knew she would tolerate no bowdlerized version. And yet, as I began, and elaborated upon the story, I found I could not myself tolerate some of its details. I told her about Macon, and our chance encounter with her brother-in-law, Thomas Crabtree, and the wait in the works outside the town, and the fateful march that ended at Griswoldville. I told her in what detail I could remember for the shock of the thing about the course of the battle, and how our squad and company and regiment were struck down around us on the sloping field before the Yankee lines. I even repeated the oft-employed likeness of the buzzing of hornets. But when I told her of Cal's wounding, I could not bring myself to describe his ruined face, or of our struggle to drag him down the hill with the Yankee balls still flying about us, or of the sound and smell of the makeshift hospital where we last saw him. And then, in the final attacks from the ravine, I gave out. I could not describe them, or the brigade's collapse, or what followed after.

I stopped. After a time, she nodded. Joan rested now in her arms, having slid down from her shoulder. Her comfortable infant snore gave rhythm and measure to our talk.

"What happened to Daddy? When?"

"There at the end."

"By the ravine?"

"I reckon so."

"What—what happened to him? How did he die?"

"They shot him."

"And Wes?"

"We run into each other back near the town, as the, the remnant rallied. He seen Granddaddy fall. I didn't."

She nodded. "What happened to Wes?"

I was some time answering. "I left him with the army. Went back to find Granddaddy and Cal."

"Did you?"

"I found Granddaddy. They captured Cal, or at least I reckon they did."

I guiltily braced for the next questions, the natural questions: *How did you find Granddaddy?* and *Where did you go after that?* and *What happened to the army?* and *How then did you come to be back here?* or merely *What then?* I thought of the way I had abused Wes and had in my turn been dealt abuse and robbery by the Yankee. But my mother said nothing. I could not stand the silence.

"I lost Daddy's pistol," I said. "They took it. Stole it from me."

She shook her head, and put one hand on my shoulder. She looked away, at nothing, for some time. I realized that dawn had come—the late grey morning light of early winter brightened the windows. Somewhere animals stirred and birds chirped, the sound of a farm awakening and girding for a day of work. My mother patted me. I was afraid to look at her after the story I had just related; when I did, I saw tears running silently over her cheeks so that her whole face shone with the early morning light.

"That's enough, Georgie. That's all right. Now get you some sleep."

I HAD RETURNED JUST IN TIME to help with the slaughter, which I took over. Even this station of the farm's year was changed. The State of Georgia and the government of the Confederacy had taken much through requisition, including two cows and our mule Herod. This year's slaughter was the work of a long morning, rather than the daylong affairs of years past.

I appointed James and Jefferson to tasks and my mother and Aunt Laura and Aunt Ellen—newly apprised of my return, and of my grandfather's death— with Jeremiah and Caroline came to assist them with the scalding and scraping. When Aunt Ellen asked, with visible trepidation, after Wes and Cal, I told her as soberly and tactfully as I could of their whereabouts and condition. I realized I did not know much. She accepted the news stoically, and we bent to our work. I drove the hogs and wielded the ax and, when James and Jefferson tired, I even slashed the hogs' gullets myself. The next day, my mother brewed a pot of coffee—she had preserved a tin against the day my grandfather might return, and ended up making it for me—and we walked to Uncle Quin and Aunt Ellen's farm, and did the same.

The work was as unpleasant as ever, the smell especially. Blood, urine, excrement, the smoke of the fire, the contents of the hogs' guts, the scalded skin and burnt hair—all reminded me of the ruined town and of the battlefield, but I hardened myself to finish the task. By the third day of slaughter, I had grown almost numb to it, but here there lay new hardships, for the third and final slaughter of the year was at my grandfather's farm.

With another cup of coffee in our stomachs to begin the day, my brothers and I set out. I was unprepared for this. The house, though visibly unchanged, seemed as emptied of spirit as his body had on the dark battlefield, as if it had known and given up some vital part of itself to participate in and complete his death. We entered and Aunt Laura fed us a thin breakfast in the sepulchral kitchen. As I ate, I cast my eye about the house, at all the things now bereft of an owner— an old hat he had left at home, boots, a couple of pocket knives, a spare pipe, and his books: the family Bible, Dr. Gunn's *Domestic Medicine*, *Ivanhoe* and *The Last Days of Pompeii*, Æsop and the *Lays of Ancient Rome*. There were more; a modest library but a dear one, and I realized only then that I should never hear him read to us again, and that, furthermore, there stood a gap between the Bible and *Domestic Medicine* where his *Book of Common Prayer* should stand, but would never return. I had not even thought to search for it among his things when I found him. Both it and the pistol were lost.

I sat suddenly awash in bitterness, and broke down crying at the table. When Jeff asked what was wrong, I shouted at him to mind his own business. And then, upon seeing his wounded expression, and thinking of the way I had attacked and impugned Wes that night after the battle, I went out, and wept bitterly.

My Aunt Laura had hired Joseph, one of the

311

MacBeans' Negroes, to keep the farm while she lived with my mother, and with his help we penned the hogs and went about our work. I worked with the ax in silence. I cannot say what happened that day, but I thought a great deal—of my father and grandfather, of my mother and brothers and, now, my baby sister— and by the time we had done and were washing the gore away, I had purposed to myself never again to lose my temper, to scorn or abuse my brothers or any man, and to behave toward them as my grandfather would have wanted.

In the battlefield shambles of the yard after the hours of butchery, hanging, gutting, scalding and scraping, as we washed over the steaming tub while our breath hung in the air, I asked Jeff to forgive me my sharpness. He did, and gladly.

That evening, as Aunt Laura fed us again, I asked her if I could borrow my grandfather's volume of Macaulay.

She nodded and thought an unusually long time for such a request. At last, she gathered herself and said, "I reckon you can have it, Georgie. Take any books you want. He'd have wanted you and your brothers to have them."

So I acquired the first books of my own.

That night, I read from the *Lays* to my brothers, mother, and sister before bed, with many heartfelt pangs as I did. Horatius proved more poignant than I remembered. From that evening onward I read to them every night until I left home for the University in Athens. Joan learned to read from Æsop and the *Lays*, and from other books I slowly acquired through my share of the paltry earnings of the farm, perhaps three per year. But they were a comfort and a guide, and such we sorely needed in those years.

MY UNCLE QUIN RETURNED in February. We learned via a boy sent running from Dawes's store, and immediately set out on foot to see him. I dreaded the moment he should ask after Wes and Cal, but purposed with myself to tell him as plainly as possible what I last knew of them. As it turned out, we would talk about much harder matters.

When we arrived at the farm, we saw the family sitting around Uncle Quin on the porch steps despite the cold. He sat with one leg stretched out and a crutch lying against the stairs within easy reach. Even at a distance I could see how much he had aged—it had been three and a half years since we had seen him. He sat patting their old bulldog, the beast calmer now with length of days, and seemed content to be home, but as soon as he looked up and marked who it was approaching, he lost all composure and held his face in one hand as if he could thus hold back sobs and cries. I should have known then, but held on to a hope that he would give us better news than he had brought. My mother, for her part, seems to have known from the moment the boy arrived saying that Quin had returned.

My father was dead, killed in the assault at

Franklin, Tennessee, two months previous, while I was yet walking home from Griswoldville. My uncle swung between weeping and rage as he described it to us, sometimes shouting through his tears. He was a man undone. I am astonished now that he had made it home in such a state, but one must never doubt a man's capacity for bottling things up.

They had deployed and gone into the attack, he told us, against prepared Yankee works, with crossfires and artillery—exploding shells, bouncing solid shot, canister, and finally double canister. For all its horrors, I realized, we at Griswoldville had at least been spared artillery. The army had advanced in brilliant order, flags flying, drums beating, and been shot to pieces, blown away by the force of Yankee musketry and blast after blast of canister. The corpses had lain in stacks on the field. My Uncle Quin had been shot through the meat of the upper thigh and lain recovering for a month; later, I examined his horrible wound: a Minié ball had torn through his left quadriceps, leaving a pair of dark indentations puckered with waxy scar tissue, a wound that never fully healed in his lifetime. As soon as he had fallen, my father had stooped to help him and been struck down, torn apart by a cloud of canister. As he had been carried to the rear and only narrowly avoided capture, despite his wound, my uncle did not know what had become of my father's body. Despite some years of searching, three visits to the battlefield, and inquiries with other surviving members of his regiment, we have never located it.

Now we truly mourned. We were doubly bereft; it was even as if my grandfather had died a second time. My mother put on mourning and tried for a time to rename first Joan and then herself Marah, but I—with the help of Aunt Laura and Aunt Ellen—did not allow her to do that. How I recall her sitting up with the baby in the night, weeping in silence, praying for mercy for her orphaned children. In time she recovered but, though still young and beautiful, never remarried.

"Somehow I knew," my Aunt Laura told me about this time, one night after we had seen my grieving mother to bed and were cleaning up the house.

"Knew?" I said.

"That your daddy was gone, too, yes." Then, imperiously, as Queen Laura, she braced herself and told me: "Not too long after you come home, I had a dream. We were all sitting down to eat at this big table, and Daddy—your granddaddy—was sitting alone down near one end. And then your daddy come in, and your granddaddy stood up and smiled at him and brought him around and set him down next to him at the table. Nobody said a word the whole time, but we were all happy as could be. Then we just kept on eating until I woke up from it."

For my part, I have dreamt of my father and grandfather over the years, and have been, by turns, grieved and comforted by such, but I have never longed for a dream the way I did that night when I lay down beside my brothers to sleep.

THE WAR ENDED and its result caused no surprise among us, but it was also a matter of little interest by that time. We worried more and more about food, and worked hard to avoid starving. The blessing of the war's end was the return of hands to farms which lay in want of them, though it took some time to recover. Beginning in May, a few weeks after the surrenders in Virginia and North Carolina, the terminus of the enemy's path of destruction through our state and the Carolinas, the roads first trickled and then streamed with men returning home. I can hardly describe what ragged figures they were; the war had not just consumed lives and property, but these men's bodies.

Among those returning, at last, came Wes and Cal singly. Cal arrived first, having recovered from his wounds and been released from captivity. He had walked all the way home. He was disfigured; the shot that had struck his face had stove in his left zygomatic bone and resulted in a misshapen cheek and eyesocket and a permanent black eye. A thick white scar, a fimbriation to the wound, edged this disfigurement. Though he still showed his former piety and good humor when in company—he joked that, thanks to the war, one need never confuse him and his twin brother again—he became in after years more solitary. He went on long walks through pecan groves and up and down the road to Danielsville with his succession of dogs and neither married nor fulfilled his boyish aspiration to become a preacher, but helped his father with the farm until Uncle Quin's death—of complications including pneumonia from his leg wound—fifteen years later.

Wes came home as we finished the late spring sowing. He was sound in mind and body, having passed, like me, through his part in the war without a scratch. I learned from those that spoke to him about it that he had rejoined the militia in Griswoldville that night and they had marched back toward Macon, before moving south in an attempt to get around the enemy in that direction. This maneuver failing, he found himself captured on the coast of Georgia near Savannah. He had no word of Cal or myself until he returned home. He set to work with us on the family farms the day after his return. He had also—in a final act of wartime requisition—brought back a mule which he had acquired in some way from the US Army, and it proved a great boon to all our farms.

Thus reunited, albeit incompletely, we continued on. We were too busy and too near starvation for the kind of reflection common nowadays, and too much had changed. There was fear for a time that our farm would be confiscated and given away, despite our having never owned slaves—a defense I had learned was inadequate in the face of the wrathful "nation." But nothing came of this fear. Thomas MacBean returned from the war mortally wounded, borne home in the bed of a cart, and died there as the summer turned to fall, having never risen from his bed. This left Pritchard the owner of their plantation, and ushered him into manhood already ruined; for Emanci-

317

pation had deprived them of all but their land and tools, and even the use of these Pritchard found himself bound to negotiate with the Freedman's Bureau, so that the land would not lie unused and the former MacBean Negroes would have work and a place to live. The plantation was divided among those that had remained—old Chapman's two sons and Pritchard's servant Anchises among them—and sharecropping has not departed since. My own brother James spent the last thirty years of his life sharecropping twenty-nine acres of MacBean land. Thomas and Pritchard's cavalry sabers were broken off to about a cubit in length for butchering hogs.

I bring Pritchard and his family into this narrative because he eventually became my family, to my lasting surprise. I have mentioned my infatuation with his sister Eliza. We had by this time become acquainted, and two years after the war's end, at a fall dance, we had our first true conversation.

I recall so much from these years so murkily—the war, for all my youth, stands out starkly against it—but that evening I recall as vividly as if it were yesterday. She wore an outmoded but well-kept dark green dress; her auburn hair, still lightened to a true red by the summer sun, and her freckles stood out brilliantly in contrast, and her lighter green eyes fairly glowed with merriment. I noticed her immediately when she arrived, and when she by happenstance wound up standing next to me by the punchbowl, I, in an even older suit that had belonged to my father and that still did not properly fit, felt like a mortal stumbling into a thicket where a goddess rested, or like a knight granted a vision of the Grail. I stood dumbstruck. She spoke to me, and as we talked, in my embarrassment I fumbled into allusions to the Knights of the Round Table and the heroes of Greek legend. I recall—I am embarrassed even in the remembering of it—offering a lame comparison of the fiddler to Orpheus. She knitted her fine red brows—with interest, as I would realize later—and asked about my literary tastes. I am certain I gave a fumbling answer, but the great virtue of ladies is their mercy, and despite all she talked to me with interest for the rest of the evening. We ended by my asking her permission to write her.

"Oh, you'll have to ask my brother about that, Mister Wax," she said, with frightening mock earnestness. "But yes."

I did ask Pritchard. He was no dancer, but attended as one of the sponsors of the festivities, and stayed mainly for the punch, of which he had drunk plentifully that night. I recall him sagging against the wall with one of his overseers and a few of the white sharecroppers—some of them twenty years his senior—and how his eyes lost their glaze when I asked. He stood up straight as if prepared to rebuff me, but then something passed across his face, he reconsidered, and he nodded, saying, "I'd be pleased, Georgie, for you to write my sister."

At that, I glanced back at her from across the dancing hall, to see her watching me. She smiled, and her eyes danced, an expression she has retained well into old age.

We corresponded. I was but seventeen—what seems to me now an absurdly young age—but we shared many interests and she was a pleasant and encouraging writer. She helped me acquire more books, and lent me many from her late father's library, and this formed the latter stage of my education. Within a year of our talk at the dance we wrote each other daily, and Pritchard would often have me over for Sunday dinners, and courteously included my family in these invitations. These meals were the best we ate for ten years. He was instrumental as well, through his late father's connections, and thanks to the intercession of

Eliza, in my admission to the University of Georgia and thus my becoming a doctor. Eliza and I were married as soon as I was graduated, and after plenty of further study and work, I had a firmly established practice and a farm of our own.

This work kept me often on the roads I had walked with my father and grandfather, and ministering to people I had known all my life. I worked myself to exhaustion in a whooping cough outbreak that passed through the county, and helped the many war wounded, Cal and my Uncle Quin among them, through their years of healing. I delivered I know not how many infants of the neighborhood, black and white, over the decades following. This became my greatest joy—to bring into the world a child, and to hand him over to a mother already forgetting the travail through which she has just passed, and remembering no more the anguish. I worked hard to improve the chances of these children and mothers living beyond that hour, and pray to have succeeded.

Eliza and I had five children of our own, all of whom survived to adulthood, and all of whom married and have children of their own; Lafayette, John, MacBean, Rebecca, and Mary Walter. I have striven hard to provide in the way my father first entrusted me in the summer of 1861, and the way my grandfather told me on that night in 1864. I pray to have done right by them and by my wife, children, and grandchildren, out of gratitude for these blessings. My brother James married Constance Magruder, a cousin of the white trash boy my grandfather and I met on the road to Dawes's store that morning long before, but she proved quarrelsome and they had no children, and he willingly gave up the farm to my brother Jeff to prevent its passing into her family's hands. Jeff married our cousin Bit, and had seven children and many grandchildren. My sister Joan grew into a lively and joyful woman, and was a great comfort to my mother through the years after the war. She married a haberdasher in Athens, a fine man with whom she had six children, and my mother moved in with them and lived there, surrounded by grandchildren and visited often by her three living sons, until her death in 1900. We buried her in the Barber's Chapel cemetery, within sight of the farm. Joan lives yet in Athens and while we see each other less and less often as the years accumulate, we write regularly—this joy in reading another gift from my grandfather. Wes married not long before Uncle Quin's death and had four sons, whom I do not know well because he and his family moved to Texas and only seldom returned. Wes died of cholera in Galveston six years later.

Though Wes and I wrote often after his move to Texas, we last spoke together a month after his father's funeral, in late November of 1880. I had just turned thirty and our fifth child had was but a month old, so when, after a large family dinner at Aunt Laura's farm, the men sat down on the porch to drink and smoke and pass the afternoon in idle talk, I had little to say of any use. At length, without preamble, as had become his way, Wes said:

"Well, it's decided. We are to move to Texas."

I sat up with a start, wrenched out of my reverie. "Texas?"

"Yes."

"Whatever for?"

Cal stood, ground out his cigar, and walked off to a stand of peachtrees he favored for their shade. Wes puffed his cigar. "Cal disagrees with my decision."

"I can't blame him," I said. "Why should you uproot and move there?"

"Signs are favorable."

"What signs? Do you mean to dowse your way to Texas?"

Wes laughed.

"It's not that bad here," I said. "Not compared to some places. You should see things around Atlanta, or—" I struggled for a way to put it. "Or anywhere between there and Savannah. Just poor whites and even poorer colored folks, climbing over each other to grow cotton in soil they've turned to powder."

"White trash and niggers, still working for the carpetbaggers," he said. "It may not be that bad but it's not that good, either. I've done all I can short of murder to raise ourselves up in the world but ain't nothing took. There's room in a place like Texas."

I had suspected Wes of nightriding during the heyday of that activity ten years before, when the state still lay under military dictatorship and it seemed every decision had to pass through a dozen Yankee bureaucrats, but this was as close as he ever came to an admission of that kind. I regarded him a moment, and puffed at my pipe.

"There's better things than rising up in the world," I said.

"Well, you can say so. You done it."

"You know what I mean. Here we can rise up together, help each other. It's the only way we got through the war."

"I know."

I watched Cal pottering about at the end of the yard and realized suddenly that Wes and I sat alone in the cool autumn air, and that the last time we had talked thus may well have been that night outside Griswoldville. Guilt overwhelmed me. I tapped out my pipe and held my face in my hands.

"Aw, Texas ain't that far away," Wes said.

"It ain't that." I turned to look at him, and he knew; he remembered. "That night, when I went back for Granddaddy—"

"No. You didn't do nothing wrong."

322

"What I called you."

He shook his head. "Things had been just a little different, it would've been me yelling at you."

I searched his face. I recall this well; it was the last time we spoke alone. He softened somewhat; the calcified mask fell away. He set down his cigar and leaned forward.

"I wish I'd gone back," he said. "What happened?"

I told him, in every detail, the only time I ever did so for anyone until I set pen to paper this last year. When I had finished, he sat back and picked up his cigar, but it had grown cold and I struck a match for him. We sat a while. As if sensing that Wes's move was no longer the topic of conversation, Cal reappeared and started back.

"That's pretty much it," I said at length.

"I always wondered what become of that pistol."

"Me too."

"You don't need to apologize for that night. You've more than made up for it."

"Made up for it?"

Wes laughed again, and smoke enfolded him. "And you don't even know it. Look at this family, and our farms—still in the family. That's thanks to you. What a rock you've become as a man, George Wax."

"It isn't like that. I had plenty of help."

"You know what I mean," Wes said.

"Well," I said at last, "it's what Granddaddy would have wanted."

"Our daddies, too."

I agreed.

Following that talk, I retained only one regret, which was that my children, and even my sister, would never know my father or grandfather. But such is life—we are here for a little while and then vanish away—and we were by no means alone in that regard, in the years following in our orphan state of Georgia.

A FINAL DETAIL: One morning a few years after the war, just as I was beginning to court Eliza, I received a parcel at Dawes's store. I had placed, some months before, an order by mail for some item wanted on the farm—I cannot now recall what. The parcel I received proved unexpectedly small, and in my surprise I opened it then and there before the store where the old men of the neighborhood still gathered to whittle and chew, and I nearly collapsed when I saw what had come. Inside were the tintype photographs that Thomas Crabtree had made in Macon, of myself and my grandfather.

It was like the visitation of a ghost. I had forgotten about the photographs in the intervening years, and to see my grandfather's face again, with the life restored to those piercing eyes, was a shock. We both looked hollowed out, ragged, malnourished even by the standards of Georgia after the war, and my grandfather looked astonishingly old—far older than I remember him—but we also seemed peaceful and confident in our arms. There sat my grandfather; a wry ghost of a grin blurred one corner of his mouth—seeing it, I could almost hear the raspy chuckle that always accompanied it—and he sat with one arm cocked on his hip the better to show his corporal's stripes. And there sat I, with my rifle and, lain across my lap, with the brass frame catching the light, my Griswold & Gunnison revolver, my father's gift.

I showed them to my mother, who tearfully kissed them both and set them on the mantle, like icons. There they remained through many years, images to remind us who knew them, and to teach those who did not, until my mother took them with her to Athens, and finally the one of my grandfather passed to me. Somewhere between the war and my mother's death, the one of myself was lost.

VII

POST

I SHOULD LIKE TO PROVIDE some details of the provenance of the preceding memoirs by my grandfather, the late Dr. George Wax, MD, of Madison County, Georgia. I am his grandson, Alexander Wax, by his third son MacBean.

My mother discovered the manuscript in a drawer of my grandfather's desk following his death last year. We had no previous knowledge of its existence. It seems he worked on it during his spare time at his office in Danielsville, and kept it there, with the result that it was not discovered until some time after we had gone through his personal papers at home. My grandmother had understood him to be working on something, but assumed it was a booklength version or compilation of his newspaper columns on home medicine, and read it with great interest before she, too, passed away last year. My grandfather, after reading the true texts of Shakespeare's plays as a man, had a great hatred of bowdlerization, and so I publish his manuscript here unexpurgated.

We found it an astonishing manuscript, both in what it included and in what it excluded. His mention of his medical career is altogether too humble, but that is in keeping with his character as we knew him. He studied, worked, and corresponded with men like Dr. Long, another Madison County native, and Atlanta's Mr. Pemberton, another veteran of the war. He met the great Negro scientist Dr. Carver twice, and used some of the latter's farm bulletins to improve the yield and quality of the family farms and vegetable gardens. He even exchanged a few letters across the Atlantic with the esteemed Lord Lister in an effort to refine the principles of antiseptic surgery. He was the most trusted doctor in three counties, and the only doctor the Negroes of the area, especially the tenants of the old MacBean place, would call for. His reputation for saving expecting mothers in danger preceded him, and brought him to the attention of Mr. Grady of the *Constitution*, who asked him to write a weekly newspaper column on medicine which, despite his grave misgivings about Mr. Grady, his calls for industrialization and Yankee commerce, his politics, and newspapers in general—a host of distrusts he never gave up—my grandfather sustained faithfully for thirty years, and regarded a God-given opportunity to help people beyond the reach of his housecalls. He used these media to help country people refine home remedies, rid themselves of ineffectual or harmful folk remedies, and more readily accept true medical treatments. So much he neglected to mention.

My grandmother—to say nothing of the rest of us—read his manuscript with interest because my grandfather said almost nothing about his experience of the war. We all knew he had fought in the militia and had seen combat, which many of us mistakenly assumed had been in the battle for Atlanta or perhaps Chickamauga, but he spoke only of the war in general or even strategic terms, demonstrating a great understanding of those, and avoided veterans' reunions. This silence had the effect of heightening the mystery surrounding his military service, as I see now that it had for his own grandfather's history. That he should not have spoken of these things to a youth like myself may be understandable; that he did not to his wife, his beloved Eliza, was even more astonishing.

Nevertheless, I did learn some things about his time in the war, and of the effect it had upon him. In addition to the occasional allusion over Sunday dinner, or in relating one of his many stories about his grandfather—one would have thought they spent decades together, rather than the fourteen years allotted them—I recollect three interesting incidents from my own childhood with him, which I shall recount here along with a sketch of my grandfather as I knew him.

He was a tall, plainspoken but courteous man who had the gentleness to deliver a baby or play with his infant grandchildren and the strength to set bones and work his farm. He loved biscuits, chicken mull, and peanuts. He weakened but never stooped with age, and his eyes remained good to the end. He dressed sharply for the office and housecalls but preferred plain clothes—dungarees particularly in the last decades of his life—for working and loitering about home, which sometimes drove my grandmother to affectionate distraction. He was generous to a fault; he lent his brother, my great uncle Jeff, the money to invest in a textile mile Pritchard MacBean intended to build with an association of Yankee industrialists, and thus helped Jeff to establish himself comfortably, though he would have nothing to do with the mill or its profits himself. He read constantly; my earliest memories of him are of sitting in his lap with a book open to some Rackham illustration of knights and ladies. Kingsley's *Hereward the Wake* was by then a great favorite of his, and he read to us as well all the books his grandfather had before the war. From him and his stories, much more than anything he ever said to me, I learned that there is true nobility in the world, but it is to be found neither in pious stories, whether true or not, of General Lee lifting baby birds back to their nests, nor in the inglorious modes of modern war, which has been stripped of right in the name of victory. He taught me yet more in the few times I remember learning about his experience in the war directly.

The first incident I recall came when I accompanied him to a lunch of chicken mull one fall at a church outside Danielsville. I was perhaps nine years old at this time. I had looked forward to the outing, not only for the food, but for the company of my grandfather, much the way he describes himself in his manuscript. We made many such excursions together when communities made pots of mull, but I recall this time because of what I learned about him.

When we had gathered on the grounds of the church, with the sweet smell of the chicken mull in the air, I sensed that my grandfather was searching for someone or something, and then that he had found it. I followed his glance and saw an old man with one leg and a battered pair of crutches seated on a bench near the mull pot. He seemed to see us in that moment, too, and my grandfather took my hand and we walked over together.

"Georgie Wax," the man said. "I'll be darned. You got my letter."

I looked at my grandfather. I had only ever heard close family use this name for him; never a stranger. To strangers he was only ever—with a great deal of admiring deference—"Dr. Wax."

My grandfather smiled and they shook hands. "Hoyt Burrell. I'm pleased to see you."

I brightened. He did seem pleased. My grandfather

introduced me, and I greeted him as Mr. Burrell. Mr. Burrell extended his hand and we shook, and, though I stood respectfully by, I let my mind wander immediately, as I foresaw a long conversation between these two old men. I looked at this Mr. Burrell. He was missing his left leg from high up near the hip. This in itself was unremarkable—there were many maimed men still about in those days, and many of them were my grandfather's patients. He behaved familiarly with my grandfather, and my grandfather spoke to him with agreeable warmth, the tone I understood adults to use with old friends.

Suddenly, Mr. Burrell turned to me and leaned forward, balanced on his one leg, and said, "Your granddaddy saved my life, you know."

This, too, did not strike me as remarkable; I had had lots of people tell me, in the roundabout way people brag on each other to children, how much my grandfather had helped them.

"No, sir," I said. "I didn't know that."

"Me and your granddaddy was in the war, you know."

Now I stared, which I knew to be impolite. All I had known up to that point was that the war had occurred long before my grandfather was a doctor. I tried to recover my courtesy. "Pardon, Mr. Burrell?"

He patted the stump by his hip and nodded to my grandfather. "Your granddaddy here helped drag me out when I got shot all to pieces by the Yanks. Lost the leg but here I am, right as rain, fifty years later."

I looked at my grandfather. He had his polite face on, but I detected embarrassment around the edges. All he said was, "That's right, Alexander."

They spoke more, and spent hours catching up over their bowls of mull. My grandfather inquired after Mr. Burrell's uncle—an allusion I now understand—and seemed pleased to learn that he had, after all, survived the war and died aged 100, cussing the Yankees and the Republican Party. Mr. Burrell himself had learned to read, after a fashion, and employed himself as a carpenter near Ila. He had three children and sixteen grandchildren, most of them sharecroppers or mill-workers, poor but honest folk. At this, Mr. Burrell lost his composure somewhat; I well remember my childish discomfort to see an old man so emotional. I was doubly embarrassed when he turned once more to me.

"And wouldn't none of that have happened without your granddaddy here."

On our way home in the dusk, holding my grandfather's hand, I asked him about Mr. Burrell and the war. He would only say that what Mr. Burrell had said was true, but did not elaborate. The last I remember him saying about it was, "We were both of us very young. I was fourteen," which, to a nine-year old, did not seem so very young.

The second incident occurred some years later, in church, and was the most explicit and detailed thing he ever said about the war in my presence. This was at the time of the Great War, of which my grandfather thoroughly disapproved; I would estimate June 1918, so that I was then just fifteen years old.

It was time for Communion; the preacher had just concluded his sermon and was preparing to administer the eucharist. I was seated six feet away from my grandfather, with only my mother, grandmother, and Aunt Joan between us, so I had an excellent view—and retain a vivid memory—of what occurred next. A man in a fine suit, with his hat in his hands in what even I recognized as an attitude of false humility, rose near the back and begged the reverend for a moment, just a moment of the congregation's time. This proved less a request than an announcement, for he launched imme-diately into a speech, which he delivered to us as he walked down the aisle toward the altar, turning this way and that to address us with a practiced air. He was one of the "Four-Minute Men" of the Committee on Public Information, recruited to drum up support for Mr. Wilson's war against the Germans. It was a rousing speech, delivered in dramatic style, invoking Nurse Cavell and the crucified Canadian and the children of the *Lusitania* as a chorus calling the Christian people of our nation to rise to the divinely ordained mission against the pagan Hun.

But it did not last quite the full four minutes, for my grandfather—who had never, so far as I could recall, spoken a word out of turn during a church service—stood and interrupted the man.

"That will be quite enough, sir," he said. "This is a house of God."

I remember the tension; the "mouthpiece of Democracy," as the Four-Minute Men called themselves, and my grandfather, the respected local doctor, with the full weight of his years and expertise and reputation behind him, staring at each other across the sanctuary. The government man recovered himself somewhat and said:

"I'm afraid you misunderstand me, sir."

"I do not," my grandfather said. "I am telling you to leave, and to take your false god with you."

"Do I take you to mean our glorious nation, which God has called to vanquish His enemies?"

My grandfather seemed to brace himself; the pew in front of us creaked where he gripped its back. This was the only time I recall ever seeing him really angry.

"I was with the Georgia militia during the March to the Sea, sir, when we met the enemy and were shot to pieces, so I reckon I know what 'the nation' will require of us. It is a jealous god and hungry for its sons to be passed through the fire. So take it with you out of this house of worship and kindly do not return."

The government man did not seem to know what

to make of that, or of the talk of the March to the Sea—this was already ancient history to the rising generations—and he looked beseechingly to the minister, who said nothing. So he tipped his hat and walked out. Some scurrilous attacks on my grandfather's character as "unamerican" and "pro-Hun" followed in letters to local newspapers, but with no result upon anyone who had once made his acquaintance. He carried on with his columns and his practice.

Nevertheless this new war did leave its mark upon our family. My cousin Lafayette, called "Fayette" by us, volunteered. He was three years older than I, who could not enlist (though I realize now that I was older than my grandfather at the time of his battle), and the younger cousins like me envied him. His father, my great uncle Jeff, intended to send him to the University in Athens and had grown immensely angry. Together with my grandfather, who approached Fayette with greater gentleness than Uncle Jeff could then manage, they tried to dissuade him, but to no avail; Fayette had gotten the bug, to do his duty to the nation against some other nation.

"Tell me, Fayette," my grandfather once said to him, "what is this 'nation?' You can know your home, and perhaps Georgia, but you can't know a nation."

"You just need to broaden yourself, broaden your mind," Fayette said. "Farms and country stores— they're going away. This is the age of industry, of science, of great nations striving against each other for Progress."

"You take a job in the mill then," Uncle Jeff said, "see how you like industry. Or try sharecropping, like your Uncle James."

Fayette burst out, "This is the twentieth century, for God's sakes!"

Uncle Jeff said, "Don't you talk back to us that way! You ain't above a little hard work."

My grandfather quieted him. "Steady, Jeff. And do try to avoid saying anything you'll regret later, Fayette. I know you've got ambitions. But what of my original question?"

"Like I said, we—we're too narrow, too close-minded," Fayette said. This *we* was a Southern instinct, much remarked-upon and therefore surely noticed by my grandfather, to avoid offense by encompassing oneself in an accusation. What Fayette meant was *you* are too narrow, *you* are too close-minded. "Our nation will not be great without unity, and unity will give us the strength to beat the Hun and make the world safe."

"From the nation to the world, now," my grandfather said, and smiled, and left it at that. Fayette would not be swayed. He died of the influenza in an Army hospital in France in January 1919.

The final incident I will relate occurred about five years thereafter, on what I now realize was the 60th anniversary of the Battle of Griswoldville.

I was now twenty, my grandfather seventy-four, nearly ten years older than his own grandfather at the time of his death. He asked me if I could do him the favor of driving him and keeping him company for a day. I answered that I would gladly do so, and he fixed a date and time to depart—before dawn on November 22—and a destination—Macon.

This was a Saturday, and the roads were crowded with automobiles. My grandfather distrusted these conveyances as loud, dangerously fast, and less companionable than a mule or horse, and he had never learned to drive one, but seemed to enjoy watching the countryside roll past in the hours it took us to drive down.

We lunched in Macon. I remember him remarking offhand that he found the city "much changed," and when I asked when he had last been to Macon, he smiled and said, "A good while ago." In the afternoon, he directed me to the Indian mound across the Ocmulgee, and to Fort Hawkins, both sites he said his grandfather had taken him to as a boy. But as we toured these places I noted a growing melancholy and distraction passing over him, and finally we climbed into the car and he pointed me down a road leading eastward. He said nothing as we drove, except once, when we reached a fork, and I asked him—for he seemed to have a fixed destination in mind, that he knew well—which road to take. He pointed right, and said, "That one," and I noted a sign that read GRISWOLDVILLE RD.

After a slow drive, with my grandfather observing the landscape intently, we arrived at a junction by the railroad tracks leading to Gordon. My grandfather stopped me. There was a white church on the left and fields full of the leavings of the fall harvest on the right, across the tracks. He seemed to search for something, a sign or clue, for some time, and then directed me across the tracks and onward.

At length we passed through some woods and turned away from the tracks and my grandfather had me slow, and at last stop. He got out and I followed.

Despite the chill fall weather he hiked downhill through thin woods between farms, and crossed a shallow, swampy creek. He did not seem to mind tromping through and soaking his feet, though I called after him to look out so he did not catch cold. Once across the creek, we climbed a low swell of ridge covered in stubble. I feared he would trip over it or twist an ankle in a furrow but he walked surefootedly up the hill, and then back and forth across the face of the slope for nearly two hours. He did not speak a word the whole time, and something kept me from speaking to him. At last, he stopped above a portion of the slope that dropped steeply away to the creek, and stood here a long while. Occasionally he turned and looked up the hill, to the quiet woods and the one or two farmhouses nearby, and then back to the ravine.

At last, he sighed deeply, and wiped his eyes, and turned and patted my shoulder.

"Thank you, my boy. Let's go home."

"Yes, sir," I said.

A few hours into our drive back, as the sun set, I asked him what that place was and what those bare fields meant to him.

"It was a battlefield. My grandfather—your great-great grandfather—was killed there."

This stunned me. "During the war?"

"Yes. Sixty years ago."

I had known his grandfather had died during the war—we had all seen the old photograph of the black-browed man in Confederate uniform—but had never known details.

"Where is he buried?"

"I don't know. Not at home."

"Like Fayette?" Fayette had been buried in France. Only his father and mother had been able to visit the grave; my grandfather had given them half the fare to sail over.

"No, not like Fayette." He seemed to think a while, and said, "If you can't encompass it with your arms, or know it like your mother's face, it's not worth fighting for, seems a good rule. Does it to you?"

I said it did, though it has taken me some years to understand why.

My grandfather retired from practicing medicine the following year, with many grateful encomia by letter and newspaper, all of which he dutifully saved and wrote in response, and spent the next years referring stubborn old patients to younger doctors. This proved particularly difficult for mothers whose children he had delivered, and who wanted him to deliver new ones, or to deliver their grandchildren. He patiently and, with sincere regret, turned them down.

I think he regretted this most because he, as he noted so briefly in his reminiscences, loved this most, and I believe this was because of his time in the war. After so much destruction and death in such a short time, to participate in new life was for him a lifelong celebration and a prayer of thanks. Every crying baby he caught cried because it had filled its lungs with the breath of life, and had been brought by God into the world to enjoy it and the fulness thereof, and something as big as the world could only be known through things that small and true.

He therefore objected to anything which diminished that life. He used his last few newspaper columns to decry the Eugenics Society, and bitterly mourned the national movement for sterilization laws. He disliked the growing tendency of doctors to treat their patients as broken machines to be jiggered, rather than miracles of flesh and life to be nurtured. A person is more than the sum of his parts, he often said, more than the gears of a mill or the figures of the actuary's tables, and a good doctor would look after a patient's soul as well as his body. This was why in the medieval era, he once told me, a doctor and a priest attended simultaneously, and why at some point the priest took over with a dying person, rather than rushing from the doctor to the undertaker. And so he not only dispensed medicines, sewed stitches, set bones, and performed surgeries, but gave his patients books which they might enjoy in their convalescence, prescribed walks (for the sunshine and the landscape, not the exercise), prayed with them or sent them someone they could pray with, wrote letters for and read letters to the illiterate, and gave his young patients candy or a trinket when they did not feel well. But his columns against Eugenics were too much for the mood of the nation, and after many letters of protest for his resistance to progress, science, and the genetic hygiene of the nation—*And he a doctor! A man of science!* his detractors seemed to exclaim as one—he was retired even from this.

When his old patients still tell me that they appreciate the doctors to which he referred them, but that something is missing, or not quite the same, I know what they mean but have not the words to express—my grandfather's life, and the life of his grandfather poured into it. I only regret that my own sons shall never know him as I did.

I SHOULD LIKE TO GIVE my grandfather the final word, and so I quote in conclusion two more writings in his own hand.

The first is a letter written to a surveyor to help settle the affairs of my Uncle Jeff, my grandfather's younger brother, following his death. My grandfather and the surveyor had corresponded regarding the boundaries of the family properties in order to help Aunt Bit divide the estate; the surveyor learned in passing that my grandfather had fought in the war and inquired for details.

The second is the final entry in the diary my grandfather kept in his study at home, made the evening before he died, at home on the farm he and my grandmother shared not far from where he grew up. His passing was unexpected—for an eighty-one-year old man—for he had not been ill or in bad health, but while this made it difficult for us, his family, we are thankful at least that he did not deteriorate or suffer, as he had seen so many do before. Only later, as we organized his papers, did we read this final entry.

I reproduce both here in full.

June 4, 1921

Dear Sir,

I rec'd your letter of the 29th ult. & apologize for the 2 day's delay in replying. The medical profession is ever interesting & I do not walk as spryly as I used to, with the result that I have had less time for correspondence than previous.

The farm you describe is the one I grew up on, & I know it intimately. The boundaries as we understood them were surveyor's lines forming a right angle at the rear of the property, in an area now wooded but which was once plowland, & the two creeks that joined below the hill, which my father kept from growing marshy by a great amount of digging, which I am sorry to say has not been kept up owing to my brother's declining health & the death of his son. The house you describe is not the original but a much finer farmhouse constructed by my late brother about 35 years ago. The present foundation is considerably larger & sturdier but is in approx. the same location as the house I grew up in. For reference, the distance between the front right hand corner of the porch is & was always 60' from the shade tree in the yard, a large oak that I am sorry to say was struck by lightning a few years ago & had to be cut down. The second farm you describe formerly belonged to a neighbor, one Mr. Hale, who was killed in the war & whose property passed to distant relations who let it to Anchises Smith, a Negro family formerly of my in-laws' place. Jefferson acquired it about the time he built the current house thanks to his early investments in my late brother in law Pritchard's textile mill south of Danielsville. The Smiths' sons still rent the place. There is no cemetery on the property as most of our people, including Jefferson & my mother, are buried at Barber's Chapel or at a newer family plot south of Royston.

You are correct in mentioning that I was involved in the war, but mistaken in that I was in the army; that is, the army of the Confederacy. I was in the Ga. militia & so saw little action, being held in reserve throughout the battles for Atl. & mostly employed in the digging of trenches & repair of railroads. The latter task kept us busy enough, as you might imagine. We did fight in an action outside Macon at Griswoldville, but you will receive little reward in looking for it in the histories, as it was so minor & inconsequential that even the victorious party seldom deigns to mention in it in their histories & memoirs. Its chief result was the destruction of some fine men including my own grand-father & did nothing to prevent the spoliation of our State. Two of my cousins were with us & one, my late cousin John C. Eschenbach, whom you may recall, was wounded & captured. I was lucky to escape with my life. My father was killed about the same time at Franklin, Tenn. Only the birth of succeeding generations have eased the troubles brought on my family by the war.

When next we meet I would be happy to answer more questions, though as I have noted one will likely find better or more interesting anecdotes among the *many other more experienced veterans of that conflict still living, though I should think the best people to talk to regarding the war are those slain in it. I pray this answer does not come across harshly. I have endeavored to answer it as truthfully as I am able. It is a thing I seldom speak of, though it is ever before my mind, esp. in dreams.*

Give my kindest regards to Betty & your children, who I pray enjoy good health.

Sincerely,

Geo. Wax, MD

March 13 1932

A dream worth recording last night: I was at home—
both here and at the farm where I grew up, as is the
manner of dreams—of an evening. I sat on the porch in
the quiet watching the sunset and the younger children
playing in the yard beside the shade tree, and was
somehow aware of a get-together going on in the house.
Eliza was there, and all our children, and James and
Jefferson and Bit and their children, even Fayette.
What is more, my mother and father were there, not as
ghosts but as I recall them from my childhood, before
the war, far younger than myself now—and finally my
grandfather. After a time he came out of the house
where the sound of cheer and fellowship was going on
and joined me on the porch. We sat in the rockers Eliza
and I used to rest in of an evening. It was, in the
dream, not that strange that he should be there with us,
these generations gathered from the quick and the dead
of the better part of a century, but I nonetheless sat
shamefaced for a time. For as long as I have missed
him, as long as I have had to live without him, I could
not now—with him here, with all the evening before us

to converse and commiserate—find anything to say. Such, once or twice a decade ever since the war, have been my dreams of him. This one seemed no different, until at last he, seeming to know my thoughts, patted me on the shoulder with his warm earth-smelling hand and chuckled in his old raspy laugh, a sound I recall as if it were yesterday. My shame lifted in an instant. We did not speak, but sat contented in the sound of family as the sun went down. ————

A pleasant enough day. A few old patients called to inquire about appts but I referred them to the young Dr in Danielsville. Alexander came by for a good visit with his boys. Both are hale and strong and I told him he had much to be proud of, as I am of him. He remarked on my improved vivacity this day. The usual aches seemed less burdensome after last night's dream. Oh what a foretaste. Perhaps another such tonight. We will see in the morning.

APPENDICES

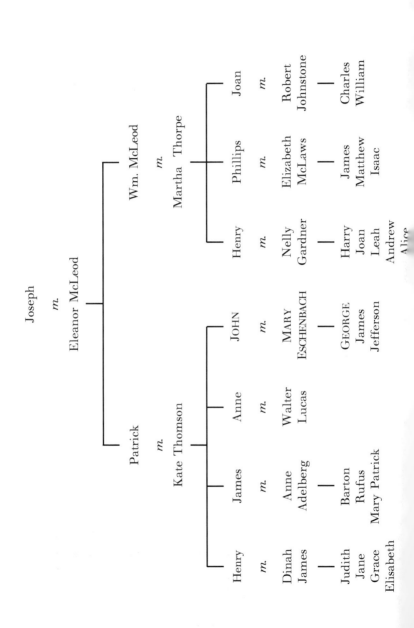

WAX FAMILY TREE, *c.* 1860

Joseph
m.
Eleanor McLeod

Patrick *m.* Kate Thomson

Wm. McLeod *m.* Martha Thorpe

Henry *m.* Dinah James
— Judith Jane Grace Elisabeth

James *m.* Anne Adelberg
— Barton Rufus Mary Patrick

Anne *m.* Walter Lucas

JOHN *m.* MARY ESCHENBACH
— GEORGE James Jefferson

Henry *m.* Nelly Gardner
— Harry Joan Leah Andrew Alice

Phillips *m.* Elizabeth McLaws
— James Matthew Isaac

Joan *m.* Robert Johnstone
— Charles William

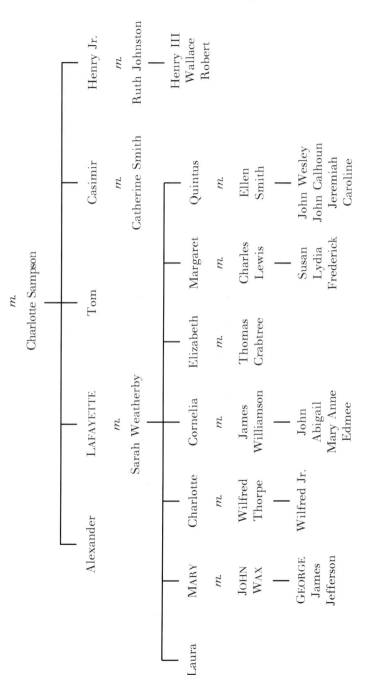

ESCHENBACH FAMILY TREE, *c.* 1860

GLOSSARY

abatis – Rows of fallen trees branches arranged with their entangled limbs facing the enemy, commonly used as an improvised defense before the invention of barbed wire.

battalion – A subdivision of the regiment composed of several companies.

big bugs – High ranking officers.

bivouac – Quickly improvised camping without pitched tents.

breastworks – Chest-high, often improvised defenses.

brigade – A unit composed of three to five regiments, though with substantial variation in size.

brogans – Heavy, thick-soled leather shoes reaching to the ankle. Issued by both sides during the war.

bummer – A forager of Sherman's Army of the Tennessee, known for their sloppy appearance and thoroughness in looting.

canister shot – Antipersonnel artillery ammunition consisting of a canister filled with small lead balls, effectively turning a cannon into a shotgun. Cannoneers commonly fired "double canister"—a double load—against infantry at extreme close range with devastating effect. Improvised canister shot could include nails, rocks, broken glass, and other odds and ends loaded into the barrel in a bag. See also *grape shot*, below.

cap and ball – A revolver firing multi-part loads consisting of a ball or slug, powder, and a percussion cap on a nipple on the back end of the cylinder. See *percussion cap*, below.

chevaux de frise – Literally "Frisian horses," a wooden defensive obstacle usually made of sharpened wooden stakes projecting from a log or beam.

common step – A marching pace of 90 steps per minute.

company – A unit notionally made up of 100 men and led by a captain.

Company Q – Slang term for the sick list.

cracker – See *white trash*, below.

desertion – The abandonment of a military duty or post without permission, especially in the face of the enemy; a crime punishable by firing squad.

Domestic Medicine – Full title, *Gunn's Domestic Medicine, or Poor Man's Friend in the Hours of Affliction, Pain, and Sickness*. A home medical almanac intended for rural or frontier families by Dr. John C. Gunn. First published in Knoxville, Tennessee in 1830 and going through more than fifty editions by the end of the 19th century.

doublequick – A marching pace of 165 steps per minute; essentially a jog.

earthworks – More permanent earthen entrenchments, as opposed to improvised defenses like breastworks.

foraging – Searching for and requisitioning supplies, especially food.

forage cap – A soft, flat-topped cap with a leather bill, similar to the kepi, but with much less structure.

furlough – Temporary leave granted to soldiers.

grapeshot – Antipersonnel artillery ammunition consisting of multiple shot or balls which, when fired, effectively turned a cannon into a giant shotgun. Devastating against infantry at close range.

hardtack – Hard flour and water crackers issued as a long-lasting field ration to armies on both sides of the Civil War. So tough it was sometimes inedible, and had limited nutritional value in the first place.

haversack – A cloth bag with a single shoulder strap used to carry an individual soldier's personal belongings and provisions, usually a few days' rations.

kepi – A soft cap with a flat top and short leather bill, originating in France but common throughout the US and CS armies during the Civil War.

line of attack – Deployment in lines one or two ranks deep for assault. Moving from marching order to line of attack was difficult and required extensive drill.

marching order – A column four men wide for long-distance movement.

Maria Monk – a.k.a. *The Awful Disclosures of Maria Monk*, a lurid anti-Catholic book purporting to be the memoir of a Canadian girl pressganged into joining a nunnery and prostituting herself in Quebec. One of the best-selling books in the United States before the Civil War.

militia – Military units raised by states, which still exercised considerable control over their deployment, as opposed to units raised by the national government.

Minié ball – A conical bullet of soft lead. Gave rifled muskets of the era greater range and accuracy, but flattened upon impact with any solid object and caused terrible wounds, especially shattered bones, which required immediate amputation.

mudsill – Rude, uncultivated people; white trash. Also a

slang term for Union troops in the western armies.

musket – A muzzle-loading longarm; by the time of the Civil War, most but not all muskets were rifled (the "musket rifle") and fired the Minié ball.

musketoon – A short, muzzle-loading musket often carried by cavalry.

percussion cap – The ignition system of pre-brass cartridge firearms; a small brass cap with a small explosive charge. Upon squeezing the trigger, the hammer would strike the cap, its fire would be directed through the nipple into the barrel, where it would ignite the main charge and fire the weapon. The system was instantaneous, as opposed to prior systems like the flintlock.

picket line – A screen of soldiers placed on guard in a line forward of the main body to provide advance warning of enemy movement.

planter – In the Old South, a member of the slave-holding elite; specifically, one possessed of land—the plantation—and twenty or more slaves. Planters formed the tiny upper class of the antebellum South.

quickstep – A marching pace of 110 paces per minute. Also a slang term for diarrhea.

repeater – A rifle that could fire multiple shots, reloaded mechanically from the breech—usually by means of a lever—from a magazine loaded with brass cartridges. The two most common and well-known repeaters during the Civil War were the Spencer rifle and carbine (seven round capacity) and the Henry rifle (15 shots), the forerunner of the Winchester.

regiment – A unit made up of ten companies formed into two or more battalions and led by a colonel.

route step – A marching pace in which the soldiers maintained their formation and intervals, but were not required to keep in step and were allowed to talk and carry their weapons in the most comfortable position desired.

secesh – Short for *secessionist*, derogatory Union slang for Confederates or Southerners generally.

skirmishers – Light infantry in open formation—Hardee's 1855 drill manual stipulates five paces between each man—deployed in front of the main body of a unit to probe or harass the enemy.

slouch hat – A broad-brimmed felt hat popular on both sides in the Civil War.

smokehouse – An outbuilding common to many farms used for curing meats with smoke.

sowbelly – Salt pork.

squad – The smallest constituent unit of an infantry regiment, consisting notionally of ten men: eight privates led by a corporal and a sergeant.

white trash – Derogatory term for the poor white underclass of the South, perceived by some—for reasons of moral degradation and "breeding"—to be lower in rank than slaves. Also called "poor white trash" and "crackers."

yeoman – In the Old South, a broad social class of non-slaveholding, non-elite, family farmers, typically living on land of between 50 and 200 acres and engaged in subsistence farming, with perhaps a few acres given to a commercial crop like cotton with much variation according to local conditions. The yeomanry constituted the vast majority of Southern whites.

yokelry – Derisive slang for the yeomanry.

HISTORICAL NOTE

The Battle of Griswoldville occurred November 22, 1864, much as depicted in fictional form here. Between 2,500 and 3,000 men of the Georgia militia, State Line, and other defense troops assaulted Union infantry on a low ridge outside the ruins of Griswoldville, Georgia. The outnumbered Union troops fought from behind improvised defenses and many carried repeating rifles like the seven-shot Spencer rifle. Failures of leadership, the courage and discipline of the militia—who kept up the attack all afternoon—and the superior position and weaponry of the enemy combined to produce disaster for the Confederates.

Initial reports counted 51 Confederate dead and 472 wounded, but this number is surely low. One of the Union regiments engaged reported around fifty dead in front of its works alone. Scaife and Bragg, in their excellent appendices for *Joe Brown's Pets*, estimate at least eighty dead and many more wounded based on casualty reports in Georgia newspapers. But these reports do not account for several of the companies engaged, so the true numbers are probably unrecoverable. From Scaife and Bragg's compiled lists I count at least 125 killed, missing, and mortally wounded.

In terms of scale and outcome, Griswoldville was a minor engagement and, as Georgie notes, the battle is seldom described in any detail in histories of the March to the Sea, being a sort of hiccup in the progress to Savannah. Several recent biographies of Sherman do not bother with the battle at all.

Exceptions which I have consulted, and which I would like to point toward out of gratitude and as possible further reading for interested parties, include short accounts in the somewhat dated *Sherman's March*, by Burke Davis, and *Nothing But Victory: The Army of the Tennessee, 1861-1865*, by Steven E. Woodworth. Another good account with good maps is a chapter in *War and Ruin: William T. Sherman and the Savannah Campaign*, by Anne J. Bailey. As I put the final touches on this book, *Rising in Flames: Sherman's March and the Fight for a New Nation*, by J.D. Dickey, was released. Dickey includes a two-page narrative of the battle, including the gruesome story of the 6th Iowa's unfortunate colorbearer, to which I made Georgie a witness. But the fullest easily available popular account comes in *Southern Storm: Sherman's March to the Sea*, by Noah Andre Trudeau, which includes a detailed and superbly written chapter on Griswoldville.

Some of my first serious research, and the most fruitful, was in reading the primary sources collected in the War Department's *Official Records of the War of the Rebellion*. The battle, which was overwhelmingly better documented on the Union side, is covered in several reports included in Series I, Volume 44.

The two most important modern resources in my writing of this book were the aforementioned *Joe Brown's Pets: The Georgia Militia, 1861-1865*, by William R. Scaife and William Harris Bragg, and Bragg's *Griswoldville*. These are well-researched and lavishly illustrated works of scholarship and proved an immense help as I wrote this novel.

Other books that proved useful in writing this story include *The Plain People of the Confederacy* and *The Life of Johnny Reb: The Common Soldier of the Confederacy*, both by Bell Irvin Wiley; James I. Robertson's more recent *Soldiers Blue and Gray*; and *The Confederate Nation: 1861-1865*, by Emory Thomas.

For folk medicine I've relied upon a minuscule amount of personal knowledge and, more importantly, on two excellent works: *Folk Medicine in Southern Appalachia*, by Anthony Cavender; and *Folk Remedies* from the Americana Library, a series of Kindle ebooks collected from the Foxfire series, a well known folklore and Appalachian heritage project founded in my home county. I also consulted *Meats and Small Game* from the same series to flesh out my understanding of hog slaughtering and meat curing learned from older relatives. Fate's method of squirrel hunting I learned from my own grandfather, who learned it from his father.

I give credit to the above books, and many others, for helping me to prepare and write this novel and especially in helping me make it as realistic and authentic as possible. I take the blame for any errors or mistakes, but I do ask the reader to remember that this is, after all, a novel—a work of fiction. Georgie, his family, and his militia company did not exist, and his unit's itinerary matches that of no militia unit that did, but I hope this book and its story are true in the most important and lasting sense.

ACKNOWLEDGEMENTS

I was first awakened to the experience of boy soldiers as a boy myself, by books in Mrs. Bourlet's fourth-sixth grade library. I recommend *The Boys' War: Confederate and Union Soldiers Talk About the Civil War*, by Jim Murphy, which I first read in her class and which I still recommend as an introduction to the American Civil War for young readers.

I am grateful to those who read early versions of this novel—from the rough draft stage all the way to final proofs—and for their thoughts, criticisms, and corrections. Thanks especially to Steve and Miles for their early feedback. There are too many more of you to thank—you know who you are.

I am grateful as well to my dad for his keen interest in this story and encouragement to finish it. I want to thank Sarah for her constant encouragement to write this novel, which she has shown interest in for years, long before words had ever been committed to paper. This book would never have been begun, much less finished, without her.

Finally, for their examples and the inspiration their very different lives have offered, I thank my grandfathers—Rabun County native J.L. McKay, who died in 1998, when I was Georgie Wax's age; and Clarke County native Ed Poss, who died at the age of ninety as I began final revisions on this book. These two men modeled wisdom, justice, and moderation for four generations, and I gratefully dedicate this book to them.

ABOUT THE AUTHOR

Jordan M. Poss is a native of Rabun County, Georgia, and a graduate of Clemson University, where he graduated with an MA in European History. He currently teaches history at a community college in upstate South Carolina, where he lives with his wife and children. He is also the author of the novels *No Snakes in Iceland* and *Dark Full of Enemies* and the novella *The Last Day of Marcus Tullius Cicero.*

Made in the USA
Columbia, SC
13 April 2020

91909836R00224